# FEEL
# THE
# HEAT

# CINDY GERARD

# FEEL THE HEAT

POCKET STAR BOOKS

New York   London   Toronto   Sydney

Pocket Star Books
A Division of Simon & Schuster, Inc.
1230 Avenue of the Americas
New York, NY 10020

Cover design by Lisa Litwack. Illustration by Craig White.

Manufactured in the United States of America

ISBN-13: 978-1-61523-618-3

As always, this book is dedicated to the men and women of the United States military—both active and retired. We owe you our freedom and our way of life. Stay safe. Stay strong.

And to my friend Sue Timmer. Because of you, I saw the beauty and majesty of the Grand Canyon from top to bottom and to the top again. Thanks for talking me into it, for being my friend, for making me laugh, and for defining the word "strong." I miss you, buddy. May you rest in peace.

# ACKNOWLEDGMENTS

Writers are a solitary lot. We spend our days alone, buried in research, pounding away at our keyboards, lost in our stories and our characters. Our contacts with the "outside" world are often limited to e-mail and phone—especially when we're mired in a deadline. I want to acknowledge all of those wonderful people who are always there on the other end of my cyber world and my cell world who help keep me connected, focused, and sane. This book, in particular, could not have been written without my sister in spirit, Susan Connell. Thanks, girlfriend, for holding on and reeling me back in when I reached the end of my rope.

I hate war as only a soldier who has lived it can, only as one who has seen its brutality, its futility, its stupidity.

—Dwight D. Eisenhower

# 1

B. J. Chase had worn her black tank top and khaki shorts for too many hours to count in the Venezuelan climate, where the heat and humidity were often measured in terms of ripe, riper, and "for God's sake, take a shower."

Restless and on edge, she tapped her thumbs on the steering wheel of a rusted-out red Jeep Cherokee, circa 1990. She felt a trail of perspiration trickle down her back. No time to worry about her deodorant letting her down now. Weeks of surveillance, back alley connections, and righteous fieldwork were finally going to pay off. The deal was going down and it was going down tonight, right here in this dark, garbage-littered back alley in Caracas.

"Provided Eduardo actually shows up," B.J. reminded herself under her breath.

Oh, yeah . . . and she had to get out of here alive once he did.

Somewhere in the distance, the feral snarls of a cat-fight rose above the rough idle of the Jeep's motor. The

driver's seat creaked and groaned when she shifted behind the wheel. She'd bought the Jeep at a used car lot
three weeks ago when she and three other DIA agents
had first arrived in Caracas. The seat was sprung; the
fenders were rusted out. Some genius had hacked off
the top at some point and done a sloppy job of welding
a roll bar to the frame. A spiderweb of cracks burst away
from a bullet hole on the passenger-side windshield.
Beneath the pitted hood, the engine knocked like a Je-
hovah's Witness rapping on a front door but the guys in
the motor pool at the U.S. embassy had done a little
tinkering and pronounced it sound. A luxury ride it was
not. B.J. didn't need luxury. She needed speed and reli-
ability and that's what the Jeep would give her if this
meet went sour and she had to burn rubber out of here.

She checked her watch and frowned. It was nearly
three a.m. Eduardo was late.

"Where the hell is he?" she muttered into the
commo mike hidden in the center of the Celtic cross
that nestled between her breasts.

"Cool your jets," Maynard's voice whispered sharply
in her earpiece.

Like Hogan and Collins, Maynard wasn't exactly
thrilled that this was her show. They were older, had
more seniority, and were openly unimpressed with her
military background, her education, and the fact that
she'd spearheaded this DIA operation from its incep-
tion back in D.C. nearly six months ago.

Nope, the boys didn't like that she'd drawn team
leader assignment. That was fine. They didn't have to

like it, just like they didn't have to be impressed. They just had to do their job, which was guard her back. And regardless of the crude message implied by the set of brass balls that had mysteriously appeared on her desk the day after her immediate supervisor, Dale Sherwood, had put her in charge, she knew they would do it.

She tamped down her impatience, then made herself draw a settling breath. She wished she had a piece of chocolate. It always calmed her but in this heat, chocolate was off the table. So was breathing easy.

She felt more jumpy by the minute. Eduardo had set up the time and place. He'd told her to come alone. Yeah, right. The three other DIA officers lurked in the shadows with a little insurance in the form of M-4s with night scopes. She had, however, followed Eduardo's instructions to park, flick the headlights three times, then kill them. Now she waited in the dark, heat pulsing from the potholed alley, sweat trickling between her shoulder blades and her breasts and soaking her shirt while her heart tripped at double time.

She had to believe he would show. Men like him— parasites without conscience or scruples—would sell out their own mothers for a helluva lot less than the twenty thousand dollars she'd already paid him for partial information. No way was Eduardo going to miss out on the other half of his forty grand, which she would trade him tonight for the rest of the info he'd promised to deliver.

Yet when she searched the darkness ahead of her all she saw were shadows. The alley was narrow and winding, flanked on both sides by an endless row of three- and four-story adobe and brick buildings. Some, she assumed, housed businesses, some residences. All but one were dark. A pale light spilled out of a first-story window several yards ahead of her. It was the only light other than the dim, pale green glow of the gauges on the Jeep's dashboard.

She lifted damp blond hair off her neck and swiped at the perspiration coating her nape. Her hair and humidity were not friends. Even though she'd used a scrunchie to wrestle the unruly mass of it into a tail, some of the thick, springy curls had escaped around her face.

"Heads up." Hogan's voice sounded in her earpiece. "There's movement, your twelve o'clock."

All of her senses slammed into overdrive. It was showtime. They were finally going to get what they'd come for. Last March a cache of controversial computer files had been recovered in Colombia tying Venezuela's president Hugo Chavez to FARC— the communist rebel group intent on ousting the U.S.-friendly Colombian government from power. The treasure trove—found on a dead guerrilla leader's laptop during a military raid—had been just the tip of the iceberg. Since then, B.J. had been setting things in motion, ferreting out contacts, paring down informants, and finally scoring tonight's meet with Eduardo of no last name. He was supposed to provide enough additional intel to make it possible for the U.S. to ratchet up the pressure on Venezuela to stop aiding FARC without having to impose sanctions on one of America's most important oil suppliers.

"Come on, come on," she muttered under her breath, then damn near jumped out of her skin when she heard the sound of footsteps on the gritty pavement.

A man appeared out of the shadows: Eduardo. Short, swarthy, black hair hanging in a long braid down the middle of his back, a gold hoop in his left ear. If he had a conscience, or if a heart beat within his chest, both were buried so deep neither had seen the light of day in a very long while.

Now it would get dicey. This is what she got paid the little bucks to do.

Her Glock 19 pressed against her right kidney where she'd tucked it into the waistband of her khaki shorts. The weight and pressure were both comforting and reassuring. So was the sawed-off 12-gauge shotgun lying lengthwise at her feet on the floor of the Jeep, stock facing the driver's door.

She pulled up on the door handle, put her shoulder into it, and pushed. The rusted hinges squawked but finally swung open. Her sandaled foot hit the pocked pavement. Mindful of both the position of the shotgun and her distance from it, she left the door open. "I was beginning to think you weren't going to sho—"

*Snick-click.*

The distinctive metallic click of a safety on an AK-47 assault rifle had her freezing mid-sentence. Her heart rate ratcheted up to triple time as Eduardo stopped abruptly about three yards in front of her, slowly lifting his hands above his head.

A man dressed in a black wife-beater and dark camo cargo pants and wielding the AK stepped out from behind him. He gestured with the business end of the rifle for her to raise her hands, too. "Up high. Let's see 'em, *cara.*"

The look on Eduardo's face told her that he was as surprised as she was. And that they were both as good as dead if she didn't do what she was told.

*Stall,* she thought, as adrenaline zipped through her blood like rocket fuel. She needed to make something happen until her backup took charge of the situation.

Very slowly, she lifted her hands, all the while inching closer to the open door of the Jeep and the shotgun that lay just out of reach on the floor.

*Where were they—?*

Oh God. Her runaway heart rate plummeted when she saw Maynard, Hogan, and Collins suddenly illuminated by the beams of three powerful Maglites, marching slowly toward her.

Their hands were linked on top of their heads. Three men walking behind them pointed assault rifles at their backs, prodding them forward. The lot of them looked ready to chew nails. They were pissed and embarrassed that they'd been caught with their pants down. Join the club.

What kind of men were they dealing with that they could get the drop on experienced DIA field officers?

She quickly decided the men either had known they were coming or had skills the DIA officers lacked.

She cut a cautious glance toward the Jeep. Knew that if she was going to make a move, it had to be now.

She dove toward the 12-gauge.

The man with the AK struck like a viper. He grabbed her arm, yanked her away from the door, then slammed her up against the vehicle.

"Not smart." He pinned her against the Jeep with the weight of his body. "Now I'll tell you again. Keep your hands where I can see them. That way no one gets hurt."

He could hurt her, she had no doubt about that. Hell, he could have killed her by now, she thought as he turned Eduardo over to one of his men. One bullet. Close range. Clean and simple.

For whatever reason, she was still fit and fine. The others were fine, too, which gave her reason to hope that they still had a prayer of getting out of this alive. To do that, she had to play heads-up ball, which meant she had to work through the adrenaline rush that mixed with fear and made her shaky, and quickly assess her adversary.

This close, it wasn't that difficult. The face that was mere inches away from hers was not a face she would expect to meet in a dark alley on the wrong side of a mission that was rapidly heading south. *Wholesome* was the word that came to mind. Altar-boy angelic—providing she overlooked the assault rifle.

She'd caught a glimpse of a tattoo on his upper arm that appeared to be a cross of some sort. It did not, however, put her in mind of altars or boys. Neither did the gold crucifix that hung from his neck and lay against a broad chest so smooth it could have been waxed.

The bright beams of the Maglites lit up the alley. She could see that his eyes were dark, almost black, like the hair that he wore cut military close. His skin was caramel toned, his face clean shaven and flawless but for a small, triangular scar that rode at the left corner of a full, sensuous mouth. She was used to assessing and cataloging adversaries on the fly. What she wasn't used to was thinking of the enemy as disarmingly handsome—or that she would be ultra-sensitive to the fact that he was plastered so tightly against her she could feel the heat radiating from his body like a pulse.

He wasn't a big man—maybe five nine, five ten—but the body pressed against hers was as lean and hard as the Jeep at her back. The steely grip on her arm was capable of inflicting pain, yet he only used it to restrain her.

Even though his English bore a Spanish accent, something about him made her think he'd spent some time in the States. He was clean, his bearing disciplined and practiced. He knew exactly what he was doing, where his men were, and how to take control. Situational awareness. Like a soldier. Like a merc, she thought, and knew that alive or not, they were still in deep trouble.

Or worse, he could be on Chavez's payroll—possibly

police, maybe even paramilitary. Chavez wouldn't take kindly to Eduardo's passing along secret government information and would sure as hell want to stop the transaction. But she knew how Chavez worked. If these were his men, she'd be bleeding out in the gutter by now, no questions asked.

So no, this detail had not been sent by Chavez. CIA maybe? This guy had the look—they all did—the skills, and the "no one can touch me" attitude. And if not CIA, then a close equivalent: badasses with a license to kill, thrill, and wreak havoc wherever they decided havoc needed to be wreaked.

Which brought her back to the immediate problem. If they were CIA then someone somewhere had screwed up royally because no way should one government agency interfere with another's sting. Regardless, his guns were still just as big and just as bad, and she was still in just as much trouble because, in her experience, spooks didn't care about rules or diplomacy.

"Let's back away from the Jeep, okay, *querida*? Easy, now," he warned in a voice that was as sultry as the night and lightly laced with that Spanish accent. Even though he spoke softly, there was no mistaking the order or the threat as he pressed the nose of the AK against her rib cage and, with a firm grip on her upper arm, guided her away from the Jeep and, thankfully, several inches away from him.

He peered around the open driver's-side door, turned off the ignition, then smiled when he spotted the shotgun on the floor. "Cute gun," he said, like he was complimenting her wardrobe—which felt mighty damn inadequate when his dark gaze raked her body up and down before he shouldered past her and plucked up the shotgun.

With hardly a backward glance, he tossed the gun to one of his men, then leaned in close and started patting her down. She gritted her teeth, readying herself to suffer pain, humiliation, and rough hands. But he surprised her again when he tugged her Glock out of her waistband then made quick and painless work of searching her.

"I *do* like a woman who knows her weapons." He glanced from the pistol to her face and smiled again as he pulled the earpiece out of her ear and tossed it away. "You have any other surprises, *mi chica bonita?*"

Smooth. Smooth and smug. While she was both surprised and grateful that he hadn't manhandled her, she could have done without the condescending attitude.

"I'm not your pretty girl."

His smile faded. "But you are my pretty problem. And you're a complication I don't have time for. Come on, let's go."

"Go where?" She put on the skids when he urged her forward.

He grunted out something that might have passed for a laugh as his men bound Maynard's, Hogan's, Collins's, and Eduardo's hands behind their backs with flex cuffs. "You don't get to ask questions. You get to do as you're told."

When he started hauling her down the alley toward

his men, she dug in her heels and latched on to the Jeep's roll bar in a death grip. "I'm not going anywhere."

He expelled a weary breath. "You don't get to call the shots, either. Now I said, let's go." He didn't mess around this time. He jerked her hard, breaking her hold.

"Look," she reasoned, fighting him at every step. "You need to let us go. You've got to know we're all American citizens."

He stopped, leaned in close, and growled in her ear, "That's not something you want to broadcast in this part of the city. But since you're so proud of the fact, why don't you tell me what four Americans are doing here this time of night?"

When their eyes met this time, a shocking heat arced between them that transcended the hottest South American night.

*Holy God,* she thought. Where had that come from? Shaken, she forced herself to hold his gaze, told herself it was only anger and adrenaline that had her heartbeat revving and every self-preservation instinct she possessed warning her to look away.

"We're with the USDA. On an agricultural exchange program." She lied like the good DIA officer she was, launching into the cover story they'd developed in the event something like this happened. She knew the cover was lame but it was all she had. Three veteran DIA officers with assault rifles and high-tech commo equipment were supposed to have ensured she wouldn't need to use it.

He looked at her like she'd grown two heads, then barked out a laugh. "USDA officials with American military-issue M-4s? I don't think so. Wanna try again?"

"Check my pocket." Anything to buy time, stall, minimize their profile until they could figure out how to either get away or stay alive until the intelligence officer at the embassy realized they were in trouble and sent a team to find them. "My credentials are in there."

"I'm sure they are. But fake IDs are a dime a dozen." His warm breath fanned her nape as he tugged her hands behind her back and secured her wrists with the flex cuffs one of his men had tossed him. "I've got a hundred of 'em. Who would you like *me* to be? The Welcome Wagon? Scooby-Doo? Or maybe you'd like me to be Batman. You choose. It'll be fun."

Oh, yeah. He'd definitely spent time in the States. The way he carried himself might be all sexy Latino swagger, and sure, he spoke with a Spanish accent, but this guy's attitude and jargon were definitely a product of American culture.

His grip tightened on her arm and he forced her down the alley and away from the Jeep.

"Where are you taking us?"

"Someplace where I can minimize the problem you're making for me."

His fingers still in a vise-like grip around her upper arm, he guided her a couple of blocks, then around a corner where two black vans sat under the pale beam of an ancient streetlight. One of the men pulled a hood over Eduardo's head then shoved him into the rear vehicle. Then they roughly tugged black hoods over Maynard, Hogan, and Collins and guided them none too gently into the other van.

Oh, God. She was next. Her captor pushed her in the same direction; the gaping darkness inside the open door had her heart slamming. She put on the brakes again. She wasn't going to give up that easily. She was losing her mole and the information she'd worked for months to uncover. She had no idea what they planned to do with them—beatings, rape, torture—

She blocked the images from her mind. This was not going to end here. She wasn't going to let it. She'd worked too hard; Eduardo mattered too much.

"You really need to let us go," she tried one last time.

"Be a good girl and that might happen."

Then he pulled a hood down over her head.

# 2

"You're making me very tired, *cara*," Raphael Mendoza grumbled as the wriggling blonde American pulled against his hold. He so did not have the patience for this.

"So much for a quick in and out," Luke Colter—aka Doc Holliday—said as he headed for the driver's-side door.

Yeah, Rafe thought. *That* wasn't happening. This whole Eduardo sting was making him weary. Wait until Nate Black, his boss at Black Ops, Inc., found out that Uncle Sam had a tag-team match going on with the Venezuelan gangster. And wait until little Miss Sunshine here went home empty-handed. The fur was gonna fly on Capitol Hill because he had no doubt that she and her boys had been sent by some lower-level spy master bent on making a name for himself through his agency staff.

"You're making a big mistake," she advised him again, her words muffled beneath the hood as she shoved against his chest.

"Won't be the first one," he grumbled, and without another word, hauled her up against him and lifted her off her feet.

She was stronger than she looked. Softer, too, not that he had the time to appreciate either discovery.

"In you go." He shoved her inside with her three amigos. Christ. With those three guarding her back, it was a wonder she wasn't dead already. "Now behave."

"Not likely," she sputtered, which made him smile. Lord knew why. He was hot. He was tired. He was pissed. But she was a fighter and he just had to like that.

Doc was already settled behind the wheel when Rafe slid into the van's shotgun seat. "We good to go yet?"

"Tell me one thing about this that's good," Rafe muttered as Doc stepped on the gas. What a goatfuck.

He glanced in the rearview mirror to see the four of them packed into the back of the van like sardines, their heads down, the black hoods covering their faces and blocking their vision. Goldilocks had scooted around until she sat with her back against a sidewall. USDA. *That* was their cover? He let out a deep breath, shook his head, and wondered what mastermind had dreamed that up.

"So," he said, because he couldn't contain his curiosity, "since we're all friends now, why don't you tell me what you're really doing here?"

"Already did," she insisted, sticking with the ridiculous cover story.

Doc grinned at him as they barreled down a series of back streets. "Whaddaya think, Choirboy? Thumb-screws or straight to beheading?"

"Both tempting," Rafe said with a weary grunt. "I really don't care—as long as we start with the woman."

Doc chuckled. "You *always* want to start with a woman."

Rafe caught her quick intake of breath. Aw, hell. He'd gone and scared her again.

"Relax, *querida*. Your pretty neck isn't in any danger. Neither are your thumbs. We'll drop you off safe and sound at the U.S. embassy. You can lick your wounds, report to whatever alphabet agency sent you down here that you were ambushed by big, bad *bandito* types, and everyone goes home happy."

Happy. Right. He was so damn happy he could spit nails.

"If you're not going to kill us," her voice came out of the back of the van, "then why the guns?"

"Guns don't kill people. People kill people," Doc, with his usual droll sense of humor, pointed out with mock gravity. "And your guys were a little too trigger-happy for comfort. We like it better when we're the ones saying stick 'em up. Works out better for us that way."

"Okay, who the hell are you?" she demanded. "And what do you want with Eduardo?"

Spitfire. Under other circumstances Rafe might have appreciated her grit, and the sweet little body and all that wild, curly blond hair. The other circumstances being she wasn't mucking up an op that had taken him and the BOIs nine months to set up.

He twisted around, scowled, and decided what the hell. He'd succeeded in scaring her. That's what he'd wanted to do. No point overplaying his hand. He reached over the seat back and tugged off her hood.

She blinked like a little bird, trying to get her pupils to adjust to the dim interior of the van.

"So it's *Eduardo*, is it? You're on a first-name basis with that lowlife? Makes a man wonder where your interest in the local *agriculture* really lies. Not a lot of pig farms in Caracas last I looked. Lotta coca farms nearby, though. That what your agricultural exchange program's about? You swapping cash for cocaine, *cara*?"

At least baiting her was marginally entertaining. So was watching her tug on the flex cuffs as if she actually thought she could wriggle free.

"Are you going to tell me who you're working for?" she shot back. Snapping blue eyes, full of challenge, met his.

"I believe I asked you first."

She glared at him.

He smiled as he turned face forward in the seat again. Yeah, she was definitely entertaining. "Just be glad it was us who found you and not Chavez's hit squad," he said finally. "Best to leave it at that."

"What do you want with Eduardo?"

He glanced in the rearview mirror, met her eyes. "Do you know the meaning of the term 'broken record'?"

"There's a simple fix for that. Answer my questions."

That wasn't going to happen. "Eduardo is a very bad man. A lot of people want him—dead or alive. So I'll repeat: You should be very glad it was us who intervened tonight."

"We're taking him in," she announced with a conviction generally reserved for someone holding the upper hand.

Doc chuckled. "Woman's got spunk. Distorted sense of reality, but spunk just the same."

"Sorry, *cara*." Like hell he was. "Eduardo is ours."

"You have no idea what your interference disrupted," she informed him, getting steamed all over again.

"*I* have no idea? *I have no idea?*" Fun and games were over. He twisted in the seat again so he could look her in the eye. "You and your three stooges here have managed to throw a wrench the size of a tank into an operation that took us months to set up. So don't tell me what *my* interference disrupted. You stumbled into a hornet's nest, *querida*. Now sit back and button it or you could still get stung."

The fierce look in her eyes relayed more than anger. "A *sanctioned* U.S. government operation trumps whatever black op you've got going on. We are taking Eduardo in."

He made a sound of disbelief. "Jesus, woman. What part of *you're* tied up and *we've* got the guns don't you understand?"

The U.S. embassy complex came into view just then. Thank God. He'd finally be rid of her and the rest of her motley crew, and he and the BOIs would be on their way with Eduardo in tow. Or they would have been, if she hadn't fired a rocket that shot straight to the heart of the matter.

"What part of DIA officer under direct orders from the Department of Defense don't *you* understand?"

He went utterly still. Tension ticked like a bomb, then blew sky-high.

Beside him Holliday muttered a low, weary "I don't fricking believe this."

*Defense Intelligence Agency? Department of Defense?* Sonofabitch.

He was fucked . . . and without so much as a kiss from a blonde bombshell with Goldilocks curls.

# 3

Three months later, B.J. stood in the middle of her mother's small apartment in Hagerstown, her thoughts drifting back to Caracas. She still got angry when she thought about that night—the shock, the humiliation, and the bigger issue, the failure. It was past time to shake it off. In fact, she'd been ordered to shake it off.

Someday, maybe she would. Not today. Today was not a good day. She let out a weary breath and tried to ignore the fact that her mother's small living room smelled of stale cigarette smoke and cheap wine. Newspapers lay in a sprawling pile on the floor; empty wineglasses left rings on the dusty end tables; a soap opera diva threw a drink in her lover's face as the TV droned on in a corner of the room.

Her mother's habits hadn't changed. Neither had the scenery or her routine. B.J. hadn't expected them to. And yet, foolishly, she still hoped. As always, those hopes were shattered when she heard her mother rummaging around in the refrigerator in the kitchen, looking for a bottle, no doubt.

Shutting it all out, wondering why she had bothered to come, B.J. lifted a tarnished picture frame from a bookcase overflowing with worn paperbacks. She touched a fingertip to her father's image. Frank Chase had been a handsome man, a real hunk in uniform. His chest was heavy with medals. He had a strong jaw, a prominent nose, and piercing blue eyes. B.J. sometimes thought she caught a glimpse of herself in those eyes. Every other physical characteristic she'd inherited from her mother.

That was where the similarities between her and her mother ended. B.J. had made certain of it.

"I hated him, you know."

B.J. tensed at the rancor in her mother's statement, which was made all the more cutting by the deep smoker's voice delivering it. She carefully set the photograph of her father back on the shelf, then turned as Janine Chase walked into the room, a full glass of wine in her hand. Dull brown eyes blinked drowsily as she sank down in a faded floral chair.

"So why do you keep his picture?" B.J. had always wondered about that.

A long silence passed before her mother blinked, then lifted her glass to her lips. "Because I loved him first."

Yeah, she had loved him. That love had destroyed her. B.J. looked across the room at her mom, wondered why she'd let life break her. She'd been pretty once; B.J. had seen photographs. Curly, platinum-blonde hair; stunning brown eyes; strong, slim limbs; and pinup curves.

Her looks were gone now. It was like she had died, too, ten years ago when Frank Chase had been killed in action. In truth, her mother's spirit had died long before she'd lost her husband.

"I still miss him," B.J. admitted quietly, and because she couldn't make herself stand still any longer, she started prowling around the room. The apartment was small, the rent was cheap. It was the best she could afford—she would never get rich as a DIA officer—and yet the guilt she felt because she couldn't provide better for her mother hung over her head like the smoke drifting on the stuffy air.

"He was never here." Her mother's voice was filled with bitterness. "How can you miss a man who was *never* here?"

Weary. These visits made her so damn weary. She didn't want to climb this hill today. "Look, Mom, I just drove down to see how you were doing, okay? See if you needed anything."

Her mother made a sarcastic sound that sent her into a coughing fit. "I need a new life," she choked out.

B.J. fought the tug on her heart that always tried to convince her that her mother should be pitied. Things didn't have to be this way. Her *mom* didn't have to be this way.

"Why didn't you divorce him?" she blurted out, unable to hide her own irritation. "If you hated your life with him so much, why didn't you just leave when you were . . ." She stopped herself from saying, "when you were young enough, alive enough to become something more than a tired drunk."

Her mother drew deeply on her cigarette, squinted through the curling smoke. "And go where? Do what? I had a high school education. And I had you. You think I could have raised you on minimum wage and tips from a waitress job? You think he would have let me go?"

Anger transitioned to compassion. It always did where her mother was concerned. "He . . . must have loved you, too . . . once."

Janine snorted. "What he loved was his almighty army. His *team*," she added bitterly. "I was just a convenience. A body warming his bed. Someone waiting at home while he went off and played war. And you," she continued, her eyes turning mean, "don't kid yourself. To him you were just an inconvenient liability."

B.J. forced herself to breathe deep, then exhale on a long, bracing breath. "That's not how I remember it. That's not how I remember him."

"Because you were a child. You remember what you want to remember. You remember how he'd come home after a deployment, pat you on the head like a good little pet, and play with you like you were some pretty doll or a wind-up toy or something."

It still hurt B.J. to know that her mother had been jealous of the time her father had spent with her. She'd never comprehend how a mother could feel jealous of her own child.

"You don't remember that he was always more than happy to leave you over and over again," her mother said.

It wasn't me he was leaving, B.J. wanted to point out. He was leaving a wife grown sour with self-pity. Or maybe Janine Chase had always been angry. Maybe that's why in between moving from base to base, B.J.'s father had volunteered for the long-term missions. The dangerous missions. Missions like the one that had gotten him killed the spring she had turned eighteen.

"Look. I've . . . I've got to get back to D.C." She couldn't do this anymore. She reached for her purse, pulled out her wallet, and counted out five twenties. "I'll call, okay?" She tucked the bills under an empty wineglass.

Flat, dull eyes pinned her by the door. "Go," her mother said with a dismissive lift of her hand. "Get outta here. Go do what you have to do. Run away. Just like he did. Damn if you're not just like him. Always running away."

B.J. paused with her hand on the door, wishing she could feel something other than relief at the prospect of leaving. Wishing her mother wasn't right. She *was* running away. She'd been running her entire life. "Take care of yourself, Mom." Without looking back, she walked out the door. She felt like she was walking out of a prison.

Her BlackBerry rang just as she hit the keyless remote and unlocked her new Jeep. She dug it out of her bag, recognized the office number, and frowned.

"I'm still on leave," she snapped, expecting to hear Cathy Watson's voice on the other end of the line. Cathy was the girl Friday, agent wannabe, chronic source of annoyance for her division of the DIA at the Department of Defense, where B.J. worked as a covert intelligence officer in the Defense Human Intelligence Service (DHS). Cathy was also a perpetual pain in B.J.'s side. Paperwork. The woman was a real stickler for it and although she was grades below B.J. on the pay scale, Cathy loved to lord it over B.J. that she wouldn't get paid if Cathy didn't sign off on the paperwork.

"How soon can you report?"

Whoa. It wasn't Cathy's smug little voice that greeted her on the other end of the line. It was her division head, Dale Sherwood.

She scowled down the street as she opened the driver's-side door and tossed her purse across to the passenger seat. "Excuse me? You're the one who insisted I take this leave," she reminded him, although her heart clattered with excitement at the prospect of reporting for duty as she settled in behind the wheel.

She was on her first vacation since she'd signed on with DIA three years ago—though it was more of an enforced time-out. Of course, the fact that she'd made the trip to her mother's pretty much told the tale. She was going stark raving mad without her work to keep her busy and her mind occupied. Not that she'd been idle. She'd used the time off to sharpen her tennis game, toning up her muscles and her evasion skills while dodging the advances of the tennis pro at the athletic club. There were only so many movies to see, she'd exhausted her interest in experimenting with new pasta recipes, and she still had three days of her two-week vacation left before she was due to report in.

"Consider it canceled. I need you back here, Chase. Give me an ETA."

Big. This had to be big for the boss man himself to call, not to mention interrupt the leave he had mandated that she take because, in his words, "You're turning into a damn drone. Go. Take some time off. Mingle with the masses. Discover what it's like to have a life. See if you can find a sense of humor."

She'd resented that last remark. She had a sense of humor. He just didn't appreciate it, just like she hadn't appreciated his parting jab. "While you're at it, get over Caracas. It's time to move on."

Caracas. There it was again. She'd replayed that debacle in her mind a hundred times in the past three months. It always played back the same: She'd failed. And she had a hot Latino Choirboy and his band of merry men to thank for it. Sure, she'd gotten Eduardo, but he'd been pissed. And suddenly, her paid informant didn't have one piece of information that could help them.

So get over Caracas? Yeah. *That* was going to happen.

"Chase?" Sherwood's voice jolted her back to the moment. "I need an ETA."

She checked her watch, then squinted against the sun as she buckled up. "I can be there in two hours if I don't run into traffic." And she wouldn't if she left right now.

She was already cranking the key when Sherwood disconnected.

Lean, mean marines in sweat-drenched PT gear were running around a quarter-mile track when B.J. arrived at the Defense Intelligence Analysis Center on the Bolling Air Force Base in Washington, D.C. Not far away, planes landed like synchronized wasps. She could see their reflections in the steel-and-glass structure as she let herself inside.

Bypassing a pair of Saddam Hussein's gold-plated automatic weapons displayed in the lobby, she headed straight for the Scud missile erected beside the elevator bank and punched the up button.

Exactly one hour and fifty-two minutes after Dale Sherwood had summoned her, she arrived at the briefing room. He did a double take when he got a look at her. She understood why. Professional white blouses and dark suits were her norm but she hadn't wanted to take the time to stop at her apartment and change out of her tank top and shorts. She suspected, however, that it was her hair that threw him the most.

As a rule, she worked hard to control the unmanageable blond curls by clipping them at her nape or twisting them into a knot. Today she'd made do with a headband that simply held her hair away from her face, letting the thick, unruly mass of it fall in wild curls around her shoulders. She'd tried cutting it once. She'd looked like a blonde Little Orphan Annie. No. Thank. You.

"Thanks for coming in," Dale said when she closed the door behind her.

"No problem."

He grunted.

Okay. Her bad. There *was* a problem. Not a big enough problem to meet at HQ at the Pentagon, apparently, but big enough for Dale's "end of the world" expression, which he generally reserved for budget cuts, or when the Homeland Security Alert Level elevated from orange to red, or, as had been the case in Caracas, when four of his best covert officers compromised themselves and blew a mission.

"You ever had someone piss all over your birthday party?" he asked abruptly as he pulled out a chair at the conference table and dropped heavily into it.

*Hokay*, she thought, narrowing her eyes and wondering where this was going. "Can't recall that happening, no, sir."

The fact was she'd never had a birthday cake, let alone a party, but she didn't think he'd give a rat's tail end about her "boo hoo" childhood. Just like she didn't figure this was about a party.

On second thought, maybe it was. It was common knowledge that the grease that made the wheels run in D.C. was generally spread at cocktail parties, dinner parties, and yeah, the occasional birthday bash. D.C. parties were places to make contacts, share inside gossip, and drop bombs of unexpected info—like the one she suspected was about to be dropped on her.

"Turned sixty yesterday. The wife insisted on a 'thing.'"

"You don't look sixty, sir."

Tired brown eyes cut straight to hers as she joined him at the table. "The world hates a smart-ass."

She *was* being a smart-ass. The division head position had taken a toll on Dale Sherwood during his tenure. He didn't look sixty—he looked closer to eighty. Fatigue and stress had dug deep hollows under his eyes and rounded the shoulders on his six-foot frame; his jowls had gone saggy and soft from too many hours spent behind a desk. His hair was as gray as concrete.

She waited, knowing he would get to the point in his own good time. She also wondered why she was the only intelligence officer present. Dale wasn't prone to secrecy in the ranks. The system didn't much allow it. As division head of DHS, he reported to the DIA director, a three-star general who would in turn report to Secretary of Defense Blaylock through the Joint Chiefs of Staff.

"So anyway," he continued, "the wife throws this party, right? More military brass than a band shows up. I spot this friend of mine—enough for you to know he's a two-star, army. Was surprised to see him because last I heard he was in Afghanistan. Turns out he's just back and he didn't come to my party for the cake."

B.J. could tell by the way Sherwood tapped his index finger on the glossy mahogany conference table that he was working his way up to agitated.

"Anyway, he corners me. Tells me he flew into Andrews three hours ago and that we need to talk. Alone. Fine. We go to my home office and he drops a MOAB at my feet."

MOAB. The mother of all bombs. B.J. crossed her legs, kept her mouth shut, and waited.

"He tells me that he got this after-action report across his desk, right? Took a couple of weeks to get there but the gist of the report is the boys on the ground intercepted a supply truck—supposedly a Russian aid truck."

"Russian aid," B.J. repeated, mulling it over. "Major oxymoron there. And let me take a wild guess. I'm betting the truck wasn't filled with Spam or bandages or contraband birth control devices."

He swiped a hand over his jaw. "No, there was no aid on board. No Russians, either. Just your stock-in-trade Taliban sympathizer who blew himself up before they could question him. In the meantime, they found a helluva lot of munitions on the truck."

This was not exactly an unheard-of event in Afghanistan. Terrorists hijacked aid trucks all the time. "And this is out of the ordinary because . . . ?"

"It was out of the ordinary because munitions weren't all they found."

# 4

Sherwood paused, gave B.J. a long, hard look. "This stays between us, Chase."

"Absolutely." The affirmation came out with a calm she was actually no longer feeling.

"Does EPFCG mean anything to you?"

She'd had some classes in high-energy physics in college, and she'd retained some basic information. The info on EPFCG had stuck because it had scared her to death.

"Electromagnetic pulse weapon—EMP—explosively pumped flux compression generator." She pulled the words slowly out of her memory banks. "More commonly known as an E-bomb. If I remember right, an E-bomb the size of a small suitcase could shut down a major city by essentially frying anything electronic. Cell phones, cars, computer networks, power grids."

Sherwood nodded. "An almost-perfect weapon—fly one over, say, New York City or D.C. in a cruise missile, set it off, and that city will be reduced to the Stone Age with no real damage to the infrastructure."

No. No damage to the infrastructure, but the chaos created by an electronic meltdown would be catastrophic, not just from a communications perspective but for commerce, health, and safety. Any cities within range could become one huge looting gallery.

She also remembered why she still slept—most nights, anyway. "But the technology to miniaturize an E-bomb small enough to deliver it . . . it's still a long way from perfected. Right?" she added, not realizing until she'd asked how hopeful she sounded.

"Right. But we're working on it. Us and half the rogue nations in the world. Supposedly we're the only ones who have it developed to the point of testing."

"*Supposedly?*" She felt her face drain of blood as the implication of that one word sank in. "Are you saying they also found E-bomb technology on that truck in Afghanistan?"

Dale looked worried. "Looking that way."

"Holy God. In a truck?"

"The techno age hasn't reached all of Afghanistan, you know that. The Taliban communication system is often rudimentary and almost uncrackable by satellites *because* they hand-carry messages. Battle plans, tables of organization, intel, and more are all stuffed in satchels and carried all over the country, sometimes by donkey, sometimes, as in this case, by a truck," Sherwood pointed out.

"So who on the ground over there would even recognize E-bomb specs?"

"Most special forces non-coms have some EOD training—explosive ordnance disposal training," he clarified unnecessarily then quickly apologized. "Sorry. Forgot who I was talking to. Anyway, they knew that what they were looking at was not status quo. Long story short, every piece of intel they recovered from that truck filtered up to the two-star, including the hard copies of the specs. Here's the kicker. The plans look an awful lot like ours."

"And ours are supposed to be top secret." No wonder Sherwood looked like he'd eaten cactus for lunch. "So, we're talking—"

"No," he said, cutting her off. "We're not talking. Not about any of this."

Of course they weren't. Welcome to life in the intelligence community.

"All the intel the military gathered on this is being run up the ranks but even with a top priority, it's going to take a while to sort things out. In the meantime, copies of the E-bomb specs are being checked out at the Pentagon for authenticity."

"So where do we fit in?"

"My friend, the two-star, trusts me to do a little behind-the-scenes work. He wants me to see if I can ferret out how plans with this type of top secret clearance got out and more important, how the breach got past NSA, before he takes it up the chain of command to the sec def.

"What I need from you," Sherwood went on after a

pause B.J. used to fully digest the magnitude of the situation, "are answers. I need an inside line to support or dispute whether it even is our technology. And if it's ours, then I need to know if the reason NSA isn't on top of the leak is due to negligence or because someone sold us out. And make no mistake—if NSA was aware of this, heads would have rolled by now."

Silence rang hollow in the wake of his final statement and struck both terror and outrage inside her. He was talking about the possibility of there being a traitor. At the National Security Agency.

Jesus.

"What do you want me to do?"

"I want you to give me a happy birthday, Chase. I want you to infiltrate the NSA, hook up with an agent inside, and find out what the hell is going on. Then I want you to report back to me yesterday."

B.J.'s heart kicked her a couple of good ones. The NSA was the top dog in the intelligence community. He wanted her to spy on the super spies. "Okay. Wait. Let's say there's actually a leak and NSA should have plugged it. Who can we—"

"Trust inside?" he interrupted, anticipating her question.

"That'd be a start," she said, unable to hide her incredulity.

"We start with a cryptanalyst by the name of Stephanie Tompkins."

The name rattled around until it finally clicked like tumblers in a lock. "Tompkins? As in . . . ?" She let her question trail off and met Dale's eyes.

"Yeah. As in her father, Robert Tompkins, was counsel to President Billings. And her mother, Ann Tompkins, is deputy attorney general. The family bleeds red, white, and blue. We can trust her. We have to trust her."

B.J. sat back in her chair, processing everything Sherwood had just told her. Still, she didn't want to believe what he was suggesting, yet she was afraid not to.

*Traitor.*

That one word stood out amid an ocean of information. They could have a traitor in their midst.

"I need to know if you're up for this, Chase."

She met his eyes and saw not only the challenge, but the quiet desperation and demand there.

"Yeah," she said with a hard nod. "I'm up for it."

The thing that always amazed B.J. about the intelligence community was how easy it was to gain access to the various divisions. Take the NSA. Following Sherwood's instructions, she'd driven to Maryland two weeks ago, gone straight through security at Fort George G. Meade, and waltzed into the NSA building with a cooked-up order directing her to job shadow Stephanie Tompkins in the Signals Intelligence division.

That had been it. A scrawled signature on an official-looking document, her badge and ID, and she'd gotten in, undercover as herself—a DIA officer temporarily and reluctantly reassigned to the geek squad of the spy world.

It helped that since 9/11, there had been a constant push, although not exactly a full-court press, for all agencies under the DOD—the NSA fitting loosely into that category—to dovetail their intelligence-gathering and operational efforts. The standing directive was to share intel, coordinate operations, and generally play well with each other.

The problem was these NSA types didn't even play well among themselves, B.J. thought with interest as she sat in on her tenth daily staff meeting and listened to the Signal Intelligence division head, Alan Hendricks, shut down Stephanie Tompkins's oral report on a possible protocol breach as a waste of time. Hendricks's reaction had B.J.'s antennae twitching like divining rods.

During the last two weeks, B.J. had grown used to Stephanie Tompkins's calm demeanor, but Stephanie wasn't her usual cool-as-a-cucumber self after the staffing either. She was fuming—if you believed pinched lips and a face that had grown red all the way up to the roots of her dark brown hair indicated fuming. In B.J.'s world, the way Alan Hendricks had discounted Stephanie's report as a waste of time was grounds for some heated name calling, pedigree bashing, and intellect questioning. But in B.J.'s world, there wasn't a lot of subtlety. She called it like she saw it and the first day she'd met him, she'd seen Alan Hendricks as a prick. Capital P. Capital R.I.C.K. More to the point, Hendricks's reaction just now was the first breakthrough B.J. had encountered in the two weeks since she'd promised Sherwood that she'd get a lead on "the matter of which we will not speak."

"*That* drilled straight into a raw nerve," B.J. said as she and Stephanie walked back to their respective cubicles after Hendricks had uncharacteristically ordered everyone to hand over their copies of Stephanie's report before he'd dismissed the troops from the staff meeting.

Stephanie shook her head and kept on walking.

Probably in shock, B.J. thought. Since she wasn't here to win friends, it was the first friendly overture B.J. had made since she'd arrived, flashed her credentials at Stephanie, and informed her of the top-secret nature of her mission.

Up until this staffing, when they'd dangled Stephanie's report as bait, then waited for someone to nibble, B.J. had been leaning toward believing Stephanie Tompkins's darn good company line about there being no incompetence, negligence, or duplicity in the NSA's SI division.

Well, that had just changed, big time. By the time Stephanie had finished her presentation, Alan Hendricks looked like he'd swallowed a nuclear reactor. Now Stephanie looked like someone had keyed her car.

It surprised B.J. to realize that she felt bad about that. She didn't know Stephanie well enough to decide if she liked her and wouldn't cultivate a friendship if she could. Years of moving from base to base had pretty much taught her that it didn't pay to get invested in any kind of a relationship. You got close, then you moved, then you got hurt. So she didn't get close.

And, no. She and Stephanie Tompkins would never be BFFs. Honest truth, B.J. hadn't known what to think about her the first time they'd met. She hadn't thought *fluff*, exactly, but even though Stephanie also dressed for success in dark pantsuits and crisp white blouses, *soft* had definitely come to mind. Soft brown eyes, soft curves, soft smile. The kind of soft that B.J. had seen men stand in line to play white knight for.

B.J. had never experienced that particular reaction from the opposite sex.

"Cold," Dave Adams had informed her over chow one day when they'd both been raw recruits at Bragg. "You've got a cold, hard heart, Chase."

"Because I won't let you get in my pants?" she'd speculated, blocking his attempt to buddy up by giving him grief.

"Because you won't let anyone get in your head," he'd said, surprising her with his serious tone. "You've got to trust someone eventually, you know."

No, she'd told him. She didn't.

"You trust someone, they're just going to let you down," she'd added, because in her experience that's the way it was. "But if I *were* going to trust someone"— she'd relented when his face had gotten all long and sad—"it would be you. Probably. Maybe."

He'd finally grinned and for whatever reason she'd been glad. That had been their last heart-to-heart. She'd made sure of it. She'd done so because there were times, vastly lonely moments when she was tempted to talk to someone, anyone. To just have someone listen, to bear witness to the pain, to tell her that time would heal.

But that was weakness. That would be self-indulgence and she didn't have time for either.

B.J. wasn't sure what it was about Stephanie that made her think of Adams. Maybe it was because, as with Adams, B.J. had grown to respect the attractive brunette's loyalty, intelligence, and work ethic. For the past two weeks as they'd worked together, Stephanie had played the loyalty card until the corners were bent.

Earlier this morning when B.J. had found Stephanie at her desk, ghost white and staring into space, she'd asked Stephanie what was wrong.

"You were right," Stephanie admitted softly. "Something . . . or someone . . . has gone terribly wrong."

Her big, soulful brown eyes were filled with so much pain that B.J. almost felt sorry for her. But Stephanie Tompkins's feelings weren't the priority. National security was.

"Tell me," B.J. had ordered, then amended, "in English, please," when Stephanie had started spouting technical jargon understood only by R2-D2 types.

"I've discovered some huge gaps in protocol," Stephanie said, regrouping. "Cryptologists look for certain patterns, phrases, repeats . . . anything out of the norm or even seemingly normal but maybe out of place. Everything is fed into a software program that filters, sorts, matches, and compiles the bits and pieces we send it. I discovered multiple deletions over at least a twelve-month period. So I searched for those deleted files."

"And?" B.J. had prompted.

"And I found them," she said, looking grim. "Hundreds of them. All encrypted communications with threads in common. If they hadn't been deleted, the program would have done its thing, red-flagged the similarities and brought them to our attention."

"Tell me about the red flags."

"Recurrent sign-offs with a code name *URA!* Communiqués between the same two IP addresses. I tracked one to Russia. Haven't managed to decipher the other address but there are multiple references to EMPs."

B.J.'s heart had practically jumped out of her chest by the time Stephanie had finished. EMPs. E-bombs. Sherwood's two-star just might be right.

"Any way to determine who deleted the data?"

"Not if they knew their business, and everyone here does."

"And yet you found the deleted files."

"Only because I'm team leader and all incoming transmissions loop through my dedicated server."

"So why wasn't the deleted info wiped clean by whoever did this?"

Stephanie had lifted a shoulder. "It's a complex, time-intensive task. Frankly, in the three years I've been here I've never back-traced deleted data, so they probably figured it was safe to leave it there. If you hadn't alerted me to a possible breach I never would have checked. Besides, asking for a clean sweep would have tipped their hand. They would have had to come to me to perform the delete process—it's a fail-safe measure. That would have been a big red flag for me and the first thing I would have done is what I just did, which led me to the inconsistencies."

*Inconsistencies*. What a nice way to say *traitor*, B.J. had thought at the time.

"What do you want me to do now?" Stephanie had asked.

"Now you write this all up in a report and present it at staffing, but suggest a possible systems failure as opposed to human intervention."

"But that's not the case."

"No. The case is, someone sold out their country. But the fact is, if the report lays that out, point blank, whoever did it will walk out that door tonight and disappear along with whatever secrets they've been sharing with the bad guys. I want this guy. I want him bad, so we're going to give him some rope . . . hopefully to hang himself."

Alan Hendricks appeared to have slipped the noose over his head in staffing just now, B.J. thought as she continued following Stephanie through the rabbit warren of walkways to her cubicle. B.J. needed to report to Sherwood ASAP, but that meant she'd have to leave the building because all outgoing calls were monitored and no one was allowed to bring their cell phone inside. She wasn't going anywhere just this instant, however, because something told her the action was about to heat up.

"I don't think you've seen the last of Hendricks today," she told Stephanie. "When he shows up play it cool.

"Stephanie?" she prodded when the other woman didn't respond. "You okay?"

"Perfect," Stephanie said in a tone that revealed just how perfect she wasn't.

"Pull it together," B.J. warned her, refusing to let herself be affected by Stephanie's misery. It was a misery she could relate to. No one wanted to believe someone they trusted would betray them.

# 5

Stephanie sank down on her desk chair, confused, angry, and suspicious of the way Alan Hendricks had shut her down. She tossed the report onto the top of her workstation that was wedged into the small, sterile cubicle, exactly the same as every other workspace occupying the vacuous, open floor in the cryptanalysis section of the Signal Intelligence Division.

Overhead, rows of fluorescent lights were interspersed with dingy white ceiling tile. Security cameras kept constant vigil. Shoulder-high, gray upholstered walls divided one cubicle from another. By design, the walls provided minimal privacy and buffered little noise. All desk phones were set to speaker only. No cell phones were permitted inside the complex. Sort of like a fortress, Steph had thought more than once.

And now that fortress appeared to have been breached.

*Traitor.*

She had fought it tooth and nail, but B. J. Chase was right. Someone right here at the NSA had sold out their country and right now the lead suspect was none other than her boss, Alan Hendricks.

Expelling a frustrated breath, she reached absently for the magic decoder ring that sat in a box on the corner of her desk, turned it over in her palm. The ring had been a Christmas gift—the kind of gift that a big brother gives a kid sister on an allowance of a buck a week. The perfect gift for that nine-year-old girl who had big dreams of being a spy.

Well, she wasn't the James Bond type of spy of her childhood fantasies. She was the kind of spy who worked nine to five in this cramped little cubbyhole, kept the true nature of her work a secret from family and friends, and, day in, day out, did her damnedest to do her job.

A job she performed well.

*And now Alan was telling her she was way off base?*

"Something is off, all right," she muttered, listening to the low drone of chatter from the neighboring cubicles, feeling the heat of her CPU and a hundred others as the AC worked overtime to keep the machines cool.

She hadn't wanted to believe B. J. Chase when she'd shown up two weeks ago. The woman was a cold fish with her facts-and-only-the-facts attitude, her one-on-one confidential briefing about a possible traitor in the NSA ranks, and her DIA orders that Stephanie was to be her inside source.

She didn't like being recruited to spy on her fellow employees. People she'd worked with for the past several years. People she trusted. People she relied on.

She just couldn't believe that Alan would sell out his country. There had to be some other explanation.

"Speak of the devil." She slid the ring back into its box when she saw Alan's bald head making its way toward her through the maze of trails that wound around the workstations on the floor.

Alan was tall and lean—and not a physically fit, runner's-body sort of lean. He drank too much coffee, smoked too many cigarettes judging by the way his clothes always smelled, micromanaged too diligently, and in general spent much of his energy making the drones' lives a living hell.

"Hand it over," he ordered, reaching over the top of her cubicle and nodding toward her report.

Stephanie suddenly felt very protective of that report. She was a disciplined cryptanalyst. She obeyed orders. She followed rules. But when he gave her that look she rammed headlong into that wall where better judgment met up with stubborn pride.

"You said to deep-six it," she reminded him, aware that B.J. was listening to every word on the other side of the cubicle wall.

He looked around to see if they were being overheard, then walked into her cubicle. "Just hand it over."

She slid the report a little left of center on her desk and a lot farther away from his outstretched hand. "What's going on, Alan?" She wanted him to tell her something, anything that would make this nightmare go away. "According to you, it's a wash. So what do you care what I do with the report?"

"I care what you do with it because you have better things to occupy your time and knowing your bulldog tenacity, you won't let this one go." He shot her a forced smile. The good boss, only concerned for his staff. "Now be a good civil servant, hand over the report, and transfer any associated computer files to me. Then what I really need you to do is get back to work on the CVX summary. Sorry, Steph, but I need it before you leave today."

Before she could react, he snatched up the report and walked off.

B. J. Chase appeared at the opening to her cubicle.

"I don't want to hear it," Stephanie warned her.

"I was just going to tell you to watch your back."

Stephanie was surprised to see real concern on Chase's face.

"The fat is about to hit the fire."


An hour later, Alan Hendricks shifted his modest compact into park, left the car running near the curb, and got out. Traffic was quiet at midday on this side street. He waited for a lone minivan to pass, then crossed the street and approached the black Lincoln Town Car.

The tinted rear window lowered silently as he approached. Sweat beaded on his forehead as he passed the report to the outstretched hand.

The silence was disrupted only by the sound of

pages being turned. Finally all movement in the back-seat stopped.

"Explain to me how an agency operating on the fundamental principle of need to know allowed this to happen. I want to know how in the *hell* an office drone by the name of Stephanie Tompkins ended up ferreting out this information. You said there was a fail-safe. That no one would find it."

The sun beat like fire on the top of Alan's head. "No one should have found it. But it's a moot point now. I dead-ended any action. It'll be forgotten by Monday. In the meantime, it won't happen again."

"You're damn right it won't."

Alan wiped a hand over his jaw, composed himself, and deflected what he knew would be the next question. "We retrieved the report and Stephanie has been told to let it drop so it's no longer an issue. As a precaution, IT will wipe her hard drive clean as soon as she leaves tonight."

"Like *that's* not going to make her suspicious."

He shrugged, a failed attempt at confidence that he was far from feeling. "We'll explain it as a unit failure. Happens all the time. When we exchange her 'fried' hard drive for a new one, data on this report will also have been conveniently lost on the backup server. Like I said. Happens all the time."

"I don't like this."

Alan didn't like it either. There was way too much at stake. Christ. How had he gotten in so deep?

"Even if you destroy all the evidence, I don't trust that this Tompkins woman will let it drop. And what about that DIA drone? Hasn't she been working closely with Tompkins?"

Alan shook his head. "Chase isn't a problem. She's just one in a long line of indifferent temporary transplants putting in their time on that damn job shadow program. Her assignment's over next week and that'll be the end of that. Trust me—she doesn't understand squat about what we do."

"You'd better be right. In the meantime, I expect you to take care of the Tompkins situation."

He swallowed. Hoped to hell he wasn't hearing what he thought he was hearing. "I told you. I *am* taking care of it."

Hard eyes stared out of the dark interior, met his with deadly malice. "You're not listening. I said, take care of it. Take care of *her*."

His heart stumbled. *Jesus*. Kill Stephanie Tompkins? He was supposed to kill Stephanie?

"You're talking about Ann Tompkins's daughter. The daughter of a deputy attorney general in the Department of Justice, for Chrissake." He swiped a shaking hand over his jaw. "And Stephanie's father—Robert Tompkins was counsel to President Billings."

Silence. Then a cold glare. "Then you'll have to be particularly careful, won't you?"

It was after six and the floor was deserted by the time Stephanie finally finished the CVX summary. Instead of taking a chance on the interoffice delivery system, she decided to walk the report up to Alan's office personally.

It wasn't just about making certain he got the report before the weekend. She wanted to talk to him, give him an opportunity to . . . damn. She didn't know. Make her believe he wasn't hiding something horrible, she guessed.

She still couldn't believe it.

"Extract your head from the sand," B.J. had told her before she'd clocked out half an hour ago. "Loyalty is one thing. It's time to face the facts."

And the facts, Stephanie knew, were going to either clear or vilify her boss.

The elevator hit his floor; she walked down the hall, then rapped a knuckle on his office door. It swung open.

"Alan?"

When she didn't get a reply, she walked inside. His computer was powered down, the screen was black.

"Bastard," she swore when she realized he'd already left. "Needed this summary tonight," she sputtered, and resisted storming out of the office.

Angry with just about everything about this wretched day, she marched back down the hall with the report, punched the elevator button, and did a little solitary fuming as the elevator descended to her floor.

She made herself take a deep, steadying breath to settle herself down. The breath left her body in a rush, however, when she stepped out of the elevator and spotted a man at her desk.

Alarm bells rang inside her head like storm sirens. "What are you doing?"

The guy jumped, then flattened a hand on his chest. "Holy crap! You scared the hell out of me."

Join the club, she thought, her concern mounting. He was little more than a kid—probably fresh out of college. His name tag identified him as Tracy Davis, IT—which meant exactly nothing to her. She'd never seen him before.

"I asked you what you're doing at my workstation," she demanded when she realized he'd torn her CPU apart and was in the process of putting it back together.

"Just replaced your hard drive." He went back to work with his little screwdriver and fastened a metal plate to the base of the tower.

"My hard drive? Why?"

Pale blue eyes glanced up at her above the thin wire frames of his glasses. "Because I got a work order. Cripes. What is your problem?"

Her problem was, there hadn't been anything wrong with her hard drive. "Let me see the order."

He gave her a huffy look, grunted, then dug around on his clipboard and produced a sheet of paper. "Satisfied?"

Alan's signature was scrawled on the order. She swore under her breath, then glanced back at the tech. "There's nothing wrong with my computer."

"You're right about that. At least there's nothing wrong now. I just installed the new drive." He stacked the old drive on top of his clipboard and rose to leave.

"But there was nothing wrong with that one," she pointed out again.

"Look," he said, sounding like he'd used up his store of patience. "The work order said it was fried. To me that means it's fried, so I replaced it. End of story."

End of story? God, she wished that was the case.

Every word that had come out of B. J. Chase's mouth during the past two weeks started replaying in her head like news footage. There was a traitor in the ranks. This hijacking of her hard drive proved it.

"When will the backup server restore the data on my machine?" she asked carefully.

"Happening as we speak. Your unit should be operational in a couple of minutes." The tech gathered his things and walked away mumbling. "Hell of a fuss over nothing, you ask me."

Oh, how she wanted it to be nothing. Her pounding heart told her otherwise. Yes, she'd been resistant to Chase's insistence that there was a traitor in their midst. Resistant, but not stupid. There hadn't been a damn thing wrong with her hard drive.

She needed to get out of here. She was already getting a late start for her trip home to her parents' in Richmond. But she needed to check for herself and see if he was telling the truth, that her data would all be restored. She sat back down at her desk, powered up her computer, then sat waiting for it to boot up.

Finally, it was all systems go. Her heart pounded like crazy as she accessed the file containing the information on her report. Gone. Her fingers trembled on the

keyboard as she typed in the path to the backup location. Also gone.

She felt the rest of the blood drain from her face.
They'd wiped out anything and everything that had to
do with the report. Alan had wanted to make doubly
sure that any record was wiped clean, which, as far as
she was concerned, was the last nail in his coffin.

It was a desperate action, suggesting that Alan was a
desperate man. She needed to get out of here and report to Chase.

But first, she had to break a few laws.

She stood up, checked the floor, listened. She was
alone.

God, she couldn't believe she was doing this.

Angling her shoulders so the security cameras
couldn't see her hands, she lifted her decoder ring out
of its box, along with the cardboard insert the ring
rested on. Inside the bottom of the little box was the
flash drive she used as temporary backup for her
work—the work Alan had just had destroyed. With her
back still blocking the camera, she lifted her purse out
of her drawer, then rummaged around for the little
cylindrical penlight she always carried. Quickly un-
screwing the seal from the bottom of the plastic flashlight, she dumped the batteries in her waste can and
hid the flash drive inside the barrel of the flashlight.

The ploy wouldn't disguise the drive from the security scanner when the guard checked her out at the
main door, but she'd think of something between now
and then to deflect his attention.

Five minutes later, she approached the security checkpoint, absently fumbling inside her purse. "'Night, Ben," she said. The scanner everyone passed through was similar to airport security scanners, only a little more sensitive and high tech.

"Oh, damn," she muttered when she "accidentally" dropped her purse and half the contents spilled onto the floor. By design, the flashlight concealing the flash drive went rolling across the polished floor, past the X-ray scanner but still in view of the watchful camera.

Ben—mid-forties, family man, working for the weekend—hauled himself out from behind the scanner with a chuckle. "Must have a hot date," he said, bending over to help her pick up her things. "Go on through, Miss Tompkins. I'll help you with that."

"Never pays to hurry," she said, sounding put out with herself.

Then she tossed her purse on the belt and together, she and Ben chucked everything back inside her bag. Everything but the flashlight, which had rolled across the room.

She stooped over, picked it up, and with Ben watching, tossed it in her purse as if, in her haste, it hadn't even occurred to her to pass it back to him to scan.

Then, counting on Ben's good nature, his long workweek, and her years of passing through security without so much as a set of nail clippers to set off the scanner, she held her breath, shouldered her bag, and headed for the door.

"Thanks, Ben." She smiled, big and wide, over her shoulder to hide how nervous she was.

"You have a good weekend," he said as he settled back into his spot and she sailed on out the door.

Stephanie's heart was still slamming when she reached her car, buckled herself in, and zipped out of the parking lot. Her palms were sweating as she hit the road and maneuvered onto the 295 on-ramp.

That's when the gravity of her situation hit her. What had she done? What in the *hell* had she just done?

And the bigger question: Why did she have the horrible feeling that "borrowing" the flash drive was the least, the very least, of her problems?

# 6

B.J. let herself into her D.C. apartment, tossed the keys to her brand-new forest green Jeep Cherokee—she was doing her bit to help the economy—on the kitchen counter, and headed straight for the freezer and the bag of Hershey's chocolate Kisses she kept there. One kiss wasn't going to do it today so she grabbed a handful and started ripping into the silver foil before she even hit the sofa.

The first piece hit her tongue and flavor burst through her mouth. She felt the tension start to ease from her shoulders as she sank into the lush red leather.

Yeah. Red. She still wasn't sure what had come over her. She wasn't an impulse buyer. She *was* a basic-black kind of girl—until she'd walked into that upscale furniture store two months ago. All she'd needed was a new floor lamp.

She ran her hand across the buttery smooth leather. No, she hadn't needed a red leather sofa, but damn, she had needed the pick-me-up.

She needed another one now. The traffic from Fort Meade to D.C. had been brutal. And despite Sherwood's assurances, B.J. had second-guessed herself all the way home. The trap she and Stephanie had laid today that caught Alan Hendricks might have also painted a big red X on Stephanie Tompkins's back.

"Stephanie's not in danger," Sherwood had assured her when she'd called him from her Jeep on the pricey new encrypted cell phone he'd issued her that ensured their conversations were secure. "Hendricks isn't going to do anything stupid. Based on what you've told me, he thinks he has his bases and his ass covered. And he knows that after his performance today, if something happened to Stephanie, the first place anyone would start looking would be his backyard. No, he'll play this safe. I'll order surveillance on him right away so we'll be there if and when he screws up.

"Listen. Good job, Chase," he'd added. "Just keep your eyes open."

She planned to, she thought as the last of the chocolate melted in her mouth. That plan included digging up background information on Alan Hendricks, which meant she had to go into the D.C. office to get it. The software that she'd need to hack through the many firewalls she'd encounter wasn't in place on her laptop. No, she needed the DIA's system to dig as deep she needed to go.

She shoved herself up from the couch. A quick shower revived her. In deference to the July heat, she

threw on a pair of khaki shorts and a black tank top—
two colors that dominated her wardrobe—and headed
out for the office.

No rest for the wicked or the terminally diligent.
She'd been labeled both.

Earlier that day a cell phone rang in a hotel room a
mile from the NSA complex.

Zach Loeffler, who was registered with the front
desk as Robert Smith, recognized the number. He
turned down the volume on the TV and flipped open
the phone. "Smith."

"Time to earn your retainer."

He'd been expecting this call. He always expected a
call. "Specifics."

He listened, then asked the inevitable question. "Ac-
cident or execution?"

"Use your imagination. If it must be newsworthy,
just make certain it appears random. Avoid any undue
attention. I'll arrange payment the usual way when you
confirm that it's done."

The line went dead.

Zach pocketed his phone, flicked off the TV with
the remote, and turned on the GPS locator he'd
planted in the target's car several weeks ago.

The vehicle was traveling south, less than two miles
from his current location. He pulled the Fort Meade
area map out of the top dresser drawer, double-checked
his bearing. He'd spent a fair amount of time studying
the area both via the map and in his car.

"Location, location, location," he muttered. "It's all about location."

But prime real estate wasn't the object of his search. Advantage was.

He had three spots picked out. The challenge would be finding the perfect vantage point.

Hell, who was he kidding? There was no challenge. He was too damn good at what he did.

He scooped his keys from the dresser and pocketed them. A golf bag leaned against the wall in the corner by the bed. He unzipped the side pouch, made sure the two magazines were both filled with 5.56 NATO rounds. Then he shouldered the bag that contained a couple of woods, a few of his favorite irons, his putter, and his custom Steyr AUG. The Austrian bull pup rifle was very compact. With the quick-change barrel detached it was so small that it looked like a child's toy, only without the cork.

"Enjoy your game, sir." A cheerful bellman stood aside as Zach stepped out of the elevator onto the gleaming marble floor of the hotel lobby.

Zach smiled and slipped on his Ray-Bans. "I intend to, thanks." Then he walked out into the Maryland summer sun.

By the time Stephanie realized she'd been gripping the steering wheel like a lifeline, her fingers were aching. She made herself relax as she drove on, wondering what to do.

Chase. She needed to talk to B. J. Chase. Before she could dial her number and tell her what happened, her cell phone rang.

"Dead?" she repeated, disbelieving, after Rhonda Burns, another cryptologist in her section, delivered the stunning news. "Alan Hendricks is dead? Oh my God. How?"

"I just heard it on my police scanner! Couldn't believe it. It got called in as a suspected random shooting."

*Alan Hendricks . . . dead . . .*

The words echoed in Steph's head long after she'd hung up the phone. She drove on in stunned silence, her fingers tightening on the steering wheel again.

*Alan Hendricks . . .*

*dead . . .*

*random shooting.*

Or was it an execution? But that was . . . crazy.

*Wasn't it?*

God. Chase was making her paranoid.

"No. Alan Hendricks getting shot to death is making you paranoid," she muttered aloud as she sped along the highway.

Her hard drive being replaced was making her paranoid.

*There are no coincidences.*

It was a code she lived by, a mantra she used to problem-solve every day. It was no coincidence that Alan had been shot to death on the same day he'd wigged out over her report. It was no coincidence that her computer had been sabotaged in an effort to hide certain truths . . . truths she hadn't yet fully pieced together.

Still, it didn't make any sense. If Alan was really the mole, then why was *he* killed? Did that mean there were others involved? And if they killed him because of her report, did that mean . . . oh, God. What *did* it mean? Was she next?

She had to talk to Chase. Her fingers trembled as she fumbled with her phone and tried to steer at the same time. She started to dial. Stopped abruptly. Cell phones could be traced. Whoever had killed Alan could be monitoring her phone and locate her.

She quickly shut off the phone, then, holding the cell phone in the same hand she used to steer, she pried open the case and pulled out the battery.

"Try and find me now," she muttered aloud, and tossed the disabled phone onto the front seat beside her, then shook her head at the desperation in that line of thinking—and the momentary, false sense of confidence. So she'd disabled her cell phone. That wasn't going to stop anyone who wanted to find her. Her car could already be bugged or fixed with a tracking device. On top of that, her Saturn had come factory equipped with both OnStar and a GPS navigation system. If she was a target a professional would already have a lock on her position. Short of smashing all the electronics embedded in her dashboard, which would also disable the car, she was a sitting duck.

Her knuckles were white again as she shot off the

parkway onto the New Carrolton exit and stopped at the first convenience store she spotted. Once inside, she bought a throwaway phone and had it quickly activated. Then she hurried into the public restroom, locked the door, and dialed B. J. Chase's number.

B.J. had just pulled into the DIA complex parking lot when her cell rang. "Chase," she answered, not recognizing the number on the screen.

"B.J. It's Stephanie."

"What's wrong?" she demanded, reacting to the panic in Stephanie's voice.

"Alan Hendricks is dead."

B. J. slammed the Jeep into park. "What?"

Stephanie filled her in on what she knew. "Jesus," she muttered. "This was no random shooting." B.J. was certain of that.

"I know. It's horrible. And there's more. I caught someone from IT swapping out my computer's hard drive. Alan had ordered it done. All the data I had stored about the report was destroyed."

"It's all gone?" B.J.'s heart sank.

"No. I managed to smuggle out a flash drive that I use for backup. I've got it with me."

B.J.'s opinion of Stephanie shot up several more notches.

"What do I do?"

Despite the lingering heat of the hot summer day, goose bumps raced down B.J.'s spine. "Have you talked to anyone else about this?"

"No. Just you. I didn't say anything to Rhonda. But shouldn't we . . . shouldn't we call someone? Tell them what we think is going on?"

"You let me worry about that. In the meantime, don't talk to anyone, okay? Not until we put our heads together and sort this out. Where are you now?"

"I'm at a gas station near New Carrolton."

"Okay, look. You can't go back to your apartment. I'm in D.C. now. I'll meet you halfway. Just keep in touch. We'll figure on a spot as we get closer. Now go. And, Stephanie, watch your back, okay? If you think you're being followed, call me immediately, got it?"

"Yeah. I've got it."

Stephanie sounded shaky and scared. Smart woman. B.J. disconnected and immediately dialed Dale Sherwood and filled him in.

"Get her under wraps somewhere until we can get this sorted out," Dale said, sounding worried. "Let me know when she's off the grid."

"Yes, sir."

"And, Chase. I'm sorry. You were right. I should have had you stick with her. I made a bad call."

Yeah. He had. But so had she when she hadn't listened to her gut.

"I'll dig up everything I can about Alan Hendricks and get back to you. In the meantime, watch your six," Sherwood added, then hung up.

B.J. hit the gas. She flew out of the parking lot and told herself not to borrow trouble, that she'd meet up with Stephanie without incident and get her tucked out of harm's way until they figured out how to proceed from here.

But her sixth sense told her otherwise. Time was critical. She needed to get to Stephanie and she needed to do it fast.

No matter how hard she tried, Stephanie couldn't shake the image of a tiny red laser light from a rifle scope centered on the back of her head. Someone was following her. She knew it long before she spotted the black four-door sedan about four vehicles back.

Oh God.

She grabbed the throwaway phone off the seat beside her and dialed B.J. "I think someone is following me."

# 7

Raphael Mendoza was a stupid, swaggering sixteen-year-old the day he jacked his first car. It was a Caddy and he was a punk on a dare. The car was hot and fast, but the cops were faster. The only reason he was free to tell the tale was because he'd known the back-streets of Little Havana in Miami as well as he'd known his way around juvenile hall. He was as good as caught, so after a merry chase he'd finally slammed on the brakes, jammed the Caddy into park, and bailed.

Then he'd run like hell and bought himself another reprieve from detention.

He'd grown up a little in the fifteen or so years since then. But he still loved a hot, fast car. As he put pedal to metal and screamed up 295 toward Fort Meade and NSA HQ, he was damn glad for his training days behind the wheel.

He needed to get to Stephanie Tompkins and he needed to get to her now.

"What the hell is holding up that court order?" he

grumbled as the speedometer on Gabe's midnight blue SUV hovered near the 90 mph mark.

Gabe Jones, his Black Ops, Inc. team member, had tossed the keys to Rafe, opting to ride shotgun. "Keep it cool, man," Jones said as he systematically filled an extra magazine with .45 ACP cartridges for his 1911-A1 pistol. "Ann will call as soon as she has it."

Cool was a little beyond Rafe at the moment. He would have liked to think they were dealing with a simple case of a mother overreacting with worry about her daughter. But Ann Tompkins didn't overreact about anything and ever since Ann had called fifteen minutes ago, desperately concerned about Stephanie, all he'd been able to think about was getting a judge to sign the court order authorizing them to tap into the onboard GPS locator in Steph's car so they could get a fix on her position.

It might not require an act of Congress to accomplish it, but it might just take an act of God to get it done in time to help Steph if she really was in trouble. He kept telling himself this was all precautionary.

Problem was, he had a bad feeling. Judging by the tense look on his face, so did Gabe.

Which brought them back to the court order. It was all about greasing the wheels. But when you had a deputy attorney general wielding the grease gun, those wheels spun fast. Usually.

He swerved around a semi, cut behind a Mini Cooper, and never altered his speed. Beside him, Gabe had started filling the extra magazine for Rafe's Sig.

Thank God for Gabe. And thank fate that he'd been at Gabe and Jenna's D.C. apartment instead of working a case out of BOI HQ in Argentina when Ann had called.

"Tell me again exactly what Ann said," he prodded Gabe, who had taken Ann's call.

"The short of it is that she's been concerned about Steph. Something was going on at work that has been eating at her."

"Ann know what it is?"

"What do you think?"

Right. Ann Tompkins worked in the Justice Department but Stephanie's NSA position dictated the highest level of secrecy. That trumped the mother card every time.

"Anyway, Ann expected to hear from Steph as soon as she left work tonight. Apparently Ann wanted her to stop at their favorite bakery in D.C. and pick up a few things for the shindig tomorrow night."

The shindig was the reason Rafe was in the States. He and the bulk of the BOI team—Savage, Colter, Green, and Black—had either already arrived or would be flying in soon because Johnny Reed had bitten the big one. The Texas golden boy was getting married in a couple of months and Ann and Bob Tompkins were throwing the happy couple an engagement party at their Richmond home. Sam Lang and Abbie were coming, too, from Vegas. Rafe had decided to fly in a day early and spend it with Gabe and his wife, Jenna, who was now back at the apartment waiting for a call telling them that this was all a false alarm and that Stephanie was just fine.

"When Steph didn't call and Ann couldn't reach her on her cell phone," Gabe continued, "Ann started calling around to see if anyone knew where Stephanie was. She reached a coworker—Rhonda somebody—and found out the woman had talked to Steph just a few minutes before Ann had tried to reach her. Before they hung up, Rhonda dropped the bomb. She'd just heard a local news bulletin. Their boss, a guy by the name of Alan Hendricks, had been killed. Shot to death. Initial report was that it was a random shooting. When Ann tried to reach Steph again, it went right to voicemail."

No wonder Ann was frantic. Something at work was bothering Steph. Now a fellow NSA employee—a man who supervised her daughter—turns up dead and Steph wasn't checking in. Given that the NSA was the spy agency to beat all spy agencies, it stood to reason that something big and bad was going down.

Since D.C. was within thirty minutes of Steph's apartment if traffic cooperated, that meant that Rafe and Gabe were the closest boots on the ground because the local PD sure wasn't going to act on a mother's bad feeling—even if that mother was with the Justice Department.

Gabe's cell went off. He grabbed it on the first ring.

"Yo. Great. Wait. Let me get a pen."

He wedged the cell phone between his shoulder and ear, fished a pen out of the glove compartment. "Okay, shoot."

He repeated a series of numbers and letters and wrote them on his palm. "Got it. We'll be in touch."

"Got the court order." Gabe disconnected, then immediately dialed. When someone picked up, he identified himself, then he fed them an access code to his cell phone. "Stream the info to this number."

He hung up, stared at the phone, then snapped it open when it rang again.

"We're in business," he said as information from Stephanie's GPS system appeared in his phone. "And there she is. Moving south on Baltimore-Washington Parkway. Looks like we're within ten minutes of her current position."

Just as critical as tracking her via GPS was the fact that she was moving. At least her car was. Rafe chose to believe it was because Steph was behind the wheel, which meant she was doing fine.

He hoped.

"Do we know where this Hendricks bought it?"

"Actually, yeah. A gas station near the Route 1 and Cherry Lane intersection. Nowhere near Steph's current location."

He wished he could consider that good news. The fact was, if whoever killed Steph's boss wanted her dead, too, he was most likely mobile. Which meant he had as much chance of reaching Steph as they did.

If he hadn't already reached her.

Rafe's gut clenched at the thought. For Ann and Bob's sake. For his own sake. He'd had sort of a little thing for Stephanie Tompkins since the first time he'd seen her almost ten years ago when he and the men who now made up BOI had first met the Tompkinses. The team members of Task Force Mercy, as tight a fighting unit as the U.S. military had ever seen, had come home to bury their brother in arms, Bryan Tompkins, who had been a tragic casualty of corruption and greed in a foreign land. The team had ended up forging a relationship with the Tompkins family that transcended blood and DNA. Since that day, Rafe had found in the Tompkinses the family he'd lost when he was fifteen.

A lifetime ago.

Yeah. The Tompkinses were family. No way was Rafe letting Ann and Bob lose another child. And no way was he letting anything happen to Stephanie.

He tromped down on the gas pedal, then touched his fingers to the gold crucifix lying against his chest beneath his T-shirt, bucking a horrible feeling that they might arrive too late.

B.J. ran a red light. She cut a sharp left, narrowly missed a cargo van, and punched it. Stephanie wasn't stupid. If she said she thought she was being followed, B.J. accepted it.

"Random shooting, my ass," she muttered, thinking of Hendricks as she raced toward Stephanie. They had to get her off the road. One shot and whoever was on her tail could take out a tire and roll the car. That would be it.

Her phone rang again. Stephanie.

"Is he still with you?" B.J. asked, not bothering with hello.

"I . . . I don't know. Maybe . . . or maybe I'm just paranoid. I thought, well, doesn't matter what I thought. I don't see anyone now."

Still, B.J. didn't want to take any chances. "Here's what you're going to do. Do you know where Greenbelt Park is?"

"Yes, it's just ahead."

"I'm almost there, too," B.J. said. "I want you to drive on by it, okay? There's a rest area just a quarter of a mile past it. Take the exit for the rest area but don't signal, don't slow down. Just whip onto the exit and drive right through, then hop the median if you have to but circle back to the Greenbelt turnoff. With luck, if you do have a tail, he'll either miss you turning off and fly on by or he'll get caught up in traffic. Either way, it'll buy a little time."

"Then what?"

"Then we meet up at the park and haul butt out of there. Tail or no tail, by the time he figures out you doubled back and he finds your car we'll be long gone in my Jeep."

Zach Loeffler loved technology. From the time he'd learned the alphabet, he'd been tapping out commands on a computer keyboard. They'd started calling him nerd when he was a skinny, pimple-faced kid in junior high. Jocks like Kevin Nowatny and Cole Landis loved to torment and belittle him. He'd never forgotten. And he'd never forgiven. It had taken twelve years but he'd been patient. He'd tracked them down—Kevin to California and Cole to Arizona. He silenced both of them with one shot from his Steyr. Fairly close range. He'd even let them see his face before he'd killed them.

No point in letting Stephanie Tompkins see him, though. He had no vendetta against her. He just had a job to do. His GPS was locked into her OnStar system, helping him make that happen.

Yeah, he loved technology.

He hung back a good quarter mile, biding his time. Like a cat playing with a mouse.

"What the hell?"

Well now. He hadn't given her enough credit. The bleep on his GPS showed that she'd pulled a little trick on him.

"Doubled back, did you, sweetheart?"

Fine. Let her run. He wasn't going to lose her. He drove on to the next exit, then headed back the way he'd come.

"Where are you going, Miss Tompkins?" he wondered aloud, then decided he had it figured out. "Nice evening for a late picnic?"

She was heading back to Greenbelt Park. He liked it. Maybe she'd lead him on a little chase. Hunter and prey. He'd read a book once about a guy who captured women, turned them loose in a forest, then tracked them like vermin and killed them. He'd never been into recreational shooting, never understood the sporting mentality. Maybe, after today, he would.

He checked the GPS again. Checked his watch. And stepped on it. This day just kept getting better and better.

B.J. tore down the approach road to the park entrance. She knew the thousand-acre park well, had hiked the lush forest of oak, hickory, and beech many times in the past three years. That's why she'd thought of it as a meeting site. It was her getaway spot. While she'd never admit to anyone that she had a nature girl side, she loved the idea of catching a white-tailed deer by surprise. She also enjoyed listening to the birds and watching the sun flicker through the poplars.

She wasn't going to be doing any bird-watching now, she thought as she skidded to a stop in front of a guardrail made of thick wooden posts and reinforced steel bars.

The guardhouse was empty. She should have known it would be this close to dusk. She'd been hoping a ranger would be on duty. He'd have been another gun if they ran into trouble.

As it was, there were only a handful of other cars parked at the far end of the lot and their owners were nowhere to be seen. More important, there was no Stephanie.

Just in case, she reached into the glove box for her Glock and her extra clip. She figured they had about another half hour of daylight. She wanted to be long gone before dark.

She checked the magazine, slipped it home, then chambered a round just as she heard a car approach on the road behind her. She stepped out of the Jeep, using it for cover just in case, as a white Saturn roared into the parking lot and jerked to a stop on the passenger side of her Jeep.

Stephanie jumped out of the car.

"Let's get out of here," B.J. said, shielding her eyes against the glare of the low-hanging sun. That's when she spotted a black four-door sedan cruising down the road.

"Change of plans," she said when the vehicle turned into the park driveway.

Stephanie followed B.J.'s gaze to where the black car rolled toward them, closing fast. "Oh, God. That's the car. That's the car I thought was following me. How did he find me so fast?"

"Too late to worry about that now. Get in my Jeep. And get down on the floor," B.J. ordered as the sedan slowed to a crawl before finally stopping at the entrance to the parking lot about twenty yards away, effectively blocking them in.

Stephanie wasn't stupid. She jerked the passenger-side door open and clambered inside.

They were pinned down. Even if B.J. wanted to make a run for it, she'd have to head straight into his line of fire.

"What's he doing?" Stephanie kneeled in the front seat.

"Waiting. Now get down," B.J. ordered again.

"What can I do to help?" Stephanie's eyes were wide and round.

"Unless you've got a submachine gun tucked under your shirt, not a damn thing. Just get down."

Stephanie immediately dropped down on the floor between the dash and the front seat.

B.J. kept her stance beside her Jeep, using it as a shield and the roof to steady her hands as she aimed the Glock at the sedan's driver's-side door.

Then she waited.

Heart hammering.

Hands sweating but steady, she sighted down the barrel of the Glock.

She couldn't see the driver. The windows were tinted black, which would have told her they had trouble even if this joker hadn't followed Stephanie on the heels of Alan Hendricks's shooting.

She had no idea what kind of firepower she was up against but she didn't want to risk driving headlong into a blast from an assault rifle, and she had to figure that was the least of his weaponry. Just like she was betting all of her marbles that he *did* have weapons. If he was here as a friendly, he'd have shown himself by now. That left only one option. He wanted to hurt them. Her, because she was in his way; Stephanie, because she was the target.

A minute passed. Then two.

He continued to sit there, the sedan idling, the windows up.

At this point B.J. would almost have welcomed some action. Any action. Her chest ached from the hyper adrenaline rush. Her arms started to tremble. Her grip on the Glock lost some of its steadiness.

"What is he waiting for?" Stephanie's tone relayed all the frustration B.J. felt.

"He's playing with us. He knows he has superior fire-power and he's banking on me doing something stupid."

"What are you going to do?"

"Something stupid," she said, deciding that two could play this game, only she was going to up the ante.

She was accurate on still targets at up to one hundred yards with her Glock. This joker sat less than twenty yards away.

She drew a deep breath.

Held it.

Took careful aim . . . and on the exhale squeezed off a single round.

B.J.'s ears rang from the blast as the report of her pistol and the crack of shattering glass echoed through the park and the rear driver's-side window of the sedan exploded.

"Next one goes through the driver's window!" she shouted, and without hesitation started counting. "In five, four, three, two—"

The sedan rolled slowly backward and away from them.

*Holy crap.* She'd figured he'd come barreling out of the driver's seat, blasting a spray of fire from an AK or an AR-15 assault rifle. Her only hope would have been a head shot—provided he hadn't gotten her first.

She let out a breath that had been stacked up in her lungs since she'd fired off that round.

He was actually leaving . . . or not.

The sedan stopped abruptly. The motor revved.

Everything seemed to happen in slow motion then, although in reality only seconds passed. The driver's-side window of the sedan slowly slid down. B.J. dove for the dirt when she saw the muzzle flash from a rifle barrel and a barrage of shots hit the ground all around her. She covered her head with her hands and rolled clear of the Jeep as the shooter slammed the sedan in drive and hit the gas.

"He's going to ram the Jeep!" she yelled to Stephanie, who had popped up in the seat again to see what was happening. "Brace yourself!"

Above the report of rifle fire, B.J. was peripherally aware of the sound of a second vehicle. Coming fast. She couldn't deal with it now. She had to stop this guy and stop him now.

She still had eight rounds in the magazine and another full clip in her pocket. She scrambled back to her feet, braced them a shoulder's width apart, and with a two-handed grip on her Glock, fired straight at the approaching sedan, popping hole after hole in the windshield as time slowed even further—so slow she could see each bullet hit.

The sedan kept coming as all around her the air exploded with the sound of gunfire. The concussion of noise, of time, of space became completely distorted as she fired and fired and fired until the clip ran dry.

As she'd practiced hundreds of times, she rapid-released the empty magazine, shoved the second clip home, and started firing again, placing round after round into the driver's-side windshield.

And the bastard kept coming!

"Hang on!" she yelled to Stephanie as the sedan slammed into her Jeep, smashing it hard into the steel guardrail. Steam hissed out from under the sedan's crumpled hood as she raced headlong toward the driver's door, firing as she ran.

The sedan was still running. When she reached it and jammed her Glock inside the open window, she understood why.

The driver was dead. He lay slumped over the steering wheel; blood oozed from a hit to his jugular and from a hole beneath his left eye. The engine screamed. The shooter's foot was jammed down on the gas pedal.

She leaned inside, struggled with the key, then turned off the ignition. Finally there was silence, except for the pinging of the cooling motor and her labored breathing. Before she could check on Stephanie, she realized she had another problem.

She jerked her head around to see a big, blue SUV skid into the lot. Dust billowed and gravel flew as it screeched to a stop not five yards away. B.J. took aim as both front doors of the SUV flew open. Two men stepped out, used the open doors as shields, and trained assault rifles dead center on her head.

# 8

"Drop the gun!"

B.J. dropped to a crouch, using the wrecked sedan as cover. Then she racked the slide on her Glock and chambered another round.

"Drop it now! Then let us see your hands."

B.J. held her ground, then damn near swallowed her tongue when Stephanie popped up in the front seat of the Jeep again.

"For God's sake, stay down!" B.J. shouted.

"But I know that voice!" Stephanie insisted. "Raphael? Raphael, is that you?" she yelled.

"Stay down, Steph!" the guy on the passenger side of the SUV shouted. "Just keep your cool and we'll get you out of this."

"Gabe! Oh, my God. B.J., it's okay. Don't shoot them."

B.J. glanced at Stephanie, then at the SUV. "You know these guys?"

"For the last time, drop your weapon!" the driver ordered right about the time Stephanie shoved open the passenger door, flew out of the Jeep, and ran toward the SUV.

A big guy—a very big guy—grabbed her as she reached the passenger side and shoved her into the SUV.

"Last chance," the driver warned her.

"B.J., *please*, lower your gun!" Stephanie yelled from inside the vehicle. "I won't let them shoot you."

And still the rifles stayed trained on her.

"Them first." She wanted to trust what she was hearing but wasn't quite ready to give up her weapon.

"Oh, for God's sake. We'll go together on the count of three, okay?" the driver grumbled, and B.J. finally nodded.

"One, two, three," he said slowly.

The sun rode the lip of the horizon now and glinted off the chrome of the SUV as the black barrels of the rifles went nose toward the ground.

B.J. cautiously lowered her pistol, stood up straight, then squinted into that blasted setting sun as the driver moved out from behind the open door. He walked slowly toward her, his rifle clutched loosely in one hand, clearly not a threat. He wore faded jeans and a white short-sleeved T-shirt that hugged a broad chest and a lot of lean muscle.

The sun had dropped so low and created such a glare that she couldn't clearly make out his features. She could see that he wasn't a big man. That his hair was dark, his face clean shaven. And as he grew closer she could see that his skin was . . . oh God . . . a soft caramel tone.

Her rapidly beating heart hitched once, then again when she made out a small scar hugging the corner of his mouth. A mouth she'd seen before. A face she would never forget.

*Holy God.* It was him, she realized when she finally came to terms with the truth. The Latino—Choirboy. The thorn in her side from Caracas.

"Sonofabitch." He stopped several feet in front of her, making the connection at the same time she did. A smile that wasn't really a smile tipped up one corner of his mouth. "Well, if it isn't Miss USDA. What in the *hell* are you doing here?"

Relief wrapped around anger and came out as sarcasm. "Right now? Wondering why I didn't shoot you when I had the chance."

"*Buen Dios, cara,* you wound a man without firing a shot," he said with a laugh that lacked any real amusement.

"She was protecting me." Stephanie joined them with the big guy at her side. She nodded toward the steaming sedan. "From him."

B.J. watched, still stunned, as the Choirboy stuck his head inside the sedan and checked the driver for a pulse. His gold cross fell out of the neck of his white T-shirt when he leaned over, catching her eye when he stood back up straight.

"*You* did that?" he asked with a look that hovered somewhere between surprise, awe, and disbelief.

"He wrecked my new ride," she said, not feeling nearly as tough as she wanted him to think she was now that her adrenaline rush was letting down. "Seemed like the thing to do."

"Jesus," he said.

"What are you doing here?" She shot his question back at him.

"You two know each other?" Stephanie cut a look between them.

"Yeah, you could say we've met." Choirboy glanced at the other man, then back at B.J. "Remember that fiasco in Caracas three months ago?" he asked without taking his eyes off her. "Meet the pain in the ass."

The big guy blinked, looked her over with renewed interest and maybe a little respect. "Caracas? Really? *You* did that?"

B.J. looked from one man to the other. "What, you guys reading from the same script?"

"Look, not that I wouldn't just love to stand here and chat about old times, but there's a good chance this joker has friends." The Choirboy nodded toward the wrecked sedan. "Sorry to have to ask you to do this, Steph, but I need you to take a look at him before we go." He gave her an apologetic look. "Tell us if you've ever seen him before."

"No. Never." Stephanie's face was ashen after looking inside the bloody vehicle.

"Then let's boogie on out of here," the big guy said.

"Fine by me," B.J. agreed.

"Me, too," Stephanie said. "I think maybe . . . maybe my wrist might be broken."

That's when B.J. noticed how pale she was. "She's going down!" she yelled just as Stephanie's knees buckled.

Bad luck and trouble, Rafe thought as he sat in the ER waiting room while the doc, a friend of Gabe's at Bethesda, tended to Stephanie's wrist, no questions asked. Yup. B. J. Chase—they'd finally gotten around to trading names—was definitely bad luck and trouble.

Although he had to give her credit. If it hadn't been for her, Stephanie would probably have been dead by now instead of suffering from a broken wrist.

What he couldn't figure was why the DIA agent was with Stephanie in the first place. And what really bugged him was why, in spite of worrying about Stephanie for the past two hours, Rafe hadn't been able to keep his attention off the restless Miss Chase as she'd practically emptied the vending machines of chocolate, then paced the white tile floor.

At the moment, she had a cell phone pressed to her ear as she walked and talked, her voice so low no one could hear, her expression never changing. *Intense. Exact. Professional.* Those were three words that absolutely described her.

But then, so did *acerbic, sarcastic,* and *cold.*

He shivered as he watched her. Now there was a major incongruity for you. Yeah, she was one cold chick, but he remembered his first impression of her that sultry Caracas night: hot babe. Pain-in-the-ass hot babe, but hot just the same. Cute curvy figure, soft in all the right places, lean and muscular where it counted. Wild Goldilocks curls, a wide sensual mouth, an energetic vitality that made a man wonder if it translated to bedroom action. There was an innate sexuality about her, all the more intriguing because she didn't do a damn thing to flaunt it.

In fact, nothing in her rigid posture, her prickly silence—except when she was stinging him with barbs—and those dark, don't-mess-with-me scowls translated to sexpot. Hell, she didn't even wear any makeup.

She was nothing like Stephanie, who was even-tempered, thoughtful, and sweet.

And yet Rafe couldn't take his eyes off her.

It was the incredulity, he supposed. He was skeptical of what she was, who she was, and why she still hadn't volunteered any info about why she was with Stephanie in the first place. And Stephanie hadn't been up for twenty questions as they'd sped to the hospital, where Gabe's doctor friend had met them at a rear entrance. So Rafe didn't have any more of a bead on the situation than he'd had when they'd set out after Stephanie—except that the prickly B. J. Chase had not hesitated to empty two full magazines from a sweet little Glock 19 into a man who'd had the poor judgment to challenge her.

He'd sized up the scene and visualized exactly what had happened there. Chase had saved Stephanie's life at great risk to her own. Woman had guts. He respected her for that, even if he didn't like her.

Beside him, Gabe talked softly to Ann and then Robert Tompkins on his cell phone, offering assurances that except for the broken wrist, Stephanie was safe.

"They okay?" Rafe asked when Gabe finally hung up.

"Shook up but yeah, I think they're breathing easier. Or they would be if they knew what was going on."

"Well, we're not going to find anything out from that one," he said with a nod in B.J.'s direction.

"What? You've given up on trying to stare the information out of her?"

"I'm not staring."

Gabe snorted. "Right."

"Just trying to figure her out," he said, wishing it hadn't come out sounding so defensive.

"It's your story. Tell it any way you want to."

He was saved from incriminating himself further when the door to the examining room opened and the doctor walked out with Stephanie. Her right hand was in a cast from the base of her fingers to mid forearm.

Rafe jumped up and rushed to her side. "How you doing?" He touched the back of his hand to her cheek. She looked pale and in pain and not entirely with the program. It broke his heart.

"She's a little groggy, but all set to go." The doc handed Gabe a prescription bottle. "For the pain," he said. "See to it she has one every six hours at least for the next couple of days."

"*She's* right here," Stephanie said as Rafe steadied her, "and she doesn't want any pain medication."

"Which is why you need to see to it that she gets it," the doc said with a smile.

He was young, clean shaven, and dressed in civilian clothes but his bearing was all military.

"Thanks, Lee," Gabe said. "Appreciate the discretion."

"It's gonna cost you, Jones. Double handicap next time we tee up."

"Yeah, and I'll still whip your ass." Gabe grinned and shook his hand. "We'll get out of your hair now."

"You think you can walk?" Rafe frowned with concern as Stephanie wove a little on her feet.

"I'm fine," Stephanie insisted.

He wasn't convinced. "Just the same, let's not take any chances." He scooped her up in his arms and carried her out to the SUV.

"White knights," B.J. muttered under her breath as Raphael Mendoza and Gabe Jones fussed over getting Stephanie to Gabe's D.C. apartment. Just like she'd figured, men turned into white knights around Stephanie Tompkins.

She'd never understood it but she'd seen it happen with Stephanie's type too many times to count.

"You'd think she broke her leg," she grumbled to herself as she and Jones stood guard and Mendoza helped Stephanie out of the car, picked her up again, and carried her into Jones's apartment building.

"You say something?" Mendoza asked over his shoulder as they all walked into an elevator.

She shot him a glare that went right over his head because he was so busy fussing over Stephanie. It wasn't that she cared how big a fool he made of himself. And it wasn't as if she wondered what would happen if the situation were reversed and it was *her* sporting the broken arm. Would he want to play white knight with her, too?

Let him try, she thought. See what he got for his efforts.

She could do without the alpha type, thank you very much. Men like Mendoza, and his buddy, Gabe Jones, for that matter, would expect to dominate, take charge, call the shots. Not happening with her. Not in this lifetime.

"Oh, my gosh!" A tall, gorgeous redhead met them when the elevator door opened. Jones had called ahead to let his wife know they were coming. "Steph. Oh, sweetie, look at you. For God's sake, hurry up, Rafe. Get her into the apartment and onto the sofa."

Whoa, B.J. thought as the redhead took charge, barking out commands to the alpha dogs, who both hopped-to like she was nipping at their heels.

My kind of woman, B.J. thought as she followed the parade into a spacious and open loft. The large living area opened directly to a generous dining area and hooked left to a large galley kitchen with contemporary cherry cabinets, gleaming stainless steel appliances, and black granite countertops.

"My wife, Jenna." Gabe smiled back at B.J. "Jenna— this is B. J. Chase."

"We'll talk." Jenna offered an apology over her shoulder. "Soon as we get our girl settled. Gabe. Hot tea. Rafe, get the pillows from the guest bedroom. Today!" she ordered with two quick, direct glares that sent both men scrambling.

I could like *this* woman, B.J. thought, but even as the notion took root, she knew she'd never invest the time or the effort to make that happen. She was the outsider here. The speck of white lint on a black sweater. This was clearly a closely knit group, one she wasn't and would never be invited to be a part of.

That was fine. That was life. Her life, at any rate. In the meantime, she was comfortable using both Jones and Mendoza. She needed to keep Stephanie safe until she heard back from Sherwood, who was arranging a safe house for her. Frankly, she couldn't think of a single place where Stephanie would be safer than right where she was at the moment.

Whoever these guys were, whoever they worked for, they weren't in the mix at NSA. Considering NSA might be the seat of the problem, it was a damn good thing. So what did that leave? She'd figured Mendoza for CIA in Caracas. CIA or a merc. Now she was leaning more toward independent contractor. Frankly, right now, she didn't care. All she cared about was that they had the skills, the means, and more important, a personal investment in keeping Stephanie safe.

Mendoza, if she didn't miss her guess, had a *very* personal investment if the way he looked at Stephanie with those Latin brown eyes was any clue.

An unexpected little twinge of jealousy caught her off guard. Way off guard.

Jealous? Of the way Mendoza looked at Stephanie? No. Not jealousy, she decided. Maybe she'd cop to a little bit of longing. She still remembered what it had been like to feel the unconditional love of someone who cared about you. And no matter what her mother said, her father had loved her.

Watching these three people who clearly loved Stephanie fuss over her—well, it reminded B.J. of what she didn't have anymore.

*Get over it.*

"I'll take those," Jenna Jones said as Mendoza returned with the pillows. "Here we go, sweetie. One for your head, one for your poor wrist. How's that?"

"I'm fine," Stephanie said, finally offered the opportunity to speak. "I appreciate all this concern, but please stop fussing over me. All of you," she added, turning her doe brown eyes to Mendoza.

B.J. was saved from watching Mendoza's reaction when her cell phone rang. She checked the display. It was Sherwood. She didn't want to talk to him in front of these people. Not until she found out more about them.

"Out there." Jenna hitched her chin in the direction of a pair of French doors behind a large dining area to the left of the kitchen. Apparently, she'd read B.J.'s expression and realized she wanted privacy.

B.J. nodded her thanks and made a beeline for the doors, which led to an outdoor terrace. Night had fallen on the city. Two exterior lights cast a soft glow as she stepped outside onto carefully laid slate tiles. They were ten stories up. Traffic crawled like ants with headlights on the streets below. This high, the exhaust smell was faint. The night air had started to cool after the heat of the day. On the terrace, lush ferns filled huge terra-cotta pots. Pansies and petunias nodded in the slight breeze. A glass-top table and a set of chairs in shades of taupe, lavender, and green occupied one end of the large outdoor space. A couple of matching chaise longues filled the other. All the signs of an affluent, comfortable couple.

"Talk to me," she said when she was sure she was out of earshot.

"Where are you?" Sherwood's tone was all business.

"D.C. An apartment where Jones and his wife— here's another name for you: Jenna—live." She rattled off the address for Sherwood to add to the cache of information she'd passed him when she'd called him from the hospital.

She'd used her phone to snap a photo of the dead shooter and his Steyr AUG rifle before Mendoza and Jones had tossed the rifle in the back of the SUV. Then she'd e-mailed the picture to Sherwood. She'd also snapped photos of Mendoza and Jones without them knowing it and sent those too, along with the names they were going by and the plate number of their vehicle. In addition, she'd advised Sherwood that Mendoza had been the man who had mucked up her Caracas operation.

She was hoping Sherwood had some answers for her.

"How's the Tompkins woman?"

"Broken wrist." She walked to the edge of the terrace, leaned a hip against an iron railing painted a pale cream. "Other than that she's fine, but you'd think she was on her deathbed the way these people are fussing over her. Speaking of them . . . are you going to tell me what you found out?"

When her boss hesitated, she felt a premonition of doom.

"You're not going to like it," Sherwood said finally.

*Not going to like it?* Sherwood was a master of understatement.

There wasn't enough chocolate in the world to make the news he delivered palatable. By the time he finished filling her in, B.J. not only didn't like it, she was quietly fuming and frustrated and wishing she'd never heard of, run into, or crossed swords with Raphael *Choirboy* Mendoza.

# 9

Rafe was waiting by the door when a silent, very pissed-off B. J. Chase stepped back inside the apartment. When she saw him standing there, she stopped short, her shoulders stiffening.

Xena, warrior princess.

He didn't know why that thought came to mind. She wasn't an Amazon. In heels she might possibly have made five-six, maybe five-seven. And she wasn't a brunette. But she was fighting mad and itching to lock horns as she squared off in front of him, her blue eyes hardening with anger.

That amazing head of wild blonde hair was backlit by the light from a wall sconce. Curls drifted to her shoulders, flared to the middle of her back, and framed her face like a halo—although there was not one damn thing angelic about the look in her eyes.

She still wore the remnants of the shootout at the park. A smudge of dirt on her right cheek. A small, triangular tear in the leg of her shorts. A skinned knee. A thin trail of blood tracked down the inside of her bare arm that he hadn't noticed before.

"You really ought to take care of that." Rafe nodded toward her arm.

She scowled, then followed his gaze, looking surprised and then dismissive when she saw it. "It's fine."

*Yeah, you're one tough cookie, aren't ya?*

"Call from your boss?" he asked carefully as he walked to the kitchen cabinets. He and Gabe had used the first aid kit often enough that he knew Jenna kept it in a drawer near the sink. He dug it out and when she didn't answer, glanced over his shoulder to see she was still glaring.

"Guess I'll take that as a yes." He ripped open an antiseptic pad. "And judging from the warm and fuzzy look on your face, I'm also guessing that he called because he's been talking with our boss."

Again, her lack of response was all the answer he needed. It also told him how much the news that she was now taking her orders from him appealed to her.

"I said I'm fine," she insisted when he squatted down in front of her.

He ignored her and went to work on her knee.

She flinched when he cupped her calf to hold her steady—and out of nowhere, he was hit by an acute and magnified awareness of everything female about her. Most of all, though, he was aware of that flinch.

That sure as hell didn't compute. He'd manhandled her in Caracas—shoved her against the Jeep, dragged her down a street, cuffed her, blindfolded her, then picked her up and tossed her sweet little ass inside the back of a van. He hadn't seen any vulnerability then. He hadn't seen it today in the aftermath of a shootout where she could have been the one killed instead of the bastard who'd been after Stephanie.

No. DIA Officer Chase hadn't shown vulnerability when they'd come barreling in, guns blazing. She'd been ready to face off with them, just as she'd faced off with an assassin. It was all the more fascinating, then, that a little non-hostile, male-on-female contact had her tensing.

He stood up, satisfied that her knee was mostly bruised and barely scraped, and started in on her arm. She flinched again when he touched her but she stood her ground.

As he wiped at the blood, she didn't say a word but she didn't pull away either. She just looked up at him with those big blue eyes full of something that could have been challenge, could have been annoyance . . . or, he realized, could have been bafflement over the fact that he was taking care of her.

That was it, he realized. She wasn't used to having anyone take care of her or sticking tight when she'd done her damnedest to warn him away. He guessed he shouldn't have been surprised by that. This one would chew her own arm off before she'd ask anyone to help her out of a bear trap.

"Can we please get this over with?" she grumbled.

He looked up and straight into her eyes. This close, he could see that they weren't merely blue. They were much more intriguing than that, with specks of silver and gray.

He finished cleaning the wound, which wasn't more serious than a long scratch. "Yeah," he said. "I think we can finish up now."

He reached behind him to the counter, snagged the bottle of peroxide and a cotton ball. "Might sting."

"Already does."

He knew she wasn't talking about the peroxide he was applying to the abrasions.

A tiny kernel of guilt wound through him. "I know you're not pleased with the arrangements. And I know what it feels like to have the rug ripped out from underneath me like what just happened to you."

"Rug? Try wall-to-wall carpeting."

"Look," he said, carefully affixing a Band-Aid, "for what it's worth, it wouldn't matter what agency was involved—yours, FBI, Homeland Security, whatever. Where Stephanie's life is concerned, protection is non-negotiable. It has nothing to do with your ability, but we won't take any chances with her safety. And since we don't know who we can trust, we're going to run the show." She narrowed her eyes. He understood that look. "Your boss fill you in on who we are and who we work for?"

"You're private contractors." Disdain dripped from each word. "You work for a man named Nathan Black out of Argentina. Got quite the 'shadow warrior' legend building."

He cocked a brow. "Do tell."

She shrugged. "I've heard the stories. I wrote them off as intelligence community legends that circulate among the ranks. Guess I have to believe them now."

"But you don't approve. What a surprise. Like most 'legit' federal agents, you hold our kind in roughly the same regard as, oh, say, roadkill, right?"

Her silence pretty much confirmed that it didn't matter that Nate Black ran Black Ops, Inc. with the precision and integrity of a special ops military unit. Didn't matter that the BOIs worked exclusively for Uncle. The "legit" warriors—those with badges and dog tags—still considered the BOIs guns for hire, cowboys, rule breakers. It pissed them off that the BOIs got a little more latitude because they worked off the grid.

"Seems everybody forgets," he went on after he'd put the first aid kit back where he'd found it, "that the jobs we take on are generally ones no one else will touch. Why, you might ask, *cara?* I'll tell you why. Because, one, they're too risky; and two, there's too much of a chance of ending up good and dead."

"You screwed me over in Caracas."

Ah. Now they were getting somewhere. The woman held a grudge. So, fine, he'd had to relent and give up Eduardo—a sanctioned DOD operation *did* trump the BOI directive—but he'd made her pay for screwing up his op. It couldn't have been easy for her when she'd filed her report.

"You kept my weapons," she pressed on. "You kept my team's weapons. And you did it out of spite. You knew what would happen."

Yeah, he'd known. The government didn't consider it good form to lose military-style weapons in a not-so-nice country. A major no-no.

"I took ten kinds of heat over it," she continued. "Had to appear before a disciplinary board. They threatened to reassign me to Nebraska, for God's sake. I'm lucky I didn't get a demotion."

"Yeah, well, I was pissed at the time."

"Gee, guess that makes it all fine and dandy."

*Right.* This was going nowhere fast. "So how long have you worked for DIA?" he asked, changing the subject.

"Long enough. You don't have to worry about me pulling my weight."

He stared at her long and hard. "Okay. If you're going to be pissed off for the duration of this op, I don't need the grief. Just say the word, I'll make a call and you're out of here."

She looked away, then expelled a deep breath and met his eyes. "I've been unprofessional. I apologize. I want in on this."

It was as close to her saying "uncle" as he was going to get. He held her gaze, finally nodded. "And I want you in. Now what do we need to do to make this work for you?"

"Answer some questions."

"Shoot."

"What's your connection with the Tompkinses?"

Rafe crossed his arms over his chest and leaned a hip against the kitchen counter. "Your boss didn't tell you?"

"What he told me was that you'd be calling the shots from this point on."

He actually felt a little sorry for her then. She was used to taking charge, taking risks, and taking orders only from DIA. No wonder the news that she was now taking orders from him had settled about as well as a jalapeño would settle a sour stomach.

He glanced over his shoulder toward the living area, where Stephanie was still resting on the sofa with Jenna and Gabe sitting and talking nearby. "Come on. Let's go back outside where we can talk.

"You thirsty?" he asked suddenly. "Because *I'm* thirsty. Hold on."

He dug into the fridge, where he knew Gabe always kept water, grabbed two bottles, then followed her out to the terrace.

"Steph had a brother, did you know that?" he asked after he'd shut the door behind them.

"Stephanie and I worked together in a strictly professional capacity."

Of course they did. No "girl talk" allowed in B. J. Chase's world. He handed her one of the bottles, then lifted a hand, indicating she should sit with him at the outdoor table.

She shook her head, unscrewed the bottle cap, and took a long drink. Then she got all matter-of-fact with him. "So. You said Stephanie had a brother. Past tense. What happened to him?"

He uncapped his own water and took a long pull. "Bryan—that was his name." He wiped the back of his hand across his mouth and saw Bryan Babyface Tompkins's perpetual grin. "Bry was part of a special military task force. A cross-branch compilation of Spec Ops personnel. SEALS, Delta, Special Forces, Rangers . . . hell, we even had a couple of spooks on the team."

"And who was *we*?"

Just because she didn't want to sit didn't mean he couldn't. He pulled out a chair and sat. "Bry, Gabe, me . . . those guys on my team in Caracas. Several others. Anyway, back then we were military. Did the dirty jobs then, too, you know?"

The outside lighting was dim but he could still see by the look on her face that she did know. Anyone in the intelligence community knew the history of American warfare. They knew about covert ops, the ones that never made the papers, never showed up on any disk or dossier. The ones that were sanctioned under the table by the president and were known only to him and the Joint Chiefs.

"What happened?" she asked, and he thought he actually saw . . . hell, he didn't know. A little softening around her eyes, a little give in the set of her shoulders as she moved to the railing and leaned against it with her back to the flickering lights of the city beyond and below them.

"What always happens to the good ones," he said, forgetting about her reaction and thinking back to that day in Sierra Leone. That horrible, shit-hole day when remote intelligence made a wrong call and sent the Task Force Mercy team into an RUF ambush. There wasn't supposed to be a handful of the murdering Foday Sankoh's Revolutionary United Front militia within a mile of their location. And Bryan, well, Bry wasn't supposed to have taken a bullet that severed his femoral artery. He wasn't supposed to have bled out while they'd been helpless to save him.

"Sniper," he finally said, more to himself than to her, as he cupped his bottle between his hands and absently rocked it back and forth on the tabletop.

*Blood. There had been so much blood. Running like a river into the dirt. Making mud. Making death.* "Doc tried. He . . . he couldn't—"

Her hand on his arm jolted him back to the Washington, D.C., night.

*Cristo.* He'd been back there. Back in that hellhole, watching Bry bleed out in the mud and the heat and the ground that ran red.

He looked down at her hand, as surprised by her knee-jerk gesture of comfort as he was by the ease with which he'd revisited Africa. He was not surprised, however, when she quickly removed her hand and drew away from him again.

He sucked in a fractured breath, shook his head, then drank again, using the time to settle himself. "Sorry. Hadn't . . . hadn't thought about that night in a while."

When he looked up, he saw something in her expression that he hadn't seen before—hadn't figured he'd ever see. Not from this tough nut.

Pain.

It knocked him for a loop, but yeah, it was definitely there. In her eyes. On her face. In her unexpected offer of comfort.

A reflection of his pain, maybe? Plain compassion? Or was he seeing her own pain?

He'd written her off as an ice princess, core of steel. But hell, he knew better than to judge people so quickly.

"Anyway," he continued, "we brought Bry home to his family. Ann and Robert Tompkins. And Stephanie. That was . . . man . . . a lot of years ago." He dragged a hand over his face, shook his head. "Ann and Robert, they sort of adopted us, I guess you could say. Just like we adopted them. And Steph, well, she was just a kid."

"So Stephanie's like a sister to you?"

That brought his head up again. He searched her face, tried to get a read on where the question had come from. Why did she give two tacos about any of his relationships?

"Yeah," he said finally. "I guess you could call it that."

He was a little confused about how he felt about Stephanie at the moment. He'd always had feelings for her. Of course, he'd also known he was never going to act on them. Why? Number one, because she'd never encouraged him. Number two, because he *needed* to think about her as a sister and he knew she thought of him and the rest of the BOIs as brothers.

"If and when you ever meet her," Bry had said one

day a million years ago when the team had been hunched over MREs in Bosnia trying to keep their fingers and their asses from freezing off, "I don't want to even see you thinkin' about laying your grubby hands on her, got it? 'Specially you, Choirboy," he'd added, grinning and nodding in Rafe's direction. "Don't you be turning on that hot Latin charm around my kid sister."

Every time he saw Stephanie, Rafe had to remind himself of what Bry had said. It wasn't that he thought Bryan would actually object to any one of the guys getting serious about her. It was more about respect for the Tompkinses. They were like the most righteous, most honorable people Rafe had ever known. He admired them. Respected them. And he knew what they wanted for their daughter. Someone connected and stable and who did not make a career out of getting shot at by terrorists.

He was not that man.

He was a *guerrero*. A warrior. And that was the only man he knew how to be.

He worked his jaw. The Tompkinses didn't know what he'd come from. He didn't ever want them to. He felt a rush of shame that he shouldn't have had to feel but was tied to by blood.

"So what happens now?"

"Now," he said, dragging himself back to a situation he could do something about, "we find out who sent the trigger guy after Stephanie and why. And then we fry the bastard."

# 10

"Have we got government hardliners at work here or rogue elements?" Gabe tossed out the possibilities for them all to consider.

While B.J. didn't like it, she was still at the Joneses' apartment at ten o'clock that night. She sat at their dining room table with Gabe and Mendoza, walking through what they knew and what they didn't about who had ordered the hit on Stephanie.

A contemporary chandelier done in polished nickel and sparkling crystal hung over the table, illuminating the grim faces surrounding it. Outside and below the terrace doors, city and traffic lights winked. In the far distance, a red light blinked on and off on a radio tower.

After considering Gabe Jones's question, she shrugged. "E-bomb technology has been a top military priority for several years. To my knowledge there have never been any dissenters among the members of the House or Senate. Funding requests have always passed unanimously, so it's hard to figure that we're dealing with a vendetta from inside."

It all came back to the E-bomb specs. Everyone in the room knew it. Per her orders from Sherwood, she'd already filled both men in on who she worked for at DIA, the find in Afghanistan that had led her to be planted inside the NSA, and about the firestorm Stephanie had created when she'd presented her report at staffing this afternoon.

"Doesn't rule out the possibility of a flat-out traitor, though," she said, aware of Mendoza's eyes on her.

"Profiteers, then," the Choirboy conjectured as he slumped back in a dining table chair, "selling out to the highest bidder?"

"That's my guess," B.J. agreed. "Sherwood's got a team scrutinizing Hendricks's PDA, office, and home phone logs as well as his professional and social network to see who he's been in contact with recently."

"What about background checks on the SI personnel?" Gabe asked.

"That too, along with anyone affiliated with E-bomb development. But it's going to take time."

"So how did they get inside?" Gabe wanted to know as he absently flipped a pen back and forth between his fingers. "And why did they kill Hendricks if he was one of them?"

"If you find the answer to that question," Jenna said, joining them at the table, "you'll probably find the rest of your answers."

Between talking with Stephanie's parents, who had called at least twice since they'd arrived, Jenna had moved Stephanie into the guest bedroom, where she was now sleeping. Next Jenna had made a pot of coffee, then filled heavy stoneware mugs and passed them around.

The Joneses made a striking pair, B.J. thought, observing them together. The nationally acclaimed investigative journalist and the elite black ops warrior. Jenna was tall and lean with long red hair, intelligent green eyes, and attitude to spare. As tall as she was, however, her husband dwarfed her in stature, but not character. B.J. figured him for around six foot four, two hundred thirty or forty pounds of lean muscle and keen intellect.

She couldn't ignore how attractive and vital they were together. Just like she couldn't help being mystified by it. By the energy they created with a simple look, a light, unconscious touch, a private smile. By the complete and utter ease they felt around each other. These two very independent spirits seemed to have somehow reached a level of trust that transcended ego and will and made them one balanced, highly functioning unit.

She imagined they thought they were in love. In her estimation love was a fallacy sparked by chemical reactions and biology. Love was an opportunity for letdown. She didn't have to look any further than to her parents to see that.

Okay. Back to business. She was taking her cues from Mendoza now, and it still grated. Big time. But she had no choice. Jenna, however, was not with the firm. Plus she was a journalist, not a trained agent.

"Is it really advisable for Jenna to be briefed on this? She's a civilian." B.J. voiced her concern when it became clear that Jenna was going to be privy to all information.

"She's with me," Gabe informed her with a hard look that flat-out said, drop it.

"She's got a valid point," Jenna agreed, then scolded her husband. "And you don't need to bully her."

B.J. didn't know what to make of Jenna defending her.

"I'm not bullying," Gabe said with a look that should have withered flowers.

Didn't bother Jenna. "You always bully, Angel Boy. It's one of those endearing qualities I love about you. The point is, you need to give B.J. a break. She's not used to playing *with* rules, she's used to playing *by* them."

"Fine." Gabe turned to B.J. "We make our own rules. Jenna stays."

Except for an eye-roll that Jenna directed her husband's way, that was the end of that discussion.

"That would be the pizza," Jenna said when the doorbell rang.

"I'll get it." Gabe stopped her with a hand on her arm when she started to get up.

"You just want to be able to say you handled dinner," Jenna said.

"And that would be different from any other night *why?*" he drawled with much more affection than accusation in his tone as he walked to the door.

"Well, he's got me there," Jenna said, not at all of-fended. "My best meals arrive via speed dial."

B.J. watched Gabe, not for the first time detecting a slight limp, and not for the first time wondering how he'd come by it. And had Jenna actually called him Angel Boy? It was none of her business but she couldn't help but wonder about the—what? Nickname? Endear-ment?

He looked more like the devil—all six feet, four inches of him—when he paused before opening the door, withdrew a 1911-A1 from the drawer of a table in the entryway, then checked the video camera monitor mounted by the door frame. Apparently comfortable with what he saw, he tucked the pistol in the back of his waistband and opened the door.

"You a cook, B.J.?" Jenna asked conversationally, but before she could answer, Gabe interrupted.

"I'm short the tip," he said from the open doorway.

"I knew he couldn't do this without me." With a smug smile, Jenna joined her husband at the door.

"What's wrong with his leg?" The whispered ques-tion was out before B.J. could stop it. She immediately regretted asking it. One, it implied that she was con-cerned, which she didn't want to be. Two, it revealed her interest in people she didn't want to be interested in—no matter how nice they were.

"A little over a year ago, he took some shrapnel pro-tecting Jenna in a bombing. Ended up with a bone in-fection. Lost the leg below the knee," Mendoza said quietly.

She jerked her head toward him, stunned by that information.

"Don't worry about Gabe," he assured her. "It slowed him down for a few months but he's one hundred percent now. That woman he married will make certain he stays that way."

She turned her gaze back to the stunningly handsome couple by the door as she digested the fact that they had been through some very rough times together.

"They're something, aren't they?" Mendoza asked as the aroma of pizza wafted into the room.

B.J. averted her gaze away from Gabe and Jenna, who were laughing and joking with the pizza delivery guy.

"Strong personalities," she said because it was true and because she felt uncomfortable suddenly. She didn't want to care about these people. Besides, small talk wasn't her thing. Finding herself fascinated by a strong male/female bond was not her thing.

The discomfort she experienced when she realized that Mendoza was watching her with unguarded curiosity was *definitely* not her thing. And earlier, when he'd gone Florence Nightingale on her and tended her skinned knee and her arm, she'd gotten short of breath. She'd been hyper-aware of the strength of his callused fingers; shockingly sensitive to his breath warming her thighs when he'd squatted down in front of her; achingly conscious of his mouth inches away from her—

"B.J."

His voice startled her.

He was smiling when she met his eyes and she fought a fleeting moment of panic, wondering if he could have possibly read her mind.

"What?" she snapped, which seemed to amuse him even more.

"That's what I'm asking. *B.J.* What does it stand for?"

Jenna and Gabe returned to the table with the pizza just then, saving her from telling Mendoza that it was none of his business. She'd been B.J. since the second grade when Bernie Watson had made fun of her name and she'd had to bloody his nose. She wasn't about to give the Choirboy access to the source of one of her biggest childhood miseries.

"Load up," Gabe said, tossing paper plates and napkins on the table. "It's going to be a long night."

Rafe pushed back from the table, stood, and stretched. "Let's call it a wrap for tonight," he suggested around a yawn.

It was close to two a.m. They'd repeatedly rehashed what they knew and what they didn't. For the most part, they made contingency plans for Stephanie's protection. They'd made lists: contact lists, to-do lists, things-to-ask-Stephanie-when-she-woke-up lists. And they'd made calls to the BOIs with instructions on what they needed put in place for Stephanie's protection.

B. J. Chase had both surprised and pleased him. She may not have liked the arrangement but she hadn't let it interfere with her job. She was intelligent and insightful and had a memory like a computer. She'd provided relevant, detailed information on her observations during her two-week infiltration of the NSA. She remembered fine points about the shooter and had had the foresight to snap his photo and e-mail it to her boss, who had dispatched a team to the scene. Hopefully they'd have an ID by morning.

She was a pro. If there was an emotion other than "prickly" bottled up inside that uptight officer, she'd given no indication she was ever going to let it loose.

"Yeah," Gabe agreed, rolling the stiffness out of his shoulders, "we've done about as much as we can do without involving Stephanie and having her interpret the contents of the flash drive she smuggled out of NSA."

"Would you mind terribly bunking in with Steph?" Jenna asked B.J., who looked as weary as the rest of them but who, Rafe knew, would have been up for an all-nighter if they'd asked it of her.

"No need," B.J. said, standing. "I'll call a cab and head back to my apartment."

"No," Rafe said, "you won't. I want you here."

"There's not going to be another attempt on her life tonight," B. J. argued.

"What about *your* life? Once the bastard who ordered the hit on Steph realizes his hired gun bought the farm there'll be another gun dispatched to find her and you. Your Jeep's at the park, remember? They'll run the plates, track you down."

He could see in her eyes that she understood this fully. She just didn't want to be there.

"I can handle myself."

God, the woman had a stubborn streak. She was making him tired.

"We are all very much aware of that," he muttered, and pissed her off again.

He hadn't intended to sound patronizing, but judging by the look on her face, he had succeeded in doing so. Too bad. "Look. We're done talking about this, okay?"

"Come on, B.J." Jenna dared to break into their stare-down contest. "I'll show you where the towels are in the guest bath. You get the first shower. I'll round up something for you to sleep in. Gabe," she tossed over her shoulder as she and a reluctant B.J. walked out of the room.

"Already on it," Gabe said. He left the room and returned with a sheet and a pillow for Rafe. He tossed both in Rafe's general direction and turned to leave. "Nightie night."

"So what do you think?" Rafe asked his friend as he shook out the sheet and spread it across what was, fortunately for him, a very large and very comfy sectional sofa.

Gabe scratched his jaw, yawned. "I think it's a damn good thing Reed decided to get married or we'd be scattered around the globe right now instead of gathering for what was supposed to have been an engagement party in Richmond."

Rafe had been thinking the same thing. But that

hadn't been on his mind when he'd asked the question. He'd wondered what Gabe thought of B.J.

"You think Chase will be a team player?" he asked, kicking off his shoes.

"I guess we'll find out, won't we?" Gabe raised a hand that passed for saying good night and headed for the master bedroom.

Yeah, they'd find out, Rafe thought a while later, as he heard the guest bathroom door open. He glanced up, caught a glimpse of B.J.

"It's all yours," she said, and scurried into the guest bedroom—but not before he'd caught a glimpse of her, wrapped in a towel, her blond hair wet and darkened. All he could do was sit there, the image of her bare shoulders burning in his brain as some amazing female scent drifted into the living room.

It didn't get any better when he made himself walk to the bathroom and strip off his jeans and T-shirt. Her scent lingered. So did the mental image of her standing where he was now standing, naked under the shower spray with clouds of steam fogging up the small room.

He got hard just thinking about it. So hard that he ached. *Hard.* For an ice princess who would rather have busted his balls than, well, than do other, much more pleasurable things involving those same balls.

She was in that bedroom now. Wearing what? Her bra and panties? Something soft and silky on loan from Jenna? His imagination ran wild. He could see her in something blue. Deep, midnight blue. Satin. A little lace. Cut low on top, high at the thigh.

God. He'd sunk to a new low. Chase wasn't here to bolster his libido. And he wasn't here to enjoy the boost. Hell, he didn't even like her and she sure as the world had a hard case against him.

"Give it a rest, Mendoza," he muttered under his breath, and turned the water on cold.

If he didn't get this little issue that shouldn't even have been an issue under control, it was going to be one long freaking operation.

# 11

Around three a.m., B.J. tiptoed barefoot out of the bedroom with her pillow. Very quietly, she let herself out on the terrace so she could escape Stephanie's restlessness.

The night was quiet and cool. The sky was big and dark and before long, she fell asleep on the cushioned chaise longue.

A voice cut into the silence. Soft, like a caress. Lightly accented and melodious, like a song. "I was thinking it would be blue."

She reluctantly opened her eyes, uncertain that she'd actually heard anything, and blinked into the dark. And there was the silhouette of a man standing outside on the terrace.

Mendoza.

"You were thinking what would be blue?" she asked drowsily, still half-asleep.

"Your nightgown."

*That* woke her up.

That and the sound of his bare feet slapping softly on the slate tiles as he walked over to the chaise. "Jenna wears a lot of blue. Thought maybe she'd loaned you something . . . well, blue . . . to sleep in."

Now she was *wide* awake. And without a clue as to what to say to that. More to the point, she didn't know what to think about the idea of Raphael Mendoza wondering what color nightgown she was wearing—or that he'd flat-out admitted it.

An even bigger problem was that she didn't know where to look. He stood above her wearing nothing but that gold cross around his neck, a pair of boxers, and a whole lot of bare skin above and below them. The boxers were so white they almost glowed against the dark backdrop of the night and the caramel color of his skin. The cross, she could see now, was actually a crucifix.

A crucifix for a Choirboy. Symbolic of a cross to bear, she wondered? A religious statement? Or simply a piece of jewelry?

Finding herself a little too intrigued, she shivered even though the summer night was warm. Even in the air-conditioned apartment, it had felt a little close. She'd been warm in Jenna's pink satin night slip. She was even warmer now. There wasn't much of a moon; only the residual light from the city below, and a pale glow from the nightlight Jenna had turned on in the kitchen leaked out onto the terrace. But B.J. could see all that muscle just fine.

Nice muscle. Wide, smooth chest. Broad shoulders, one of which sported the tattoo she remembered from Caracas. Yet another cross of some sort. She couldn't make it out clearly in the dark but she could see it was unusual.

And she didn't understand why she was lying there like a lump instead of telling him to leave her the hell alone.

She swallowed hard. Shadows darkened his face so she couldn't see his expression as he loomed above her. Probably a good thing because that meant he couldn't see hers either, which was hovering somewhere between embarrassment, surprise, and appreciation.

What he could see, however, was that the night shirt Jenna had loaned her was not blue. It was pink and cut like a tank top and fell only to about mid-thigh. She was as covered as if she were wearing a pair of shorts and a summer top, but there was the issue of underwear. She wasn't wearing any. Well, except for the brand-new thong Jenna had also loaned her.

"What are you doing out here?" he asked around a yawn, and in a uniquely male action, flattened a palm on his chest and rubbed with a casualness totally at odds with the tense intimacy of their situation. She watched in fascination as his big rough hand and long fingers moved in a circular pattern. His bicep bulged with the action; the network of veins in his forearm expanded.

"Stephanie was restless," she said, tearing her gaze away and tugging self-consciously on the hem of the nightshirt. She sat up, leaned forward, and adjusted the back of the chaise so she was barely reclining instead of lying down. "I thought she'd sleep better if I let her have the bed to herself."

Without an invitation, he sat down on the foot of the

chaise. This close she could see that he was smiling. His teeth were straight and white, his lips full and sensual.

"Why, that was mighty considerate of you," he said with an edge of teasing in his tone. "One could almost say you did a nice thing, *cara.*"

*Cara.* The endearment had ticked her off in Caracas. It should have ticked her off now. Instead it added to the intimacy of the moment.

"I thought I'd sleep better, too," she said crisply, not wanting him to get the idea that Stephanie was the only reason she'd brought her pillow outside, even though it basically was. "And I *was* sleeping." *Until you showed up.*

If he caught the implied accusation and her invitation to go back inside so she could get back to sleep, he chose to ignore them. Instead, he watched her with those dark Latin eyes of his as if she was the biggest puzzle he'd ever encountered.

"What are *you* doing out here?" she asked, turning the tables on him. "Other than speculating about my sleepwear."

Apparently he didn't have it in him to look guilty. "I heard you slip outside. Kept waiting for you to come back in. Got to worrying when you didn't, so I thought I'd better check."

"You're my boss," she said, trying not to choke on the concept and the words, "not my babysitter. I'm fine. You can go back inside now."

He smiled, shook his head. "Why is it that you always think you have to play the hard-ass?"

She blinked at him. She didn't know what ticked her

off more: the question or the amusement on his face.

"You know, it's the middle of the night," she pointed out, "and I really don't care to have this conversation. Most of all, I don't care to have this conversation with you. I might have to work for you, but I don't have to engage in idle chitchat."

His white teeth shone bright in the darkness when his smile widened. "Now see, that's what I mean. You're a hard-ass, B. J. Chase. Admit it."

"I'm a hard-ass?" she challenged. "Why? Because I'm tired? Because I wish I was in my own bed? Because I wish I was sleeping and you won't let me?" She stopped, dragged an unsteady hand through her hair. "Look. I got shot at today, okay? Some jerk with a Steyr made scrap metal out of my new Jeep. And another jerk," she added pointedly, "is determined to keep me from getting a couple of hours' sleep before I have to get up and start what promises to be another stellar day."

She was shaking now, as much from anger as from a delayed shock that had, unfortunately, kicked in now. She didn't get shot at every day. She didn't face down assassins. She didn't act as a living shield. And she sure as hell didn't kill people.

"Hey, hey," he said gently, and scooted up closer until his right thigh pressed flush against her left. He planted his hand on the chaise cushion near her right hip, so he was leaning over her, cocooning her with his heat and his body. And while his tactic could have been threatening, she understood that he was trying to offer her something to hang on to.

He touched a hand to her hair. The teasing smile was gone. "Easy, *cara*. It's okay."

His gentleness almost broke her. *White knight*. He wanted to play white knight for her. For a moment that scared her to death; she wanted to let him.

She managed to get ahold of herself. By sheer force of will, she kept herself from leaning into the support he offered. No way was she going to let him see her fall apart. She'd be damned if she *would* fall apart. And she wasn't about to accept any help from him. "Go away. Leave me alone."

He didn't budge. "Because you think you're super-woman?" He cupped her face in his hand. "You think you're not entitled to a little meltdown?"

No. She wasn't entitled. And she wouldn't let a latent case of nerves get the best of her. She wouldn't let him get the best of her, either. She shoved his hand away and recovered the only way she knew how, with more anger.

"You'd like that, wouldn't you? You'd like to see me break—"

"Whoa. Just . . . just whoa, okay? Jesus. Where is this coming from?"

He looked concerned and puzzled and convincing. And for a moment, she almost cut him some slack before she reminded herself that it was so much easier to be angry than to be weak.

"I thought we'd gotten past Caracas."

This wasn't about Caracas but it was fine with her if he thought so. She angled away from him, showing him her back, and drew her knees up to her chest. "Still working on it."

"Look, I know I should have cut you some slack. You were just doing your job."

She wrapped her arms around her legs, dropped her forehead onto her knees, and refused to be affected by the regret in his voice. "You're damn right I was."

"And it wasn't your fault that your op interfered with mine." He heaved a deep breath. "I apologize. Again. Okay? Taking the weapons . . . it was a lousy thing to do to you."

She felt his hand in her hair then, dragging it slowly away from her face in an invitation for her to lift her head and look at him. The intimacy of their situation hit her again. They were alone in the night. Alone in the dark. Her heartbeat drowned out the faraway traffic sounds and the low, distant drone of hundreds of air-conditioner units humming away in the night.

She should have pulled away. But his touch was surprisingly gentle. His accent was a little heavier as he softened his tone and his attitude and his hand slowly stroked her hair.

Her reaction was unsettling and strong. Ache in her breasts, unsettling. Wanting to lean into him, strong.

It had been so long since she'd had human contact—real physical contact. Her dad had been a hugger. He'd hug her so hard sometimes she'd thought her ribs would break. And she'd loved it.

She missed it.

And sometimes, alone in the night, in the dark in

her bed, sometimes she thought about another kind of physical contact. The contact between a man and a woman. The ultimate physical connection. No, she didn't believe in love but she did believe in the basic human need to mate, to join, to seek assurance and sustenance and renewal in contact. In sex.

It had been a long time since she'd made that kind of connection. Longer still since she'd made one worth missing. It made no sense that this man reminded her of all that.

"I'm sorry, *querida*."

Oh God. There he went again with those Spanish endearments.

She had to get away from him or he was going to see something she never let anyone see. Need.

She didn't *need* anyone. At least she didn't want to.

On a deep breath, she lifted her head. The hand in her hair stilled but stayed exactly where it was. When she looked over her shoulder at him, his eyes searched hers in the dark. Only inches away. But worlds and worlds away from what she really needed.

"If I accept your apology will you leave me alone so I can get some sleep?" She somehow mustered the will to gather her hair in her hand and drag it out of his loose grasp.

He was quiet for a long moment before he finally smiled. "That might work."

Her breath hitched out, riding on the tension of the near catastrophe. "Fine. Apology accepted."

Gentle humor colored his voice. "Did that hurt so badly?"

"Actually, yes. It did."

He chuckled. "But I feel so much better."

"I'm happy for you."

"Good night, *cara*," he said softly, and stood. His movements were too natural to be staged as he extended his arms up over his head on a huge yawn. Every muscle in his body tensed with the motion. His thighs bunched, his abs tightened, his rib cage expanded. Her mouth went dry and, *God help her*, her thong got wet.

She was in a bit of a daze by the time he finally lowered his arms and turned to go back inside. She watched him walk away, held her breath until he finally reached the terrace doors.

*Thank God.*

But then he paused with his hand on the door latch and turned back to her. "Will you tell me if I guess?"

"Guess . . . what?"

"What B.J. stands for."

That's when she realized she was *still* holding her breath.

"Bonnie Jean?" he suggested on a grin when she said nothing.

The man was infuriating. And yet, against all odds, she had to fight to keep from smiling. "Good night, Mendoza."

# 12

"Hey, Rafe."

"Hey, you." Rafe looked up when Stephanie walked into the kitchen the next morning. Her brown eyes looked tired, her long brown hair hung soft and loose around her shoulders. She was dressed in her rumpled white blouse and black slacks from yesterday. She looked pale and drawn but she still came up with a smile for him. "How you doing this morning?"

"Okay," she said. "Feeling like a slug. You all shouldn't have let me sleep so much yesterday."

"You needed it. Besides, we're going to work you hard today so the special treatment is over." At least he let her think so. He'd keep an eye on her and if she started wearing down, he'd send her off to rest. "Let me get that," he said, intervening when she opened a cupboard door and reached for a coffee mug.

"You don't need to take care of me."

"Just indulge me. It's not every day I get to cater to a damsel in distress."

She rolled her eyes but gave him the all clear by

walking over and sitting down at the dining table. "I talked to Mom and Dad," she said.

"I wish we could let you see them," he said, reading the look on her face. "We can't risk it. Whoever's after you is bound to have someone watching them, expecting that they'll lead them to you."

"I know. I understand. So do they. They just don't like it very much."

No, Rafe thought, he didn't suppose they did but it was a precaution they needed to take. "We'll be moving you soon, then we'll see what kind of communication we can set up that's safe, okay?"

"How long is this going to go on?" Her brows knit together in worry when he brought her the coffee.

"Wish I could tell you. But we're going to get to the bottom of it. You trust me on that, right?"

She nodded. "You know I do." She sipped her coffee, then glanced around the empty apartment. "Where is everybody?"

"Gabe and Jenna haven't made an appearance yet. B.J.'s out on the terrace."

He could see her out there, sitting alone at the table. Sipping coffee, staring into space, a brooding look on her face.

"She was amazing yesterday," Stephanie said quietly. "I've never seen anything like it. She . . . just took control. She told me what to do, where to go, and then she faced down that . . . that assassin like bullets bounced off her or something."

He understood where this was coming from and sat

down at the table with her. He covered her hand with his. "Yeah. She kept her cool. She did her job."

"And I did nothing."

She was suffering from survivor's guilt even though no one she cared about had been hurt. "*Nothing* was the best thing you could have done. You're not trained to deal with those situations. Hell, few people are. She's a pro, Steph. You gave her the room to do what she needed to do to keep you both alive by keeping your head, following her orders, and not making her worry about whether or not you'd do something stupid."

"This is your life, isn't it?" Her big brown eyes searched his. "You . . . you and the guys. You're involved with this sort of thing all the time."

He didn't say anything because there wasn't anything to say.

"I don't know how you do it."

"And I don't know how you apply that amazing analytical mind of yours to cracking codes. The idea of tackling an encrypted message scares the socks off me."

She finally smiled at that. "That's hardly the same thing."

He squeezed her hand. "The point is, we all have our strengths."

"You and B.J. and the guys, yours is a different kind of strength. I'm humbled by it. Bry . . . Bryan had it, too, didn't he?"

He touched her cheek. "Yeah. Yeah, he did."

She forced a smile.

The terrace door opened then and B.J. walked in. Her gaze flashed to his, then to his hand covering Stephanie's, to his palm caressing her cheek.

Her face flamed red. "Sorry," she said, and turned to go back outside like she'd interrupted a lover's tryst.

"B.J., wait." She stopped with her hand on the door when Stephanie called out to her. "It's way past time I thanked you for what you did yesterday."

B.J., ever the tough, cool customer, just shrugged and made a beeline for the coffeepot. "We got out of there alive. That's all that counts."

"Again, thanks to you." Stephanie rose and walked over to her. Then before B.J. could figure out a way to escape, Stephanie wrapped her in an embrace and hugged her. "Thank you," she whispered.

Rafe watched, as touched by Stephanie's gesture as he was by B.J.'s difficulty accepting it. For the longest moment, she just sort of endured Stephanie's display of affection and gratitude, standing as stiff as a post, a trapped expression on her face, her body poised to bolt.

Rafe wondered what had happened to make her so distrustful, not only of everyone else's actions but of her own reaction to them.

Finally Stephanie pulled away. She smiled at B.J., who still looked a little flummoxed and uncertain. "I'm sorry. I didn't mean to get all gushy. Can we blame it on the pain medication?"

Looking relieved that the contact was over, B.J. gave her a clipped nod. "We can."

Jenna and Gabe walked into the kitchen right then.

"The rest of the guys ought to be here any minute," Gabe said. He'd barely gotten the words out of his mouth when the doorbell rang.

Jenna, who was a toucher by nature, slung an arm around B.J.'s shoulders. "Brace yourself. The A team has just arrived."

Rafe was too busy watching B.J. stiffen at Jenna's casual familiarity to take offense to the redhead's good-natured jab.

Gabe, however, couldn't let it pass. "Dissed by my own wife. You just lost certain privileges over that remark, darling dear," he informed her, walking toward the door.

"Empty threats. Always with the empty threats." Jenna left B.J. and followed her husband to the door. She patted him on the ass on the way, then squealed in delight when the rest of the BOIs walked in the apartment.

Luke "Doc Holliday" Colter, Johnny Reed, Wyatt "Papa Bear" Savage, Mean Joe Green, and finally Nate Black himself crowded into Jenna and Gabe's apartment.

Jenna hugged each one in turn until Gabe intervened when Reed, always the ladies' man, lingered a little too long.

"You've got your own woman," Gabe grumbled.

Reed just grinned his slow Texas grin, forked the blond hair back from his eyes, and pulled Jenna closer. "But I like this one, too. You gettin' tired of that oaf yet, sugar?"

"He is a trial sometimes," Jenna confessed, "but he has his uses. How's Crystal?"

Reed's smile widened at the mention of the woman he'd be marrying in a month. "Amazing. And the only woman who could tear my heart away from her is you. Here's an idea. Drop that joker and the three of us can move to Utah and make a real big love."

"You are so full of it," Doc put in, then sobered when his gaze landed on B.J. A crooked, searching smile tipped up one corner of his mouth. "We've met."

"Caracas," Rafe supplied before B.J., who looked a little shell-shocked by the sheer number of BOIs, could respond.

"Right," Doc said with a snap of his fingers. "That's it. What the—"

"She's the reason Steph is alive," Rafe explained.

With that statement, all eyes turned to B.J.

If Rafe read the look in her eyes correctly, right about now B.J. was feeling like a cat in a cage in a zoo. And she didn't like being the center of attention.

She was literally saved by the bell when the doorbell rang again.

"For the love of Mike," Gabe said after checking the camera monitoring the hallway and swinging the door open wide. "Sam Lang. If you aren't a sight for sore eyes."

"Senator, please. Panic is not the answer." Alex Brady attempted to calm his client. "Even though things appear to be unraveling a bit, these are minor setbacks.

You've got to keep a cool head." Coffee cup in hand, he walked to the window of his fourteenth-floor hotel room and looked out over the beltway traffic, waiting for the diatribe he knew would follow.

"Minor setbacks?" the senator repeated. "What planet are you on? Your man, Loeffler, the man who was supposed to take care of loose ends, is dead. Stephanie Tompkins is missing and her car was at the scene of Loeffler's shooting. Half a dozen of the best guns *my* money can buy are scouring the D.C./Fort Meade area, yet fourteen hours after she disappeared, the only clues to her whereabouts—her car and a smashed Jeep—have been confiscated by local law enforcement. Minor setbacks? Don't insult my intelligence."

Alex Brady had done work for this client before. The money was good. Almost good enough to make up for the shit he had to take as the point man. "We're working on finding the owner of the Jeep." Find the owner, find a trail to the Tompkins woman. "And I've spoken with a camper at the park who heard gunshots, then a crash. He watched from the woods while he dialed 911."

"I trust you were discreet when you questioned him."

Alex clenched his jaw, let the insult go by. He prided himself on discretion. That and providing results. And doing things his own way, which was why he and the Baltimore PD had parted ways several years ago. Public service was for Boy Scouts and suckers. He was neither.

"He assumed I was a Fed. Anyway, he said there were two women at the scene. A dark blue SUV arrived after the gunfire, two men on board. After some discussion that he couldn't hear, both women got in the SUV with the men and they made fast tracks out of there."

"You asked about license plate numbers, right?"

Again, he exercised control. The senator was angry and desperate. He'd make allowances. "We have a partial on the SUV. I've got a guy at Motor Vehicle running what we've got. I expect to hear from him soon."

"And I expect a resolution to this soon. Do not let this go on much longer."

"I'll be back in touch."

"Damn right you will!"

The senator slammed down the phone. Alex listened to the dial tone for a moment before flipping his cell phone shut.

Money, he reminded himself as he dialed Jenkins to get an update on the hunt for Stephanie Tompkins. Money was the motivator and the payoff.

In this case, it was too much money to tell the illustrious senator to fuck off.

The senator stared out the window for a moment, then picked up the phone again and made the dreaded call to Colombia. A flunky answered on the third ring and the senator spoke the code word. "*Ura.*"

"*Momento.*"

Several long minutes passed before Emilio Garcia came on the line. "Senator. To what do I owe this pleasure?" the head of the Garcia drug cartel inquired in heavily accented English.

There was nothing for it but to come right out with it. The Colombian drug lord would find out soon enough anyway. "A complication has arisen."

Silence, then a carefully measured question. "What kind of complication?"

"A cryptologist within the NSA appears to have stumbled onto a limited number of the encrypted communications that transpired between us and our Russian counterpart."

Another silence. This one rang with rage. "I had understood our bases were covered on that front."

"Yes, well, they were."

"Define *limited*."

"Unknown at this point in time. The cryptologist in question was to have been contained; however, she somehow managed to escape."

"You assured me there would be no discovery on your end, Senator." Emilio's tone had grown clipped.

"I realize that. And the situation will be controlled shortly. I'm calling only as a courtesy as I did not wish to have you come by this information from another source—a source that might not appreciate the lengths being taken to recover and prevent any leakage of information."

"A courtesy? How very thoughtful of you." Sarcasm dripped from each word. "I do not, however, want courtesy from you. I want results."

"Which you will get. In the meantime, what's the status of the project?"

"For what purpose do you require this information?" Emilio made no effort at all to conceal his contempt.

The gall of the bastard. "I was not aware that I needed a reason to request updates. Further, I will remind you that if all had gone according to schedule on your end, there would be no need for us to have this conversation as the attack would already have taken place and we would be out from under potential scrutiny. Now what is the status of the project?"

"Nearing completion." While there was still an edge in his voice, Emilio leveled his tone. "The technology is about to be tested. It is a very delicate process. My engineers inform me that everything will be operational within seven days, at which time we'll be able to turn the device and the sub over to Abdul Azeem."

Seven days. An eternity. "And Azeem?" The Afghani sheik had the ear and the trust of bin Laden. He would command this attack on the U.S.

"Impatient," Emilio admitted. "But he will wait. He has no choice."

None of them had a choice at this juncture. They were all in too deep to change course now.

# 13

Less than twenty minutes after the BOIs arrived at Gabe and Jenna's apartment, everyone teed up to move Stephanie to the safe house. Everyone but Gabe, who would drive Jenna to the airport.

"Macho boy thinks I can't get myself on a plane to West Palm," Jenna said, the affection in her eyes undercutting her tiny bit of annoyance.

"That's macho *man*, dear," Gabe clarified with an arch look. "And I'm not taking any chances when it comes to getting you out of here safe and sound."

They weren't taking chances with anything. The plan was for Jenna to spend a little down time in Florida with friends, Amy and Dallas Garrett and their family, who were close with the entire Black Ops team from the sound of it. Also from the sound of it, Jones felt Jenna would be in good hands with the Garretts in the event some of this mess with Stephanie slopped over on her.

In the meantime, Black was now calling the shots for the team. "Green, you're in the car with me and

Steph. Lang, Colter, and Savage, you're point car." He nodded toward Rafe. "You, Reed, and B.J. will cover our six. Everyone good with this?"

They were.

He checked his watch. "Okay. Head out, Rafe. You've got twenty minutes."

Twenty minutes to get to B.J.'s apartment, grab a change of clothes and replenish her ammo, then double back here and join the parade.

"No offense," B.J. had said when they'd offered to supply her with their ammo, "but you military types carry full metal jackets. I want my hollow-points."

Reed had whistled. "The lady not only wants to tear a big hole, she wants to let the air out."

"The lady," B.J. had clarified, "trusts her own loads. Plain and simple."

As shooters, they'd understood even though they hadn't liked it much.

"It'll take fifteen minutes to get there and back. Twenty tops. That's all I'm asking."

And that's what she'd gotten, thanks to Black. "Good chance to see if they've put a tail on B.J.'s apartment. So watch yourselves," he'd warned.

"Call when you're back and we'll head out and meet you in the parking lot," he said now as B.J. followed Rafe and Reed to the door.

Jenna stopped her with a hand on her arm. "Don't let 'em push you around," she told her by way of good-bye.

B.J. acknowledged Jenna's warning with a nod. "That's not going to happen."

Jenna grinned. "My money's on you." Then she pressed a chocolate bar into B.J.'s hand.

She glanced at it, then back at Jenna.

"Rafe said you have a thing for chocolate."

B.J. wasn't used to warm fuzzies from other women and felt way out of her element fielding one.

"Thanks for the hospitality." It was the best she could do.

As Jenna closed the door behind her, B.J. realized again that Jenna Jones was a woman she could grow to like. What she couldn't figure was why Mendoza had been talking to Jenna about her. Or why something about that knowledge didn't suck as much as it should have.

"What'da ya think?" Reed asked on their second pass around B.J.'s apartment building in one of the rental Suburbans the guys had driven to Gabe's.

"I think I need my ammo," B.J. muttered from the shotgun seat beside Rafe.

Rafe didn't much care that she was impatient. He hadn't been about to take a chance that some badass with a bad gun was staking out her apartment.

"It's clear," he said, which earned him a big sigh of relief from the passenger seat as he pulled into the lot. They'd barely rolled to a stop when she bounded out of the car and sprinted up the building's steps.

"Damn woman," he sputtered as he slammed the car into park and tore out after her.

Reed chuckled. "I'll just man the boat," he said from the backseat as Rafe jerked open one of the double glass entry doors and followed B.J. inside.

He caught B.J.'s arm and jerked her around to face him just as she opened the stairwell door.

"Will you slow the hell down? You're not a one-man show here. This is a team effort, remember? Or did you have a change of heart about being a team player?"

She actually looked contrite. "I'm sorry. Really," she added for emphasis. "Habit, okay? I'm used to calling my own shots."

"And I'm used to working with a tight team. You don't go anywhere without backup, got it?"

She nodded. "So can we do this?"

"Go," he grumbled, and followed her as she sprinted up three flights of stairs, then stopped outside her apartment door.

He put a finger to his lips, mouthed, "Stay back," and drew his Sig from the shoulder holster he'd strapped on over his T-shirt and covered with a loose cotton shirt. Then he nodded for her to unlock the door.

He shoved it open and, leading with the Sig, checked all the rooms. "It's clear."

"I'll just be a minute." She shouldered past him and headed for her bedroom.

Rafe locked up behind them, then checked out her apartment while he waited. Small, pin neat, and unexpectedly colorful.

The red leather sofa surprised him. So did the wild splashes of color in her choice of artwork. No pastels for this lady. She liked vibrant, saturated reds and blues and aquamarines. Even her bedroom was decorated with lots of color but in there she'd gone for rich gold, earthy green, and warm burgundy. And about a hundred pillows on her bed.

So she liked her creature comforts. Not that he'd expected her to sleep in a box. Not that he'd expected to be thinking about her and a bed. Her in a bed.

"I'm almost set." She rushed back out of the bedroom, catching him in full speculation mode.

"I thought you were going to change," he said when he saw her.

She looked down at herself after she'd tossed an open duffel on the kitchen counter.

"I did."

Hokay. So her fun with the color wheel was limited to her decorating, because damn if it didn't look like she'd traded one pair of khaki shorts and a black tank for another.

He watched as she squatted down to access a lower cupboard, drew out several boxes of hollow-point cartridges, and tucked them in the bag with some toiletries and a change of clothes.

"Lotta ammo."

"You ever met a woman who travels light?" She

zipped up the bag and headed for the door. She was ready to burst back out into the hall when she stopped short and waited for him.

"Quick study." He shouldered by her and, Sig drawn again, checked the hallway. "We're clear."

They didn't stay that way for long.

"Company?" Rafe asked when they joined Reed in the car and saw he'd dug the HK MP-5 mini sub out of his go bag.

"Maybe. Tan Buick," Reed said as B.J. retrieved her Glock from under the seat, then dug into her bag for her ammo. "Pulled in right after you went inside."

Rafe checked out the vehicle that sat several rows down from them. There were two men inside. "Recognize the car?" Rafe asked B.J., who shook her head and started filling her magazine.

"Doesn't belong here," she said.

"Let's see if they want to play Follow the Leader." Rafe pulled out of the lot and eased onto the street.

"Yep," Reed said after they'd driven a couple of blocks and the Buick fell into the line of traffic behind them. "Bastards want us to lead them to Steph. Looks like it's time for fun with Dick and Dickhead. Better buckle up, B.J.," he added with a grin. "Nothing the Choirboy likes better than putting on his Dale Earnhardt face."

Rafe punched the gas, swerved between two cars, and hung a quick left on a yellow light at the next intersection. They took the corner on two wheels as horns honked, brakes locked, and fists shook.

Couldn't be helped. The streets were congested here. The last thing they needed was for bullets to start flying and for some hockey mom to catch a round.

"And?" Rafe asked as he barreled down a side street.

"And the guy can drive. They're still with us."

"Hook a left, then a right," B.J. said, twisting in the seat to see how close the tail was. "Drive about a mile and we'll get out of the thick of the traffic. If I remember right, there's a block of condemned buildings, old manufacturing plants. Should be an alley we can pull into."

"I love a woman who's into showdowns."

"In case you hadn't noticed," Rafe said as he alternately gunned the motor and stood on the brakes as he maneuvered the two turns, "Reed has never met a woman he didn't love."

Reed swore after looking behind them. "Those SOBs are sticking like ticks. Like to know what they've got under the hood."

They hit a series of potholes, jolting them against the seatbelts as Rafe flew through a red light. The nose of the big Suburban scraped the pavement when they hit another dip and he had to wrestle the wheel to keep the car under control.

"Up there," B.J. said, pointing to the right.

Rafe slammed on the brakes, cut the wheel sharply right, and nosed the Suburban into the narrow alley.

Reed reached behind him into the cargo area and grabbed an M-4 assault rifle. He handed it over the front seat to Rafe and the three of them bailed out, took defensive positions at the front of the vehicle, and waited.

They didn't have to wait long. The Buick roared past, slammed on the brakes, then backed up when its occupants spotted the three of them in the alley.

"Fifty yards?" Rafe asked, sighting through the M-4's scope.

"Give or take," both B.J. and Reed said at the same time.

"Piece of cake." Rafe set the rifle to full auto, then emptied a full magazine into the Buick.

The concussion of sound was deafening as round after round pummeled the car, shattering windows, blowing tires.

"Jesus," Reed swore, sticking a finger in his ear as they watched the Buick limp away as fast as the two flat tires could take it. "I'm going to be deaf for a fucking month."

"Say what?" Rafe asked with a grin as they hauled ass back into the SUV.

"We gonna finish it?" Reed asked as Rafe pulled out of the alley.

Down the street, smoke billowed out of the shot-up Buick; sparks flew on the pavement as the metal wheel rims spun on ruined rubber.

"They've called reinforcements by now. Let's just get back to Gabe's and get Steph moved before they catch up with us again."

They arrived back at Gabe's apartment with a minute to spare on their twenty-minute limit.

"Any problems?" Nate asked when Reed called to let them know they were outside.

"Nah. But I am going to file a complaint with the city about the potholes," Reed said, then laughed when B.J. rolled her eyes.

Two minutes later, Stephanie, flanked by the BOIs with guns drawn, hurried outside and into the cars and headed out of town to the safe house.

Testosterone. Testosterone. Testosterone. These guys had it in spades, B.J. thought as she sat with them at a huge oak table and observed their briefing session at the safe house. When they moved, they moved fast, as was evidenced by the fact that it had only been two hours since the lot of them had delivered Stephanie to the safe house with the precision of a well-oiled machine.

A military machine, B.J. couldn't help but think as the three-car caravan had employed dozens of evasive tactics to ensure that if anyone was tailing them, they were subsequently lost in a sea of traffic and exhaust.

Jones had just arrived for the tail end of the briefing. The safe house was a small one-story ranch in the country, far outside the Beltway and well beyond the Maryland suburbs. It was isolated but defensible—the point men in the group had been busy and had assembled a small arsenal and enough ammo to ward off an invasion if it came to that.

As soon as they'd arrived Green and Savage had gotten busy placing trip wires and motion sensors around the perimeter to alert them to any unwelcome guests. Doc and Sam Lang had set up a laptop computer in the main living area, then connected it to the surveillance cameras that they'd mounted on all four corners of the rectangular house. B.J. had also noticed that the house was situated near a crossroads in the event they had to make a quick getaway. No one was going to get within one hundred yards of the place without detection.

The refrigerator and pantry were well stocked. One of the three bedrooms had been set up as an intelligence center complete with a desktop and another laptop computer, high-speed modems, and cloaking devices to keep uninvited cyber eyes from intercepting their communications. Stephanie was, at this moment, searching and analyzing the data on the flash drive she'd smuggled out of the NSA.

The entire setup was impressive, though how they'd managed to arrange this in advance of Stephanie's arrival was baffling. Just another reminder of the expansive resources and network of Black's operation and of the Tompkinses' clout.

B.J. looked around, trying to get a better read on the men gathered there beneath an overhead light that was centered above the table. Outside the late-morning sun shone bright, but it felt more like evening inside. The shades were all drawn and the curtains all pulled tight.

Nathan Black made a formidable presence in the room. She judged the tall, and she suspected deceptively slim, man with the dark hair to be in his mid to

late forties. His calm, controlled demeanor was that of
a natural leader. The rough-and-tumble men sitting
around the table clearly thought the former marine
non-com officer walked on water and made it rain, and
those men were no shrinking violets. He was all hard
angles and intense eyes, except for a moment when
Jones asked him about a woman named Juliana. He
softened then—only a little—but B.J. caught it and the
fact that this Juliana meant something special to both
Black and Jones.

Wyatt "Papa Bear" Savage, she'd been told by Mendoza when he'd made introductions, was former CIA.
He was a big, burly man with a soft southern drawl
and a pleasant and unremarkable face most people
wouldn't remember. A highly desirable trait in a CIA
operative or a black operator. Savage seemed more
than content to occupy that background position.

At first glance Johnny Reed—whom the rest of them
often referred to jokingly as Golden Boy or "dead bach-
elor walking"—appeared to be a lot of flash and swagger and little else. But the thing B.J. recognized was
that this was an elite group of men. They would suffer
no fools. That told her that there was much more to the
former force recon marine than met the eye. She also
recognized that the ridiculously flirty grins he occasionally shot her way were mechanisms he used to ensure that others underestimated him.

Luke Colter, whom all the guys called Doc or Holliday, was a former navy SEAL and the team medic. He
had a tall, rangy cowboy look going on and was almost

as big a flirt as Reed. But there was intelligence and passion behind his easygoing smiles and she had no doubt that he was, also like Reed, an invaluable member of the team.

Mean Joe Green—it seemed most of them had a nickname—was a hard one to get a read on. Like Savage, he was also former CIA. He was silent, thoughtful, and if his skin wasn't so clear and she wasn't certain that Black wouldn't tolerate it, she would have sworn that the man was on steroids. He was built like an Abrams tank and without a doubt, she would not want to be on his bad side.

Aside from Mendoza and Jones, the final man at the table was Sam Lang. From what she'd gathered, Lang, former Delta and almost as tall as Jones, was no longer with the team. He'd retired recently to raise horses and babies in Nevada with his wife, Abbie. Apparently, however, Stephanie's troubles had lifted the moratorium on his combat days. B.J. had gathered that he'd left a very pregnant Abbie behind and joined the team at Abbie's insistence. It was yet another indication of how important the Tompkinses were to these men.

These were the men she'd been ordered to work with.

It could have been worse. Sherwood could have taken her off the case altogether. After Caracas, it wouldn't have surprised her if he did. So she was grateful that she was still on board—if not resentful at the shift in power to Black's crew.

"So," Black said, after Mendoza had filled in the entire team with the sketchy details, "in a nutshell, what we know is that we've got stolen E-bomb technology floating around the world. We have a traitor at NSA who intercepted and hid cyber-traffic that should have been passed on to DOD alerting them to the theft of the technology. We know that the same traitor was most likely responsible for ordering the hit on Stephanie. We have Alan Hendricks, Steph's supervisor at SI, acting suspicious, so we have to figure that at the very least he knew about the leak and was covering it up, or was involved in some way. But then Hendricks ends up dead, either deemed nonessential or a screwup by whoever is pulling the strings.

"What we don't know," Black went on, "is who's pulling the strings and what they plan to do with the technology."

"And when they plan to use it," Mendoza added.

Nate looked grim when he turned to B.J. "Get Sherwood on the line. While I'd sure as hell like to give them a target and a date, it's time for DIA to alert the Joint Chiefs that we're facing the very real possibility of an imminent attack."

An hour later, after Black and Sherwood had talked for the second time, Black said, "Here's how it's shaking down. Sherwood ran the info up the chain of command. With no established target, no established attack date, and no real handle on the viability of either the functionality or the method of delivery of an E-bomb, we're still in fact-finding mode. DOD, however, will jump-start a covert top-security-level internal analysis, but they're expecting us to continue to run our off-the-grid investigation."

Which meant, B.J. knew, that everyone was relying on Stephanie to uncover something for them to work with as she continued to wade through those encrypted messages.

Her phone rang right then. It was Sherwood again.

"We've got a name for the shooter," she told the group, hanging up after Sherwood had filled her in on the positive ID. "Zach Loeffler. He's in the system as a known gun for hire. They were able to trace him through ballistic matches from the slugs they recovered from his Steyr. It's custom made and apparently his signature weapon."

"Loeffler. Name sounds familiar," Mendoza said thoughtfully. "We need to access our database, see what we can find on him."

Black nodded at Reed. "Get Crystal on it."

"Might be better coming from you," Reed suggested.

Doc made meowing noises and punctuated them with a grin. "Pussy. The man is afraid of one hundred pounds of dynamite," he informed B.J.

"Damn right I am," Reed agreed without apology. "You've never seen my fiancée ticked off. I have. Right now, she's royally pissed that we cut her out of this op."

"Guess we know who's going to wear the jockstrap in that household," Doc added, to which Reed just flipped him the bird.

"If you haven't figured it out yet," Mendoza told B.J., "Crystal is soon to have the undesirable title of Mrs. Johnny Duane Reed. She's also the newest member of the team. She took over the commo and security systems and is working on our data files."

"Guys."

Conversation around the table stopped when Stephanie walked into the room. B.J. couldn't help but feel a twinge of sympathy for her. The dark circles beneath her eyes were evidence that both stress and fatigue were taking their toll. The tightness around her mouth relayed the pain her wrist must have been giving her, especially after she'd been working the computers.

"You okay, Steph?" Black rose and went to her, his brows drawn together in concern.

"I'm fine."

Stephanie had just scored more points in B.J.'s book. She was far from fine but she was holding up.

"I might have found something," Stephanie said, "but I'm not sure what it means yet. And I won't know until I talk to a friend of mine, Ben Brommel, who works at the Pentagon."

"Steph," Black cautioned her.

"I know. You don't want to take the chance of someone finding me through a phone call, but it's critical that I speak with him. And Ben's okay. I'd trust him with my life."

Black looked from Mendoza's concerned expression to the rest of the sober faces circling the table.

"I can get Sherwood to run a quick check on Brommel," B.J. suggested, recognizing that they were waffling for Stephanie's sake but knowing that time was critical.

"And waste more time," Stephanie protested. "Look. Trust me on this. Ben is solid. Sic DOD on him if you must but do it later. I need to talk to him now."

After a brief hesitation, she got a nod from Black.

"Use my secure phone." B.J. handed Stephanie her cell phone.

"Answer no questions," Black warned as Stephanie headed back toward the computer room. "And keep it as brief as possible."

# 14

*Ura!*

Everything from her fingers to her toes and parts in between had tingled with alarm the first time Stephanie had read the translation over a week ago:

*Ura. The Russian army battle cry traditionally thought to mean "Hurrah!" Coming from the Turkish word for "kill."*

*Kill.*

She'd known then . . . known deep inside that B. J. Chase had been right, that someone inside NSA was a traitor. She still couldn't believe it was Alan. And that he was dead. That someone had tried to kill her. Her wrist throbbed and ached, reminding her she had reason to believe it and more.

It all seemed like a nightmarish dream. What she'd just uncovered after finally cracking the sub-code of the deleted messages were dozens of communiqués from a base in Russia to an address that she still hadn't pinned down. There were still a lot of puzzle pieces missing but she had high hopes that Ben could give her the final one.

She drew a deep breath as she waited for him to answer.

"Brommel."

She jumped when he finally came on the line. "Hey, Ben. It's me."

"Hey, you. How's the spy business?"

It was a standing joke between them. He'd ask about her job and she'd reply, "The spy business is its usual virtual snore." That was because day after day, week after week, month after month, decoding and deciphering reams of encrypted cyber-communications was about as far from playing spy as Ben was from being straight.

"I need your help," she said. "And I need you to not ask questions. I've got a problem. A big one, and for now, I really need you to just trust me. I'll explain everything later."

"Okay," he said, after a moment's hesitation. "What do you need?"

She pulled some key words from the communiqués in question and read them to him. "Do these terms mean anything to you?"

"Jesus, Steph," he whispered so tightly that she could visualize him, shoulders tensed, head low, as he hunched over his cell phone. "Where the hell did you get that? No one—and I mean *no one* outside of a very tight, sworn-to-secrecy-or-they're-gonna-die group—is supposed to know about that project."

"Then why did I pick up the lingo on a coded com-
muniqué that originated in Russia?"

Silence, then a weakly uttered, "Mother of God."

Stephanie had no sooner left the tension-filled room
than Reed asked cheerfully, "Anyone but me
hungry?"

They were big, active men. Stood to reason they'd
have big appetites, B.J. thought, and she very much
doubted that any of them had had more than coffee for
breakfast.

"I could eat," Savage said.

"There's a surprise." Doc grinned at the big guy.

Mendoza tipped back, balanced his chair on the
back legs, and glanced B.J.'s way.

Oh, yeah. Here it comes. They're going to expect
me to cook, she thought. But before she could formu-
late a semi-civil version of "bite me," he surprised her.

"Hope you like bacon and eggs. It's my specialty," he
announced, bringing his chair back down to the floor
and rising.

"*I'll* do the bacon," Reed informed him, pushing
away from the table. "You always burn it."

"I'll take four eggs, over easy." Doc put his order in
with a lazy grin.

"You've apparently mistaken me for a short-order
cook," Mendoza said over his shoulder. "You'll eat 'em
how I fix 'em."

But less than an hour later when the cooks served up
heaping platters of bacon, toast, and eggs and a huge

pitcher of orange juice, B.J. noticed that Doc got his four perfectly cooked, over-easy eggs.

"Too bad you're so damn ugly," he informed Mendoza as he chowed down, "or you'd make some lucky woman a good wife."

"Better grab and growl," Reed told B.J., "before these primates lick the platters. No such thing as ladies first with this crew."

"I'll just . . . um . . . go get Stephanie," she said, a little too fascinated by the sight of all that food and all those men and all the nonsense going on among them.

You'd think they were in the midst of a party instead of a life-or-death situation. The good-natured insults kept flying as she walked out of the room. On one level she understood it. Humor was a coping mechanism for some people. And there was the fact that these guys had been through many fires together. Was there a point in time, she wondered, when it all became rote? That the idea of possibly taking a bullet, of taking a life, became such an integral part of their existence that fear no longer factored into the mix?

No, she didn't buy that and thought back to yesterday—God, was it just yesterday?—when she'd killed a man. A sick knot clutched at her stomach. No one could get used to that. Didn't matter that it had been life or death.

It had to be that way for these men, too, she suspected. No matter how much they'd done, how much they'd seen, how many times they'd escaped

death, what they did would never become status quo.
They were just better than most 'at concealing their
nerves.

What struck her most about these men, however, was
that they seemed more like brothers than coworkers. In
a fleeting moment of longing, she realized that, in part,
it was the absence of that sense of brotherhood, of community, of belonging, that sometimes made her feel so
empty inside.

"Stephanie, come get something to eat," she said
from the open doorway of the computer room.

"In a minute." Stephanie's head was down, and her
good hand held a pen that flew over a stack of paper.

"In a minute, it might all be gone," B.J. warned her.

If Stephanie heard, she ignored her.

"Don't be too long," she suggested, then walked
back into the middle of that sea of men.

Not five minutes later Stephanie joined them, her
fist full of papers, her eyes wide and alarmed.

"Steph?" Nathan Black rose and went to her. "What
is it?"

She shook her head. Swallowed. "It's bad. It's really,
really bad. I cracked the sub code on those communiqués Alan Hendricks dumped from the system,"
Stephanie said. "And I kept finding the same references
to Black Ruby."

"Black Ruby?" Nate's brows knit together. "Sounds
like a military project."

"Exactly. That's why I needed to talk to my friend at
the Pentagon."

Rafe glanced at Green, who had moved to the laptop and was checking the exterior cameras shots. The
big guy had a very hard look on his face. Nothing new.
But when Green glanced at Steph, Rafe saw more than
generic concern. It was such a shocker, Rafe stared for
a moment. Long enough for Green to catch him at it
and immediately turn his gaze back to the cameras.

"Ben was horrified when I asked him if he knew
what it meant, because, according to him, Black Ruby
is a top, top secret heat beam research project. He described it as Star Wars–type technology: an invisible
heat beam that's fired from a high-powered ray gun. It's
a totally non-lethal, invasive crowd-control device that
can be used to disburse unruly crowds by producing a
blast of heat so fierce people run from it, but it leaves
no long-lasting effect. But there's another application.
It can act as a cloaking device."

"A cloaking device?" Rafe asked the question that
was on the tip of everyone's tongue. "For what?"

It was B.J. who drew the disturbing conclusion.
"The delivery and deployment of an E-bomb."

Silence. Total and complete.

Everyone in the room stilled, their gazes switching
from B.J. back to Stephanie as they digested the magnitude of the news.

"Jesus," Savage said finally.

"You're sure?" Black asked, even though his expression relayed that he already knew the answer.

"I'm sure. The communiqués are from an IP address
in Russia to someone somewhere—I still haven't

uncovered the destination—and they are all about Black Ruby and E-bomb technology."

"So they're in the talking stage," Gabe suggested.

"Not just talking," Stephanie said. "Assembling."

It was as if everyone in the room quit breathing.

"These communiqués are filled with orders for components, tweaking of applications, and progress reports," Stephanie continued.

"Were you able to determine the status of their progress?" Nate asked.

She swallowed hard. "They're nearing the end of the testing stage."

"How can that be? It wasn't more than two weeks ago when those specs for the E-bomb showed up in Afghanistan."

"They may have only been *found* two weeks ago, but it looks like the technology and the Black Ruby technology were both stolen over a year ago. Maybe longer. Many of the messages I've been decoding started twelve months ago. That's how long Alan was hiding data."

"Steph—have you found a target?" Rafe's heartbeat drummed in the silence.

She shook her head. "I don't know where," she said. "But I do know when. Seven days from today."

The tension in the room was suddenly so thick a chain saw couldn't have hacked through it.

"So, we have unknown terrorists, a known target date, an unknown target, and the technology to launch an E-bomb that could cripple the entire electronic grid of a major city," Black summarized into the silence.

"It's worse than that," Stephanie said. "Remember the blackout of 2003?"

Everyone remembered. A cascading blackout destabilized the Niagara-Mohawk power grid as far north as Canada and as far west as Detroit and Cleveland.

"Millions of people were without power for several days," Nate said.

"Take that times one hundred if whoever is behind this manages to use an E-bomb to take out that same power grid, or any one of a number of grids that provide electricity to the U.S. and Canada," Stephanie said. "Virtually everything electrically powered will be dead. Forever. There's no coming back. No repairs. No possibility of getting the power grid back online.

"One bomb, in the right place, could shut down half the country. Think about it. Airports. The stock exchange. The Internet. All finance. All computer records. Gas pumps." The list that came to mind was staggering.

"Who the hell is behind this?" Gabe's face was beet red with anger.

"It wasn't Alan Hendricks," B.J. concluded. "He was just a chess piece they were pushing around the board."

"Someone higher up then. Someone with a high level of security clearance and a reason to sell out their country," Lang put in quietly.

"A reason?" B.J. said, sounding disgusted. "Money is always the reason."

Stephanie shook her head. "I still can't believe there could be a traitor inside our ranks."

"And yet, Alan Hendricks was in it neck deep," B.J. pointed out.

"We've got to look at a higher level," Nate said.

"Lots of special interest groups out there lobbying. Lots of foreign money making its way into greedy hands," Reed agreed.

"B.J., call Sherwood again," Nate ordered. "Fill him in on what Steph discovered so he can pass it on. And Steph, we need the destination IP address. We need to know where those communications are going. What can we get you to make things happen?"

Stephanie looked uncomfortable.

"What is it?" Black pressed.

She hesitated. "If I had encryption software, this would go a lot faster."

"No way can we breach NSA security," B.J. said, reading the minds of everyone in the room.

Stephanie met B.J.'s eyes. "You wouldn't have to. I've got software loaded on my laptop at home. It's just something I use to practice with. But it would be too dangerous to go get it."

"Would it help you?" Black asked.

She gave a reluctant nod.

"Where do we find the laptop?"

"On it," Rafe said after she'd told them where it was. He grabbed an extra magazine for his Sig, along with a set of car keys. "Chase, you're with me."

Maybe it was fatigue. Maybe it was blowback from going head-to-head with a paid assassin yesterday and playing hide-and-shoot with the goons in the tan Buick earlier this morning, but B.J. felt as jumpy as a kid at fright night at the movies.

Holding her Glock in a two-handed grip, she followed Mendoza cautiously down the hallway on the fourteenth floor of Stephanie's D.C. apartment building.

It had to be the fourteenth floor, she thought grimly. Everyone knew it was really the thirteenth floor. It wasn't that she believed in any of the unlucky number thirteen crap, but with the way her luck had been running lately, this was an additional strike she didn't need going against her.

"Here it is," Mendoza said, reaching the door to apartment 14G. He produced Stephanie's apartment key from his pocket.

B.J. drew a bracing breath, then, gun held low, hustled to the opposite side of the door and flattened her back against the wall. Mendoza gave her a nod, then carefully turned the key. The tumblers made a soft thudding sound and the door slid open half an inch.

"On my go," he mouthed, drawing his Sig, then, with a final cautious glance, he started counting backward from three.

On one, he kicked open the door and charged inside. B.J. followed as they quickly checked the foyer. The apartment was dark, lights off, drapes drawn.

"Clear." Mendoza hitched his head toward the living area.

They moved in together, guns drawn, him high, her low, ready to shoot if they met resistance. B.J.'s heart thudded hard and fast.

"All clear." Mendoza shoved his Sig into the belt at the small of his back after they'd cleared the rooms one at a time.

"But hardly clean," B.J. said after flicking on a light switch.

"Jesus," Rafe swore when the overhead light illuminated the shambles.

The room had been thoroughly and ruthlessly trashed. Sofa cushions slashed, lamps broken, artwork ripped from the walls.

"Think they were pissed?" he muttered.

"Or desperate." B.J. holstered her Glock in the leather sheath beneath her arm.

"Moment of truth," he said, and headed for the bedroom.

B.J. followed, stepping over the debris as he walked straight to the clothes closet and the heavy metal safe that sat askew on the floor.

"Looks like when they couldn't crack it, they tried to drag this sucker out of here," he said. "Bad boy must weigh close to a thousand pounds."

"Here's to distrustful women everywhere," B.J. said, and watched Rafe work the lock with the combination Stephanie had given him.

"Hurry it up," she said, her nerves and her sixth sense working overtime. She'd had too many close calls lately.

One of these times, her number was going to be up. "It couldn't have been that long ago that the bad guys were here. I'm betting they'll come back with some C-four. They've got to figure there's something in that safe of use to them."

"Not anymore." Rafe grinned as the last tumbler clicked into place and the safe door swung open. A laptop computer was tucked inside, along with what looked like insurance and other legal papers. "Jackpot."

He grabbed the laptop and closed up the safe. "Let's go—"

*Boom, boom, boom!*

B.J. didn't think. She just reacted. She threw herself on top of Rafe, knocked them both to the floor beside the bed, and drew her Glock.

"Stay down," she ordered when he groaned. "I said, stay down, damn it," she repeated, driving a knee into his back, and with the Glock drawn, levering herself up high enough to see over the bed, the only barrier between them and the bedroom door.

On the floor, Mendoza was gasping in pain as he rolled to his side and into a ball. "Can't . . . brea . . . the . . ."

Whoops. He must have landed on the edge of the laptop and had the wind knocked out of him when she'd pushed him down. Which meant she was on her own until he recovered.

*Boom, boom, boom!* rattled the walls again.

B.J. ducked down, then belly crawled to the foot of

the bed, where she could get a clear shot at the door.

Then she waited, adrenaline zipping through her blood.

But nothing happened. No guys with guns burst through the door. No AK rounds shredded the mattress.

*Boom, boom, boom!*

"Shit. Shit, shit, shit," she muttered, finally realizing the source of the noise.

She hauled her sorry self upright, walked over to the window, and hooked a finger on a drapery panel, pulling it aside. Looked like lunch break was over on the high-rise construction site across the street.

*Boom, boom, boom!* reverberated through the apartment again as the heavy-duty equipment went about the business of transforming steel girders and cement and rerod into living space.

A low curse from the bedroom jarred her back to Mendoza.

"Crap." She walked back into the bedroom, knowing she'd never hear the end of this. "You, um . . . okay?" she asked carefully as he levered himself up to a sitting position.

He slumped against the wall, gingerly rubbing his chest with the heel of his hand. "I didn't hear any shots."

"Yeah . . . well. False alarm."

He shot her a dumbfounded look. "Say again?"

She lifted a shoulder, saw the pain still drawing his face tight. "Construction. Across the street. Sorry."

He glared at her.

"I'm a little tense, all right?" she pointed out in her own defense.

"Like I'm a little pissed?"

"Yeah," she said. "Like that."

"Do me a favor. Next time you want to play conquering heroine, warn me first so I can get the hell out of Dodge."

"I said I was sorry."

He grunted.

She held out a hand. He grasped it and she helped him to his feet. When she would have let go of his hand, he held on tight.

"I'd say this makes us even for Caracas." His dark eyes flashed before he finally let go, retrieved the laptop, and stomped toward the door.

Yeah, she thought, working hard, suddenly, to suppress a smile. Maybe they were even now.

They made the trip back to the safe house in record time and record silence. All the while, she thought about the look in his eyes—hard and hot and she wasn't sure what else. She thought about the strength of his hand, how he'd held hers, how her skin still tingled from his touch.

One look at the BOIs' grim faces, however, was all it took to ground her back in the reality of traitors, national security threats, and an unavoidable ticking clock.

"Thanks," Stephanie said when Rafe handed her the laptop.

"What else can we get you?" Nate asked.

"Time," she said grimly, because she knew as well as the rest of them that time was the one thing they didn't have. "I could use some help charting and recording," she added.

"Mendoza—that would be you," Nate said.

"I can help, too."

When Green also volunteered, it surprised everyone in the room—possibly everyone but B.J. because she'd seen the look in Green's eyes when he'd thought no one was watching.

Green had a thing for Stephanie. Interesting

"First you eat," Green ordered Steph, which raised a few eyebrows and questioning looks. Only when he was satisfied that she'd refueled did he let her get back to work.

"Get me results, people," Nate said. "And get them fast. We cannot let this happen."

# 15

"Colombia," Stephanie said within the first hour of searching with the aid of her software. "The other IP address is in Colombia."

Rafe's expression hardened. "You're sure?" he asked quietly.

"Positive. Give me a little more time and I'll get account names for the addresses."

"Good work." Green squeezed her shoulder.

"Something wrong?" B.J. asked Rafe when Stephanie and Green had their heads together again over a series of graphs and charts Stephanie used to organize the deciphered messages.

He glanced at her, his dark eyes cold. "I'll go make some more coffee."

What in the heck is that about? she wondered. Maybe he was still ticked at her for laying him out.

"Rafe's from Colombia," Green said.

B.J. turned back to see Green looking over his shoulder at her. She didn't know what surprised her more: the warning look on Green's face—as in "don't press it"—or the fact that he was talking at all. It hadn't taken long for her to discover that Green was a man of few words.

"He doesn't talk about it. But there are bad memories there." With another meaningful look, he turned back to Stephanie.

*Bad memories.*

B.J. knew about bad memories—she had her own to deal with.

Everyone had a story. She wondered what Rafe's was. It was none of her business. She didn't *want* it to be her business, because she didn't want to care. But when he returned to the room a short time later with a fresh pot of coffee and a hollow look in his eyes, she realized that she did. She did care.

And that scared her almost as much as the prospect of a terrorist with an E-bomb targeting the United States.

B.J. immersed herself in helping Stephanie for the next several hours in an attempt to distance herself from Rafe and her uncharacteristic reactions to him. Distance was always the answer. It would have worked this time, too, if everything hadn't changed around six p.m.

"I've got it! The name attached to the Colombian e-mail account is Emilio Garcia."

When Stephanie announced Garcia's name, no one was overly surprised. Garcia was a Pablo Escobar protégée who had learned his lessons well from the most notorious drug don in Colombia. Pablo was long dead—killed in a covert U.S. operation that had taken years to come to fruition. However, Emilio Garcia and many others like him had carried on the lucrative trade after his death. Garcia, in particular, had ties to several terrorist groups.

Rafe alone showed no reaction.

"Reed. Get this info to Crystal," Nate said after Stephanie's announcement. "See what she can dig up. B.J., call Sherwood."

An hour later, they had more answers . . . and every one of them was bad news.

"Okay, Tinkerbell," Reed said after putting Crystal on speakerphone.

"Give us your worst, darlin'."

"I'm going to nutshell it," Crystal said, "because you don't have time to hear the gory details. Garcia has been in regular communications with a Russian by the name of Serge Bartrev. Former KGB, current Russian mafia. Known collaborator with our favorite fugitive, bin Laden. Missing Soviet missiles, anyone? Gosh, I wonder whose fingerprints you'd find on them when they turn up in some cave in Afghanistan.

"Anyway, lots of back scratching going on between Bartrev and Osama's camps—which would possibly explain why the E-bomb specs showed up where they did."

It was pretty easy to piece together the basics after that. Throw Bartrev, bin Laden, and the head of the largest drug cartel in Colombia in a bag, shake 'em up, and you've got a recipe for terror—all of it aimed at the U.S.

By the time Crystal was finished with her report, B.J. understood why Crystal Debrowski had been added to the BOI team. She was intelligent, focused, and as tenacious as a bulldog when she dug into a task.

"Good work, Tink," Reed said.

"I'm still working on your list of senators and congressmen," she said, "but I hope to have it soon."

"Keep digging, babe."

"We've got to get down there," Gabe said to the room at large after Crystal had signed off, "figure out a way into Garcia's camp, find out what the bastard is up to."

"Suggestions?" Nate glanced around the room.

"Infiltrate Garcia's organization?" Savage suggested.

"Right. Without an in, it could take months to get a foot in the door."

"We have an in."

All eyes turned to Rafe, who'd been quiet until that point. He scrubbed a hand over his jaw. "Cesar Munoz is my uncle. He married my father's sister and is Emilio Garcia's banker and close personal friend."

Stunned silence followed his announcement, giving B.J. the distinct impression that she wasn't the only one who was shocked by Mendoza's news. Emilio Garcia was the top dog of the cocaine empire in Colombia. Cesar Munoz, one of Colombia's most powerful men in banking, had been suspected for years of laundering Garcia's dirty money. The two names were often linked together in reports that came across B.J.'s desk at DIA. And Munoz was Rafe's uncle.

Finally Nate spoke up. "What have you got in mind, Rafe?"

No other questions. No recriminations, just quiet acceptance that you can pick your friends but you can't pick your relatives. In that moment, B.J. understood just how deep the bond was among these men.

"It's been almost fifteen years," Rafe said, his face and voice solemn. "Seems like a perfect time to get reacquainted with the family, maybe get involved with the family banking business. Should be cause for celebration, don't you think?" he added, his tone edgy.

Nate nodded. "Lot of opportunities for social gatherings. Introductions to business associates."

"Yeah," Rafe agreed. "Associates like Emilio Garcia."

Alex Brady wanted to chuck his cell phone across the room. But the senator was just winding up to rip him a new asshole. He had no choice but to bear it.

"There has not been one mention of Stephanie Tompkins's disappearance in the newspapers." The senator's voice grated across the airwaves in an irate, accusatory tone. "Nothing. Not even a whisper of a rumor in a town that runs on gossip. How do you explain that?"

Alex pinched the bridge of his nose, dug deep for patience. "I don't."

"Well, what does it *say* to you?"

"That the Tompkinses are private people who have chosen not to share their dilemma with the media, perhaps?"

"Wrong! Ann and Robert Tompkins dote on that girl. If they believed she was missing and in danger, they'd have every law enforcement agency on earth searching for her! So it tells me that they've been in touch with her. That they know where she is and that she's intentionally flying under the radar."

That's what Alex thought, too. "I've had men watching the Tompkinses' house and Stephanie Tompkins's apartment since this started." He didn't bother to report that they'd also blown a chance to have the DIA agent, B. J. Chase, lead them to Stephanie. "She's not there and they haven't made any trips that have led us to her."

"Watching? Your men are merely *watching*?"

God, he hated having anyone tell him how to do his job. "We are also monitoring their Internet activity and their phone lines. These people are smart. They're giving nothing away."

"They have to be communicating with her somehow!"

"I'm certain they are. Look, we're all over this, okay? Now I'm sorry, Senator, but I've got another call coming in. I'll be back in touch."

Alex broke the connection and took the incoming call when he recognized his man Smith's number. "Tell me something I want to hear."

"Caught up with another person on the list of the Tompkins woman's friends. A Ben Brommel. Pentagon employee. The guy thought I was hitting on him so I used it, brought up her name as a mutual friend. Brommel gets all quiet and nervous then and all of a sudden he makes excuses and splits."

"He knows something."

"Yeah, that's what I figure. Smith and I are tailing him now. Looks like he's on his way home."

Finally, Alex thought. A promising lead. "Get back to me after you've had your little chat. And Bryant . . . no witnesses."

Stephanie was taking a well-deserved nap; some of the guys were cooking dinner; others were cleaning weapons, shooting the breeze as they waited. Only Rafe had distanced himself from the activity by slipping quietly out of the house when he'd thought no one was looking.

No one was. No one but B.J.

She found him outside standing alone under the shade of a tall tree that looked like it had been there since the beginning of the last millennium. It was very late afternoon now. The July sun burned warm on her face. What breeze there was lightly rustled the low-hanging limbs, heavy with waxy leaves, and carried the scent of dust and summer and the faint promise of a much-needed rain.

If he was aware that she'd come looking for him he didn't show it. Instead, the expression on his face held the weight of time. Hard time.

A twig snapped under her foot when she was within a few feet of him. He had to have heard her but he didn't look her way. He just leaned back against the broad tree trunk, his arms crossed over his chest, his thoughts a million miles away—or at least several thousand miles away in Colombia, she suspected.

"You should go back inside," he said without looking at her.

"Yeah, I should," she agreed, stopping beside him. "And I will. In a minute. I need some air."

He looked across the flat farmland. She looked at him, wishing she didn't feel so compelled to do so. But it was hard not to look at him, a dilemma she found as baffling as her interest. He was a man. Just a man . . . who made her think of all the things missing from her life.

She wasn't sure what she'd come out there expecting. That he'd tell her what was eating at him? Which meant she was totally and thoroughly out in left field somewhere. She had her own baggage. She didn't need to share the weight of someone else's.

And yet she still stood there, teetering on the brink of inviting him to unburden his heavy load. Of telling him that she had broad shoulders and that she might be able to help.

*God. What was she thinking?*

Raphael Mendoza was nothing to her. So he was a hot Latino stud. He had a pretty face and a buff body. He liked to tease. He felt pain. He harbored secrets. None of which had anything to do with her.

They weren't friends. They weren't lovers. And they weren't ever going to be, either. For all she knew he had a case for Stephanie.

Just because he stirred something inside her that she'd never allowed herself to feel or explore didn't mean she was going to act on it. There was something much bigger at stake than what was happening with the ill-timed reawakening of her libido. She needed to get her head back in the game, reestablish her basic ground rules, and maintain her distance for her own self-preservation.

And she needed to do it now. She started walking away.

His soft voice stopped her.

Rafe had always known his past would catch up with him at some point. Never in a million years had he figured he'd be spilling his deepest secrets to a DIA agent who fancied a Glock 19, pissed him off, screwed with his head, and turned him on like a spotlight.

And yet, here he was.

"I grew up in Medellín," he began hesitantly. "I don't know how much you know about the history of Colombia, but for decades the country was torn apart by ongoing political warfare."

"I've read about La Violencia," she said quietly, surprising him with her knowledge of the terminology for a very ugly period.

"La Violencia had actually ended years earlier, but even in the years that followed there was constant guerrilla warfare between the Liberals and the Conservatives, who still take their politics to extremes. Add in FARC and ELN, and everyone suffers from the violence and the poverty. Everyone but my family and the circles we ran in."

He paused, shrugged. "I was a kid. I wasn't aware, and I didn't question. We had money and I liked it. If I asked for something, I got it. We lived in villas, threw big-ass parties, drove top-of-the-line cars, had a private jet, traveled. My sister and I . . ." He paused again, thinking of Eva, feeling the pain of loss before pulling himself back together. "We went to private schools. Indulged, spoiled children of an obscenely wealthy father."

He leaned down, snagged a waxy leaf off the ground, started shredding it. "I had just turned fifteen when everything changed."

He forced himself to go back, to revisit memories that he'd never completely forgotten but that he had worked every day to suppress. "I was visiting my *abuela*—my grandmother—in Bogotá. She wanted to take me shopping for a birthday gift." He saw his elegant and fashionable *abuela* in his mind. Her dark hair had been stylishly streaked with gray and pulled back in a classic chignon. Her clothes were from only the most upscale boutiques in the city. And her skin had been as soft and smooth as silk. "But we never went.

"My uncle called just as we were leaving the house." He stopped. Swallowed. "My father and mother and my sister . . . they'd all been murdered."

He'd never forget the horror and grief on his grandmother's face after she'd answered the phone that morning. She seemed to age twenty years in that moment.

His stomach roiled thinking of how his mother and sister had most likely been tortured and raped and his father forced to watch before they were finally killed.

"I'm so, so sorry." B.J.'s voice was hushed, filled with shocked disbelief and an uncharacteristic sympathy.

Hatred for the men who had brutalized and murdered his family coiled in his belly. Among his many regrets was that he could never extract his own pound of flesh for what those men had done.

"What happened next," he pushed on, "is still a blur but my grandmother threw my things back into my suitcase and rushed me to the airport to get me out of the country. She put me on a plane to a friend's in Miami right after she shoved a wad of cash into my hand and told me to give it to her friend for my care until she could send more. News arrived shortly after I got to Florida that my grandmother had been killed, too—a bomb leveled her home and killed everyone inside."

"My God. Who—"

"Killed my family?" he finished for her, then confessed the ugly truth. "I don't know. Business competitors sending a message to Garcia that they could hurt his 'family' anytime? A warning to get out of rival territory? Pick a reason."

He turned his head and met eyes brimming with both questions and concern before she put it together. The wealth, the extravagance, the execution of his family.

"Your father was a member of the drug cartel?"

He looked away, still struggling with the possibility that his father, whom he had idolized, had been a player in the same dirty game as the men who had ordered his death. "As far as I knew then, he was a top exec at one of Uncle Cesar's banks." He lifted a shoulder. "But I've since learned that while my uncle keeps up a respectable banker façade, there's no getting around the fact that he's tied in with the cartel. With Garcia."

He stared into space. "I still don't want to believe that my father was involved, too. But maybe even back then, I just didn't want to know."

"You were a boy."

Yeah. But he'd grown up real fast after that.

"I was also dead, as far as anyone knew. They assumed I died in the bombing that killed my grandmother."

"If this was a hit by the cartel, why wasn't your uncle killed, too?"

"That's the million-dollar question, isn't it? Maybe Garcia protected him? Maybe he cut a deal for his life? I'll probably never know."

She was quiet for a time before asking, "So your grandmother's friend in Miami . . . she took you in?"

"For as long as the money lasted. She kicked me out a few months later. Can't say as I blamed her. I was pretty angry."

"More like devastated and disillusioned," she said, and he heard the compassion in her voice.

Yeah. More like that. His family had been violently

killed. He was in a strange country. On top of it all, he'd had to live with the fact that the man he'd looked up to and wanted to be like had likely been a criminal who made moral and business decisions that were responsible not only for his own death but the deaths of everyone in the world Rafe loved.

"I fell in with a pretty rough crowd," he went on, still not exactly sure why he was telling her this. "Lotta scrapes with the law."

"So what changed?"

"I got tired of living on the streets. And I finally wised up. On my eighteenth birthday, I did the best thing a young Latino male without U.S. citizenship could do. I joined the army. They turned me into something more than a punk kid with a chip on my shoulder and a death wish."

"Where was your base?"

"Fort Benning."

"Bragg."

He cocked a brow. "You? Army?"

She nodded. "I was an army brat. Following in the old man's footsteps seemed like the thing to do."

It all kind of made sense now. Her no-nonsense delivery. Her in-your-face attitude. Her discipline.

"Let me guess. You were an officer."

"Non-comm. College came later."

"And then DIA. Impressive."

She looked at him sideways. "Right. You were a Ranger, then moved on to an even more elite spec ops unit when you were recruited for Task Force Mercy, and *you're* impressed with *me?*"

Several things occurred to Rafe at once. One, he'd told her the worst about his past and in the process it felt like the weight he'd carried for years had eased a little instead of gotten heavier. Two, they were conversing. Like adults. Like normal people, instead of engaging in verbal skirmishes.

Three, someone had done their homework—most likely her boss, Sherwood—if they'd uncovered his affiliation with a highly guarded unit like Task Force Mercy. And finally, yes, he was impressed with her.

"Wait," he said as a file from his memory bank shuffled forward. "Chase. I ran into a Chase in Somalia several years ago." He dug deep, willing the rest of the information to break loose. "He . . . he was a master sergeant. Delta. Frank." It finally came to him. "Frank Chase."

Her face softened. "My dad."

"I'll be damned. We ran a few joint ops with his squad. He was a helluva soldier. Helluva man. I was sorry when I heard that we lost him."

"Yeah." She pinched her lips together, slowly nodded. "Me, too."

They both grew silent then. Rafe suspected that like him, she was a little lost in her thoughts and in her memories.

"I don't know why I told you all of that," he said, suddenly feeling very much the fool.

"I . . . I'm glad you did."

He stared at her long and hard, looking for some emotion to go with her words. Such a hard one to figure.

"You'd better go back inside."

She slowly nodded. Then she left without another word. Probably wishing she'd never come out here, he figured.

Well, that made two of them.

Or it would have if he had an answer for the coil of longing that had tightened in his chest when he watched her walk away.

They spent what was left of the night and the next morning planning and prepping for all contingencies. Sherwood and his staff would check out the Russian connection and continue to try to covertly ferret out the person or persons who had misappropriated the E-bomb technology in the first place.

Green would remain Stateside on protection detail for Stephanie. Reed, Lang, Savage, Colter, and Black booked flights to Bogotá tomorrow, where BOI had contacts that could hook them up with the weaponry and commo they'd need to back up the op. From there they would travel to Medellín and start searching the perimeters of the Garcia network in a secondary attempt to locate the facility that housed an assembly plant for the E-bomb and the Black Ruby cloaking device.

By six p.m. that night, Raphael Mendoza was on a jet bound for Colombia, where he would attempt to reintroduce himself to his family.

And that distance thing B.J. had banked on? It wasn't happening. She was on the same flight with Rafe, sitting right beside him in first class, embarking on what would most likely be the most dangerous ride of her life.

# 16

"You have to start thinking of yourself as Brittany. And you have to stop flinching every time I touch you."

"I know what I have to do," B.J. informed Mendoza stiffly from the window seat as the second leg of their flight lifted off from Miami heading for Medellín.

It would take a little time to get used to her new persona, mostly because she looked like a hooker. And not the grand-per-night call girl kind who wore Vera Wang and messed up the sheets in upscale apartments with Wall Street types.

Thanks to Johnny Reed, who had volunteered to drive her into the city to oversee her shopping and transformation from bland DIA officer to her new role as gold digger, B.J. now sported long acrylic nails that matched her siren-red toenail polish. She wore rings on at least four fingers; huge, dangly gold hoops in her ears; bracelets and bangles on her wrists. The only essential element of her new wardrobe was a Linea Pelle Dylan Croco handbag that cost more than her monthly apartment rent.

"Gotta look the part to play the part, darlin'," Reed had drawled with that lazy grin of his. "Besides, we can hide a transmitter in the bottom between the insert and the leather in the purse." The transmitter would be their only source of contact once Reed, Lang, Jones, Colter, Savage, and Black arrived in Medellín tomorrow morning.

"Because it's a radio transmitter, the bad guys can detect it if they check you for bugs when you first get into the estate," Reed had gone on.

"So keep it off when I first enter the compound," she'd surmised.

"Right. Before you leave, we'll set up a time every day for you to turn it on for five minutes so we can get a fix and then you turn it off. Any time you leave the estate, turn it on so we can follow you. Got it?"

She got it—and much more. Her suitcase was packed with a wardrobe straight out of Victoria's Secret's Naughty Nights catalog and it had cost a small fortune. The dresses were short, tight, low cut, and slinky. The underwear barely was. The shoes were strappy, stiletto, and painful—*fuck-me shoes*, Reed had called them, pronouncing her fit to pose as the sexpot fiancée of a man whose priorities were all about money, power, and sex. She didn't even want to think about the bikini he'd picked out for her.

Rafe's physical transformation was no less dramatic than hers. The first time she'd seen him he'd been wearing cammo cargo pants and a wife beater. Since they'd met up again, he'd worn a white T-shirt and well-worn jeans. As of today, Raphael Mendoza had shucked his casual attire for pleated, cream-colored linen pants and camel-colored Italian loafers that he wore without socks. His short-sleeved shirt was of the finest silk, a pale sky blue. He let it hang loose over his trousers and it was buttoned only to mid-chest.

His gold crucifix gleamed against skin so smooth and free of chest hair it crossed her mind again that he might wax. Raphael Mendoza in the persona of this slick, fashion-conscious Latino would definitely wax. The Choirboy, however, would sneer at the idea.

It was the Choirboy who looked at her now, all business, his brows pinched together in a scowl, reminding her that he had a right to be concerned about the way she reacted to him. She breathed in deep through her nose, then exhaled slowly through her mouth.

"Okay. Look." She figured she owed him an apology. "I'm sorry for being so short. It's just nerves. And this damn dress. I'll get past it, okay?"

"I never should have agreed to let you come along," he said, turning away.

That was no news flash. From the moment they'd all gotten their heads together to come up with a plan to infiltrate Garcia's operation, Mendoza had nixed the idea of the two of them going in as a couple. She'd eventually won the argument.

"You show up out of the blue," she'd pointed out, "after an almost fifteen-year absence, you've got to have a reason and you've got to have a decoy. I can be both. You've been running a small but lucrative financial firm that took one shady risk too many. You badly need a financial transfusion. So you go to your uncle, wanting help from his bank. It makes sense. It also makes sense that you've got a taste for the finer things. So does your fiancée—"

"Who has you pussy-whipped and panting," Reed had interrupted, building on the ruse, "and is pressuring you to claim what's rightfully yours. A piece of the family 'business.'"

"They'll watch you like a hawk until you earn their trust," B.J. had continued. "Me they'll dismiss as arm candy. I'll be about as suspect and threatening as a layer cake. I have to go along and you know it."

They'd all known it. Even Mendoza, who'd finally, grudgingly relented but with several caveats.

"I run the op. You do what I say, when I say, and you take no stupid risks."

"You run the op," she'd echoed, and after a long, angry glare, he'd finally agreed.

Which had brought them to this juncture in their Colombian getaway. B.J. drew a steadying breath. Mendoza was right about the flinching. She had to get used to him touching her because the people they were trying to fool would see through their scam in a heartbeat if she didn't nail the role of his possessive and clingy fiancée.

"Oh, and for what it's worth," Rafe said, drawing her attention away from the endless sky outside the window, "from where I'm sitting there is absolutely nothing wrong with that dress."

She snorted. That's because from where he was sitting, he could probably see all the way to her navel. It took everything in her not to tug on the scrap of material that passed for a bodice and drag it over her breasts. Not only did she not want to give him the satisfaction of seeing her squirm, he was right. She had to get used to it.

She would have killed for a piece of chocolate. It might have helped her make the transition from B. J. Chase to Brittany Jameson, disinherited wild child of the Pennsylvania Jameson Department Store Jamesons, failed model, failed fashion designer, but winner of a three-karat, emerald-cut diamond engagement ring and Raphael Mendoza's heart. Brittany was shallow, she was spoiled, she was demanding, and now that she had her hooks into the CEO of a hot new financial brokerage firm based out of Vegas she wasn't about to let him out of her sight—especially once she'd learned of his wealthy Colombian family and had seen a chance to enhance her lifestyle by having her fiancée join the family business.

At least that was the cover story. In addition to planting Internet articles about Brittany Jameson and her family, Crystal was hard at work even now, creating an identity for Rafe as one of those shady financial gurus who lived on the edge and by their own set of ethics. They'd also called on Ann Tompkins, who was in the midst of an ongoing criminal investigation of a prominent but clearly corrupt CFO of a major savings and loan corporation. Ann had promised to cut a deal with the defendant if he would vouch for Rafe's identity in the event Munoz put out any feelers about Rafe's dealings.

The fake background wouldn't hold up under lengthy scrutiny but it would buy them a few days to get in, find out what they could about Garcia's operation through the Munoz family connection, and get out. Hopefully they'd be armed with the information they needed to find and destroy the facility manufacturing the E-bomb and the Black Ruby cloaking device.

Long shot? At best. But if and until Stephanie pinpointed the location of the facility as she continued sifting through and decoding hundreds of encrypted messages, it was all they had to run against a fast-ticking clock. They now had six days and counting.

"Cocktail?" The flight attendant intruded on B.J.'s thoughts.

"None for me, thanks." Rafe turned on a dazzling smile as he reached for B.J.'s hand, brought it to his lips, and kissed it. "Darling?"

He was testing her.

Fine. It was showtime.

"Brittany" smiled. "You know I can't resist champagne, baby," she said, turning toward him in her seat, reaching for him in such a way that her dress gaped open even further, giving him a real eyeful. She lightly stroked his chest, played with the gold cross nestled against his skin in the open neck of his shirt. Then she leaned in close and bussed her nose along the rim of his ear.

She felt a shiver ripple through him. Felt his muscles tense and his heartbeat kick up beneath her palm.

"I'll be right back with your champagne." The attendant barely managed to suppress an eye roll.

"You do that," B.J. told her.

For good measure, she caught his earlobe between her teeth, let it slide between them as she slowly pulled away. Then she settled back in her seat and tried to pretend that the heat and the touch and the taste of him hadn't affected her.

"Well," he said, his voice sounding strained. "I'd say you've gotten past your problems with the . . . um . . . touching thing."

"Thought you needed a little demo to set your mind at ease."

Hoping she didn't sound as breathless as she felt, she gripped the armrests to steady her hands so he wouldn't see that she did, indeed, still have a huge problem with touching him. And smelling him. And feeling his powerful reaction eddy through his very responsive body.

"Do . . . ah, do we need to talk about this little chemistry thing that's going on between us?" he asked.

No, they did not, B.J. thought, fighting panic at his admission that he'd felt it, too. They just had to get through it.

Rafe willed his eyes to focus.

When the woman decided to prove a point, she did it with a very sharp pencil—and a wicked, wanton mouth.

His pulse slammed at about two hundred per; his hands clenched into fists to keep himself from reaching for her and taking her little game several steps further. She'd not only called him out, she'd taken him to task and damn near to the limit of his self-control.

He was glad he'd worn pleated pants and that his loose shirt covered his lap and camouflaged the tenting action going on underneath it.

*Madre de Dios.*

He should have gone out and gotten himself laid. Several times. Several ways. But a hard-won maturity had crept up on him over the past few years. Once upon a time—when he'd been young and randy and in a constant state of rut—sex without strings had been not only the method of choice but the status quo. He hadn't been looking for commitment. He hadn't been looking for romance. Hell, he wasn't looking for it now, but now a woman had to mean more to him than a quick tumble and a fast good-bye. Trouble was, his line of work didn't allow for much more than that, which meant it had been a damn long time since he'd spent any quality time with a woman.

The fact was, until he'd tangled with one B. J. Chase, aka Brittany Jameson, there hadn't been another woman who had interested him enough for him to even consider advancing to the getting-to-know-her-better stage. Stephanie didn't count, he realized now. While Stephanie had represented what he'd thought was his ideal and he respected and admired her, he now understood that he'd never loved her that way.

Not in the way that made it right. The way Gabe loved Jenna, the way Sam loved Abbie, and God help them, the way that wild man Reed loved Crystal to the exclusion of his own life. He would die for her—almost had. Just like Gabe and Sam would die for their women.

When and if the time ever came, that's what he wanted. A love to die for with a woman who would do the same. He did *not* want to love some sharp-eyed shrew who just happened to make him hot. And Chase was a shrew even if he had detected those little glimpses of vulnerability suggesting there was more than met the eye.

The attendant arrived with her champagne.

"Not a minute too soon." "Brittany" smiled widely in anticipation of the champagne.

*Dios santo.* She had the sultry blonde act down to a science. He'd never gone for the playgirl types. But that smile. He'd wondered if he'd ever see her smile and now she'd delivered twice in the last few minutes.

So it was manufactured. Didn't diminish the impact. All those sharp, brittle edges melted away. Ice-chip-blue eyes turned simmering hot. Her skin even warmed and those wide, wicked lips revealed a toothpaste ad smile that could have sold anything from lipstick to liquor to sex and only made him more intrigued. If she could affect him like this with an act, what, he wondered, would happen if he ever got a genuine smile?

Jesus. He was running in circles. He wanted to know more. He *didn't* want to know more. He didn't like the woman. He *wanted* to like the woman. What was he, sixteen?

Rest. He needed rest. So did she.

"Better try to catch some shut-eye," he suggested. None of them had gotten much sleep in the last forty-eight.

"You don't have to tell me twice." She sipped her champagne, set it on the tray, then settled back and closed her eyes. He did the same. Yet an hour later, he was still awake. But B.J. was asleep.

She looked small and vulnerable and almost child-like with her feet tucked up under her hips and her head lolling to the side. A tenderness washed through him that he couldn't explain and didn't understand as he watched the sunlight streaming in through the window play against her cheek and set golden sparks shimmering in her hair.

She stirred, trying to get more comfortable. He didn't even think about it. He slipped his arm behind her and around her shoulders and drew her close to his side. She made a sleepy, sighing sound and snuggled right up against him, her head on his shoulder, her hand on his chest, and settled back to sleep.

And the damnedest thing happened as he rested his cheek on the top of her head. A feeling of peace came over him. It felt so natural to hold her this way. Like it was something he did every day. Like it was an intimacy he had a right to feel and indulge in. Like it was something he wanted to have the right to do.

# 17

"Took you long enough." Alex opened his hotel room door to let Smith inside. The shooter's alias wasn't exactly original but Alex didn't care much about originality. He cared about results.

"Talk," he said, ignoring Smith's sideways glance toward the minibar.

"It didn't take much to flip Brommel and get him to admit he heard from the Tompkins woman. She called him yesterday."

"She tell him where she was?"

Smith shook his head. "If he'd known, he would have told us before he died, trust me."

Alex knew that Smith was one of those guys who enjoyed the wet work. Brommel would not have gone out easily, poor bastard.

Smith dug into his pocket. "Brommel's cell phone," he said, handing it over. "The incoming number was blocked but I figure you've got someone who can get a fix on the approximate location, right? Then it's just a matter of tightening the noose."

Yeah, Alex had someone who, for the right price, could access the information. A cell phone call could be pinpointed simply by finding the closest cell towers and calculating the signal strength. It wouldn't put them on top of Stephanie Tompkins but it would get them in the right neighborhood. After that, process of elimination would help them find her.

"I'll be in touch." He checked his watch as he walked Smith to the door. It was almost one a.m. "I should have something for you in a couple of hours."

Stephanie opened her eyes slowly, then groaned in pain when she tried to turn her head. God. Her neck was killing her.

Very carefully, she lifted her head, then reached up and peeled a sheet of paper off her cheek. Why was there paper stuck to her cheek?

Because she'd fallen asleep at the computer desk, she realized, clawing a little further into consciousness and working the stiffness out of her body.

That's what she got for taking one of those damn pain pills. They made her sleepy. And a little woozy.

She wondered what time it was but was so tired she could barely focus on the clock on the lower right corner of the monitor. Three sixteen a.m. Late. Or early, depending on your perspective. She wondered how B.J. and Rafe were doing but knew they were capable and smart and good at what they did. She also knew she was frightened for them.

For herself also, for that matter. But she couldn't

think about that now. Beneath the cast, her arm throbbed and pounded like ten headaches. She went in search of an ice pack to wrap around the cast, which might reduce the swelling. Then she needed to get back to work. She still had hundreds of messages to decode. Time was the enemy and there had to be something more in there . . . something to help lead B.J. and Rafe and the BOIs in the right direction.

The house was quiet. Ghostly quiet now that everyone was gone but her and Green.

Green. He was a tough one to figure. He was a quiet man. She'd always been intrigued by the former CIA agent with his aura of mystery, his quiet competence. Of all the guys, he was the one who raided her father's library whenever the BOIs came to visit. And he had always been the one she thought about after they'd gone.

Where was Green?

"Joe?" she called from the hallway, suddenly concerned.

She jumped when a table lamp by the sofa in the living area burst with light.

"You okay?" He bolted up off the sofa.

"Other than the heart attack, yeah, I'm fine," she stuttered, holding her good arm to her breast. "Sorry . . . sorry I woke you."

He ran a hand roughly over his eyes, blinked away the sleep.

"Combat nap. Don't worry about it. Damn. Look at your hand."

"It's okay," she lied, then looked down and saw what he saw. Her fingers were swollen like sausages. "Or maybe not."

"Sit down," he ordered, jerking his head toward the sofa. "We need to get it elevated and iced. Be right back."

She watched him walk away from her and into the kitchen.

He was barefoot. Why that struck her as . . . well . . . sexy, she didn't know. But something tickled her stomach at the sight of those big bare feet. Something that made her see him as more of a man rather than just a warrior. A man who had feelings and vulnerabilities and, well, bare feet, just like any other man.

She sat down. She realized she wanted to get to know him better. Better? That was a laugh. She didn't know him at all. She decided that was going to change. She'd almost died yesterday. She could die tomorrow if whoever wanted her killed found the safe house and got past Joe. These past couple of days had taught her what Bry's death should have. Life was precarious and precious and she really didn't have all the time in the world to experience it.

Joe returned to the living room carrying not one, but two ice packs and a towel.

*Seize the moment.*

Bry had lived by those words. It was past time she carried on in his absence.

"Lift your arm." Joe sat down beside her, all business. "Let's use this towel to protect your cast so it doesn't get wet."

With unbelievable gentleness, he wrapped the hand towel around her cast, then grabbed a throw pillow and placed one of the ice packs on top of it before carefully lowering her arm onto the pillow. Satisfied with the placement, he covered it with the other pack.

"Thanks." She smiled up at him.

He scowled and avoided meeting her eyes. "You're working that wrist too hard."

"If there was another option, I'd take it. But there isn't. I have to keep after those messages."

"Not right now you don't. You have to sleep. Why don't you lie back? Catch a few winks."

"I'm awake now, and too wired to sleep."

"Then you'll rest your wrist—minimum half an hour. We'll see how the swelling is then and decide whether you go back to work."

"Fair enough," she agreed because her wrist really did hurt and because he was pretty cute giving orders.

Cute? Green? Oh man, he'd love that.

"So, bet you never thought you'd be demoted to playing nursemaid."

He still wouldn't look at her. "I've pulled worse duty." He stared at the laptop on the coffee table in front of the sofa. A constant stream of shots from the outside security cameras scrolled by in an eerie green glow. She recognized the pictures as views through night vision cameras. "Besides, I volunteered."

That was news. Interesting news. Interesting enough to make her heartbeat step it up a bit.

She watched him as he leaned forward, moved the

laptop a little closer, then settled back beside her.

Most people wouldn't call Joe a handsome man. Not like Rafe and Gabe and some of the other guys were handsome. And he definitely wasn't pretty, like Reed, who could be a huge box-office draw as a heartthrob.

No, his jaw was too hard, his lips too narrow, giving him a bit of a sinister look. A Mean Joe Green look. His eyes were hazel, deeply set, and mysterious. Add the high cheekbones and a strong, prominent nose and it made for a very interesting face. And no windswept hair for this man, this no-nonsense man who kept his light, sandy brown hair cut military short. It looked great on him.

Most impressive of all, though, was his build. He was honed and hard and pumped up in all the right places. Not body-builder pumped, but close.

"What do you do to keep in this kind of shape?" she asked.

He glanced at her, his brows drawn together like he was thinking, What? Did she really ask me that? Just as quickly, he looked away, clearly uncomfortable to have any kind of attention directed at him.

He clasped his hands between his widespread knees. "I've just always kept fit, I guess."

She laughed. "Fit? Is that what you call it?"

"Well, yeah." He leaned back against the sofa again. "What do you call it?"

Sexy. Hot. Buff. That and more came to mind but what she said was, "I call it hard work."

"I never think of it that way. And I asked you to lie back."

"Fine," she said, deciding that maybe it was time to rattle Mr. Green.

She shifted sideways, leaned back against the over-stuffed arm of the sofa, and lifted her feet until she was semi-reclined with the pillow on her lap and her legs bridged over his lap, while her butt nestled up against his big, solid thigh.

Blame it on the drugs. Blame it on fatigue. Blame it on the notion that she wanted to see how he'd react.

And react he did—without saying a word.

His entire body stiffened. He just sat there, staring straight ahead, like he was afraid to move.

"Happy now?" she asked, wondering where this shameless flirt had come from. It wasn't that she hadn't had her share of relationships, some not worth talking about, some she'd probably always remember. But she was not and had never been a flirt nor the aggressor.

Maybe it was just time to force Green's hand and see if she was the only one interested in exploring a relationship. She'd noticed the way he'd been watching her when he didn't think anyone was looking.

"You're not much of a talker, are you?" She wasn't sure why she felt such an urge to bait him. Or maybe she did know. Still water and all that. She wanted more glimpses of what lay beneath the surface.

"Not much, no," he agreed.

"Why is that, do you suppose?"

He finally looked at her. Looked at her long. Looked at her hard. "Guess I just don't have much to say. And you're supposed to be resting."

Evade, evade, evade. He was skilled at the tactic. "This is restful. The quiet. The night. You. You're very comfortable to be around."

He shot her a doubtful look.

"Okay. Maybe *comfortable* isn't quite the word. How about *safe*? I feel safe around you."

He actually smiled.

"Why is that funny?"

"It's funny because usually I make people nervous."

"Ah. The Mean Joe Green persona."

"That would be it."

"And you perpetuate it."

He shrugged. "I don't have to. You're looking at me, right? This face doesn't exactly say nice puppy dog."

She smiled. "Yes, I am looking at you. And no, I don't think puppy dog. Should I?"

"Rottweiler, maybe." He smiled again and she was charmed.

"Is that what you want people to see?"

"Most of the time, yeah. I guess I do. And most people don't bother to look further."

"I'm not most people. What I see is a stand-up man, a man who would die for his friends and put his life on the line for me. It humbles me, Joe. And it scares me. I don't want anything happening to you because of me."

"Nothing's going to happen to me."

"Because you're good at what you do."

"Because if something happens to me, that means they got to you. That's just not going to happen."

"Because I'm a job."

"Because you're important," he said, meeting her eyes.

Unspoken were the words *to me*. He didn't have to say them. In that moment she knew. His eyes said it all. She was more than a job to him.

The room got very quiet then as they both processed that fact.

"Joe?"

"I'll go fix something to eat," he said abruptly. "If you're not going to sleep you at least need to refuel."

Then, with a dexterity that astounded her, he lifted her legs off his lap and shot up off the sofa without disturbing her arm.

As he headed for the kitchen, she felt an immeasurable amount of power because she seemed to be capable of making this big, strong man run away like his tail was on fire.

Way over his head, Joe thought as he dug around in the fridge for the makings of a sandwich. He'd gotten in way over his head with Stephanie and way out of his element.

He attacked. He didn't retreat. Yet he'd done everything but wave a white flag when he'd tucked tail and run away from the woman with the amazing, expectant eyes and the bottomless bag of questions.

He wasn't a talker. Hell, he wasn't witty. Puppy dog?

Rottweiler? Where the hell had that come from? He'd been flirting, and it wasn't right.

Not with Stephanie. Stephanie was . . . just what he'd said she was: important. The more he was around her the more he realized just how important she was to him.

And there were more things wrong with that way of thinking than there were hours in a decade. He was a loner by choice as much as necessity. His work didn't exactly allow for long-term relationships. Hell, he'd already lived longer than he'd have bet on. So no, a woman—a good woman—like Stephanie couldn't factor into any equation involving him.

*Comfortable. Safe.*

He wished she wouldn't have planted that seed.

Because, damn. It had taken root. And damn, it made him wonder about all the what-ifs he never let himself think about.

"Joe?" Stephanie looked over her shoulder to see that he'd poked his head back out of the kitchen.

"Problem?"

"I don't know. Is that supposed to do that?" She nodded toward a control panel of sorts they'd mounted on the wall. One of the green lights was suddenly flashing red.

In three strides he was back at the laptop.

"Something or someone tripped a wire in the right rear quadrant." He tugged a pistol out of the waistband of his jeans and doused the light. Then he reached for his boots and quickly pulled them on. Only the eerie green glow from the laptop monitor cast light into the room.

"Could it be an animal?" she whispered hopefully.

Before he could respond, another light started blinking red, then two more in rapid succession.

"Oh God," Stephanie gasped. One animal, maybe. Four, not a chance.

Just then the shadowy form of a man appeared on the laptop's monitor.

Joe knelt in front of the computer, clicked a few keys, and the screen scrolled through a full cycle of the cameras set up around the perimeter of the building. He clicked some more keys. As the lenses zoomed out to encompass a larger area, he attached a sound suppressor to his pistol, the action so automatic he never lifted his gaze from the screen. Every view showed a similar shadowy figure hunched and walking slowly toward the house.

"You know what to do and where to go."

Yeah, she knew even though when they'd gone through a practice drill in the event the grounds were breached, she had hoped she'd never have to put the plan into play.

He pulled a wire out of his pocket, gripped it in his teeth, and grabbed what she recognized as an AR-15 automatic rifle that was loaded and ready from the hallway.

"Don't come out for anyone but me," he ordered, settling a pair of night vision goggles over his eyes. "And if you're not sure it's me, shoot."

"Be careful."

But he was already out the back door, shutting it behind him so quietly, she didn't even hear him leave.

Trembling with terror, she ran to the kitchen, withdrew the Glock that he had loaded and shown her how to operate that morning. Then she hurried to the back entryway and tucked herself into the tiny broom closet they'd cleaned out for her. Once inside, she sat down on the floor, her back wedged into the corner as he'd told her when he'd briefed her on defensive actions in the event the house came under attack.

And then she waited, in the dark, her heart beating so hard she could feel it in her throat and in her ears and in her throbbing wrist, which, thanks to the adrenaline boost, she didn't even feel anymore.

The only thing she felt was terror.

Of the dark. Of the unknown. And for the man who was out there right now, risking his life to save hers.

When you grew up a country boy in the South, the son of a marine and avid outdoorsman, you learned how to hunt. Joe had been a hunter his entire life. He especially liked hunting night predators, the cowardly kind that preyed on the weak. What he didn't like were the odds. He was going to do something about that right now.

The trip wire sensors had been set one hundred yards from the house, four long, individual filaments, all set to trigger independently no matter which point was breached. Because Stephanie had noticed the instant the first wire was tripped, he was ahead of the game. There were four of them and there was no way in hell a single one of these bastards was going to get within fifty yards of the house.

He ran at a crouch toward the first perimeter that had been breached. The ground there was flat and empty. A small copse of trees no more than twenty yards long ran along a dry creek bed less than fifty yards ahead. He'd walked the entire property at least twice the day before. Had memorized each berm, rock pile, and culvert.

He reached the trees just as he heard someone stumble, then curse. He saw him an instant later. Stupid bastard was wearing a suit and carrying a sawed-off shotgun. Amateur.

In the darkest part of the night, unless the shooter had excellent night vision, there was no way he could distinguish Joe from the tree trunk he leaned against.

He waited, judged his proximity by the sounds the guy made lumbering clumsily through the dry summer grass, then stepped out behind him just as he passed. Before the guy knew what hit him, Joe hooked a forearm around his throat in a stranglehold, shoved his Sig in his back, and fired. The Sig made barely a pop, muffled by the sound suppressor and the guy's bulky body. He twitched, flailed, then went limp. Joe slowly lowered him to the ground, then, crouching low, set off again at a run in search of the next predator.

# 18

Nothing. Stephanie could see nothing. She could hear nothing. Nothing but her irregular breathing and the beating of her own heart as she hid in the stuffy closet. Perspiration trickled down her back; her palms were sweaty on the pistol grip.

The adrenaline had let down a while ago. Her wrist screamed in pain, but she refused to give in to it as she gripped the gun with both hands, the barrel braced in the tight vee between her bent knees.

How much time had passed? Five minutes? Ten? She didn't know. She'd lost all point of reference. How long had Joe been gone? Long enough to . . . to kill those men? Long enough to get killed?

And then she heard something.

She jerked her attention to the closet door, hyperaware of every sound outside of her little hidey hole.

Someone had entered the house.

She swallowed hard, her heart beating so fast she thought it would explode.

*Joe. Please, please be Joe.*

And then she heard nothing.

No. Something. Someone breathing. Then the snick of metal against metal. A gun, she realized. Someone had injected a bullet into the chamber of a gun.

Footsteps. Slow. Cautious. Careful.

It could still be Joe, she told herself, working to regulate her breathing so she wouldn't hyperventilate and pass out. He could be checking the house to make certain no one else was inside. He wouldn't call out to her if that was the case. He wouldn't want to give away her location.

So she sat. And trembled . . . and gasped when the door swung open.

The silhouette of a man filled the doorway. A small man.

Not Joe.

He raised a rifle to his shoulder.

She screamed.

And she fired.

And fired.

And fired until the gun was empty and she was wild-eyed with shock as a man lay twitching at her feet.

"Stephanie."

Terrified, she scrambled further into the corner.

"Stephanie. It's okay. It's Joe. You're okay. Steph. Look at me."

A light flicked on.

"Look at me!"

An order.

She looked up.

Joe. Oh God.

"Joe!" She reached for the hand he extended, rose on wobbly legs, and flew into his arms.

Hard, strong arms wrapped around her, then lifted her off her feet. Joe stepped over the body and carried her into the living room.

"He . . . he—"

"I know. I'm sorry. He never should have gotten to the house."

"I . . . I . . . is he . . . d-dead? Did I k-kill him?"

"Don't think about it."

"The . . . the others—"

"Are no longer a problem."

*God, oh God, oh God.*

People were dead. Men were dead. She could be dead . . . if not for this man.

She was shaking violently now. Even in her agitated state she knew it was a form of shock.

"Steph?" He set her on the sofa, knelt in front of her, and gripped her face between his big hands. "I know you're scared, baby. But you've got to pull it together, okay? We've got to get out of here. As soon as they figure out that their goons are out of commission, they'll send reinforcements. Are you with me?"

She nodded, then almost started crying again when he used his thumbs to gently wipe the tears she hadn't even known were sliding down her cheeks.

"Good girl. Now come on. Let's get your computer and your papers and make tracks."

"Wait." She covered his hands with hers. His face was inches away. His hazel eyes were narrowed with concern and something . . . something that told her he wouldn't stop her if she leaned in and kissed him.

So she did. She kissed him. She poured her terror and her gratitude and her heart and her soul into a kiss that had him groaning deep in his throat, drawing her against him again and taking everything she gave him in that kiss. Giving back more.

She wanted it to go on and on. She wanted to lose herself in this moment where time stood still, where bad guys weren't trying to kill her, where something felt good and right and vital.

She clung to him when he pulled away. He met the questions in her eyes with a smile that transformed his face to something beyond handsome, something that said he didn't want to end it either.

"To be continued," he promised, then leaned in and kissed her again. Fast and hot and hard. "Now we really have to go."

Cesar Munoz's gated villa nestled like an Old World Spanish castle on the rim of a lush green mountainside that overlooked the valley and the sprawling city of Medellín. Rafe had made the decision to arrive unannounced. He'd also wanted to arrive in style. The perception of success was often all about showmanship, and the stretch limo and chauffeur he'd rented this morning fit the bill. Plus, his uncle had always been into high drama. Rafe's resurrection from the dead would definitely provide it.

"*¿Qúe quiere?* What business do you have here?" the uniformed guard demanded when the limo rolled up to the guardhouse and stopped in front of the locked gates.

"Raphael Mendoza to see his uncle Cesar," the chauffeur announced as Rafe had instructed.

Yeah, high drama, Rafe thought, breathing deep to steady himself as they waited for a response. It was supposed to have been for his uncle's benefit. He hadn't counted on feeling the effects of it himself. And yet he did.

Nostalgia clutched at his gut as memories assaulted him. How many times had he come here for family celebrations? For parties by the pool, to make out behind the cabana with the daughter of one of his father's business partners? To watch his mother and his aunts laugh and cook in the big chef's dream of a kitchen, taking it over from the kitchen staff so they could provide their families with their own special style of cooking?

How many times had he and his father gone horseback riding with his uncle and his cousins Felipe and Rodrigo? It always ended in a horse race that his cousins resented when they lost to Rafe.

It would be interesting to see his cousins' reaction to his reappearance. He expected resistance on that front—provided he could overcome this first obstacle.

Nearly fifteen minutes later, the guard leaned out the small window. "Señor Munoz has no nephew. You must leave now."

Rafe had expected this. He lifted the chain holding his gold crucifix over his head, handed it to the chauffeur. "Ask him to please show this to my uncle."

Rafe had noticed the bank of security cameras inside the small guardhouse, had seen the lenses expand to look inside the limo. No doubt, the guard had an interior camera he could use to photograph the crucifix.

"Every male child born into the family was given this exact same crucifix at his first communion," he told B.J. quietly as they waited. "The gold is twenty-four karat, the design unique to a local craftsman commissioned exclusively by the family. He'll recognize it."

Several more minutes passed before the guard stepped out of the guardhouse. He handed back Rafe's crucifix, then motioned for them to get out of the car.

"Is this really necessary?" B.J. fell into the role of Brittany when the guard asked Rafe to empty his pockets and B.J. to turn over her purse. "We're being treated like criminals!"

She held her breath while the guard looked through her purse, concerned that he would spot the false bottom and discover the transmitter.

"It's just precautionary, *cara*," Rafe assured her, glancing apologetically at the guard. "My uncle is a very important man. And you must remember, for the past fifteen years they thought I was dead. Until we meet face-to-face, Cesar can't be certain I am who I say I am."

"Well, it's insulting," she said indignantly.

"*Discúlpeme, señorita*." The guard looked sheepish as he handed the purse back to her.

"He took my cell phone!" she cried, hiding her re-
lief that the transmitter had not been discovered.
"Baby . . ." She clutched Rafe's arm. "I *need* my phone.
I have to be able to text my sister and check on Peanut.
I have to know how my little baby is doing."

Peanut was the imaginary dog they'd settled on as a
tool to relay coded messages to the BOIs in the event
she was allowed to keep her phone. If Brittany called
her "sister"—in this case, Crystal—who was "babysit-
ting" and asked one of a set of prearranged questions, it
would cue Crystal to their current circumstances.

"I'm sure you'll get it back," Rafe placated her,
handing over his own phone to the guard.

"*Gracias.* Now, please get back in the car."

After walking around the limo, then getting down
and peering under the carriage, the guard returned to
the gatehouse. A few seconds later, the gates swung
open.

"We're in," Rafe said, sounding relieved.

"Alice falling down the rabbit hole," B.J. murmured,
her sigh relaying both relief and tension now that they
were on their way into the inner sanctum.

"Just stick to the plan," Rafe whispered in reassurance. "We'll be fine."

"Said Custer to his cavalry."

He pushed out a surprised laugh. "Here I thought
you didn't have a sense of humor."

"There's a lot you don't know about me."

For damn sure, he thought as they advanced slowly
up a wide driveway made of stone pavers and lined

with towering palms. For one, he was just getting to know what an amazing actress she was.

"Holy God," B.J. said under her breath a quarter of a mile later when the limo rolled to a stop in front of the villa.

Rafe understood her reaction. He'd spent half of his childhood here yet the opulent grounds and buildings never failed to elicit some kind of reaction. Today it was nostalgia, determination, and regret.

The sprawling, three-story, Spanish-style villa was constructed of stone blocks, adobe, ornate grillwork, terra-cotta tile, and what seemed like hundreds of gleaming arched windows. While his family's home had also been extravagant, he'd always thought of Cesar and Aliria's villa as a castle. Clearly, it affected B.J. the same way.

Flowers and flowering shrubs of every color and description bobbed in lush beds on either side of the driveway, filling the air with a fresh floral scent he remembered from his childhood. Orchids dripped from palm trunks where they'd taken root. Sundogs played in the water spewing from a huge, ornate fountain sculpted in the shape of a dolphin.

"So crime does pay," he heard B.J. murmur as he got out of the limo, then walked around to help her.

She took the hand he offered and stepped outside, looking in awe at the massive *casa* and perfectly manicured grounds. And for a moment, he didn't see anything but her. Not his youth. Not the familiar sights of home. Just her.

She'd left her hair loose and wild; a warm breeze whipped it around her face.

"Fits the image we're shooting for," he had told her when she'd walked into his hotel room this morning. They'd booked adjoining rooms when they'd arrived last night, had a quick dinner in the hotel restaurant, then stayed up late hammering out the details of their strategy.

Yeah, her hair fit the image, he thought again as she stood there in her four-inch red stilettos; a short, clingy, yellow, strapless, sarong-style dress; and red-rimmed sunglasses with lenses the size of small coasters. Her lipstick matched the shoes, which matched her nails and generated as much red-hot heat inside him as the sun that blazed down from a cloudless blue sky.

"You look stunning," he said because she did and because, he assured himself, he was merely playing the part of the love-struck fiancé.

"I know, darling." Her smile was all devotion and confident seduction as she looped her purse handles over her right arm, then wrapped her left arm around his waist and snuggled close.

He'd dressed for the Colombian heat in white linen pants and a pale pink gauze shirt. He could feel the warmth of her body pressed against his side. Specifically, the heat and pressure of a very nice breast as he wound his arm around her waist and drew her against him.

"They're watching, you know," he whispered, lowering his mouth to her ear.

She stood up on tiptoe and pressed her mouth to his. "Would I be doing this if they weren't?" Then she kissed him. A long, hot, wet kiss that sent his blood south and his head reeling.

*Cristo.* She was killing him. "Let's just do this."

"Yes, let's," she agreed on a bracing breath.

Arm in arm, they walked toward the entryway and straight into a past Rafe had been dodging for fifteen years.

# 19

The Colombian people were as diverse in appearance as they were in culture and class distinctions. B.J. had already discovered this in their brief contact with the local populace in Medellín. Cesar and Aliria Munoz belonged to a small group of wealthy, fair-skinned Colombians who dominated the economic activity of the country. Rafe's aunt Aliria looked basically the way B.J. had pictured her. She was a slight woman, still slim and lovely at sixty-five. She wore her jet-black hair stylishly cut, just as she wore her clothes with an understated elegance.

Cesar Munoz's hair was snow white, his neatly trimmed mustache lightly peppered with black. He was around five foot eight or nine, fit and trim, and he greeted them wearing a white shirt and pants and brown sandals. Cesar struck her as shrewd, intense, and deeply distrustful. Hard. Strong. An enforcer. But when his skepticism and doubt finally gave over to astonished belief at the realization that Rafe was, in fact, the son of his wife's brother and that he was alive, Cesar Munoz embraced him, then spoke rapidly in Spanish.

"Thank God for this miracle. You're alive!"

Rafe's aunt Aliria stood by quietly, tears filling her eyes, wringing her hands to keep from reaching for Rafe until Cesar finally released him so he could stand back and look his fill.

"Tía Aliria," Rafe murmured, enfolding her in a gentle embrace.

"Raphael. Sweet child. You . . . you look just like your father."

The affection was genuine and lavish. From where she was standing, B.J. understood that it went both ways. For Rafe, this was a reunion with a family he had loved. A family that, when his life had blown apart, he had no idea was made up of criminals.

Never more than now, she understood the meaning of the word *bittersweet* as they stood in the grand foyer under an exquisite crystal chandelier that looked like it belonged in the lobby of a five-star hotel. Vibrantly patterned, hand-woven Colombian wool rugs adorned the gleaming marble floor. A medieval custom hand-carved wooden staircase wound up three floors and led to a ceiling that rose to the roof.

The villa not only looked like a castle from the outside, the appointments inside ranged from elegant to extravagant to gauche. Sumptuous fabrics, lush leathers, rich brocades and velvets adorned furniture, walls, and windows. Expensive artwork was everywhere—modern oils, ancient-looking vases, and marble busts of Spanish conquistadores perched on lavishly carved pedestals. Intricately woven tapestries were artfully hung on the wall adjacent to the grand staircase.

And there was gold everywhere. Gold leaf. Gold fili-greed woodwork. Gold cherubs on ornately carved ta-bles, in the pattern in the wallpaper, in the corners of the crown molding.

"Tío Cesar. Tía Aliria," Rafe addressed them re-spectfully, pulling B.J. close to his side. "This is the woman I love. My fiancée, Brittany Jameson."

They were still in shock, still processing the astound-ing news that the nephew they had thought long dead was really alive, but they turned to B.J. For a moment, just a moment, she wanted to reassure them. Instead, she flashed a smile that could never be mistaken as sincere.

"*Hola. A . . . grad . . . able en . . . con . . . trar . . . le.*" She was actually fluent in Spanish but no one here was going to know it by the way she intentionally garbled the greeting.

"Did I say that right?" She blinked up at Rafe, all hopeful and pleased with herself and expectant. "Or did I screw it up again? I've been practicing," she as-sured the Munozes, turning back to them with a mar-ginally apologetic look. "But the truth is, *yo no hablo español*," she admitted in a way that clearly expressed that everyone present should speak English anyway be-cause it was simply the civilized thing to do.

The Munozes tried to hide it, but they were clearly appalled by her brash manner.

"Why aren't they saying anything?" she added in a stage whisper that could have been heard in Cambodia.

"It's okay, *cara*." Indulgence dripped from each word. "I'm sorry, Tío Cesar, Tía Aliria. Brittany has been trying to learn Spanish but no matter how hard she tries, she has been unable to grasp even the slightest nuance."

"We are the ones who should apologize for not speaking English," Aliria offered graciously.

"Oh, thank God." B.J. sighed in relief. "I'm so relieved. Rafe," she scolded, tapping him lightly on the chest. "Why didn't you tell me they spoke English? Men." She flashed a conspiratorial "girl to girl" smile at Aliria. "They just never share the important things."

"Raphael," Cesar said, unable to stop staring at his nephew. "I still cannot believe it. I cannot believe that fate has brought you back to us."

It was a tender moment. One that a sensitive woman would have stepped away from and let unfold.

Brittany Jameson was not that woman. "This place is amazing!" she exclaimed. "It's like a museum. Or a Vegas casino!" she exclaimed, pleased with her analogy.

Aliria flinched at the insult. Cesar glared, his black eyes judgmental and hard.

"Again," Rafe said, his indulgence waning a bit, "you'll have to excuse Brittany. Her excitement, it sometimes outdistances her manners. And she's exhausted. It feels as if we've been traveling for days."

"What did I say?" she demanded, clearly feeling maligned. "I was complimenting their home."

"It's all right," Aliria said stiffly. "And again, we are the ones who should be apologizing. You are weary.

And here we have not even offered you something to drink."

"Wine would be lovely," B.J. said, earning a scowl from Rafe.

"It's a little early, don't you think, *cara?*"

"Raphael." Cesar intervened just as Brittany was winding up to get indignant. "Raphael, please say you are here for a long visit."

"It is my hope, yes."

"*Bueno.* You must stay with us."

Rafe was about to make a pretense of declining when B.J. interrupted.

"Of course we'll stay!" She beamed at Aliria and then at Rafe. "It would be rude not to accept such a generous invitation. You can send someone to the hotel for our luggage, right?"

"We will have it no other way," Aliria insisted, her voice filled with warmth and affection as she smiled at Rafe. "We have much to catch up on. There is much we want to know, Raphael. How you survived the bombing. What you've been doing all these years. And of course, we want to know about you, too, Brittany," she added dutifully.

"See, it's all settled." B.J. squeezed Rafe's arm, then turned a bright smile toward Cesar. "Now, about that wine . . . not that I'd turn down champagne, mind you."

"So this is how the other half lives," B. J. murmured more to herself than to Rafe as she stood on their own private balcony just outside the lavishly appointed bedroom that had been made ready for them.

Two stories below, spread out over sweeping green grounds and surrounding a huge terrazzo patio, were two swimming pools, each boasting three Jacuzzis. There were brightly canopied social areas, lush gardens, what appeared to be a conservatory, and even a man-made waterfall. Farther out were the stables and an adjoining pasture dotted with horses. She could make out tennis courts beyond the gardens and a full nine-hole golf course. A helicopter sat on a helipad at the rear of the stables.

The balcony outside their bedroom suite was huge. They stood at its far edge, looking out over the grounds, and because they were so far away from the house, felt marginally free to talk. Rafe had pointed out before they had arrived, "Cesar is no fool. He may or may not be glad to find out I'm alive, but because of Aliria, he will welcome me home. I am a stranger to him now. You can be certain that until he is satisfied he can trust me, he will take precautions. And after all these years away, he'll suspect that I have an agenda."

That's why they had immediately slipped a CD into the sound system to muffle the sound of their voices in the event that Cesar had bugs planted while they were waiting for the room to be made ready. As much as Rafe would have liked to search the room, they didn't dare. A surveillance camera could be hidden in the TV or the alarm clock—anywhere.

Out here, however, as long as they were careful, and

the CD played a Latin beat in the background, they could talk softly.

B.J. glanced at Rafe, who stood close beside her, his palms planted on the polished marble railing. He'd grown very quiet once they'd been shown to their room. She could see the strain on his face caused by the struggle with his memories, with his love of family, and with the mission they were on.

"Your aunt loves you very much," she said, sensing what was weighing on him.

He lowered his head. Breathed deep. "My father was her only family. She thought she'd lost everyone."

"And you feel like you're betraying her," she whispered.

He didn't have to respond. A horrible sadness filled his dark eyes.

"Cesar is quite a businessman," he said, moving on. "I imagine the boys are deep into the business now, too."

The boys—that would be the cousins he had told her about, Felipe and Rodrigo. They had been teenagers, too, when Rafe had escaped to Miami.

"Were you close to them?"

"We were very competitive. Girls, cars, sports. But yes, we were close."

And that hurt him, too. She didn't know why she felt compelled to comfort him. Or worse, why she followed through with that compulsion. "We're not here to destroy anyone," she said, lowering her voice even further.

"No, we're just here to use him and my aunt." He

breathed deep. "Look. I know why I'm here. You don't have to worry that I won't hold up my end of our bargain."

"It never occurred to me that you wouldn't. I just recognize that this is going to be difficult for you."

"Yeah, well, when is anything ever easy?"

In her experience? Never. Raphael Mendoza also spoke from experience. She'd lost her father, yes. Had never really had a mother, not in a functioning capacity at any rate. Raphael had had it all. Loving family. Wealth. The good life. And then he'd lost it all. His mother, his sister, his grandmother, and his father, whom he had loved and clearly revered, only to later learn his father had not been who he had thought he was.

He could have lost himself, too. From what he'd told her, he almost had until he'd wised up and gotten his life together. She respected him for that. Saw some of herself in him as they'd both had only themselves to rely on.

And now here they were. Relying on not only themselves but each other.

"Do you think they suspect anything?" she asked quietly, toeing off her heels. Her untouched champagne flute sat on the rail.

He turned to face her, leaned back against the rail, and crossed his arms over his chest. The balcony was shaded by an awning. A cool breeze rustled his gauzy shirt. He'd propped his Ray-Bans on the top of his head and looked every bit the hot Latin lover with his poet's face and caramel skin tones and hard body. For an instant, a sweet, sharp instant, she wished their relationship was real.

"After that act you put on?"

Right. The act. Touching him. Kissing him. It was all just an act. God. She had to focus. She had a job to do. "You don't think it was too much?"

He pushed out a laugh, took her hand, and led her to a small table. "No, *cara*," he whispered, leaning close. "It was perfect. They'll be so absorbed in being annoyed by you they'll never perceive you as a threat. You should pretty much have free rein at the estate. And I am certain you will be able to convince them you want introductions to their friends." Their friends being Emilio Garcia and his associates.

"And of course, they'll do what they can to accommodate me, since I'm going to be a member of the family and all," she said, deadpan.

He smiled and reached for her left hand, the one sporting her "engagement" ring. "Here's to a long and happy union," he whispered, lifting her palm to his mouth and kissing it.

A shiver of sexual heat eddied from the middle of her palm to her breasts, then spread to her belly. It's all an act, she reminded herself, and closed her eyes, achingly aware of her tight, hard nipples pressing against the fabric of her dress. When she opened her eyes again, he was watching her mouth. Openly. Intensely. Hungrily.

If possible, her nipples got even harder. Painfully hard. That look in his eyes . . . *that* was no act.

He wanted her.

She'd known it for some time now. Hadn't wanted to deal with it or the fact that for the first time in a very long time, she felt that low, deep pull, that sharp, sweet ache that she'd conditioned herself to ignore.

The memory of the kiss they'd shared in the driveway came back to her with alarming clarity. His lips were so soft, yet so firm and so amazingly warm and welcoming and exciting.

*"They're watching, you know,"* he'd said.

*"Would I be doing this if they weren't?"*

She'd thought she'd known the answer then. Now, not so much.

She was in deep trouble with this man. The trouble became even deeper when in the next instant, he stood and pulled her into his arms.

"In case someone is watching now," he whispered, searching her eyes.

There was no one on this balcony but them. There was no need to put on a show for anyone. That's what she should have told him.

But she didn't. She couldn't. And worse, she didn't want to.

"In case someone is watching," she murmured, and lifted her mouth to meet his.

# 20

Rafe wasn't sure what he'd expected. Resistance, maybe. Tolerance, possibly. An act, most definitely. But this wasn't an act. This was a sweet, astonishing surrender. A generous, willing acquiescence from a woman who lived, breathed, and practiced total control and rigid restraint. A woman who suppressed her feelings, her emotions, even her own sexuality with the diligence of a castle guard.

She wasn't guarding anything right now. Now, she was all about compliance and participation as her mouth opened beneath his and she finally, finally, let him taste her without pretense or playacting tempering the way.

She melted into his kiss, accepted his tongue, moved into the erection pressing against her belly. When he backed her up against the wall and pressed his hips deeper into her, she made a sound in her throat that damn near buckled his knees.

It was a sound of total submission, without restrictions. A sound of pleasure and invitation and of a longing so desperate and demanding it stole his breath.

Closer. You couldn't have slid a strand of her hair between them and still, he wanted to get closer. Couldn't get enough of her taste and her scent and the silk of her skin as he slid a hand down her leg, then tunneled under her dress. He encountered nothing but bare thigh, bare sweet ass, and a thin scrap of damp lace covering that part of her he would willingly crawl naked over glass to taste.

He lowered his head to her throat, tracking kisses along the pulse that beat wildly there. She gasped when he covered her with his hand, cupped her where she was wet and hot and . . . vulnerable.

He stilled when she rocked against his hand. Stiffened like a tree trunk. Swore against her neck.

Vulnerable.

There it was.

There was the reason he had to stop and he had to stop now.

*Cristo.*

He sensed the instant she came back to herself, when she realized he'd put on the skids. The next moment, desire transitioned to regret, then embarrassment, and finally self-disgust.

And he couldn't let her feel any of those things. This was too important. She was too important.

"Get. Off. Me," she grated out through clenched teeth.

Ah, that was the B. J. Chase he knew and . . . well, that he knew.

"It's all right, *querida*." He backed away but only slightly, pressing a tender kiss on her temple. "In fact, it was more than all right."

"That didn't just happen," she managed on a shaky breath, her entire body stiffening.

"Oh, but it did. And it was amazing. When the time and the place is right, it will happen again."

He touched a hand to her wild beautiful hair, stroked it back and away from her face, her incredible, stunning face, as a war of emotions battled for dominance. "Don't look like that. Don't overanalyze it. Don't be angry about it. Not with yourself. Not with me. But do remember it. And think about what it will be like between us when we finally have our time together."

She opened her mouth to deny that possibility, he was certain, but he placed two fingers over her lips, rubbed them lightly back and forth along with the motion of his head. "When the time is right."

Then, marshalling all the self-control he possessed, he stepped away from her. He walked into the bedroom, headed straight for the bathroom. He turned on the shower, stripped naked, and ducked under the rainwater shower spray.

He stood, rock hard and jutting, his hands flattened against the tile wall, his head lowered between his arms. Every muscle in his body was drawn tight and taut. He shook all over from the need to have her, cursed himself in English and Spanish for not taking her then.

She'd been his. She'd been wet and willing and . . . vulnerable, he reminded himself again. And she would never have forgiven him for taking advantage of that vulnerability.

He didn't want her that way. He wanted her to come to him. He wanted the choice to be hers. Without coercion. Without duress. And absolutely without the weapons of anger and blame to hide behind afterward.

In the meantime, they had a job to do. Until it was over he would suffer. It was small consolation to know that she would be suffering, too.

B.J. stood exactly where Rafe had left her, leaning back against the outside wall, her breasts rising and falling with her erratic breaths, aching with need and embarrassment and anger.

She was a professional, for God's sake. She was there on a mission. How could she have let him get to her like that? Why had she let things go so far?

She wasn't one of those weak, simpering women who let a man dominate her or a sexual creature who was ruled by her libido. In short, she wasn't Brittany Jameson.

She had a mind. She had a backbone. She had a . . . oh God. She had a major problem.

Raphael Mendoza had just turned her on like a faucet and all she could think about was the touch of his hands on her body, the taste of his tongue in her mouth, the promises he had made.

She was tired, was all. They'd been on a whirlwind ride for the past few days. She was strung tight with tension and needed an outlet for all the pressure. Enter the hot Latin lover, ready, willing, and able to take the edge off. How . . . *generous* of him.

Bastard.

Or not, she admitted, touching her fingertips to her lips and feeling them warm and swollen from his kisses.

He'd walked away, hadn't he? He'd left her before things had gotten totally out of hand. A bastard didn't do that.

Why in the *hell* had he gone all sensitive? Because there was much more to Raphael Mendoza than met the eye, she admitted on a deep breath. Much, much more. And therein lay the crux of her problem. He moved her. Emotionally. Physically.

So what now? She was strung as tight as a piano wire. She couldn't go on this way. They had to perform for the Munozes, for God knew how many others before this was over. The way she was now, she'd jump like she was shot if he so much as touched her again.

Because she wanted him to touch her. Silence rang in the wake of that unvarnished truth.

Her heart was beating like crazy as she stepped back inside the bedroom. She heard the shower running in the bathroom.

And relief was ten steps away.

Before she could think about it, before she could analyze and argue and talk herself out of it, she reached behind her back and tugged down the zipper on her strapless dress. She stopped long enough to let the dress fall to the floor and shimmy out of her thong.

And then she stopped for nothing.

Rafe couldn't shake the image of B.J. backed up against the wall where he'd left her, her eyes cloudy with desire, her lips swollen from his kisses, her breasts rising and falling above the fabric of her sarong dress.

The shower sure as hell wasn't helping. He suspected that nothing short of having her was going to help. And that wasn't going to happen. At least not yet.

But then he heard the bathroom door open and close. And he knew it could only mean one thing.

He whipped his head around and there, standing naked and proud in the vortex of steam swirling through the room, stood B. J. Chase.

*Madre de Dios.*

She was exquisite. Slim, toned legs; softly flaring hips; small, trim waist; and breasts so beautiful he could weep. Tightly peaked berry brown nipples jutted from delicate aureoles. Lower, where she'd been wet when he'd touched her, where he ached to touch her still, soft gold curls guarded her most feminine place.

Physically, yes, she was exquisite, but it was the look in her eyes that held him in thrall.

This was a woman on a mission.

This was a woman who knew what she'd come for and had no reservations about taking it.

Gone was the vulnerability. Gone was the denial

and the pretense and the façade she hid behind so well.

This was B. J. Chase in the raw. Raw emotions. Raw desire. Raw and real.

He could have played this a dozen different ways. Only one held any appeal.

He held out his hand.

Without hesitation she stepped into the shower and took it.

"Why?" He had to know.

"Because I want you," she admitted on a ragged whisper. "Because I need you."

It was all over for him then. Any valiant notion he might have harbored that he could still find the strength and the will to turn her away vanished like the space between them.

He dragged her hard against him, buried his hands in that wild tangle of hair, and lowered his mouth to hers in a kiss that told her everything she needed to know about how badly he wanted her, right here, right now. She stood flush against him, with the water raining down and her wet hair cascading over his hands and his thigh pressed between hers.

He backed her up against the shower wall, skimmed his hands down her sides, spanned her waist—because he could, because he needed to, because he had to touch her everyplace, everywhere, and because she let him. She encouraged him with her throaty groans, her open-mouth kisses, and her possessive hands as they skated over his shoulders, down his back, then lower to his hips, where she squeezed and urged him with the rock of her hips and a whispered plea: "Please, please, come inside me."

And he wanted to. More than breathing, he wanted to enter that tight sweet heat with nothing coming between them. He came within an insane moment of doing just that when clarity staged a comeback.

"What, wait, what are you doing?" She moaned when he pushed away from her.

"Taking care of business," he said on a growl as he took her hand, grabbed a towel on the way out the door, and dragged her with him to the bedroom.

He drew her against him again, kissed her deep before letting her go. He tossed the towel on the bed. "Lie down," he ordered.

And it *was* an order.

Fire flared in her eyes and he could see she was considering defying him. He wasn't having any of it. He reached out, clutched a handful of wet hair, and drew her toward him again. "Lie down," he whispered against her mouth.

Her breath fluttered against his lips, erratic and sweet as he cupped her breast in his palm, then tweaked her nipple. She shivered, swayed . . . then lay down on her back on the bed at his urging.

Submission. It was a hard pill for her to swallow.

He'd never been into dominance. But he needed submission from this woman. Total surrender. Absolute acquiescence. Nothing less would do. Because resistance would mean she didn't trust him, and he needed her trust in this. He needed it because he knew that without trust, he would lose her to inhibition, resistance, and shame.

He wanted none of that from her. None of that for her. And he would not let her go there. Not with him. With him, it was all about pleasure.

"I want to do things to you, *cara*. Many, many things," he murmured, kneeling over her on the bed and lowering his mouth to her breast. "I want to lick you. And suck you. Here," he whispered, laving his tongue over her tight nipple, then sucking her into his mouth.

"Tell me it's good," he demanded, moving to her other breast and indulging himself in her silken skin and responsive body.

"Tell me," he urged again as he slid lower and swirled his tongue around her navel, nipping lightly, leaving a trail of moisture as he moved lower still.

"It's . . . it's good . . . ," she managed with a gasp, and arched her hips toward his mouth, begging for more, inviting him to take her.

"Very, very good," he agreed, moving between her legs and finally capturing that part of her he'd fantasized about since he'd held her at gunpoint three months ago in a dark alley on a hot Caracas night.

He kissed her hungrily, clutched her hips in his hands, and held her against his mouth, nuzzling between velvet folds.

She tensed and gave a low groan when he licked her there, then flicked the tip of his tongue over the swollen bud of her sex and savored the intoxicating taste of her, the lush heat and shuddering sighs. It was like igniting a wildfire. Flash, crackle, and burn. He could feel her climax rising through her body, urged her on with a total and thorough dominance that had her gripping the bedspread with clawing fists, then rising up on her elbows, her head thrown back as she reached for him, strived with him, then flew for him as he took her over that sharp, taut edge of pleasure.

He held her while she fell apart, gently nuzzling, leisurely indulging in the scent of woman and sex and sweet, sweet surrender. After one last kiss, one last taste, he rose above her. Her eyes were closed, her arms flung wide, as he reached across her body to the nightstand and his shaving kit. He pulled out a condom, pressed it into her lax fingers.

She slowly opened her eyes.

He smiled down at her. "Put it on."

Her fingers trembled as she opened the packet and, with a renewed urgency, sheathed him. Every muscle in his body clenched as her small fingers caressed him, measured him, then guided him home.

Nothing felt as good as this. No woman felt as good as her. And as he eased in and out of her, he couldn't imagine anything ever feeling as good again. She was as tight as a fist. As sleek and wet as rainwater. And at the moment, she was his.

*Surrender.*

She gave it again as she lifted to him, matched his rhythm, and took him deep inside.

"Come for me," she demanded, digging her fingers

into his buttocks and asking for more. Asking for harder. Asking for everything he wanted to give, and taking without reservation.

"Come for me," she demanded again, the cords in her neck extended as she wrapped her legs around his waist and increased the speed of her matching thrusts.

A wildcat, he thought as his climax boiled up inside, then shot through him like an electrical current. Powerful, hot, primal.

He collapsed on top of her, burrowed his hands under her hips, and ground his pelvis into hers, wringing out every ounce of pleasure, prolonging the rush that he wanted to go on and on and on.

"*Cielo dulce*," he murmured against her throat and kissed her there.

"Sweet heaven," she agreed after a deep, contented sigh.

Surrender, he thought again—only this time he wondered who had truly surrendered to whom.

# 21

B.J. was vaguely aware of a shrill ringing sound.

Flat on her stomach, she opened one eye, squinted to her right, and stared at the bare muscular back of Raphael Mendoza as he lifted up on an elbow and twisted toward the nightstand to answer the phone.

"*Hola,*" he answered quietly after snagging the headset off the receiver. "*Sí. Sí. Gracias.*"

He hung up and lay back, looked her way. When he saw she was awake, he smiled. "Sorry. I tried to catch it before it woke you."

"It's okay," she said, and fought a "What have I done?" moment as she looked into those beautiful dark eyes and at his kiss-swollen lips and thought about all the places that mouth had explored on her body.

While embarrassment probably should have been the appropriate response, a wild rush of arousal shot through her body at the memory of all that had happened in this bed.

He turned on his side, facing her. Caressed the small of her back, drawing lazy circles with the tip of his fingers.

"You okay, *cara*?" he asked gently.

She turned her face into the pillow, groped for the sheet, and pulled it up over her head. "Never better."

He laughed and that skillful and clever hand skimmed up her back, then slowly down again. "Yeah, I can see that. Is that why you're hiding from me, *mi amor*?"

*Mi amor.* My love. Okay. This got straightened out right now.

She scooted to the far side of the bed, jerked the sheet with her, then wrapped it around her as she struggled to stand. "In the first place—"

He cut her off with a finger to his lips, warning her to keep her voice low in the event the room was bugged.

She shuffled quickly to the CD player, turned it on loud, knowing it would garble any conversation if they were being listened to.

"In the first place," she began again in a whisper as she moved back to the bed, "I'm not your love. That was chemistry, tension, adrenaline—whatever label you want to put on it. In the second place, it was unprofessional. And it's not going to happen again."

Okay, this might have been easier if she'd left the damn sheet and taken the blanket instead. While she'd wrapped the sheet around her like a dust cover, he was lying there on his side, his head propped on his hand, gloriously naked, outrageously male.

And he was smiling, the bastard. The gorgeous, sexy bastard.

God, he was beautiful. From the unusually crafted cross tattoo on his upper arm, to the gold crucifix dangling from his neck, to the caramel skin covering sinew and sleek muscle, to the steely heat of his penis that even now swelled with arousal, he was beautiful. There was no other word for it. Stunningly, excessively beautiful.

He patted the bed in invitation. "Why don't you come back and we'll talk about it," he murmured, all soft and seductive and smug.

If by any chance there was a hidden camera in the room—and God, she tried not to think about that possibility after what had just happened—it would simply appear that they were having a lover's quarrel.

She backed a step away, telling herself it was for his benefit, not hers. "What did I just say?"

"That something's not going to happen again. I thought perhaps you meant you weren't going to swaddle yourself like a mummy again."

She wished he'd quit smiling. "Don't be obtuse."

"So, you're saying you didn't enjoy making love to me?"

"Look, it was exactly what it was. An outlet for nervous energy. Something had to happen or I was going to blow it. So I took one for the team, okay?" she said, knowing that even in whispered tones she sounded like a raving bitch.

Instead of getting all indignant, he laughed. "For the team, was it? I think, *cara*, that on this, you might be wrong. I was there, remember? I don't recall any self-sacrificing moments."

He was still smiling, damn him. He knew the effect he had on her and he made no effort to cover himself and help her out.

"But," he continued, his dark gaze holding hers as his voice turned all smoky, "if it helps you to think otherwise, then by all means, knock yourself out. Only this is what I think. I think that I scare the hell out of you.

"No." He lifted a hand, cutting her off before she could push out an incredulous "In your dreams."

He pushed up on one arm, leaned toward her to make certain she could hear him. "I think that I make you feel things that frighten you. I think I make you want to take a chance. But you don't do that, do you? You don't take chances when it comes to protecting yourself from anyone who might expect something in return. Well, let me say this. And I want you to listen and believe. I'm not your enemy. Stephanie and Jenna, both of whom you would like to embrace as friends"— he lowered his voice even more—"they are not the enemy either, but still you hold them at arm's length."

"I know who the enemy is," she whispered.

"Do you?"

Her eyes filled with tears. She didn't know why. She . . . okay, damn it. She did know. He was right. She did hold herself apart from many people because yes, yes, the thought of opening herself up for rejection and loss scared her to death.

But sometimes, *sometimes,* the fight made her very, very tired.

"Do you?" he repeated gently. "Do you really know who the enemy is?"

"We are *fighting* the enemy," she hissed. "That's what I know. That's why we're here. That's the only reason we're here."

He wasn't smiling anymore. "Am I your enemy then?"

Yes, damn it. He was. He was an enemy to her sanity. He threatened every rule she'd ever imposed for her own self-preservation. He made her want things and question what she knew to be true.

God. She couldn't think about this now.

"What you are is a complication I don't need," she whispered when what she wanted to do was yell. "And what *we* are—what we did—is just what I said it was. A necessary release. For the good of the operation."

He watched her for a long time, then finally nodded. "All right, *cara.* I'll respect your boundaries."

She eyed him warily. "Thank you."

"You're welcome. But so you know, when we get out of this, *if* we get out of this, I'm going to blow so many holes in that wall you've built around your heart that you'll have no choice but to let me in."

She couldn't think of anything to say to that. Couldn't have spoken if she wanted to. The look in his eyes stunned her. He was serious. He meant what he said.

"Right now, I have to get dressed," he said in a normal voice as he rolled to the other side of the bed and stood. "That was Cesar on the phone. He wants to meet with me before dinner. A little one-on-one conversation."

The man had no shame. No inhibitions. He stood there in all his naked glory, still semi-erect and altogether magnificent.

"I suspect he wants to know my reason for showing up here after all these years. Guess it's time I tell him. Oh, and Tía Aliria has invited you for cocktails and hors d'oeuvres poolside."

"I . . . I, ah," she stammered, wanting to look away but unable to, "will behave like a perfect fiancée."

The look in his eyes as he watched her from the other side of the bed was almost her undoing. And when he walked around that bed and enfolded her in his arms, sheet and all, it was all she could do to keep from melting into him.

"Don't be afraid of this. Don't be afraid of me. There are much bigger things to fear."

He set her away from him then, searched her eyes like he was looking for the Holy Grail there. "But there is something, one thing I desperately need to know."

She held her breath, waited, and finally he asked, "You must tell me what B.J. stands for."

She didn't know what she'd expected, but it sure as the world wasn't that. Her face must have registered her surprise because he immediately broke into a grin.

What an unusual man, she thought in that moment. With one well-timed burst of insight, he'd put things back in place between them. Gave her an opening to fall back into their verbal sparring because he sensed that she needed that common ground to steady herself.

"Nice try," she said, and actually found herself smiling back.

"Bobbie Jo?"

"Forget it."

"Bethany Jill? Belinda June?"

"Don't you have a meeting to attend?"

"You're no fun, Chase." He dropped a kiss on her forehead and headed for the bathroom.

Nope. No fun at all, she agreed, and watched what was possibly the nicest ass and the most intriguing man she'd ever known disappear behind the bathroom door.

Rafe blew a plume of cigar smoke—Honduran, Cesar had told him, custom made—into the air in the dimly lit room. This was Cesar's inner sanctum, part library, part office. Cesar sat behind a huge antique mahogany desk. Floor-to-ceiling shelving behind the desk stored everything from priceless bound volumes to a small original Picasso and a few Chagalls. Next to the desk stood a workstation complete with computer, fax, printer, and modem.

The small talk was over. Rafe understood that even before Cesar finally mentioned the pink elephant sucking up all the oxygen in the room.

"So, Raphael, you have been alive in the United States for fifteen years. Yet you have never been in touch. Never returned to Colombia. I have many questions."

"I would expect you to," Rafe said as he rolled the tip of the expensive cigar in an ornate glass ashtray, then tapped off the ashes. "For many years, fear kept me away. I knew that if I returned, I would also be killed. As long as whoever killed my father thought I was dead, then I was safe in America. But then I matured, became involved with my own business, and time passed, you know?"

He drew on the cigar again, pausing to let the smoke drift toward the coffered ceiling. "I have been wanting to return for years. I want to claim my place in the family business, Tío Cesar. I have always wanted that. But I wanted to wait until the time was right. I wanted to bring something of worth to the bank and all its highly profitable auxiliary businesses so they would understand that I can be a viable member of the business."

"And besides your father's name, what does Raphael Mendoza bring?"

"A profitable Las Vegas–based operation."

Cesar's eyes reflected exactly what Rafe wanted to see. Interest.

"My business is small in contrast to yours but lucrative, just the same. I can offer this to the family. I can offer a conduit to a market that could multiply by thousands of branches with the connections I have in Nevada."

Cesar said nothing, but Rafe could see he had his attention and his interest. After a long, thoughtful moment, Cesar lifted a hand in a gesture for Rafe to continue.

He'd taken the bait. Now Rafe just had to reel him in.

"You do realize, it is not my decision," Cesar said after Rafe had outlined his fake Vegas operation and his plans for expansion—with the help of an infusion of capital from his uncle's business, of course.

"I want you to see this." Rafe produced a totally bogus annual business report. "Look it over," he added. "And I expect you to check me out. You could start with him." He gave his uncle the name and number of the financier Ann Tompkins had cut the deal with.

Rafe knew he was on board then. If Cesar wasn't interested, he would have given him a flat-out no.

"I know that Emilio will have the final word," Rafe said as Cesar thumbed through the report.

Cesar didn't bat an eye when Rafe mentioned Emilio Garcia, the godfather of the cartel. The man whom Rafe and B.J. had come down here to find.

"I will arrange a meeting," Cesar said, and that was the end of the discussion. "Now, we've kept the ladies waiting long enough. Please, go ahead and join them at the east pool. I'll be there in a few moments."

Right after he searched the web for information, Rafe figured, and hoped to hell that Crystal had planted enough bogus intel to convince Cesar that the line of bullshit Rafe had just fed him was the truth.

"Uncle Cesar," Rafe said, hesitating at the door. This wasn't part of the plan. This was personal. So personal it had been eating a hole in his gut for years. "My father . . . my family. Who took them away from me?"

Cesar blinked slowly, leaned forward behind the

desk, and propped his elbows on the leather blotter. "Their murderers have received what they deserved. I saw to it personally. You must trust me on this," he added, apparently seeing the lingering question in Rafe's eyes. "Just as you must trust that some things are best left buried."

Buried with his mother and his baby sister, who were innocent of all crime. Buried with his father, who was ultimately responsible for their deaths.

He breathed through the knot clutching at his chest and left the room, shutting the door behind him. His hands were shaking as he turned the knob; his heart raced on a runaway ride to nowhere. For most of his adult life he had thought of extracting revenge. For the past several years, when time and technology had permitted, he had quietly investigated the Munoz bank and the Garcia drug cartel, searching for clues as to who had been responsible for murdering his family. The lack of information hadn't surprised him. The cartel was cloaked in secrecy.

*"Their murderers have received what they deserved. I saw to it personally. You must trust me on this."*

His uncle had felt the need to insist on trust. Why was it, then, that Cesar had not looked him in the eye when he'd said it?

# 22

Rafe almost choked on his wine when he spotted B.J. as she emerged from the double French doors of the house. The woman knew how to make an entrance and this one was on par with a pole dancer out to collect a helluva lot of tips.

Hips swaying, boobs bouncing, dressed in little more than three triangles and some string, she sauntered across the huge, tiled patio toward him and his aunt and uncle.

Her four-inch heels were made of some kind of clear plastic or acrylic material with a big fuchsia flower attached to the strap at her ankle; her wide-brimmed floppy hat and sunglasses matched her teensy weensy hot pink bikini, and the gauzy white translucent swim poncho was less coverup than it was tease.

*Madre de Dios*, was she trying to kill him or help him?

He glanced at his aunt and uncle. The faces greeting B.J. as she made her long, hip-swaying way across the tiled patio were not happy faces.

"Look at the three of you," she cooed with a huge smile as she joined them at the table. "What a lovely family picture you make. You're still a handsome son of a gun, you know that, Cesar? *Muy macho*," she assured him with a flirty smile. "And, Aliria, I would just love to get you to my hairdresser. Why the things she could do—"

"Brittany," Rafe said sharply. "We've been waiting for over an hour."

"Well, darling," her smile grew tight with annoyance as she circled the table and planted a kiss on his cheek, "you wouldn't have wanted me to make an appearance unless I was all put together. It took forever for this nail polish to dry." She splayed her fingers in front of his face, then leaned down and nibbled on his ear. "It's passion pink. Because I know how much you like my little pink—"

"Brittany." He silenced her again, smiling apologetically at his shell-shocked aunt. "We're having dinner. This is not a pool party."

She stood up straight, then affected an injured but valiant smile. "Oh. When you said to meet by the pool, I naturally assumed . . . well. It doesn't matter what I assumed now, does it? I didn't realize I was supposed to *dress* for dinner. I'll just go change."

"Brittany, wait." He snagged her arm.

She jerked out of his grasp. "I said, I'll change." She shot a glare at Rafe while he wondered what in the hell she was up to.

"Excuse me," she said curtly to Cesar and Aliria. "I'll just be a few minutes."

For the longest moment, all Rafe could do was watch the sweet bounce of her almost bare ass and wonder about the things he did not know about B. J. Chase.

He finally shook his head to clear it and found both Cesar and Aliria staring at him as if they were trying to figure out what in the hell he saw in her.

"Women," he said, offering up a sheepish smile. "Who can figure them out?"

It was all about timing. As soon as she hit the house, B.J. slipped out of the ridiculous heels—if she ever ran into Reed again, she had a *lot* to thank him for—sprinted up the stairs to their bedroom, and changed into the green silk slip dress she'd laid out on the bed. She ditched the hat, jammed a flower from the bedside bouquet in her hair, grabbed a pair of white heels, then ran back down the stairs, where she ducked around the corner and headed straight for Cesar's office. If her cell phone was anywhere, she suspected she'd find it there. Earlier, she'd turned on the transmitter she'd hidden in her purse to notify the BOIs that they were in and so they could get a fix on their location. But they needed to check in with Crystal and see if there was anything new to help them.

She'd been waiting for just the right time to slip away after tracking the pattern of movement of the household staff. She'd figured out that this was their break time, which they spent out back at a small sitting area reserved just for them. It gave her this small window to check out Cesar's office.

"Damn," she sputtered, trying the office door. Even though she'd anticipated it would be locked, she'd still hoped for a break. Slipping a hairpin out of her updo, she went to work. It was a simple interior lock, not designed for heavy-duty security, and it took her all of thirty seconds to spring it.

She slipped inside, closed the door quietly behind her, and headed straight for Cesar's desk. It, too, was locked, but after checking all the usual hiding places, she found the key tucked in a small box affixed to the bottom of the center desk drawer.

"Bingo," she murmured when she found her cell phone in the first drawer she opened. "Be there, Crystal," she whispered after sending the first text, then held her breath while she waited for a reply.

Her heart kicked with relief when no more than thirty seconds later, Crystal answered. Less than two minutes after that, B.J. had replaced the phone, locked up the desk, and let herself out of the office. Then she breathed deep to collect herself, slipped on her shoes, and headed back for the pool and her waiting "fiancé." He wasn't going to like the news Crystal had passed on.

While Crystal had nothing new on the investigative front, her other bit of news wasn't good. Whoever was pulling the strings back in the States had found the safe house. Only because Green was so skillful was he able to get Stephanie out of there alive. Now they were on the run.

"Tick. Tock." Crystal had written in her text.

Yeah. No one knew better than B.J. that the clock was ticking.

No one, possibly, but Rafe, who searched her eyes with a scowl when she joined him and the Munozes at the table.

"Happy now?" she asked, and executed a little twirl for him.

"You look lovely." Rafe held out a hand for her, then gave her a reassuring squeeze before pulling her against his side. "And we have a surprise for you."

*Brittany* quickly forgot that she was in a bit of a snit. "Really?"

"There's going to be a party in our honor."

She all but squealed in excitement. "You know how I love parties. Where? When?"

"The day after tomorrow at a business associate of Tío Cesar's."

She made her eyes as big as her smile. "Business associate?"

"Emilio Garcia," he supplied, and if possible her eyes grew wider. "When Uncle Cesar informed him that I was alive and in Colombia, Señor Garcia insisted he be allowed to throw a welcome home party."

"I understand he's a very important man." She flashed a conspiratorial smile at Cesar. "*Muy importante*," she added in her clumsy Spanish, her expression relaying how pleased she thought they should be that she'd made another attempt to speak their language.

"It will allow you an opportunity to meet many friends and family," Aliria said, ever the gracious hostess. "In the meantime, let's eat our dinner, shall we? I've had the chef prepare something special in honor of Raphael's return."

"That is so sweet," Brittany said. "Raphael deserves something special, don't you, darling?" She pressed a kiss on his mouth, then made a huge production of waiting by her chair until Rafe rose and pulled it out for her.

Satisfied that she was properly arranged and looking gorgeous, she smiled around the table, then lifted her wineglass in anticipation of a toast. "Isn't this just so lovely?"

"You did what?" Rafe demanded, hoping he hadn't heard her right when B. J. told him she'd broken into Cesar's office.

They had excused themselves shortly after dinner, Brittany pleading a headache. Now they stood in the bathroom with the shower running full blast to ensure they couldn't be overheard. Which was a damn good thing because he was close to yelling.

"Are you going to tell me that if the opportunity came up, you wouldn't have done the same thing?"

He glared at her.

"I didn't think so. Well, I created an opportunity."

In spades, he thought, thinking about the way she'd looked in that bikini. Especially how she'd looked walking away.

"Look, I told you—I call the shots. You don't go all Rambo on me, you got it? If you're going to pull something like that, I need to be in the loop."

"Fine. Point taken. It won't happen again. In the meantime, do you want to hear what I found out or not?"

*Cristo*, the woman had balls. He covered his mouth with his hand, skated it up over his head, and clutched the back of his neck, trying to settle himself down. Finally he nodded.

"And they're both okay?" he asked after she'd told him about the text conversation with Crystal, who had relayed news of Stephanie and Green's narrow escape.

"Apparently, but it was a close call."

He turned his back on her, paced two steps away, then turned back. "We've got to get in touch with Nate and the guys. See what they've dug up. Something's got to shake loose on this. We're running out of time."

"I know," she said. "I was thinking that 'Brittany' could insist on a shopping trip to Medellín tomorrow. She'll need something snazzy for the big party—and I can make a side trip to an Internet café. Crystal can either put me in touch with the guys or give me a report on what, if anything, they've found out."

Rafe thought about Cesar. About the way he hadn't been able to look him in the eye when he'd told him he'd dealt with the men who had killed Rafe's family. And Rafe knew that Cesar was too shrewd to take the story of his Vegas operation at face value. If he hadn't already, Cesar would soon be running a check on Rafe's Vegas alias. Until his uncle was satisfied with the "truth" of Rafe's story, Cesar would continue to watch him like a hawk. "Brittany," too, but to a lesser degree and mostly because B.J. had done such a good job of presenting herself as an obnoxious airhead.

"He'll insist on his own chauffeur taking you. And he'll watch every move you make."

"Don't worry. I'll find a way to slip away."

Yeah, he thought. She would. She was capable and smart and, damn, he wished he could get the picture of her in that tiny scrap of a bikini out of his head. Wished he could shake the constant images of them naked in the shower together, and in the bed. The amazing taste of her.

"My cousins are coming tomorrow," he said, because she was too close and he was too hard and if he didn't focus on something else, he was going to break his promise about respecting her boundaries until this was over. "It should be an interesting reunion."

"No doubt," she agreed. "What's the plan at Emilio Garcia's?"

"Same as it's always been. I'll look for an opportunity to get into his office, attempt to access his files, and hopefully find the info we need."

It wasn't much of a plan. It was more like a desperate marriage of guesswork and necessity. They were grasping at straws here but the options were few and far between. They had only a scant few days to ferret out the information they needed to find the facility manufacturing the E-bomb, disrupt the delivery of said bomb and stop the attack on the United States, get Stephanie out from under the gun, and oh yeah, find and expose the traitor.

He'd worry about getting them out of there alive when the time came.

"I'm going to take a shower," he said abruptly. "Unless you want to join me again—and believe me, you're more than welcome—you might want to close the door on your way out."

Myriad emotions flickered in her eyes. Longing. Indecision. Regret.

Resolve finally won out and she turned and left the room.

He stood in the shower until the water ran cold. When he finally opened the door to the bedroom, the lights were out. A sliver of moonlight gilded the slight form under the covers on the far side of the bed.

He crawled into the big king, crossed his arms beneath his head, and stared at the ceiling, listening to her breathe. Knowing she was awake, knowing she wanted him to think she was sleeping.

He lay there. Stared into the dark.

He was home. After fifteen years, he was home.

A hollow emptiness suddenly consumed him. An emptiness he hadn't let himself feel since he was a lost boy crying in the dark for his family.

# 23

Even before Stephanie and Joe crossed the Potomac last night, it had seemed like they'd driven for hours when Joe turned west on 66, then veered off onto 81 and finally onto a secondary road. Time, like reality, had become distorted when Stephanie's life became the stuff of those spy novels she'd devoured as a girl.

*Be careful what you wish for.*

Yeah, she thought, staring at the ceiling of a rustic cabin nestled in the woods somewhere in rural Bath County in southwest Virginia. Be careful what you wish for, you just might get it. People were trying to kill her because she was helping to stop a terrorist plot and expose a traitor. Bullets and bad guys came with the territory, unless she and Joe could outrun and outsmart them.

So far, so good. They'd arrived at this out-of-the-way spot in the earliest part of the morning, awakening a grumpy innkeeper who'd given Joe the keys to the little cabin at the far end of the trail.

"It's as far from the road as he had available," Joe

had said as he'd opened the door and stood aside for Stephanie to enter.

She'd been too exhausted to take much more than a cursory glance at the worn pine floors and slightly shabby furniture before she'd used the bathroom and collapsed on the first bed she saw.

That had to have been a while ago, she thought, because sunlight from a low-hanging sun streamed in through a small double-hung window. Outside she could see the green of trees swaying in a summer breeze. Inside, she smelled bacon. And coffee.

Joe.

Feeling like death warmed over, she slogged her way out of the bed and stumbled into the main area of the cabin—which consisted of the living room, dining area, and kitchen—to see him, standing in those sexy bare feet again and wearing nothing but a pair of soft faded jeans and a few droplets of water from what must have been a recent shower.

His back was to her as he cooked, which worked out just fine because she was fascinated by that broad, bare back and by the tattoo that ran from the nape of his neck to the spot on his spine where it disappeared beneath the waistband of his jeans.

The tattoo was a mix of cobalt blues, scarlet reds, powder whites, and rusty golds. It snaked sinuously down his backbone, all sleek knots and vibrant strokes.

A ribbon, she realized. A red, white, and blue ribbon braided with letters and numbers and—*oh God*.

"Bryan."

She hadn't realized she'd spoken out loud until he twisted around, saw her standing there.

"Bryan," she repeated, walking toward him. "Bryan's name is on your back."

Not just Bryan's, she realized when she reached him and touched her finger to her brother's name. There were many names, many dates—a dozen at least—and she felt her heart stumble when she recognized the date that Bryan had died.

Joe turned slowly so he was facing her. He looked self-conscious and somber and apologetic. "I wanted to make certain no one ever forgot," he said, watching her face.

"All of them? You lost all of them?"

He clenched his jaw, looked over her head, and she knew he saw the horror of the deaths of each and every one of the men who had been his brothers in arms.

"I'll go put a shirt on," he said, and started to move away.

She stopped him with a hand on his arm. "You are so much more than meets the eye," she whispered, then wrapped her arms around his waist and held him. Just held him, to let him know that he didn't have to carry that burden of pain alone.

His arms came around her slowly. He lowered his cheek to the top of her head, breathed deep. For the longest time they just stood that way, holding on, holding tight, sharing a moment of reassurance that although those brave men he'd memorialized were dead, the two of them were alive.

"The bacon is going to burn," he said finally.

"Well, we can't have that," she said with a smile and reluctantly pulled away. "I need a shower."

"Watch the hot water faucet. It's very sensitive."

She nodded, turned to go.

"Wait." He stopped her, held a finger in the air that said hold on, then rummaged around in the cabinets. "We don't want that cast getting wet."

He produced a plastic bread wrapper and a roll of silver tape, then fit the wrapper over her hand and taped it on so that the water couldn't seep through to her cast.

It made her smile. "Yet one more use for duct tape. Bry used to carry a roll with him everywhere he went."

"You say that like everyone doesn't."

Oh, my God, would you look at that smile, she thought, grinning back at him. Who knew.

"Like I said. There is so much more to you than meets the eye."

"Take your shower," he advised, looking self-conscious again. "The eggs will be done when you come out."


"So you figure we're going to be here awhile?" Stephanie nodded toward the counter where Joe had unloaded a couple sacks full of groceries he'd apparently gone out and bought while she'd been sleeping. She'd finished off the last of her breakfast, which was actually an early afternoon lunch. Now she sat at the small pine dining table sipping her coffee, wearing a white terry-cloth robe she'd found hanging on the back of the bathroom door.

"Hard to tell." Joe stared at his coffee mug, absently running the pad of his thumb over the lip. "I figured better safe than sorry and the less we go out, the less chance of being spotted."

"Did I dream it or did you call someone while we were on the road last night?"

"Sherwood. I let him know what happened at the safe house. He was going to send a team out to, well, clean up, and see if they could get any leads from the, ah . . ."

"Bodies," she finished for him. "Got it."

She was responsible for one of those bodies.

"Don't think about it," he said. She brought her head up as she blocked out that horrible picture of life-less eyes and blood everywhere. "Don't think about it," he repeated.

She nodded. She didn't want to think about it. She didn't want to think about anything but tomorrow or the day after when all of this would hopefully be be-hind her.

"This is good," she said, finishing off her breakfast. "Do all you guys cook this well?"

"Colter burns everything he touches. Savage knows his way around a grill but that's about it for him. But yeah, the rest of us cook."

"Good to know." She lifted a coffee mug to her lips. "You're a handy man to have around, Joe Green."

For God's sake, she was running for her life, but she couldn't seem to stop herself from flirting with this man. Maybe it was a derivative of gallows humor catching up with her. Maybe her mind just couldn't take any more terror and flirting with Joe Green was simply an excellent diversion.

Or maybe he was just a very special man.

Last night at the safe house, when she'd kissed him . . . she kept thinking about it. In the shower, knowing he was just in the other room—God, she kept hoping he'd strip off those jeans and join her.

That wasn't her. She wasn't ruled by her libido.

At least she hadn't been until she'd kissed him.

*To be continued.*

He'd made her a promise. On the backside of a blistering kiss, he'd promised that he wasn't nearly through with her. When she looked up and met his eyes, she could see that he was thinking about that promise now, too.

When he realized she'd caught him staring, however, he shot up from the table and busied himself gathering up their dirty plates. "How's the wrist?"

Okay. How did she interpret this? Was he having second thoughts? Did he think that she was? Because he clearly didn't want to go there, she followed his lead.

"It feels pretty good today."

He shot her a doubtful look.

"Really. Look. The swelling in my fingers is almost totally gone. And I even managed to rinse out my . . . um . . . underwear," she finally finished, then wished she'd never brought her underwear into the conversation.

Oh, well. He'd know it soon enough anyway since her bra and panties were hanging over the shower curtain rod drip-drying.

"Just the same," he said, his back to her as he ran water in the sink, "it would be smart to ice it again."

The man was in misery. He could no longer look at her. Which meant one of two things. Either he was embarrassed by the talk of women's undies—and she hardly thought a man who faced death for a living would be taken down by a few scraps of satin and lace—or he was having a hard time keeping his hands off of her.

She decided to go with door number two. And she also decided to give him some time to get used to the idea of what now seemed inevitable between them.

Besides, she needed to get back to work. Too many people were depending on her.

"I don't suppose there's such a thing as Internet access here."

"I made sure there was when I booked the cabin."

She should have known. "I'll get to work, then."

A couple of hours later, Stephanie said, "You know, something has been bothering me about this from the beginning. I couldn't figure out how the Russian connection fit in. I mean, the Afghans and the Russians have been enemies for years."

"So you're wondering why U.S. specs for E-bomb technology were found in Taliban hands and apparently about to be shipped to Russia," Joe concluded.

"Exactly. It doesn't make sense. So I'm thinking we were off on that one."

"What does make sense?" Joe asked, apparently sensing she'd figured it out.

"Something that got lost in the rush to get Rafe and B.J. to Colombia. Remember that even though it was only a month or so ago that those specs turned up in Afghanistan, the encrypted communiqués that Alan Hendricks had deleted dated back over a year. All of them mentioned the E-bomb technology."

"So, you're thinking—what? That it was just a fluke that the specs were on that truck?"

She nodded her head slowly. "Yeah. I'm thinking the specs have probably been passed around to the highest bidder for over a year now. And for most rogue nations, the specs are worthless. They don't have the facilities or the manpower or the money to tackle a project that complex."

"You now feel the Russian connection is irrelevant?"

She shook her head. "No. The Russian connection is very relevant. Just for a different reason. Look at this."

She showed him her notes. "Do you recognize any of these terms?"

He read through the list. "Looks like a parts list."

"Exactly. I did a web search. They're submarine parts. All shipped from Russia to Colombia."

"What the hell?" His brows knit together in momentary confusion before it hit him. He shot up from his chair. "The bastards plan to deploy the E-bomb from a sub—with the parts coming from Russia. Jesus. It makes perfect sense," he said, scrubbing a hand over his head. "Other than funneling them through Mexico, do you know the preferred method of smuggling drugs into the U.S. from Colombia?"

"I'm guessing submarine?" she said. She felt dizzy; her head was spinning.

"Exactly. The same type of sub they use to smuggle coke would be perfect for delivery and deployment of an E-bomb. It's the ultimate stealth weapon. Underwater, no radar profile; above water, still no radar profile unless someone gets lucky and is flying over with an airplane that has look-down radar. And these subs the Colombian drug cartel uses to transport coke are often smaller and can fit into places that our attack boats can't."

Stephanie felt her blood run cold. "With the stealth subs transporting the E-bombs and the Black Ruby stealth device cloaking them once they're deployed, our surface-to-air defensive missiles don't have a chance to intercept them."

Joe paced back and forth, stopped abruptly. "Rafe, B.J., and the BOIs—they're looking in the wrong place. They won't find the manufacturing facility in Medellín. Find the sub; find the bomb. It's got to be in a seaport city. Cartagena, maybe. Possibly Barranquilla—"

"Or any one of a dozen cities along the Colombian coast," Stephanie interrupted. "I need to get back to work on the coded messages. There's got to be a reference somewhere, something to point us to the right port."

"In the meantime, we've got to get this info to Crystal so she can relay it to the guys. Between her and Nate and the crew, hopefully they can get it to Rafe and B.J."

"Before it's too late," Stephanie added unnecessarily. Joe and everyone else associated with this op knew that the clock was ticking like a bomb.

"Nothing," Stephanie said after three more long, frustrating hours of combing through the coded messages. "If there's a reference to the location of the facility, I missed it."

Joe wasn't buying that. He'd seen how hard she worked, how thorough she was. And how exhausted she was as she lay her head on the table.

"You didn't miss anything," he assured her. "You fine-tooth-combed each and every message. The information just isn't there."

"I need to go over it all again."

"No," he said with a forceful scowl when she straightened in the wooden chair and dragged the hair back from her eyes. "You do not."

She propped an elbow on the table, rested her head in her good hand. "I can't just sit here and do nothing while they're flying blind down there."

"Flying blind is one of their favorite things to do," he said, trying to get her to ease up on herself. "If these guys aren't outnumbered and outgunned and fumbling around in the dark, they just don't have any fun."

"Fun?"

"What? You think we do this for the money?"

Finally she smiled. "So what you're saying is that you're all loose cannons."

He spun a chair around backward, straddled it, and crossed his arms over the chair back. "I'll let you in on a little secret. There are many who maintain that BOI stands for something other than Black Ops, Inc."

"Okay, I'll bite," she said when he didn't elaborate. "What do they say it stands for?"

"Black's Obnoxious Idiots."

A bigger smile. Soft and sweet and finally, not quite so tense.

"The guys know how to handle themselves," he assured her. "B.J., too. And you read Crystal's response when we e-mailed her. She'll get hold of them. She'd already made contact with B.J., right? At least B.J. had made contact with her. The woman is resourceful. She'll figure out how to reach Crystal again. In the meantime, you've given them something to go on. You've done what you needed to do. The rest is up to them."

"Okay. You've convinced me. They're going to be okay."

Still, he saw the lingering fear in her eyes.

"My money is always on them."

Her valiant determination to believe damn near broke his heart. He was so out of his element around her. He always had been. From the first moment he'd set eyes on Bry's kid sister ten years ago, he'd been trying to figure out why it felt like his bell had been rung, cracked, and de-clappered all in one righteous peal. It was like he didn't have any defense mechanism in play or had no contingency plan to help him deal with the things he felt just looking at her.

He wanted to protect her and ravage her at the same time. Those staid, proper business suits she wore drove him crazy. And when she sometimes wore her thick brown hair pulled back in a severe bun, it was all he could do to keep himself from backing her into a corner somewhere, ripping the pins out of her hair and the clothes off her body.

Animal. If she knew how he thought about her, she'd think he was an animal.

Even now, as she sat there in that damn white robe with the lapels gaping open, exhausted and in pain, he wanted to do things to her. Bad things. Amazing things.

"Joe."

Her soft voice jarred him out of his dark thoughts.

"If you keep looking at me that way, I'm going to have to insist that you take me to bed."

*Holy Christ.*

"I'm . . . I'm sorry. I didn't mean to be disrespectful. Look, um . . . I think I'd better go get some air."

He shoved up from the table, the wooden chair legs scraping on worn pine, and bolted for the door.

"Joe."

*Holy, holy Christ.*

He stopped, his hand on the doorknob. But he didn't turn around. He couldn't. For her sake, he couldn't, because if she still had that look in her eyes, he was going to—

"Joe." A whisper.

A soft hand on his arm.

"Don't go."

He turned then because he had to see her face. Had to let her see his face. One look at the hunger, the need, she'd see wisdom in letting him go.

But God, oh God, she didn't go anywhere. Instead, she reached for the belt on her robe and untied it. A sultry shrug of her shoulders and it was open, then lying on the floor.

"Jesus." He swallowed hard. "Stephanie—I don't—"

"Want me?"

"Christ, no. I mean, yes. Yes . . . I want you, but—"

"But what?"

"This . . . this isn't right. You've been traumatized. You've been—"

"Joe." She pressed her fingers to his mouth, silencing him. "Don't make me hurt you."

And then she smiled. A smile so warm and sexy and filled with need that he surrendered. Flat-out. No protest. Surrender.

He moved in close against her, wrapped her in his arms, and lifted her off her feet.

"I'm taking you to bed," he said, a final warning, just in case she'd somehow misread his intent.

She laughed at him. All amused and happy. "I am so glad we finally got that straightened out."

# 24

B.J. figured that Aliria had probably been right when she'd told Brittany that the El Tesoro shopping center in the El Poblado barrio was the best in Medellín. It was also beautiful. Waterfalls rained down in the middle of a palm tree garden surrounded by upscale stores and even a miniature railroad. She stopped for a moment as a beautiful couple danced a sultry tango on the open plaza.

"Would you just look at them dance," she gushed to the chauffeur, who had stuck to Brittany like a tick. She'd been shopping for over two hours now and the only time she'd managed to get out of his sight was when she slipped into a dressing room to try something on.

So far, she'd bought a pair of shoes, two dresses, and a supply of Santander chocolate—a Colombian delicacy that might just save her life. She was running out of opportunities to slip into the Internet café she'd spotted when they'd first arrived.

"Jose—it is Jose, right?" she asked with her sweetest smile as she absently rummaged through her purse.

"*Sí*, señorita."

"Jose, I can't seem to find my wallet. Oh, dear." She walked over to an outdoor café table, set down the purse, searched the bag in earnest, and turned into a drama queen. "It's not here. Someone must have lifted it out of my purse when I wasn't watching. Oh, my God! How did this happen?"

She turned angry eyes on him. "Isn't that what you're here for? To make sure something like this doesn't happen to me?"

Poor Jose wasn't sure what to make of an agitated and loud American woman. "I . . . I speak only small English," he stammered.

"You understand money? *Pesos? Muchos dólares?* Well, my money is gone. My wallet is gone! You need to find my wallet!" she demanded, then acted as if a thought occurred to her. "Or maybe . . . maybe it wasn't stolen. Maybe I left it in one of the stores!"

One of about twenty-five stores she'd made certain she'd visited.

"Go!" she demanded, making shooing motions with her hands when he just stood there. "What are you waiting for? Go find it. I cannot possibly walk any farther today." She pointed toward the café. "I'm going to use the restroom. Restroom?" she repeated when she could see he didn't understand. "*Servicios.* I'll wait for you there."

Jose looked torn. It was either stay with her and risk her wrath and the potential of a big scene—which B.J. knew Cesar would not want—or do as she asked. She decided he needed a little more incentive.

"Do you think that Señor Munoz will be happy when I tell him my wallet was lost or stolen while you stood by and did nothing?"

That did it. He bowed slightly, then took off down the long line of shops.

B.J. hurried over to the Internet café, found a table in the back, quickly accessed the e-mail account Crystal had set up, and typed her message.

ONLY A FEW MINUTES. NO DISCOVERY HERE. DO YOU HAVE ANY INTEL?

Since Crystal had her e-mail account set to sound an alarm when a new message was received, B. J. was confident of a quick reply. Still, it seemed like an eternity while she waited, watching the entry to the café, expecting Jose to show up at any moment.

"Finally," she whispered when the new-message icon popped up.

She opened it quickly, hoping that Stephanie or Nate and the crew had discovered something of use to them. Her heart sank as she read it. Stephanie had discovered something, all right. On the heels of disappointment, a renewed sense of urgency kicked in.

She had to get back to the villa and talk with Rafe. She closed the e-mail account, spotted a display of computer accessories by the cash register, and quickly bought a flash drive. She tucked it in her purse and rushed out of the café just as a harried Jose ducked into a store.

She headed in his direction. "Jose! Good news! I found it! It was in my purse after all."

The look on his face would have been laughable if she hadn't been so anxious to get back to Rafe.

"I'm tired. Take me home, please," she said, and started marching toward the parking area.

Half an hour later, they arrived at the villa to find Rafe on the back patio smoking cigars with Cesar and two men that she assumed were his sons.

The three younger men were quick to rise when she sashayed out onto the patio, all flirty eyes and piqued interest. Cesar rose slowly. Not because of his age, she knew, but because he felt little for her but disdain.

"Well, hello." She beamed at the handsome brothers, noting their strong resemblance to Cesar, all the while trying to figure out how to get Rafe away from them. "Looks like you're having a party without me."

"Felipe, Rodrigo"—Rafe addressed his cousins as he wrapped a proprietary arm around her waist—"my fiancée, Brittany Jameson."

"Señorita." Felipe was all bold eyes and Latin charm as he claimed her hand, then kissed it.

Brittany laughed in delight.

Rodrigo showed more reserve and extended his hand to shake hers. "Señorita," he said, his smile much cooler than his brother's. "Welcome to Medellín."

"My goodness," she said, sounding breathless, "good looks and charm certainly run in this family. Better be careful, Raphael," she teased, "or one of your cousins will turn my head."

Rafe's laugh was tight as he played the marginally jealous fiancé. "Brittany, *mi chica bonita*, I'll give you three reasons why that will never happen. Maria is one and Belicia is two. Both will gouge your eyes out if you look at their husbands the way you look at me."

She affected a pouty moue at the discovery that they were married; the playful American, pretending to be disappointed. "And reason number three?"

He jerked her hard against him, a brittle smile on his face. "You will not like the punishment if I ever catch you cheating on me."

Then he kissed her, all dominant male, a stag marking his territory.

"Well, my." She wrapped her arms around his neck. "Maybe we ought to find a private place to continue this conversation."

She pulled slowly away from him, trailed a pink-tipped nail down the center of his chest as she backed away.

"Gentlemen," she said. "A pleasure."

Then she walked back into the house, hips swaying in a blatant invitation for Rafe to follow.

"You'll excuse me," she heard him say to Cesar and his sons. "It seems there is a matter of great importance that requires my immediate attention."

Later when they were alone on the balcony with their arms wrapped around each other so they could whisper safely, B.J. filled him in on the information Stephanie had relayed to Crystal.

"Has Crystal contacted Nate and the guys with this info?" Rafe asked.

"Yeah," B.J. said. "They've packed up and moved

out of Medellín. Nate, Reed, and Lang headed for Cartagena. Savage Jones and Doc Colter moved out to Barranquilla."

"If the facility is in either one of those cities," Rafe said, "the guys will move heaven and hell to find it, especially now that they can isolate their searches to just the seaport instead of combing the entire city."

"And if it's not in either city?" B.J. asked, because they both knew that concentrating the search on Cartagena and Barranquilla gave them, at best, two chances in twenty of being in the right place.

"That's why we're walking into the fire tomorrow. Emilio Garcia will have the answers. It's up to us to find them."

Unspoken was the very real threat that they were running out of time.

While the Munoz villa straddled the line between opulence and overkill, the Garcias had gone to the far side of the equation, Rafe thought the next day as the early afternoon sun glanced off gleaming windows and golden archways.

"Okay, now when I say Vegas, I don't think anyone can dispute me," B.J. said so only Rafe could hear her as they walked up the villa's Roman coliseum-esque entrance behind Cesar and Aliria.

Rafe had to agree. Emilio Garcia's villa and grounds reminded him of Caesars Palace in Vegas. Once they'd been admitted past the high-tech security gates, the Munoz limo, carrying the four of them—Rafe, B.J.,

Cesar, and Aliria—had crawled slowly up a curving drive bordered with dancing fountains and freestanding Roman columns. More columns—these towered to the roof of the three-story villa—flanked the wide bank of white marble steps leading to the entryway.

"Holy gilded cage," B.J. managed under her breath as they stepped into a grand foyer.

The room was roughly the size of a basketball court. It was open from the front doors to the back, with a botanical garden/aviary complete with a thirty-foot waterfall taking up most of the floor space and reaching to the high ceiling. Beyond the wall of glass that faced the back of the house, Rafe could see party tents and tables and above the rush of water, he could hear a band playing.

Waitstaff stood like sentries in pristine white uniforms just inside the intricately carved double doors offering flutes of champagne and an exotic array of hors d'oeuvres.

"Your mouth is open," Rafe whispered, leaning close to B.J.'s ear.

"Yeah, I imagine it is," she agreed.

"Our host," he murmured with a nod as the crowd parted.

Emilio Garcia strolled toward them through a sea of guests milling around the foyer enjoying the birds and the flora and the huge golden koi swimming in the lagoon at the base of the waterfall.

Unlike Cesar, who had remained fit and trim, Emilio wore his life of indulgence in the form of extra weight on his short frame. He put Rafe in mind of Brando in the classic *Godfather* film. His jowls were soft, his girth wide, his gray hair thinning on top— which Emilio apparently felt he could make up for by wearing it long and tied with a braided leather lace at his nape. A huge diamond stud winked from his left earlobe.

In one hand, he held an unlit cigar; in the other he held a thick fat glass filled with what looked like scotch. Both arms were open as he met Cesar for an embrace. Then he politely bowed to Aliria.

Rafe stood back, waiting, while Emilio sized up first Rafe and then Brittany over Aliria's shoulder.

"And you would be the guest of honor." Emilio drained the scotch, then openly appraised Rafe. He set his glass on a tray as a waiter magically appeared, then just as discreetly faded away.

Rafe gave a respectful bow of his head. "Your generosity leaves me speechless. As does the grandeur of your magnificent home."

"You look like him," Emilio said after studying Rafe with narrowed eyes. "We have missed your father. What happened to your family . . . a horrible tragedy. No amount of sympathy can express my regret."

Again, Rafe nodded, schooling his expression to hide his hatred for Emilio and everything he stood for. "*Gracias.* This is a great honor. Please permit me to introduce you to my fiancée, Brittany Jameson."

A quick spark of carnal interest flared in Emilio's eyes when he turned his attention to B.J. Rafe understood the drug lord's reaction. When she'd finally made an appearance after purposefully keeping them waiting for over half an hour, Rafe had been struck silent by the sight of her walking down the stairway at Villa Munoz, dressed in her finest afternoon party wear.

He hadn't been certain what she'd been going for with the short, white strapless dress that showed off her smooth shoulders, hugged her slim hips like a glove, and showcased her amazing legs, but he knew what effect it had on him. Instant arousal.

His first thought had been, Can she breathe in that dress? His second was, Can *I* breathe standing next to her? Turned out he could, with great difficulty, once he'd gotten over the initial shock. God, she was stunning.

She'd clipped back the hair on the left side of her face and tucked it behind her ear along with a lavender orchid. He suspected that her intent had been to bring order and civility to the mass of golden curls; instead the hairstyle only emphasized how incredibly, wildly sexy she was.

As if he needed a reminder of that. After she'd filled him in on Stephanie's report and they'd discussed their plan of action today, he'd spent another long night far too aware of the fact that they shared a bed but nothing more. He couldn't remember when his willpower had been subjected to such extreme tests.

Just like he couldn't remember when another woman had turned him on this way. Her gold hoop earrings matched the bangles circling her wrists, which tinkled softly as she lifted a hand for Emilio to kiss. "It is an honor, sir," she said in her best Brittany attempt to show restraint. If her smile hadn't been so wide and her eyes so full of dollar signs, she might have pulled it off.

As intended, Emilio picked up on her signals. Rafe clenched his jaw when Emilio bent over her hand, ever so subtly taking advantage of his proximity to her cleavage, which was magnificent. Somehow, she'd managed to plump up her breasts so they all but burst from the molded cups of her dress.

"You Colombian men are all such charmers," Brittany purred demurely, touching her fingers to the solid gold slave necklace surrounding her neck.

"We are merely appreciative of true beauty," Emilio said, switching to English. "And speaking of true beauty, may I present my lovely wife, Sofia?"

Sofia Garcia stepped dutifully forward. "Welcome to our home."

Her English, like her makeup and hair, was perfect. Her smile appeared rehearsed, that of a woman used to living in her husband's shadow as well as accustomed to his flirtations.

"Your home is breathtaking." Brittany returned Sofia's perfunctory handshake and somehow managed to look envious and awestruck. "You ought to get Cesar to build one of these, Aliria," she said brightly, walking toward the atrium/rain forest.

"Señora Garcia." Rafe attempted to draw Sofia's attention away from Brittany's rudeness. He accepted the hand she offered and lightly kissed it. "We cannot thank you enough for opening up your lovely home to us. Thank you so very much."

"*De nada*. It is our pleasure. Now, please," Sofia said with a sweep of her arm, "let us move on outside so we can introduce you to everyone."

"Actually," Brittany said in an aside to Sofia, "I could really use a visit to the powder room."

"Of course. I'll show you—"

"Oh, no, no. I don't want to take you away from the rest of your guests. Just point me in the general direction and I'll find it."

"Certainly." Sofia gave her directions for both the downstairs and upstairs facilities in the event either was occupied.

B.J. leaned into Rafe, kissed his cheek, and winked at Emilio when she caught him watching her. "You go on ahead, baby. I'll just be a minute. I'll find you."

"Don't be long," Rafe said, watching her walk away, that damn dress accentuating every curve. "And don't get lost," he added indulgently, planting the seed of expectation that she might be a while.

Then he did a little silent praying that she would find Emilio's office right away so her absence wouldn't be suspicious. And so help him, if she went solo on him again and broke into the office on her own, he was going to wring her gorgeous neck—provided Garcia or one of the many goons he'd spotted positioned discreetly around the villa didn't beat him to it.

"Promise me," he'd insisted last night as they'd finalized their plan. "You do nothing without me knowing it."

"I already promised," she'd said testily. "We both look for opportunities to get into his office. If I see one, I only take it if it's possible to alert you. Just make sure you do the same."

It was like planning an assault on a terrorist camp with firecrackers. All they had going for them was smoke and mirrors with no guarantee they'd find anything to help them even if they got out of there without being caught.

*Desperate times. Desperate measures.* He'd been there before—but never with a woman he cared about. And the thought of her doing something reckless and getting herself hurt or worse . . . God, it ate at his gut.

"Rafe," she'd said when he'd pulled her against him last night, not giving a damn that he'd promised to keep his distance. "You need to trust that I can handle myself."

Yeah. He had to trust in something. Just like he had to pray that they didn't strike out. They were down to seventy-some hours and counting.

# 25

"There you are." Breathless and full of herself, Brittany walked into Rafe's embrace when she spotted him with Felipe and Rodrigo and their wives visiting around a poolside table. A small band played salsa music nearby. "My goodness. The Garcias certainly know how to throw a party."

Rafe introduced her to Maria and Belicia as children squealed in the background. Another band at the far side of the pool with a Shakira wannabe at the mike entertained the teens. Not ten yards away, a beautiful couple dressed in brilliantly colored native Colombian costumes danced and swirled to a sultry rhythm, providing yet another form of entertainment.

Food and champagne and every other drink imaginable flowed like water. While they'd barely just arrived, it was clear to B.J. that several of the partygoers had been heavily partaking of the Garcias' hospitality.

"It is so impressive that Emilio could gather so many guests on such short notice," she observed as a continuous stream of laughter rang through the crowd of what

B.J. estimated to be at least three hundred people. "And all for us," she added, sounding beyond important and pleased.

Felipe smiled. "No one would think of missing one of Emilio's parties."

Yeah, B.J. thought. That was probably because their lives wouldn't be worth a plug nickel if they declined an invitation from the drug lord.

"What is that music they're dancing to?" she asked Rafe.

"*Cumbia*. It's a mixture of Spanish and African."

"You must teach me," she insisted, using it as a ploy to get him alone so she could tell him what she'd discovered.

"Excuse us, please." He grinned at his cousins. "It would seem my lady wants to dance."

Instead of attempting the *cumbia*, however, Rafe twirled her into his arms and pulled her close. To anyone watching, they were lovers swaying to the beat of their hearts. And many were watching, she realized.

As Rafe turned his liquid brown eyes and seductive smile on her, she understood the envy in the eyes of the single—and some of the married—women in the crowd. She could almost feel the tip of the blade they'd have liked to shove in her back.

There was no denying that he was an incredibly beautiful man, a man who would turn heads no matter where he went or how he dressed. But never more so than in this setting, surrounded by powerful men and privileged women, had she understood the full impact of not only his physical appearance but of his bearing on both women and men. Everything about him said confidence, competence, and power.

"What did you find out?" he whispered close to her ear as his hard body moved sensuously against hers.

She leaned back, smiled into his eyes like a besotted lover, and reminded herself once again that this was all an act. "There was only one locked door on the main floor. Fourth door on the east side of the atrium. That has to be Emilio's office."

He pressed his lips to her forehead and she felt a shiver ripple through her despite the warm Colombian sun. "Guarded?"

"No." She nestled her cheek against his chest and felt just a little too contented there. "Now that the party has moved outside, the house is practically empty."

A shriek of laughter, followed by a loud splash, sounded from the adult pool. Someone had apparently fallen or been pushed in. "Everyone's getting pretty happy." Rafe took her hands in his, kissed them, then looped them around his neck. "Emilio's parties are notoriously wild."

Speaking of wild, all this close body contact and playacting was taking a toll. Her heart went crazy when his large, warm hands skated down her ribs, then lower to caress the small of her back. She felt the hard thickness of his erection swell against her belly.

"Sorry," he murmured with a slow, sexy smile. "I don't seem to be able to control myself around you, *mi amor.*"

"Um . . ."

He chuckled. "Blushing? How sweet."

She couldn't believe that he thought it was funny. "Will you just get your mind back on the operation?"

"Trust me, *cara*. I know what's at stake. But you can blame yourself for distracting me. That dress . . . every man here is panting after you and calling me a lucky bastard."

"Well let's hope you do get lucky," she said, needing to derail this line of conversation, "or that I do." One of them had to get into Emilio's office.

"Let's let the party play out awhile longer," he said, swaying to the music. "The mellower our host becomes, the easier it will be to get past his guard."

"Speaking of our host," B.J. said, spotting Emilio over Rafe's shoulder, "he's heading this way. Looks like he's bringing a contingent of his lieutenants with him."

"Must be time for the big talk." Rafe smiled into her eyes. "You may be looking at the newest member of the Munoz/Garcia bank and drug cartel."

"Either that or they're going to fit you for cement shoes."

"And would that bother you, *cara*?" His eyes searched hers, sober for a change, no hint of a smile on his face now. "If something were to happen to me, would that bother you?"

Yeah, it would bother her. Damn it. She had fought it every step of the way, but she would care if something happened to Raphael Mendoza. She still had too much of a self-preservation instinct, however, to admit that weakness to him.

"Depends on whether or not you took me down with you."

One corner of his mouth tipped up in a crooked smile. "Such a hard, cold heart. And such a pretty liar," he added, letting her know he was on to her. "You would care very much, I think."

Then he kissed her and walked off to meet Emilio.

Yes, she thought, watching him go, she would care very, very much.

Over two hours had passed since Rafe had gone off with Emilio, Cesar, and the other men. B.J. had kept a distant eye on them where they were clustered in a group at the far end of the paved terrazzo, cigar smoke rolling, heads nodding, a small contingent of muscle standing close by protecting their privacy.

B.J. had made Brittany-esque attempts to ingratiate herself with the women and flirt with the men, all the while watching the villa, looking for an opportunity to go inside and get into Emilio's office. She'd managed to dump glass after glass of champagne into various potted plants while everyone around her was happily getting a party buzz on.

Even among the family and friends, however, there emerged a pattern of cliques as clusters of people mellowed out here and there on the lavishly appointed grounds. Many had changed into swimsuits and were splashing in the pool. The children were all in the care of nannies and twilight was setting in.

Now, B.J. decided, was the best opportunity they were going to get. She wandered as close to the men as she dared, laughing too loud as she visited, touching too easily—in short, apparently drinking too much and feeling the effects. She got Rafe's attention, waved giddily, then blew him a kiss—her signal that she was going in.

She didn't stick around to see his response. She already knew what it would be. He'd have given her a "no go" signal because he felt he should take the risk, but the bottom line was she had the opportunity and it was now or never.

She wandered aimlessly toward the villa, made a big production of snagging a full champagne flute from a waiter passing by with a full tray, then, with a tipsy walk, angled toward the far side of the villa where the landscaping was thick with tall shrubs, pineapple and coconut palms, and trellises lush with flowering bougainvillea. Careful to make sure she wasn't being watched, she tucked in behind a trellis, then ducked around the side of the house where she'd spotted an entrance door on an earlier pass.

Without wasting another second, she hurried down the hallway, checked to make sure no one was inside, and entered the grand foyer. So far so good. If anyone did intercept her, she was simply admiring the waterfall.

Heart kicking up as the risk grew greater, she approached the locked door, slipped a pin out of her hair, and went to work. This lock was more stubborn than the lock on Cesar's office—either that or her hands weren't as steady.

"Come on, come on," she pleaded as her hands started to sweat. Finally, the lock gave.

After one final look over her shoulder, she opened the door, slipped inside, and locked it behind her.

"Oh, yeah," she murmured as she quickly scanned the room. This was Emilio's private domain. Heavy glossy wooden furniture, imported Persian rugs, walls filled with erotica. Priceless erotica, she imagined, but porn just the same. No surprise there. Emilio had struck her as a pig at first sight.

In the center of the room was a desk roughly the size of a banquet table. Bookcases and pedestals were filled with more erotica, bronzes, ceramics, and earth-tone pottery that suggested they were possibly pre-Columbian artifacts. Among them were some compelling nudes but it went downhill from there to women on women, men on women, men on men . . . bestiality.

She shivered and quickly sat behind the desk. She opened up the laptop computer, desperately ignoring the nine-inch anatomically correct porcelain phallus perched on the edge of the desk near a silver tray that held a bottle of scotch and a single glass.

The screen came to life. No surprise that Emilio had chosen a graphic sex scene as his wallpaper.

"The man is a pervert," she muttered, quickly opening up his document folder.

She scrolled through the folders, looking for something that might alert her to the one she was looking for. Her heart almost leapt out through her throat when a folder jumped out at her: URA.

It was the code word Stephanie had discovered. This had to be it. She opened the folder, every cell in her body tensed in anticipation of someone bursting into the room at any moment.

"Oh, my God," she mouthed as she opened the first of ten documents in the folder and quickly scanned it. She didn't have time to read it thoroughly but she knew that they would find everything they needed. The trick now was copying it and getting out of here so they could read the documents later.

Her fingers were trembling on the mouse as she closed the document, then the folder. She reached between her breasts, where she'd been carrying the flash drive all day, and hurriedly plugged it into a USB port.

"Hurry, hurry," she whispered, waiting for the data to copy and breathing a serrated sigh of relief when it finally finished.

She tucked the drive back into her dress and returned the computer settings back to the desktop and closed it. Then she hurried around to the front of the desk, took one last look around to make certain she'd left no telltale signs.

That's when she heard footsteps outside the office door.

Her heart stopped when she recognized the sound of a key in a lock.

* * *

Brittany was sitting on top of the desk, facing the door, her legs seductively crossed, her skirt hiked up high on her thighs when Emilio Garcia walked into the room.

He stopped abruptly when he saw her. And in his eyes she saw a killing rage.

"What took you so long?" she asked with a sly smile, then made an elaborate production of recrossing her legs and planting her palms behind her hips on the desk.

"What are you doing in here?" Rage cooled marginally to suspicious but intrigued anger.

"Emilio . . . Don't be coy. You know why I'm here." She tilted her head coquettishly and arched her back, a not so subtle attempt at seduction. "I'm waiting for you. Or did I read you wrong when we first met?"

She slid slowly off the desk, making sure he got a good eyeful. Averting her eyes, she reached behind her, ran her fingertip suggestively along the length of the porcelain phallus before looking back at him from beneath her eyelashes.

"I saw the way you looked at me," she said. "I saw what you wanted to do to me."

While he still looked suspicious, she could see the carnal heat in his eyes along with the effects of the scotch he'd been drinking all day. She turned her back to him, holding her breath, hoping that he was watching her ass instead of puzzling out her real reason for being there. She prayed to God that Rafe was on the way. He knew she was in here and he would have been watching Emilio. What they were going to do to get out of this, she didn't know, but in the meantime, all she could do was stall.

Willing her hands not to shake, she uncorked the crystal stopper on the bottle of scotch and poured two fingers. Glass in hand, she turned back to him.

"I thought we could continue the party in private."

Her mind raced a mile a minute as she dipped an index finger into the scotch, brought it to her mouth, and licked it.

He advanced toward her, lust in his eyes.

"Have you forgotten you have a fiancé?"

She smiled, shrugged. "Why settle for a foot soldier when I can have a general?"

He liked that. He liked it a lot. The bastard.

It took everything in her not to flinch in revulsion as he reached out, ran the tip of his finger down her cheek, across her jaw, then trailed it along the length of her throat. "So, you will fuck me while your lover waits for you."

She affected a wounded look. "You make it sound so naughty." Then she smiled, fighting panic as his hand slid around to the back of her neck. He grabbed a fistful of her hair and jerked her roughly against him.

His breath reeked of cigars and scotch. His body smelled of sweat and sickeningly sweet cologne. "I must ask myself, are you worth the trouble?"

Her breathlessness wasn't an act. She was scared to death but she couldn't let him see her fear. "Oh, I'm worth it. But if you like, take your time. Think about it. You know where to find me when you decide."

She started to move away, thinking maybe this was her ticket out of there.

His fingers tightened painfully in her hair.

"Or maybe you should prove your worth to me now."

He reached for his belt with his free hand and pushed her to her knees. "Put that pretty mouth to work, *puta*. Then we shall see."

# 26

Rafe was half out of his mind. From the moment Emilio had ended the meeting he'd been trying to wade through the throng of well-wishers and get to B.J.

Damn her! She'd gone Rambo on him again, refusing to wait for his okay. He knew what she was doing. She was in the drug don's office—and Emilio was heading straight toward the villa.

He smiled and patted backs and shook hands and kissed cheeks and bit back his panic as he worked his way toward the house, constantly tracking Emilio. As long as he'd been in sight, Rafe had held it together. But he'd lost Emilio by the buffet table, only to catch a glimpse of his back disappearing through the atrium doors.

He had to get into the villa now.

"Raphael."

Cesar's voice stopped him.

*Damn it.*

He froze, pasted on a smile, and turned to his uncle. "Wonderful party," he said.

Cesar nodded, his gaze hard on Rafe's face. "And the meeting with Emilio. It went well, I think."

"Yes. Yes, it seemed to."

"I believe he will be contacting you very soon with his decision."

"My hopes are high," Rafe said with a nod. "You must excuse me now. The wine," he said, implying that he needed to relieve himself.

Cesar smiled and clapped him on the back. "Go."

He was already gone, sprinting inside, then finding the fourth door on the east side of the atrium per B.J.'s report.

The door was open a crack when he reached it. When he saw Emilio's hand knotted in B.J.'s hair, heard her gasp of pain as he pushed her to her knees, he almost lost it but knew if he did that he'd get them both killed.

He drew a bracing breath, then burst into the room. "Emilio?"

The don paused in the process of unzipping, slowly turned around. And said nothing.

Rafe made a big show of taking in the situation, then drawing the only conclusion a man who wanted into the organization could draw.

His eyes grew hard as he turned them on B.J. He stalked toward her, grabbed her arm, and dragged her to her feet.

"You whore! You fucking bitch!"

Brittany whimpered.

"This? This is what I can expect from you? To force yourself on any man with a cock? On a man as important as Emilio Garcia?"

"He . . . he made me," she wailed, tears streaming down her face.

"Shut up! You think I believe anything you say? I could kill you for this," he spat, pouring it on. Emilio had to buy this. He had to buy that Rafe could kill her, not just for cuckolding him but for the insult to the drug lord.

B.J. took all her cues from him. She whimpered like a spoiled, scared brat. "Please, you must believe—"

Rafe drew his arm back and slapped her across the face. "I said, shut up."

He hated hurting her. But his anger had to look real or they could both end up dead.

"Emilio. I beg your forgiveness." Rafe closed his eyes, breathed deep, dug for composure. "I sincerely hope this will not influence your decision concerning our business discussion."

Emilio looked from Rafe to Brittany and back again. "You need to find yourself a good Colombian woman. A woman who knows her place," Emilio said, and Rafe could sense that he not only embraced the opportunity to lay all the blame on Brittany but was relieved that Rafe's anger was not directed at him.

"Apparently," Rafe said, glaring at B. J. as she wept quietly. "Again," Rafe said, embarrassed, "my apologies. You will understand, I hope, that I feel the need to excuse myself from the lovely party." He jerked B.J.

roughly against him. "I have business with Brittany that I must attend to."

"Certainly," Emilio said. "I'll have a car sent around front to take you back to Cesar's."

"Thank you. And if I could impose on you to inform Cesar that Brittany developed a headache and I had to take her home. I do not wish for him to leave the party early on our account."

"Of course," Emilio said.

Rafe nodded his appreciation, then dragged Brittany toward the door. "You may not have any pride but you will not embarrass me further by wailing in front of the other guests or the driver. Now pull yourself together."

He apologized once more to Emilio and forcefully ushered her out of the room.

"Remind me not to tick you off for real," B.J. whispered when they were settled in the back of the limo with the privacy glass closed and the radio turned up so there was no chance the chauffeur could hear them.

Rafe stared straight ahead, his jaw tight, his hands clenched into fists on his thighs. "Oh, trust me. I'm pissed."

Okay. She'd walked into that one. She'd known he would be angry. Just like she'd known he would come for her.

"Look, Mendoza—"

He held up a hand, cutting her off. "Do not say a word."

He looked at her then, and the anguish in his eyes almost destroyed her. "You made me hurt you."

The slap. Yeah. She'd known he'd be beating himself up over that. "I'm fine. And it was necessary."

"None of it would have been *necessary* if you hadn't decided you had to play hero and take on Emilio by yourself. What would you have done if I hadn't gotten there?"

She'd been about ten seconds from faking a drunken stupor and passing out on the floor, that's what she would have done. "I knew you would," she said simply.

The minute the words were out of her mouth, the stark unvarnished truth of them hit her like a blow. It was true. She had known he would come. She'd trusted him to come. Without question.

The realization stunned her. On past ops she had always relied on her backup because they'd been paid to do the job, just as she had. It was all for the good of the op. But with Rafe, it was different. She'd inherently known it was different. She'd understood that duty or not, he would have come for her, because he had feelings for her.

One part of her wanted to embrace the idea. Another part, the part that guarded her from disappointment and pain—didn't want any part of it . . . didn't want the responsibility of knowing someone would willingly put his life on the line for her simply because, well, because she was important to him.

She'd seen just how important when he'd burst into Emilio's office. She saw it now, in the thousand-mile stare that told her he was so angry he couldn't talk or he might explode; in the rigid posture that told her that it took all of his control to keep from punching his fist through the window.

She didn't know how to feel about that. She didn't know what to think or what to say. So she said the one thing that put everything back in perspective.

She leaned in close, as if she meant to kiss him, a show for the chauffeur in the event he was watching. "I found the files," she whispered.

When he whipped his head her way, she touched her fingers to her bodice, tugged the flash drive out just far enough for him to see it, then tucked it away again. "Didn't have time to read them but I copied them to the flash drive. We'll need to get to Cesar's computer as soon as we get back."

"Well," he said after a long moment, "as long as you got results for risking your life, it was all worth it then, wasn't it?"

Okay. So he wasn't past his anger yet.

She breathed deep, deciding to quit while she was behind. The rest of the drive back to the Munoz villa passed in angry silence, both of them, if not content, at least resigned to be alone with their thoughts.

And the thought B.J. kept coming back to was that while her confrontation with Emilio Garcia had terrified her, the idea of letting Raphael Mendoza into her life scared her to death.

It took a while for the maid to come to the door of Cesar and Aliria's villa to let Rafe and B.J. inside.

Clearly, because of the party the staff thought they would have the evening off and had either retired early or gone home.

"*Por favor*," Rafe said with a smile as B.J. hurried up the stairs ahead of them to their bedroom suite. "Don't trouble yourself. We don't need anything, and Señor and Señorita Munoz aren't going to return for hours yet."

"*Gracias*, Señor."

He watched the maid walk back to the servants' quarters. Hopefully that was where she'd stay. They needed to be able to access Cesar's office and his computer to read through the documents B.J. had copied.

He bounded up the stairs then stopped just outside their bedroom door. He had to get control of himself. He was still so angry at B.J., so full of fear for her. If Emilio had . . . he stopped himself, forced back the image of Garcia's hands on her.

"Get past it," he muttered, and opened the bedroom door.

*Cristo.*

She'd already stripped out of her dress and was standing there in a white thong, hurriedly arranging a skimpy lemon yellow tube top over her breasts.

All that pale, fragile skin. All the things Emilio could have done to her . . .

He snapped then.

All the anger and fear and love—yeah, *love*, damn it—she'd stirred in him with her careless bravery boiled to the surface like a lava flow. Blazing hot, out of control, unstoppable.

She'd barely registered that he was there when he dragged her into his arms, slammed his mouth over hers, and kissed her, long and hard. When he finally came up for air, her breath was as ragged as his and he hadn't relieved nearly enough of the tension that had built up inside of him.

Breathing hard, he knotted his hands in her hair, pressed his forehead to hers. "Another time, another place," he ground out, "and I'd have you naked and flat on your back."

Her eyes were wide with shock . . . and something else. Desire. "But it's not another time. And we have to get out of this place."

Breathless. She made him breathless. And stupid.

"Screw it. We both know there might not be another time."

He saw in her eyes that she understood that too as he backed her up against the wall, jerked down her top, and filled his hands with her breasts. She gasped, sharp and aroused, as he lowered his head and took her into his mouth.

"I am so not through being pissed at you," he murmured as he skimmed the thong down her hips.

"Yeah. I . . . Oh God . . . I got that," she whispered against his mouth as she frantically unbuckled his belt and shoved his pants down around his ankles.

Then he was inside her, slamming into her. She gripped his shoulders, hooked a leg around his hips, and cried out when he grasped her ass and lifted her. Frantic to go deeper, to somehow make her understand the depth of his fear, the strength of his arousal, he lost total control. He shot into her on a hoarse groan, all fury and fire and emotion rife with passions he couldn't even name.

Only heartbeats had passed since he'd taken her— yet a lifetime of need and discovery had just passed between them.

He held her close as they both came down from the rush. "You okay?" he whispered gruffly, his face pressed into the soft hollow of her throat where her pulse thrummed, fast and wild.

"I'm sorry," she murmured as he slowly lowered her to the floor. "I'm sorry I scared you."

"Yeah." He touched a hand to her face. "Me, too."

He kissed her again. A kiss filled with apology. "Steady?"

She laughed. "Never again."

"That's what you're wearing?" Rafe asked when she walked out of the bathroom less than five minutes later, readjusting her top. She'd somehow managed to shimmy into a pair of skintight, lime green spandex Capri pants.

"It's either this or one of those ridiculous dresses. Remind me to thank Reed for his brilliant wardrobe choices," she sputtered, slipping on a pair of gold espadrille sandals.

Okay. So they were both short on work clothes. He'd have to make do with what he was wearing, too.

She grabbed the flash drive from the bed and they headed out the door and ran quickly downstairs.

"This is becoming a habit," B.J. said as once again she picked the lock on Cesar's office door.

"I see a great future for you as a cat burglar," Rafe murmured dryly as they hurried inside the office and made a beeline for Cesar's computer.

B.J. found the key and unlocked the top desk drawer, then retrieved her cell phone while they waited for the computer to boot up.

"Jesus." Rafe cupped his palm over his jaw and squeezed after B.J. had loaded the folder from the flash drive and started scrolling through the documents she'd copied from Garcia's laptop. "The details are all here."

And the plan was chilling. So were the players. They'd suspected all along that Emilio Garcia and the drug cartel were merely middlemen, brokers, as it were, making a huge profit by helping whatever terrorist group was fronting the cash and would carry out the plan.

"Crystal was right," Rafe said when he saw the name of a known bin Laden associate pop up in a document. "There's our Al Qaeda connection. Sheik Abdul Azeem."

"Azeem? From the U.S. embassy bombing in Madrid last year?"

"The same."

"We've been waiting for him to rear his ugly head again."

"Looks like the wait is over. I can't believe some sonofabitch in the U.S. government sold our technology to this bastard." But the fact was, someone had. "Check the next document. We need to find the location of the facility."

Emilio was a stickler for detail—the drug don would no doubt use the documents as insurance in the event his money didn't come through. The next document they opened contained meticulous accounting of costs for the development of the project, for equipment, salaries, parts, shipping—all to a warehouse in Santa Marta.

"That has to be it," B.J. whispered, not wanting to attract any of the staff who might happen to wander by Cesar's closed office door. They were working in the dark with a penlight and the computer screen the only light in the room. "The facility is in Santa Marta. Look—building specs. I'll bet there's a blueprint in here somewhere."

A few more clicks and she found it.

"Gotta be the whole shebang," Rafe said after seeing how large the building was and its proximity to both a railroad line and the seaport. "Looks like they put all their eggs in one basket," he said, studying the blueprint for the building.

"I agree. See this? This part of the building is designated for E-bomb development, this part," she added, pointing to the screen, "for the Black Ruby cloaking device."

"And there's the missile storage," Rafe added.

"Is that a crane?"

He nodded, studying the diagram. "They'd need some way to load the missiles onto the sub," Rafe surmised.

"Quite the operation."

"Won't be when we're finished with it. Print that," he added, referring to the blueprint.

That plant would cease to exist provided Nate and the guys had been able to get the munitions they would need to breach a facility that size.

"It's going to be heavily guarded," B.J. pointed out.

"Understatement," he agreed as she hit the print button and then went on to another document.

B.J. breathed in sharply when she read it. "Oh, my God. There's the target. Stephanie was right. It's the Niagara-Mohawk power plant."

She glanced up at Rafe as he leaned in closer, a re-newed sense of urgency enveloping them both. The bastards were going to hit the plant near Syracuse, New York, and go for total and permanent blackout over a third of the United States. Only unlike the 2003 tem-porary blackout, there would be no recovery from this attack.

"When?"

"I'm looking . . . Oh God. The launch of the missile carrying the E-bomb is scheduled for midnight on the twentieth. Less than sixty hours from now."

Face grim, Rafe scanned the rest of the document, looking for more info.

"There it is," B.J. said, slumping back in the desk chair. "The sub carrying the bomb is due to leave port from Santa Marta at six a.m. on the eighteenth and travel up the eastern seaboard the next two and a half days. Rafe . . . that means the sub is leaving tomorrow morning!"

Rafe snagged the copy of the blueprints from the printer. "Pull the flash drive. We've got to get out of here, contact the guys, then hope to hell we can charter a flight to Santa Marta."

"But we still haven't found the U.S. connection."

"That'll have to wait until we have a chance to review the rest of the data. Right now we have to get to Santa Marta, intercept that sub, and keep it from leaving. And we've got exactly"—he checked his watch; it was closing in on eight p.m.—"ten hours to do it."

He could see that she didn't like the idea of leaving that piece of the puzzle unsolved. That made two of them. "Look, Green's taking care of Stephanie. I'm not worried about her. And we *will* find the traitor. One problem at a time."

Only their problems were just beginning.

The office door swung open. The light flicked on.

And Cesar Munoz walked into the room.

The Ruger Blackhawk he held in his hand was pointed dead center at B.J.'s chest.

# 27

"This is how you repay my hospitality? By breaking into my office?"

"Tío Cesar. I . . . I hardly know what to say. I beg your forgiveness." Rafe shot a chastising glare at Brittany. "I just found her down here. I have no excuse for her behavior. I don't know what she was thinking."

He had to sell Cesar a bill of goods and he had to sell it like his life depended on it.

"I was worried about my poor Peanut," Brittany cried, managing to make her lower lip quiver as she took her cue from Rafe. "I only wanted my cell phone. See?" She held it aloft, trying to look repentant. "My little baby . . . my Peanut has to be wondering where his mommy is. I just wanted to call my sister and check on him."

"Her dog," Rafe explained with an embarrassed if indulgent eye roll. "Peanut is her poodle."

"I just miss him so much," Brittany exclaimed, tearing up.

"That's no excuse for what you've done," Rafe said between clenched teeth. "Again, my apologies, Tío Cesar. I will deal with her, I assure you."

He grabbed B.J. by the arm and made a move for the door.

"Stay where you are," Cesar ordered. "I think perhaps I should deal with her."

Rafe affected a wounded look. "Tío Cesar, I understand your anger but I assure you, I can discipline my own woman."

"Then perhaps I should simply deal with both of you."

Now was not the time to quit selling. "I don't understand."

"What do you really want here? Who sent you?"

This was going south fast. "No one sent me. And you know what I want. You know why I'm here."

"What I know is that you had many opportunities to return to the family before now. So I must ask myself, why now? Just as I must listen to my gut. I have learned much of treachery over the years. I have learned to question what seems too good to be true. You have been dead to me for fifteen years, Raphael. Now you will talk, or you will die again. You and your *puta*. I will gladly start with her."

Rafe moved in front of B.J.

Cesar shrugged. "As you wish it then." He cocked the trigger on the .44 Magnum revolver and took aim.

The office door opened.

Still holding the Ruger on Rafe, Cesar looked over his shoulder and saw his wife enter the office.

"Put down the gun, Cesar."

It was Aliria as Rafe had never seen her before. Anger and resolve cast her face in stone. Only the tremor in her hands as she held an ancient cannon of a handgun in a two-handed grip gave away that she was also frightened.

Cesar looked from Aliria, who now stood to his right, to the gun in her hands. He laughed, like he was looking at a joke. "This is no business of yours. Leave us."

"Put down the gun, Cesar," she repeated, her voice clear and strong. "Or I assure you, I will shoot you."

Outrage darkened Cesar's eyes. "You will do nothing. Just as you have always done nothing."

"You are right," she said, stepping closer. "I stood by and watched you turn my brother into a criminal against his will, drawing him so deep into your dirty business that he could not get out." A single tear slipped down her cheek. "I watched you turn my sons into criminals. My sweet baby boys are now corrupt beyond redemption. But I have reached my limit, Cesar. I will not allow you to kill the only thing left of my brother."

"You knew what I was when you agreed to marry me."

"I knew," she conceded. "And may God forgive me for that. Not a day has gone by that I haven't mourned all that decision took away from me. All that *you* took away from me."

She held the gun level with Cesar's chest, but her hands were shaking so badly and her breathing was so erratic Rafe was afraid she would pass out.

"You love the power and the prestige I give you."

"But I hate myself. My integrity is gone. My freedom, gone. My brother. My mother." More tears fell but she squared her shoulders, looked him straight in the eye. "I know it was you who had them killed. My brother wanted to leave the cartel. He could no longer live with the guilt. So you had him executed."

Rafe felt his blood run cold. *Cesar? Cesar had killed his father?* Beside him, B.J. gasped.

Cesar shook his head. Sneered. "Put down the gun, Aliria. I demand it. You know you aren't going to shoot me. You're as spineless now as you were when I married you."

"No, Cesar. You have mocked me for the last time. I am no longer your slave. And I am no longer willing to stand by while you destroy my own blood. When Rafe came back to me, I decided then. Enough is enough. And you will not take the last of my family from me."

She drew a steadying breath . . . and pulled the trigger.

The explosion of sound hit the room like a bomb.

But it was the picture of Cesar, a circle of crimson spreading over the middle of his chest, that paralyzed Rafe. It felt like he was watching in slow motion as Aliria reeled from the recoil. Smoke curled up out of the gun barrel. An astonished look of disbelief and awareness of his own mortality froze on Cesar's face as he slowly crumpled to the floor.

It was B.J. who finally had the presence of mind to

spring into action. She dropped to her knees, pried the Ruger from Cesar's hand, and checked for a pulse.

She looked up at Rafe, shook her head.

Cesar Munoz was dead.

Rafe carefully approached his aunt. "Tía Aliria," he said gently, knowing she needed his support but not quite capable of grounding himself.

"Go now," Aliria said, snapping out of her shock. "You must go now."

"We have to help you with this," Rafe insisted. They couldn't leave her here with Cesar's body. It wouldn't be long before the staff would come running. They couldn't know that she'd killed him; she would be the next target of the cartel.

"I dismissed the security guards. Only the household staff is here. And they are loyal to me. It will be a very long time before Cesar's body will be discovered."

In that moment, Raphael knew she had been planning this day for a very long time. His heart broke for her, this gentle woman he remembered from his childhood. This sister of his father who had often worn bruises she'd tried to hide with makeup.

"I am so sorry." He carefully removed the gun from her unsteady hands.

She turned misty eyes up to him. "Forgive me."

He drew her into his arms. Held her. "There is nothing to forgive."

"Only a lifetime," she whispered against his cheek, and kissed him. "Now go."

"Rafe." B.J. touched a hand to his arm. "She's right. We have to leave."

He held his aunt a moment longer. "Be safe," he whispered to the only family he had left in the world.

"What do you mean, the Tompkins woman escaped?"

Alex Brady closed his eyes and lowered his head as the senator's anger ripped through the phone lines. "My men were outmanned and outgunned."

"In other words, you fucked up!"

"Look." Alex had had it. "I've lost a total of five men on this wild goose chase! All valuable assets, all difficult to replace. And the only thing fucked-up about the entire operation is that you were certain that Stephanie Tompkins's protection detail would be pushovers. Rent-a-cop types, if I remember your assessment correctly. Instead they're like some ninja warrior super squad. That's your fault, not mine. And if you want me to continue the search, it's going to cost you."

"It's already costing me."

Alex grunted. Then he named a figure.

"You've got a lot of nerve."

"No," Alex said. "I've got a lot of overhead."

"I'm not paying that price."

"Fine. Been nice doing business with you."

He hung up. Tossed the phone on the bed and started throwing his things in his duffel. He was done with this mess.

The cell phone started ringing almost immediately.

He ignored it. It was time to get out of town. At this point, the illustrious senator could offer him Fort Knox and he'd still walk away.

Far away. In fact, Barcelona sounded like the perfect spot to count his losses and regroup. The cell phone was still ringing when he took one last look around the room.

"Screw you, Senator," he muttered with a great sense of satisfaction, then let himself out the door. It was only nine p.m. If he hurried, he could still book a night flight to Spain.

Emilio Garcia could hear the party still going strong as he sat behind his desk in his office, sipping scotch and pondering Raphael Mendoza's future. And yes, thinking about his *puta* of a fiancée. Raphael had dragged the lovely whore out of there over half an hour ago and Emilio was still hard, still hungry, and still thinking about the slut's amazing body and lush mouth.

Women. Sex. Power. All three came to him like breathing. Free. Easy. Constant.

But now he had a decision to make. He clasped his hands together and tapped his index fingers against his chin. What to do? Mendoza wanted into the organization. Cesar seemed to approve. But something . . . something didn't feel quite right.

His phone rang, jarring him out of his pondering. He considered letting it ring and rejoining the party but then he saw the number on the caller ID.

Frowning, he picked up.

"*Hola*, Senator."

"We have a problem."

The keys to all six vehicles parked in Cesar Munoz's garage hung in a row just inside the door like soldiers. Rafe had grabbed the keys to a black brute of a Hummer and they'd made tracks straight to Medellín and the airport. Beside him in the front seat, B.J. had called Nate and filled him in on what they'd found on Garcia's computer. Then Nate had called Savage in Barranquilla so they could all mobilize and move on up the coast to Santa Marta.

"Time?" B.J. asked when the charter flight that Rafe had paid through the nose for landed at the Santa Marta airport two hours later.

"Almost eleven," he said as they walked briskly toward the terminal across a tarmac lit by floodlights.

Eleven o'clock. They were down to seven hours before the sub left port.

"Over there," he said when he spotted Savage, Gabe, and Doc waiting by the arrival gate.

Gripping B.J.'s elbow, he steered her over to the guys, saw the look on Doc's face when he got a look at B.J. in her skintight spandex and tube top, and had to bite back a warning.

Doc let out a low whistle.

"Do not say a word," she warned under her breath.

"I was just going to welcome you to Santa Marta."

She shot him a "yeah, right" look as they rushed out of the terminal and headed across the parking lot.

"Okay. So maybe I *was* also going to mention that those duds beat any op gear I've ever seen."

"There," she said with a tight smile. "You feel better now that you got it out of your system, don't you?"

Doc grinned. "Yes, ma'am. I do."

When Rafe shot him another glare warning him to back off, Gabe barked out a laugh. "So that's the way—"

"Zip it," Rafe interrupted, wishing to hell these guys didn't know him so well. Gabe had taken one look and he'd seen the way it was for him where B.J. was concerned. Nothing for it but to bear it.

"What's Nate's ETA?" Rafe asked as they approached a tan cargo van. Since Cartagena was twice the distance from Santa Marta as Barranquilla, he already knew that Nate would arrive later.

"They'll be here within the hour. As soon as we set up an FOB, we're to call him with the location and he'll join us."

Savage settled in the shotgun seat while Doc got behind the wheel and Gabe, Rafe, and B.J. climbed into the second seat.

"Nice toys," Rafe said after twisting around and looking under the tarp that covered most of the cargo area. The back of the van was full of automatic weapons, handguns, and ammo.

He had to grin when he spotted a Glock 19 and a

box of hollow-points. Someone had been paying atten-tion. B.J. would be a very happy girl.

There were also several pairs of night-vision goggles. The NVGs would come in handy since the night sky was overcast. "This it?"

Doc grinned over his shoulder. "What do you think?"

What he thought was that Nate would have a few surprises—most likely in the form of explosives.

"Let's roll," Rafe said.

Forty-five minutes later they'd located and checked into a decrepit, seaport no-tell motel a quarter of a mile from the target facility. Doc was just returning to the single dingy room with bags full of food and bottled water when Nate, Reed, and Lang pulled up in an older-model SUV.

It was five minutes to midnight.

"You doing okay?" Rafe asked B.J. when he caught her merely nibbling at her food.

She gave him a quick but not very reassuring nod. "I'm good."

She's lying, he thought. She was not good.

"We're slipping outside for a sec," Rafe said over his shoulder. Taking B.J. by the arm, he walked her to the door.

The night air smelled of sea salt, fish, and diesel from the cargo ships lined along the wharfs. A pair of hookers trolled the corner across the street. A drunk sagged against a building, head down, an empty bottle at his feet.

"What's wrong?" Rafe asked as B.J. leaned back against the motel wall.

"I told you, I'm fine. I'm just . . . regrouping is all. Getting my head together."

Okay. He got that. They'd been riding on the serrated edge of danger for days now. What he also got was that they'd both cheated death too many times to count on this op, and that was what was bothering him.

"Look," Rafe said, facing her. "Maybe you should sit this one out."

She looked up at him like he'd just suggested she cut off an arm. "What are you talking about? I'm not a quitter."

He rested his hands on her shoulders, squeezed gently, and said what he needed to say. "No. You're no quitter. But you're not a part of the team either."

Stunned silence. Then a knowing nod. "You mean the *boys'* club? Well, sorry. I can't do a damn thing about the fact that I can't stand up to pee."

"B.J." He shook his head, squeezed her upper arms. "That's not what I meant."

"Then what *do* you mean?"

Great. He'd wanted to reason with her and all he'd done was piss her off. Hell, maybe he ought to just go with it. "I don't want you on the op," he said flat out.

"Thanks for the vote of confidence." She jerked out of his hold.

He caught her. Hung on tight. "Damn it, B.J. It's not that I don't think you can hold up your end. You've more than proven that you're capable."

"Then what is the problem?"

All he could do was come out with it. "The problem is I can't trust you not to go Rambo on me again. Wait," he insisted, giving her a little shake when she tried to break away again. "It's not just you and me this time. There are six other men—six of my brothers—counting on everyone to be a team player. You pull one of your solo stunts and someone could die."

She closed her eyes, looked away before meeting his gaze again. "You know what your problem is? You have control issues. Wait. I'm talking now," she informed him when he would have interrupted. "I did what needed to be done at Cesar's and at Emilio's. I'm not stupid. I know how to minimize the risk, and I know when the risk is worth it. I would never take a chance that would jeopardize an op or the life of anyone involved in it. You're just ticked because what I did was effective and because you didn't get to micromanage every second of my time."

He stared at her long and hard. "Okay, fine. I'm pissed," he said, and then admitted, "because I'm scared to death of losing you. Damn it, B.J.," he went on, more gently now. "If something happens to you, I'll never forgive myself."

He drew her close, bent his head to kiss her. She jerked away like he'd hit her instead, stumbling before she caught herself.

"You are not my keeper," she whispered vehemently, her voice shaking. "You are not responsible for me. *I'm* responsible." She tapped a fist to her chest, eyes wide, her stance defensive. "I have *always* been responsible. Me. Just me. That's the way I want it. That's the way it's going to stay. So you don't have to worry about losing me, Mendoza, because I'm not yours to lose."

He stood in the darkened night and watched her whirl around and jerk open the motel room door.

"Nice work," he muttered, disgusted with himself. She was exhausted, fueled by adrenaline, about to put her life on the line—again—and he'd added to the mix by pressuring her about the one thing she feared more than death. The only thing he'd accomplished by bringing her out there to reason with her was make her more determined to finish the job she'd started.

He stared at the closed motel room door. Accepted that he'd lost that battle. When this was over—and by God, they would all get out of it alive—he was going to get her alone somewhere, lock her up if he had to, and convince her that she had nothing to fear from him. Nothing but love. Nothing but total commitment.

Yeah, he thought, slogging back toward the room, like *that* wouldn't scare her.

# 28

The party wound down and the last guest left by two a.m. "Go on to bed," Emilio told his wife when she came looking for him in his office. "I'll join you soon."

At two thirty, however, he was still sipping scotch, staring moodily into space. The senator's phone call had disturbed him. She and her hired thugs had failed to contain the Tompkins situation back in D.C. The woman was still at large. And Emilio knew that the longer a problem was left to breed and grow, the greater the chance of a security breach.

His BlackBerry vibrated in his pocket.

Only one person who had this number would dare to call him at this hour. His head of security.

"*Dígame,*" he said, then listened with a growing sense of anger.

Outrage boiled in his gut as Hector reported his findings on Raphael Mendoza.

So, Emilio thought after disconnecting. Raphael Mendoza was not who he pretended to be. Face recog-

nition software—the finest money could buy—had been
used to find a match. Yes, there had been information
about the Vegas financial wizard on the web. But there
had also been information about a young Sergeant
Raphael Mendoza, formerly of the United States Army,
and an older Mendoza photographed grieving at the
graveside of a fallen comrade, one Bryan Tompkins, son
of Robert and Ann Tompkins, brother of Stephanie.

He flipped his BlackBerry over and over in his hand,
thinking. He had known in his gut that Mendoza was
lying. Stephanie Tompkins and Raphael Mendoza
were more than passing acquaintances. And the timing
of Mendoza's visit to Colombia, of his *puta's* unex-
plained appearance in Emilio's office at the very time
Emilio stood to receive an obscene amount of money
from Azeem once the submarine left port at Santa
Marta—he checked his watch—in a little over three
hours, was coincidental at best.

Emilio believed in exactly two things—money and
power. He did not believe in coincidence.

He leaned forward suddenly, opened up his laptop,
scrolled through the documents until he reached the
URA file.

He felt his face go pale when he checked the view
details. The file had last been opened this afternoon,
just prior to the time he had found Brittany Jameson
waiting for him in his office.

"Where are they?" Emilio demanded in rapid-fire
Spanish twenty minutes later after pounding on Cesar

Munoz's door and waking up the household. Four of his trusted men had accompanied him to ensure that Mendoza and the woman would talk long before they died.

"They all left." Aliria clutched her night robe to her breasts. "Cesar didn't tell me where. The three of them, they left together."

"When?" he bellowed.

"I'm not sure. One . . . maybe two hours ago?"

Furious, Emilio stomped out of the house, checked the garage. The Humvee was gone.

"Take me to the airport," he commanded as the five of them piled into his Lexus SUV. "Call ahead and have my plane made ready."

He had a very bad feeling about this.

"They'll need a destination to file a flight plan," his driver said as he dialed.

"Santa Marta," Emilio said darkly. He knew he would find Raphael Mendoza in Santa Marta. But first he had to protect his investment.

For the next hour the lot of them poured over the blue-prints B.J. had printed in Cesar's office. Then they piled in the vans and made two drive-bys of the facility with NVG binoculars to get the lay of the land and a feel for security. Another two hours back at the motel hammering out contingencies, and they decided on the final assault plan.

The warehouse was constructed of concrete and steel. A dozen surveillance cameras were mounted under the eaves of the steel-reinforced roof. They'd counted twenty exterior security guards all toting AK-47s, the terrorist weapon of choice.

"Ideas on how the hell we're going to get inside? The damn building is reinforced like a missile silo," Doc said, frowning.

"It'd take a freight train to breach those concrete walls," Lang put in in his usual understated tone.

"Maybe we'll just have to find one," Savage said.

Four hours after checking into the motel, B.J. looked up at Nate when he gave her her assignment. "Seriously?"

"Like Reed always says." Nate glanced at Reed.

The cowboy smiled. "Go big or go home."

"*Big* being the operative word," she said, then set her mind to the task.

Rafe hadn't said a word to her since their little "chat" outside. She'd overreacted, she knew that. But damn it, she thought as they started gearing up, she couldn't deal with it. Not with his worried looks. Not with his caring. It was too much. *He* was too much. Too much to handle. Too much to count on.

So she'd slept with him and yeah, it had been amazing. Now he *thought* he cared about her. She apparently didn't suffer from the same delusion because she knew what happened when this was over. If they got through this alive, he'd go back to Argentina. She'd go back to DIA, and that would be the end of that.

Just like she'd told him. She took care of herself. Always had. Always would. That rush of longing and sinking sense of loss she felt every time she thought about the possibility of never seeing him again? Well, she'd deal with it. Because that was what she did.

"Commo check," Nate said.

She glanced around the motel room while a series of "Check. Checks" rolled out as they confirmed their radios worked. They were all in black T-shirts and pants and face black. Black baseball caps sat on their heads and they were loaded down with enough guns and ammo to start a war. Tactical-level body armor sat on the floor by the door.

Since Nate had had the foresight to pick up an extra set of clothes, she was dressed exactly as they were. She'd tucked her hair up under a cap, strapped a k-bar to her thigh, tucked a Glock in her waistband, and pocketed two extra magazines for her M-4 rifle.

"Everyone solid on their assignments?" Nate asked with a hard look around the room.

He was met by grim nods. "All right. I've got T-minus one hour, forty-five minutes and counting. Let's do this."

They parked the vans in a narrow dead-end alley between two abandoned warehouses approximately one hundred yards away from the target facility, which was located at the far end of the major shipping wharfs. The facility was old, one story, as large as a football field, and at first glance appeared vacant. The fairly new twelve-foot-high chain-link fence topped with coils of barbed wire, however, suggested otherwise. It was a lot of security for an abandoned building.

The streets were deserted; the six a.m. sub launch was one hour and twenty-three minutes away. The sun would make an appearance in one hour and ten minutes. They wanted to be long gone before either happened.

Rafe rolled out of the back of the first van, fixing his NVGs on top of his head. He cut a glance at B.J., who was definitely in her Xena mode. Five feet six inches of tightly coiled concentration, high-octane determination, and single-minded focus. She actually did look like a female version of Rambo in her face black and ball cap, the M-4 clutched self-assuredly in her small hands, her bullet-resistant vest zipped up tight at her chin.

She glanced over at him. He gave her a nod. A silent vote of confidence. A signal that he'd never doubted that she had his back. Just like he had hers.

Across the road in the railroad yard dozens of boxcars lined the labyrinth of crisscrossing tracks. Closer to the opposite end of the wharfs, a steam locomotive chugged and clanked as rails were reset and cargo was loaded. Another sat on the tracks nearby, the roar of the steam engine a loud and constant disruption in the dark. Commerce in Colombia was no different than in the U.S. It never slept. And this morning, the noise was going to work to their advantage by camouflaging the racket they were going to make. One more chugging locomotive in this active rail yard would never be noticed.

"Okay, boys and girl," Nate whispered, "you know where to go."

Doc and Savage shouldered the heavy scuba gear they'd picked up back in Barranquilla. Reed and Lang carried the limpet mines and C-4. Nate and Gabe's backpacks were full of frag grenades, and Rafe and B.J. handled extra ammo. He looked for signs that she might buckle under the weight but she squared her shoulders and sucked it up.

And Rafe fell a little deeper in love. Okay, yeah, and deeper in lust.

Single file, moving in a running crouch, they scuttled across the empty street and straight for a specific locomotive engine that sat at the far end of yet another dozen sets of rails. These tracks led to the closed bay of the warehouse.

Rafe was certain that the facility had never had a delivery like the one they were going to get tonight.

Like bees swarming a clover field, they buzzed around the dormant engine, made sure no one was on board.

"Go," Nate said, and Savage climbed up into the cab. Once aboard, he reached for the scuba gear and explosives. Next came the extra grenades and extra ammo.

Then Savage held out a hand for B.J.

"Wait." Rafe stopped her from climbing aboard by pulling her into his arms. He kissed her hard and quick. "Give 'em hell, Chase."

He gave her a boost and Savage tugged her the rest of the way up and inside the cab with him.

Seconds slogged by like hours as Rafe, Doc, Gabe, Reed, Lang, and Nate guarded the perimeters around the engine, waiting for Savage to fire her up.

Their entire plan hinged on this hulking two-hundred-ton monster, so when the engine hiccupped and then clattered to life the lot of them expelled a silent breath of relief.

"Piece of cake," Savage said when he climbed down five minutes later. He'd found a heavy-duty pair of wire cutters in the engine's toolbox and tossed them to Gabe. "We've got twenty minutes until the boiler's hot enough to build up any speed."

"Then that gives us twenty minutes to level the playing field," Gabe said, and they all headed for the chain-link fence.

Rafe couldn't help himself. He grabbed Savage's arm, stopped him. "She going to be able to handle it?"

Savage shot him a look. "She can handle you, can't she?"

Fuck. He hadn't known that he'd been so obvious.

"Yeah," he admitted as he joined the rest of the guys at the fence. "She sure as hell can."

From her lofty perch in the locomotive, B.J. watched the guys as one by one they squeezed through the hole Gabe had cut in the fence. Per the plan, they split up, four advancing to the left, three to the right. Through the green glow of her NVGs they looked like eerie little alien spiders scrambling in the night. Rafe was in the group with Doc and Jones. She recognized the way he moved. She watched them until they ducked out of sight behind a stockpile of wooden pallets.

The plan was for them to take out the surveillance cameras first. The security guards would be next. Seven against twenty. She didn't like the odds and the fact was there could actually be more guards they hadn't spotted on their drive-by recon. For certain there were more inside the huge warehouse, which they were counting on her to breach all by her little ole lonesome. Well, her and Betsy here, which was the name Savage had given the locomotive engine.

"Temperamental as a contrary woman," Savage had said in that soft southern drawl of his as he'd flipped switches and spun dials and coaxed the engine to life as if he did it every day.

"My granddaddy was an engineer," he had told her as he'd made adjustments and checked gauges. "Nothing made me prouder than riding those rails with him."

"I take it he taught you everything he knew?" B.J. had asked, feeling overwhelmed by the complexity and the size of the enormous machine.

"Almost." Savage had winked at her then. "No need to worry. I'll walk you through everything you need to know."

And then he had.

"Driving a steam locomotive is a rush! Feels like riding a dragon," he'd informed her as he caressed the controls. "The steam chuffs, smoke swirls, the engine shudders, and you feel like you're guiding some living, breathing beast that you control with sheer muscle. There's no power anything on this baby. An eight- or ten-hour shift on the footplate will test a big man—but you only need eight to ten seconds, so you'll be fine," he'd told her.

She hoped he knew what he was talking about.

"That big lever running horizontally across the cab from left to right is the throttle. You're going to use it to open a valve that controls how much steam is piped into the cylinders. Now, see that bar at the bottom right, the one that's about a yard long?"

Yeah, she'd seen it.

"That's the Johnson bar. When I contact you, you're going to lever that sucker forward . . . but not all the way, got it?"

She had it. Once she engaged the Johnson bar, the engine was going to charge forward. The locked chain-link gate would be no match for the steam engine loco-motive. Neither would the steel-reinforced door of the warehouse that was rolled down and locked tight. B.J. and Betsy didn't care.

"Now, this is key," Savage had added. "You've got three hundred yards before you ram through the closed bay door. This sucker isn't going to stop on a dime. So as soon as you get yourself some forward momentum, count on inertia to do the rest. Halfway to the building, power down. You don't need speed. You need muscle and this beautiful old lady will glide right on through in damn magnificent fashion. And we'll be there waiting for you. Me and Rafe and the boys."

She checked the water glass now as he'd instructed her, was relieved to see the level was rising, which meant the steam was also rising. Then she glanced out the window into the dark. She couldn't see them anymore. But she knew what they were doing.

Leveling the playing field.

She touched her fingertips to her lips. Still felt Rafe's kiss. Damn that man. That controlling, amazing, make-her-knees-weak man.

"Don't get yourself killed, damn you," she whispered into the dark.

He wouldn't. He'd be fine. They'd all be fine. She had to believe that. Just like she had to keep her head in the game because Casey Jones was not at the wheel. She was.

*Jesus.* She was going to drive a fricking train.

# 29

"I might have known you'd be the one to end up bleeding," Doc sputtered in a low whisper when he, Rafe, and Savage caught their breath by the big steel door of the warehouse where the railroad tracks disappeared inside.

They were all breathing hard, adrenaline pumping, and in Rafe's case, blood as well as Doc covered the wound with QuikClot to slow the bleeding.

"Just wrap some gauze around it," Rafe grumbled, embarrassed that one of the guards had gotten a lick in before Rafe had been able to take him out. "It's only a scratch."

"To match that bad itch you've got for a certain DIA agent," Doc concluded as he cut a length of gauze off a roll with his trauma shears, then quickly bound it around Rafe's forearm.

"Now?" Rafe groused, wiping the sweat from his forehead by rubbing it on his shoulder. "You're going to give me shit *now*?"

Doc taped the bandage in place, then shot Rafe a candy-eating grin. "It just wouldn't feel right if I didn't."

"Heads up," Savage said, and all three of them squared off, guns ready.

"Hold fire." It was Nate. "Sit rep."

"Except for Lover Boy taking a blade in the arm," Doc reported, "we're good. Nine guards. All out of commission."

Nate nodded, both approval and confirmation that he, Gabe, and Reed had neutralized the rest of the exterior security detail. "You okay, Mendoza?"

"I am fucking fine," he muttered. "Colter's a drama queen."

"Speaking of queens." Savage nodded into the dark toward the locomotive chugging away in the distance. "That woman is royalty in my book."

"She had enough time?" Nate asked.

Savage checked his watch. "Twenty minutes exactly."

"Then raise her on the radio."

"Roger that. Savage to Casey Jones," he said into the commo mike attached to his shoulder. "Lock and load, darlin'. It's curtain time."

"He called her darlin'," Reed said, dying to get a rise out of Rafe.

"He calls *you* darlin'," Rafe grumbled back. "Anything you two want to share?"

"An eight a.m. flight back to the States," Lang said, then jerked his head toward the tracks.

"Atta girl." Savage sounded like a proud papa bear as the locomotive started barreling down on the building.

"Let's go," Nate said, and they all ran to meet the oncoming engine.

Rafe was the first to latch on to the handrail and hike himself up on the ladder as the engine chugged slowly forward. He held out his hand and, one by one, helped the other guys on board.

"This," Reed said, catching Rafe's outstretched hand and pulling himself up on the moving train, "is what us Texans call a real yee-haw moment!"

"And what do you consider adequate perimeter security?" Emilio asked Abdul Azeem in English since they did not speak each other's languages.

Azeem's silence, Emilio knew, was one of disapproval. The sheik had already been on site at the facility for the launch of the sub transporting the E-bomb, which was scheduled for exactly thirty-four minutes from now. He had not been pleased when Emilio had called him in-flight from Medellín to Santa Marta and informed him he would be arriving to share concerns.

The dark look on his face when Emilio was admitted into the facility by way of a side door a mere five minutes ago reinforced the sheik's displeasure. Emilio did not care about the sheik's pleasure. He cared about his investment, and everything from the senator's call to Raphael Mendoza's sudden disappearance told him that his investment was in jeopardy.

"I can assure you," Azeem said finally, "all precautions have been taken to ensure this site is secure."

"Then you won't mind showing me your command center."

Azeem glared, then reluctantly nodded. "As you wish."

Emilio followed him down a long corridor that led to an open warehousing area filled with equipment and conveyor belts. "The assembly station," Azeem explained as they proceeded another twenty yards. "Inside." Azeem unlocked a door and opened it wide. Two men sat at a bank of blank monitors, all of them working frantically at the controls.

A look of alarm crossed Azeem's face and he stepped hurriedly over to the control panel. "Why are the surveillance cameras dark?" he demanded.

The frantic technician rattled off something in Arabic that Emilio didn't understand. A heated and frantic exchange followed.

"What's happening?" The knot of dread that had been clutching at Emilio's gut since he'd discovered Raphael Mendoza had chartered a flight to Santa Marta coiled tighter.

"The cameras all went black several minutes ago and these fools did not deem it necessary to inform me."

"Check with your exterior guards," Emilio ordered. "Do it now!"

Azeem pulled a two-way radio out of his pocket. Spoke into it. Repeated his question once. Then again.

"They are not responding."

Emilio snagged an assault rifle from the rack by the door and tossed it to Azeem. "This facility is under attack!" he roared, and grabbed a weapon for himself. "Alert the interior guards, you fool!"

He headed out the door at a run just as a horrendous screech of metal scraping metal echoed through the cavernous warehouse. The building shuddered, almost knocking him off his feet. The far corner of the steel roof sagged, ripping through electrical wires and sending sparks skittering and crackling through the expanse of the room. The lights flickered, then died.

Emilio steadied himself, then, murder in his eyes, stalked across the warehouse.

He didn't have to ask himself who was responsible for this attack. He'd known that Raphael Mendoza was trouble. His mistake had been not listening to his gut soon enough.

Mendoza's mistake had been thinking he could lock horns with Emilio Garcia and live to talk about it.

"Hurry!" he demanded. "They intend to stop the sub. We can't let that happen."

B.J. was still gripping the Johnson bar with both hands, putting all of her weight into it as the engine finally screeched to a stop inside the building. Concrete dust rolled in billowy clouds all around them. Gnarled sheets of steel, chunks of concrete, and trailing electrical wires rained down, crashing against the locomotive as the chaos of the collision slowly ebbed to the low hiss of the steam engine and the settling of the broken building.

Reed grinned over at her as they all gathered their gear and ordnance. "I love a woman who knows how to make an entrance."

She couldn't help it. She grinned back. "That was almost better than chocolate."

Reed gave her a high five and was about to pull her into his arms for a big bear hug when Rafe shoved the scuba gear into his chest. "Go make like a fish, pretty boy."

"How many times have I told you jokers I don't like water?" Reed groused as they piled out of the engine.

Doc clapped him on the shoulder as he slung his own scuba gear over his back. "Cry me a river. Oh, wait. We've already got an ocean. And a date with a sub. Now shake a leg. It's twenty-nine minutes to launch."

B.J. shouldered her pack of extra ammo, wouldn't let herself think about the white bandage on Rafe's forearm or the blood that had seeped through the field dressing. She couldn't think about it now, not and keep her head in the game.

Nate had pulled the blueprint out of his vest. He studied it with the help of a Maglite, looked up, flashed the strong beam around the building, checked the map again.

"Fifty yards dead ahead, a left, two rights, and a left," he said, pocketing the map. "Jones, Savage, Lang— you're on point. Mendoza, B.J., and I will guard the rear after Reed and Doc. Go."

With Gabe and his Maglite leading the way, they set off at a run, dodging fallen steel girders, chunks of concrete, and downed power lines.

"Rafe! Your seven o'clock!" Nate yelled just as a burst from an AK echoed through the building.

Rafe whirled and took a knee as the rest of the team kept moving. B.J. dropped to her belly. Beside her, Nate did the same. Together the three of them fired toward the muzzle flashes of at least five rifles, an explosion of sound and concussion and men screaming. And then silence.

"Go," Nate ordered, and the three of them rose and sprinted to catch up with the others.

Adrenaline overload. B.J. shook with it. Tried to regulate her breathing to control it. It was a rush. It was a pain. It was keeping her on her feet and threatening to buckle her knees. She was on autopilot now, hyper-aware and ultra-alert to even the most minuscule movement.

A tingle raced down her spine. She stopped, spun, shouldered her rifle, and fired just as a muzzle flash burst into the dark. She heard the sound of metal clattering onto cement, the heavy thud of a body hitting the floor.

For a moment she froze, locked in a dimension where reality warred with necessity and short-wired her brain.

"B.J.!"

Rafe.

His shout snapped her out of her stupor. *The fog of war.* The phrase zipped in, then right out of her mind as she kicked into gear and raced to his side.

"You okay?" he asked urgently.

"Good. I'm good."

They both knew she wasn't. No one was good when they were getting shot at. When they were shooting back.

"Go," he said, shoving her ahead of him, making sure he was pulling up the rear, where he was the most vulnerable to attack.

It took them ten minutes of firefights to reach the rear of the warehouse. A trail of bodies lay in their wake.

She shut out the screams of pain, the proof of mortality, as they burst out onto the wharf and took out the four guards assigned to keep the sub secure. They still had a job to do as they hit the warm night air that smelled of everything bad the seaport had to offer: dead fish, diesel, rancid flotsam that lapped against the creosote-treated pilings.

And there, no more than fifty yards from the dock, they could make out the humped back of the submarine where it rode, fully emerged in the inky black water.

"Thar she blows," Doc said.

Nate checked out the sub with night vision binoculars. "As we suspected. She's already armed."

He passed the glasses to Doc, who then gave a running commentary as he checked things out. "Missile bays are open. Check that. They're closing as I speak."

"They'll be taking her down any minute. Double-time it," Nate ordered, and they made a protective circle around Reed and Doc as they scrambled into their scuba gear. The waters of the Caribbean were warm enough this time of year to forgo their wetsuits. Time wasn't going to allow it anyway. They tightened the straps on their air tanks, checked the regulators, and stepped into their flippers. Without a word, they jumped off the wharf, wet their masks, and settled them over their eyes and nose.

"Pass down the limpets," Nate said when Doc gave the signal that they were ready for them.

Six mines in all, B.J. knew. Doc, a former Navy SEAL, was well schooled and highly experienced in underwater demo. He and Reed would set the limpet mines in critical spots around the hull of the sub, set the timers, then make like torpedoes and get the hell out of there.

Nate held up ten fingers for Doc and Reed to see.

Ten minutes. They had ten minutes to put the limpets in place or every inch of ground they'd fought to take would all be for naught.

"Let's go," Nate said as soon as Doc and Reed disappeared underwater. "We've got a plant to destroy."

And most likely several more waves of resistance, B.J. thought as they headed back inside to finish the job they'd started with the train.

It wasn't good enough that they stop the sub. They had to destroy the entire facility and everything in it to ensure their operation was shut down for good.

An auxiliary generator had kicked on while they'd been on the dock. Flickering, murky light illuminated a warren of hallways. Red warning lights blinked on and off above exit doors. The shrill *werup, werup, werup* of interior alarm sirens echoed through the space like screeching gulls, lending an eerie, grating urgency that set B.J.'s teeth on edge.

"Break into pairs so we can cover more ground." Nate divvied up the C-4. "Savage, you're with Lang. Take the southwest quadrant of the building. Gabe, you're with me. We'll hit the northwest."

That left her with Rafe and the northeast part of the structure since they'd already decimated the southeast section.

"Rig the blasts for fifteen minutes. Radio if you run into trouble, otherwise we'll meet you at the vans."

*If* they ran into trouble?

Rafe must have read her thoughts. "Almost home," he assured her, and they took off at a sprint.

"Clear," he said, and plastered his shoulders against the wall again after he'd taken a peek out into the corridor.

B.J. inched around him, then headed down the hall. Twenty yards later, they switched. "Clear," she told him after checking around the corner. They worked their way quickly through the maze of hallways until Rafe was satisfied they'd infiltrated deep enough into the northeast portion of the building.

"Stand back." He kicked in a door, entered with his rifle at his shoulder while the sound of round after round of automatic weapons fire reverberated in the distance. The guys were taking fire.

"They're fine," Rafe told B.J., reading her mind. His face grim, he shrugged out of his backpack and dug inside for the C-4.

B.J. stood over him, facing the door, her M-4 locked and loaded. No one was getting past her to get to him. She'd die before she let that happen.

*She'd die before she let that happen.*

The thought had been knee-jerk. Involuntary.

And the fear factor that had been fueling her every move since this night began kicked up a notch because she realized in that moment that it was true. She *would* die before she let anything happen to him.

Damn it. God *damn* it! She'd fallen in love with Raphael Mendoza. And yeah, she'd have sooner dodged a bullet than dealt with that untenable truth.

"We're set," he said, jerking her from one source of terror to another. "Let's get the hell out of here."

He didn't have to tell her twice. He took point, made sure the coast was clear, then led the way back down the trail of hallways. All they had to do now was make it across approximately fifty yards of open warehouse and they were out the door.

"Keep low," Rafe said, ducking down to a crouch as they scuttled across the open area, totally exposed.

She was about ten yards behind him when she heard several rapid-fire rounds of gunfire. A sharp pinch stung her upper arm, followed by a shockwave that rocketed down her bicep. Her fingers went numb. She watched with a disjointed sense of reality as the M-4 tumbled out of her hand and the floor rose up to meet her face.

The next thing she was aware of was a tugging pressure on the back of her vest, of multiple rounds of spent shell casings flying around her face as she was dragged across the concrete floor.

"I've got you," Rafe yelled above the *tat tat tat tat* of his M-4 and the *thump thump thump* of the answering AK-47s.

# 30

Rafe dragged B.J. behind a forklift, propped her up against the wheel as AK rounds zipped over their heads and ricocheted off the heavy piece of machinery.

"I'm okay," she said, struggling to sit up. "I'm okay now."

"Lie still," he barked, whipping out his Ka-Bar and slicing off the two top Velcro straps securing his Kevlar vest. He had no idea how badly she was hit but she was bleeding too damn much. He willed his hands to steady as he located the wound, breathed a small sigh of relief that the bullet had missed bone and gone straight on through her upper arm.

He found his packet of QuikClot, made a mental note to thank Doc for insisting they all carry it, and dumped it over the wound. Then he ripped an empty pocket off his cargo pants, folding it into a dressing of sorts.

"This part's gonna hurt," he said, and tightened the inch-wide Velcro straps over the makeshift bandage, securing it tightly.

"I'm good," she whispered, biting back a yelp of pain.

"We've gotta get out of here," Rafe said, reaching for his rifle.

A booted foot came out of nowhere and kicked it away.

A uniformed guard stood over them, the business end of his AK pointed dead center at Rafe's forehead.

The man on the guard's right was tall and slim, dressed in Western clothes. Rafe would have recognized Sheik Abdul Azeem in or out of traditional Afghan robes.

Emilio Garcia, covered in dirt, his expensive shirt tattered and torn, flanked the guard on the left. "You're not going anywhere."

B.J. forced herself to lie still and close her eyes as Rafe rose slowly to his feet, his hands beside his head. Slumped against the forklift's tire, she lay in the shadows and assessed the strength in her right hand.

The feeling had slowly come back, along with a searing pain in her upper arm where Rafe had tightened the dressing.

"You will pay with your life for the millions you have cost me." Emilio's voice was gravelly from exertion and eating smoke.

"Only millions?"

Garcia didn't find Rafe's flip response amusing.

"So, Azeem," Rafe said, all up close and friendly. "Next time you see Osama, tell him I said to go fuck himself for me, would you?"

Azeem lashed out, backhanding Rafe across the mouth. "You will not speak his name, infidel."

Rafe staggered, steadied himself, then wiped the blood from the corner of his mouth with the back of his wrist.

"He always this touchy?" he asked Garcia.

"So brave," Garcia spat. "We'll see how brave you are when I start slicing her apart. I'll make sure I cut very small pieces, make the pain last."

"It's too late, you sick bastard. You already killed her."

"Truly? Then it won't bother you if I empty my magazine into her."

He moved around Rafe, lifted the AK to his shoulder.

Rafe roared and threw a body block on Emilio that slammed him to the floor. B.J. heard the sickening smack of Garcia's head hitting the concrete floor as she drew her Glock and fired in Azeem's general direction.

Then she rolled out of his line of fire just as the nose of the guard's AK jerked upward and he toppled to the floor, dead. She'd been aiming at Azeem but the rounds from her Glock must have taken him down. Azeem took aim at Rafe. B.J. screamed a warning, then emptied her clip into Azeem as Rafe rolled Garcia's limp body on top of him, using it as a shield.

Azeem dropped to one knee, clutching his gut. B.J. shot out from behind the forklift, kicked the rifle out of his hand, then swung back around and drove her heel straight into his jaw. Then she slammed her foot down on his throat and pinned him on his back to the floor.

"I want a name," she said, meeting eyes filled with pain and terror.

She was peripherally aware of Rafe rolling Garcia off him and staggering to his feet.

"Tell the lady what she wants to know," he advised Azeem.

"Yeah," Savage's voice echoed across the empty warehouse. "Tell her what she wants to know."

Three more silhouettes appeared out of the dark behind him. They all made a circle around Azeem, their M-4s all pointed dead center at his head.

"Tell me who your U.S. government contact is."

Azeem pushed out a hoarse croak as blood pooled on the floor beneath him.

"Say again," B.J. demanded, lifting her foot off his throat.

When she heard the name, B.J. felt like someone had punched the breath out of her body.

"Sonofabitch," Gabe swore.

Yeah, they'd been looking for a traitor. And yeah, they'd been looking in their own government. But the hard fact was that none of them really wanted to believe it. They'd wanted a different explanation. They'd wanted to believe in good guys.

Abdul Azeem had just forced them to deal with the ugly truth.

"What are we going to do with him?"

"It's already done," Rafe said quietly.

B.J. looked down.

Sheik Abdul Azeem, a religious fanatic, a terrorist responsible for the deaths of thousands, was dead.

Rafe carefully removed the Glock from B.J.'s hand. She hadn't even been aware that she was still holding it.

"Let's get the hell out of here."

Reed and Doc were waiting in the vans, motors running, when the six of them materialized out of a darkness that hovered on the cusp of dawn. No sooner had they climbed inside than an explosion shook the earth and sent a shock wave reverberating through the surrounding area. B.J. watched through the van's windshield as two additional charges detonated, raining fire and billowing black smoke and flying debris a quarter of a mile in all directions. By nightfall there would be little left of the facility but smoldering ash.

They'd just pulled out onto the street when a fourth concussion of sound thundered from beyond the wharf. Even at this distance, a wash of sea spray splattered the windshield in a blowback from the charges Reed and Doc had set to destroy the sub and everything in it.

"Time to go home." Rafe put his arm around her and pulled her close.

"Yeah," she whispered as the adrenaline let down and left her with no defense against his embrace. "It's time."

"Hard to believe I had to get tough with you to get you to take me to bed." Completely comfortable in her nakedness, Stephanie lay back on the pillow, smiling at this beautiful man with the sensual hands.

Magic hands that performed magic acts.

She'd never been this way with a man before. Wanton. Uninhibited. Never known she was such a sexual creature. But then, she'd never known Joe. Not like this.

"Umm. Yeah. Right . . . there." She groaned in pleasure as Joe sat cross-legged in front of her, one of her feet flattened against his naked chest, the other foot swallowed up in those big, sensual hands as he massaged her arch.

She knew she was supposed to be frightened. She knew she was supposed to be far more concerned about what was happening in the real world. But she didn't want to face that world right now. She wanted to lose herself in this one.

Lose herself in this beautiful, amazing man as she'd been lost in him for the past two days and nights.

"I've always had a crush on you, you know," she admitted as he extended his massage to her calf.

He smiled, slow and . . . yeah, sweet.

"What's that mean?" she asked, curling her toes into his chest.

"It means I've always had a crush on you, too."

"Oh, yeah? So when were you ever going to let me know about that?"

His hands moved to her inner thigh and she shivered as his fingers brushed against her pubis.

"Guess we'll never know, will we?" He touched her then. Gently parted her thighs, caressed her until she arched against his fingers as they slid in and out of her.

"Joe . . ." She sighed his name, felt the heat coil tight and low. "God . . . Joe . . ."

And then he was there again. Inside her. Filling her. Thrilling her. Reminding her that this was the only place in the world she wanted to be.

"Tell me this isn't just about sex," she whispered later when he held her close, stroked her back, settled her as she made the slow, liquid descent from a Joe Green–induced high.

His hand stilled. And for an instant so did his breathing.

She pushed up on an elbow. Searched his face, saw nothing that she wanted to see there. Devastated, she looked away. How could she have been so wrong?

"Sorry," she said, telling herself she wasn't going to lose it. "I . . . well. I guess I put my foot in that one."

"Stephanie—"

"No. No, it's all right," she interrupted when she realized how uncomfortable she'd made him. "That was my bad. Forget I said anything."

"Stephanie." His tone demanded that she look at him. "It's not just about sex."

She searched his face. "But?" The qualifier was as big as an elephant.

"But you don't know who I am. You don't know what I've done."

Ah. Now she got it. "Don't know who you are?" Between making love and eating and sleeping and making love again, they'd talked and smiled and shared huge pieces of their lives with each other. "Joe, I know everything I need to know about you."

She sat up, pulling the sheet with her and tucking it under her arms. "Look. I know that up until these past few days we haven't spent that much time together. I know it's crazy but I feel like I know you better than I know myself.

"Bry . . . he used to write me about you guys, you know? He talked about you a lot. About how quiet and intense you were. About the strength of your character. About your big muscles and your bigger heart. So don't tell me I don't know you."

The look he gave her broke her heart. Not for her, but for him.

"You don't know what all I've done."

"You're right. I don't know. But I know this. What you did, you did because you had to. You didn't do it by choice. You didn't do it for yourself. You did it for something greater. Something important. Something that was right, not something that was wrong."

He crossed his hands behind his head, stared at the ceiling. "I'm not the man your parents would want for you."

Oh, my God. There it was. "Joe. They adore you."

She dropped the sheet, leaned over him, kissed him. "I adore you."

He finally looked at her. Touched a hand to her hair. A love so strong and tender welled up inside of her when she saw the longing in his eyes.

"You adore me, too." This she now understood. "We'll take it slow, okay?"

He smiled then. Surrendered. "So, what's your definition of slow?"

She laughed. "We'll figure that out as we go along."

He pulled her down next to him, held her against his side. "That'll work."

They'd just drifted off again when his cell phone rang.

"Green."

Stephanie watched his face as he concentrated on the call.

"What? What's happening?"

"That was Nate. They did it. They destroyed the bomb and the facility."

"Thank God." She hugged him hard. "Where are they? Are they okay?"

"Yeah. Yeah. B.J. and Rafe both had minor scrapes but they're okay. They're on their way home."

"Thank God," she said again. "This means we can go home, too."

"Not just yet," he said. "There's the little matter of taking care of a traitor."

At sixty-three, Senator Joan Bentley was still an attractive woman. She wore her straight, ash blonde hair in a stylish bob, exercised daily, and credited her size-four suits and low blood pressure to Pilates.

She preferred a good pinot noir to a chardonnay, liked her steak rare and her lobbyists generous. While she had been elected on the Independent ticket, she was known on the hill as a bipartisan player. She often found herself in the position of being the swing vote that could make or break a politician's favorite piece of legislation.

She enjoyed the power that afforded her. She enjoyed the perks that allowed her to live the lifestyle of her choosing. And while her divorce five years ago had been cause for concern, her reelection team had put a magnificent spin on the whole unfortunate incident by painting Freeman Bentley as a womanizer as well as a blood-sucking leech who depended on her generosity for his support. In the end, she'd won the sympathy vote and cruised to victory in a landslide for her fourth term in office.

If asked, she couldn't tell you the exact moment when she had made a decision that had forever altered the course of her life, but it had all started with Freeman. He had contested the divorce, of course. Getting rid of him had been costly; his insistent threats of blackmail were untenable. That was the first time she'd called Alex Brady and his team.

Freeman hadn't gone softly into that good night. His death, determined a tragic suicide, had been widely covered in the press. Even in death, he'd been a ball and chain around her neck.

Next came the opportunity to invest as a silent partner in her brother's brilliant Ponzi scheme. It had netted her millions. And when, on a goodwill visit to Turkey, she'd received a message from a cabinet minister requesting her discretion and her presence at an unsanctioned meeting, the investor in her sensed an opportunity was about to be put in play.

Of course, there had been no Turkish minister waiting for her when a car and driver had picked her up and delivered her to a secret location. None other than Sheik Abdul Azeem had greeted her and any kernel of patriotic red, white, and blue she still embraced gave way to the color of the sheik's money.

She thought about all these things now as she walked the halls in the Pentagon on her way to a meeting with Secretary of Defense Blaylock. While it was a bit unusual to be summoned to his office, it had been inevitable that she would eventually get a call to meet with him since she did sit on the defense appropriations committee. Her ties there had given her a direct pipeline to NSA and Alan Hendricks.

So no, she wasn't concerned about this meeting. Except possibly that it might keep her from her biweekly appointment with her manicurist.

There was no way in hell she could be tied to Azeem's terrorist plot. Failed plot, apparently, because the sky hadn't fallen as planned. She'd been trying to reach Garcia for over twelve hours to find out what the hell had happened. Someone had obviously fucked up.

Frankly, that was fine with her. She'd gotten her money and she hadn't been looking forward to the inconvenience of dealing with the fallout from the E-bomb. The Tompkins woman was still a worrisome detail but Hendricks would eventually take the fall for that and the dead couldn't defend themselves.

Finally, she reached the sec def's office. She ran a hand over her hair to smooth it and rapped on the door.

"Come in."

She smiled broadly, extending her hand as she approached the secretary's desk. "Secretary Blaylock. Good to see you."

Only when she was met with silence did she have the presence of mind to glance around the office. All the blood drained from her face when she recognized the three other individuals in the room.

Dale Sherwood from DIA.

Anne Tompkins from DOJ.

Robert Tompkins, whose face had become so famous when he'd been the advisor to President Billings.

She'd been blindsided.

A profound panic sent her heart racing. She was swamped by a wave of dizziness and disbelief as she turned slowly back to Secretary Blaylock.

His mouth was moving but the sudden ringing in her ears—her own death toll—drowned out his words.

The door opened and a uniformed officer entered the room.

Over. It was all over.

Everything she'd worked for. Everything she'd planned.

Prison. Oh God. She could not go to prison. They'd eat her alive there.

She sank down in the nearest chair before her knees gave out on her.

And then she prayed for a fatal heart attack.

# 31

"Thanks, Stephanie. Yeah. Yeah, I'm doing fine. Sure. We'll be in touch. And Stephanie. I'm sorry about your friend."

B.J. slowly hung up the phone. Careful of her arm, she leaned back against her sofa.

It was over. Stephanie had just called to let her know that Senator Bentley had spilled it all.

Greed. A four-term senator had sold out her country for greed.

B.J. was so tired. Tired of "patriots" who skewed their views of democracy for their own gain.

*"It's not like Nine-Eleven. No one was going to get hurt."* That was how the senator had twisted logic to soothe her conscience.

*"E-bombs kill electronics, not people. It would ruin the electrical infrastructure, that was all, an infrastructure that was already in shambles. So in the end, the attack would have been beneficial when we rebuilt."*

Never mind that the entire economic structure of the United States—already stressed to the max—would have collapsed, leaving the country vulnerable not only to a physical attack but to a financial takeover by a totalitarian government. Life as we knew it would have been over. Democracy would have been over.

And people *had* died. Lives *had* been affected. Stephanie had almost been killed and now she had to live with the knowledge that her friend Ben Brommel was dead because she had involved him in the search for the traitor.

B.J.'s own life had been affected. She'd experienced Raphael Mendoza and she would never be the same again.

It had been almost twenty-four hours since they'd landed back in D.C. She checked her watch. Twelve hours since she'd last seen Mendoza.

Doc had cleaned up her arm and treated it before they'd boarded the plane home.

"You need to see a doctor."

She could see in Rafe's eyes that he agreed but hadn't let the concern sway her.

"I will. When we get back."

He must have understood that she wasn't budging so he hadn't pushed. But as soon as they were wheels down and they made arrangements for a car, they headed straight for Gabe's doc friend at Bethesda, who had patched her up, shot her full of antibiotics, and ordered her to come back in two days so he could redress the wound.

"I'll be fine," she'd insisted when Rafe had brought her back to her apartment.

He'd wanted to stay. She'd known he wanted to stay. Just like she'd known she had to insist that he didn't.

"Okay. You want space. I get it," he'd finally said, his face worried and grim, and him not one bit happy about leaving. "But you call, okay? You need anything, you call."

She hadn't called.

She wasn't going to call.

What had happened between them in Colombia— well. It had happened. She couldn't take it back. But she couldn't look back either.

She could not let herself think about that man. That gorgeous, intriguing, soulful-eyed Latino. She closed her eyes. Let the pain wash through her, a reminder of what was at stake here.

Too much heartbreak. Too much pain. She wasn't ready—didn't think she'd ever be ready—to open herself up to either again.

That's why she put up walls. Fortified herself with emotional barriers. Raphael Mendoza was not going to breach them. She had a life to live and she knew exactly how that life was going to go.

Did it hurt to know Raphael wouldn't be a part of it? Yeah. It hurt a lot. But not nearly as much as it would hurt if she let him in and then he left her when he'd decided their love affair had run its course. Or when a bullet hit something vital and he ended up dying in some terrorist-infested jungle, or blown up in a bombing, or—

Stop.

She made herself stop because the thought of Mendoza dead ripped through her heart like a knife.

Bottom line, someday, some way, he would leave her. Just like everyone who had ever meant anything to her had left.

A single tear rolled down her cheek. She brushed it away angrily. She wasn't going to cry over what might have been. And then she ran over in her mind what she was going to tell him when he showed up—and he would show up—at her apartment. An hour later, when he rapped on the door, she was ready for him. More to the point, she was ready to say good-bye.

Rafe was so nervous his hand was shaking when he knocked on B.J.'s apartment door. *Cristo.* He didn't get this wired when he prepped for an op. Which told him exactly how important this woman was to him, and how difficult the fight was going to be.

"Just tell her how you feel," Jenna had said, covering his clasped hands with hers as he'd sat at the dining room table in the Jones's apartment that morning. "Speak from your heart. There's nothing more honest than that."

He couldn't believe he'd spilled his guts to Jenna. Maybe because he'd witnessed how deeply she and Gabe loved each other, yet in the beginning Gabe had run scared in the other direction.

"And whatever you do, don't give up. If you love her don't give up just because she's scared."

He'd never given up on anything in his life. He wasn't about to start now.

The door swung open.

"Hi," he said, and knew the instant he saw her face that he was in for the battle of his life.

"Come on in."

She stepped aside. And she wouldn't look him in the eye.

She wasn't wearing a speck of makeup; those amazing golden curls cascaded wildly around her face. She was barefoot in a pair of worn jeans and a simple white tank top. Yet she looked more alluring and sexy and real than Brittany Jameson in a hot pink string bikini.

She also looked bruised and distant, all of the shields protecting her emotions locked down tight. Yeah, the battle of his life was about to start.

"How's the arm?"

She lifted a shoulder. "Little sore, but it's fine. Yours?"

"Minor scratch. You're watching for signs of infection, right?"

"I said, it's fine."

Okay. She knew how to take care of herself and she didn't want to talk about it. He got it.

When she walked into the small living area and eased down on the sofa, he followed her. Took a seat on a leather barrel chair facing her.

"So when are you heading back to Argentina?"

Brittle and blunt. That was B.J.

"We had R and R coming even before Colombia. And the Tompkinses still intend to throw that engagement party for Reed. So I'll be sticking around for a while."

The look that crossed her face told the tale. She was not happy to hear that bit of news.

"Make sure you tell Reed congratulations for me. I didn't know what to make of him at first but the pretty boy kind of grew on me."

He smiled. "Yeah, Reed's a piece of work but he's a damn good man."

"They all are," she agreed with a nod.

Silence crept in like the sunlight sifting through the partially closed blinds covering her living room windows. Silence and a building sense of good-bye.

He didn't want good-bye from this woman. And he had to man up and face whatever resistance she was going to lob his way.

"Look. B.J." He hiked himself forward on the chair, propped his forearms on his thighs, and leaned toward her. "Can I just say something flat out?"

She swallowed hard, still wouldn't meet his eyes. "I think that maybe good-bye would be the best thing we could say to each other."

Even though he'd expected resistance, her words still hit him like a bullet. "Just like that? You don't even want to talk about . . . us?"

She glanced at him, then quickly averted her gaze. But he saw something in that glance. Longing. Regret. Sorrow. He wanted to fold her into his arms and hold her. Just hold on and tell her everything would be okay if she'd just let him in.

But she appeared so fragile right now, he was afraid

that if he touched her she'd shatter into a million pieces. "What happened to you?" he asked gently. "What happened to you that you are so afraid to trust in something good?"

Her eyes grew glassy with moisture but she didn't break. "I'm not afraid."

"Right. I know. You're not afraid of anything. Nothing but me. Nothing but the possibility of us."

She stared at the hands she'd clasped in her lap. "There is no us."

"But there could be," he said, wishing she would look at him. "There could be if you'd just let it happen. And don't you dare try to tell me that what happened between us in Colombia was nothing."

He still had a vivid image of her in his mind, her head thrown back, her eyes closed as she climaxed and trembled and fell apart for him.

She picked up a throw pillow, hugged it to her breast. "What happened was a casualty of the circumstances."

"Oh, right. Heat of the moment," he concluded for her, not able to hide his anger. "Tensions ran high. Lives were on the line, and all that bullshit."

"Yes, damn it," she said, reacting to his tone. "All of that. And it's not bullshit. Sometimes . . . sometimes the moment feels like the only reality. Sometimes you need that moment to get you through."

"So you're saying that any time you get in a dicey situation you sleep with your partner."

"Don't be absurd."

"Then don't lie to me. It meant something. *I* mean something. *We* mean something."

She closed her eyes, shook her head. "I . . . I can't do this."

"Why? Just tell me why."

She tossed the pillow aside and shot to her feet. He stood and stopped her with a hand on her good arm when she would have walked away from him.

She lowered her head, spoke to the floor. "I want you to go now."

His head fell back in frustration. "How can I fight something I can't see? And how can you *not* want to fight for this?"

"Because I'll lose!" Her eyes swam with tears when she finally looked at him. "And I don't fight battles that I can't win. Not anymore."

"Not any*more*? Are you listening to yourself? Damn it, B.J., you're still fighting those battles. Battles you lost a long time ago. Battles that have nothing to do with me. Yet I'm taking the heat for the beating someone else gave you."

She jerked out of his hold and walked to the door. "You don't get it."

He breathed deep. Cupped his fingers around his nape. "Damn right I don't. I'm offering you something good. Something you can count on. And you're letting past pain dictate your future."

For an instant, just an instant, he thought he saw a flicker of hope. And then it was gone. She swung open the door. "Just go. Just, please, go."

Defiant, prideful, she fought back the tears.

She wasn't going to break.

Instead, she'd broken him.

"Good-bye, B.J. Have a good, lonely life."

B.J. stayed in her apartment with the blinds shut tight and the phone unplugged for two days. She slept. Dry-eyed, she stared at the walls. Occasionally, she remembered to eat. On the morning of day three, she declared herself cured of Raphael Mendoza.

Well, if not cured, at least capable of functioning. She rode her bike, jogged, tried out a new recipe. And she did it all by rote. But at least the sharp pain she felt in her chest every time she thought of him had mellowed to a dull, tolerable ache. The hollow and futile echo of longing had been muffled by a numbing fog. And she'd wallowed in self-pity long enough.

She was due to return to work tomorrow after her short medical leave. Today was about fulfilling another duty. She arranged for a rental car and headed out of the city.

"Mom? You home?" She let herself into her mother's apartment with her own key when her mother didn't answer her knock. Of course she was home. Her mother never left the house. Thanks to the corner market that delivered her groceries, cigarettes, and wine, she never had to.

She stepped further inside and was hit by the stale odor of cigarette smoke and booze. The TV blared in the corner.

"Mom?"

She finally found her in the bedroom. For a heart-stopping instant, B.J. thought she was dead. Her mother lay flat on her back, fully dressed, an empty bottle of wine lying on the floor by the bed.

Then her chest rose.

B.J. honestly didn't know if she was disappointed or relieved.

The first time she'd found her mother this way, she'd been eight years old. She'd been so scared she'd hidden in her bedroom closet. That's where a neighbor found her the next day, her panties wet, her eyes matted shut from crying.

Her mom had gone away for a while then and B.J. had stayed with some nice people until her daddy had come home. When Janine came back from the hospital, things changed for a while and B.J. had thought she was safe again.

She was twelve the next time she'd found her mother that way. And she'd grown up a lot. She called for help. Over the next several years, she'd made many such calls.

She wanted to feel indifference as she watched her mother. She wanted to just walk away. But she couldn't because in spite of it all, she still loved her mother.

So she stood there and stared as she thought of all the loneliness, the bitterness, the pain that was her mother's life. The anger and isolation her mother had chosen.

And in a horrible moment of clarity she saw her own future. A future filled with loneliness and bitterness and pain—all because she was too afraid to take a chance on something good.

"My God. Oh, my God," she whispered, and dropped to her knees beside the bed. Then she lowered her head and finally let the tears come in earnest. They spilled out like a flood then, hot and wet and heavy.

She cried for herself, for the father she'd lost, the man she'd just driven away.

She cried for her mother, for her wasted life, for the choices she'd made.

She cried until her chest hurt, until her throat was raw, until her eyes burned and ached and there weren't any tears left to shed.

"Hush little baby . . . don't . . . you cry. Momma's gonna . . . love you by and by . . ."

Her eyes were blurry as she lifted her head, saw her mother's sad, tired gaze fixed on her as she sang a long-forgotten lullaby. "Don't cry. Don't cry, baby. Momma loves you. It'll be okay."

# 32

It was clear from the look on Jenna's face that she was beyond surprised when she opened the apartment door and saw B.J. standing there at nearly half past ten at night. "B.J. Hi. Come on in."

"I'm . . . I'm sorry to intrude. I know it's late." By the time she'd gotten her mother sobered up, fed, and bathed, it was already after eight. She'd pushed the speed limit all the way back to D.C. and driven directly to the Jones's apartment. "I . . . I was hoping Rafe might be here," she said hopefully.

Jenna hesitated, then finally nodded. "Yeah, yeah, he's here. He and Gabe are out on the terrace having a beer."

B.J.'s pulse picked up. Part relief. Part dread. What if she was too late? What if Rafe had decided she wasn't worth the effort? She breathed deep. It didn't matter. She needed to do this.

"Um . . . I'd really like to talk to him," she told Jenna, who was clearly hovering somewhere between curiosity and concern about what this was going to mean for Rafe.

In the end, Jenna took a chance. "I'll just tell him you're here."

"Wait." B.J. stopped Jenna when she turned to go. And then she did one of the hardest things she'd ever done in her life. She asked for help. "I need a favor. I . . . would it be possible for me to see him alone? On the terrace, maybe?"

Jenna hesitated again, then leveled a look at her. "You're not going to hurt him again, are you?"

Her heart sank. "No. I'm not going to hurt him. I'm just hoping he'll listen to me."

Jenna's expression softened. "You can do this," she said gently.

B.J. pushed out a nervous laugh. "God, I hope so."

"Hold on. I'll go get rid of the king of the castle and clear the way for you. Then Rafe's all yours."

All hers. The idea still scared her to death. But so, now, did the prospect of a future without him.

In that desperate, defeated moment when she'd wept beside her mother's bed, the loneliest, most hopeless moment of her life, her mother had responded to her pain. She'd reached out. Offered comfort. Offered love.

Love . . . from a woman who had been lost to B.J. for as long as she could remember. Her mother had somehow found it in herself to be a mother to her. To care and protect and comfort.

Love . . . from a woman who had been lost even to herself. In B.J.'s darkest moment, her mother's humanity had emerged from the ashes of a desolate life and she'd taken a chance that her daughter wouldn't reject her.

And in that precious moment, B.J. had understood: If a soul that lost could find the courage to love again, then how could she continue to deny love's existence? How could she not take a chance to find love for herself?

"All clear," Jenna said as she stepped back into the apartment with Gabe in tow.

Gabe's stern scowl let her know that the jury was still out where she was concerned. It reinforced something Rafe had said to her. "They're my brothers." And brothers looked out for each other—just as Gabe was looking out for Rafe.

"Don't pay any attention to him," Jenna said as they headed for their bedroom. "My money's on you."

B.J. smiled her thanks, drew a fortifying breath, and stepped out onto the terrace.

Rafe reclined on the chaise longue, nursing his beer, looking at the night sky as if he really gave a crap about the stars. Stars were for lovers. Without someone to watch them with, they were just a bunch of stupid, overrated balls of fiery gas.

"Thought Jenna had dragged you off to bed," he said when he heard the terrace door open, then close. He cranked his head to the right, expecting to see Gabe.

His heart stopped when he saw B.J. instead.

Slowly, he sat forward, swung his feet onto the slate tile. And said nothing. He just stared, wanting to draw a dozen good conclusions about why she was there, afraid to let himself explore even one.

"Hi." She walked hesitantly toward him.

"Um . . . yeah. Hi," he said cautiously.

"Nice night."

Okay. The unknowns were killing him and small talk was not a game he wanted to play. "You came here to talk about the weather?"

She stepped closer, stopped when she was standing directly in front of him. "I came here to talk about stupidity. Specifically mine."

Relief. Hope. Love. They rose up in his chest, filled the emptiness there as her eyes filled with tears . . . tears that glittered like the brilliant, beautiful stars scattered across the heavens.

He held out his hand—and she gripped it like a lifeline. Without a word, he pulled her close, wrapped his arms around her hips, and buried his face against the warmth of her belly.

"Thank you, God," he murmured, and breathed in the scent and the heat and the wonder of this woman.

"I didn't realize I had so much anger inside me." Night shadows played along her bedroom walls as B.J. splayed her fingers across the solid breadth of Rafe's bare chest. She turned her head to kiss his shoulder. "Didn't know how heavy it was, how crippling, until I let it go."

He folded her hand in his, brought it to his lips, and kissed her fingertips. "You don't have to be angry any-more."

She believed him. Because she trusted him. And in-stead of feeling burdened by that trust, she'd never felt so free.

They'd left Jenna and Gabe's an hour ago and come straight to her apartment, where they'd ripped each other's clothes off and tumbled into bed. Where he had thrilled her and consumed her and taken her places she wanted him to take her again and again.

Then they'd talked. In the mellow aftermath of spent, desperate passion, she told him about her child-hood. About her mother's addiction. About her feeling of rejection.

"I'm so sorry." He'd held her as gently as he would have held a child. "I'm so, so sorry."

Until Rafe, no one important to her had held her as if they felt her pain. As if they wanted to absorb the weight of it, relieve her of the burden.

"It was a long time ago," she'd whispered, and felt as though she no longer had to carry her grief alone.

She'd seen Rafe rough, seen him clever, seen him outsmart and outwit the enemy. But she'd never seen him this gentle. She was right to trust him. Right to take a chance.

And now that she'd opened up to the possibility of loving him, she wanted to know everything about him. Starting with the dramatic tattoo on his arm.

"It has special meaning, doesn't it?" she asked now, tracing her fingers over the crossed stakes entwined with bloodred veins.

"For my family," he said simply. "For the loss."

Yes. They both knew loss.

And now they both knew love.

She rose up above him, reached across to the night-stand, and turned on the light.

"I want to see your face," she said simply, and watched his eyes go dark. "I want to see the love." She lowered her head and kissed him. "I need to see the love," she murmured, pressing kisses across his brow, along his temple, then traveling back to his mouth and pouring all her love and trust into a kiss that laid her bare. Told no lies. Breached all barriers. Surrendered to the need to give herself over to him completely.

"I love you," she whispered, letting herself say it for the first time. "I love you," she mouthed, trailing kisses across the smooth expanse of his chest, the taut, quivering muscle of his abdomen.

He hooked his hands under her arms, drew her back to his mouth, and devoured her. Pleasure and tenderness and the encompassing sense of coming home brought tears to her eyes again as he rolled her to her back and entered her. Slowly. Deeply. Without the urgency of their earlier passion, but with all the intensity of a man laying claim to and being claimed by the one woman who could make his life worth living.

\* \* \*

"So why do they call you Choirboy?"

Rafe groaned. She wanted him to talk? Now? While the shower rained down around them and she was using her busy, busy hands to lather, rinse, and repeat her teasing, sensual caresses all over his body?

He pushed out a sound that was part laugh, part pure unadulterated joy, and in answer to her question launched into a warbling and comically dramatic, *"Ah . . . sweet mystery of life . . . at last I found you . . ."*

She giggled. B. J. Chase giggled. It was the happiest sound he'd ever heard. He was the happiest man he'd ever been, until . . . *Ah, God* . . . she went down on her knees in front of him. Pressed feathery kisses to his belly. Skimmed her tongue along the ridge of his erection and worked him into a frenzy.

"B.J." He knotted his hands in her hair as she took him into her mouth and with a selflessness that humbled him, indulged him in degrees of carnal pleasure he'd never imagined existed. Her lips and tongue induced unbelievable sensations from every erogenous zone in his body.

Her mouth was magic. Her hands sheer torment, as she took her time and took him places he'd remember until the day he died.

"Sweetheart . . . ah . . . God," he moaned as she finessed him to climax, then rode with him until he was thoroughly and magnificently spent.

He collapsed back against the shower wall. Dragged her to her feet. Held her tightly against him. Then he laughed. Exhausted. Wrung-out. Happy.

"Well," he managed when he caught his breath. "Guess I don't have to wonder what B.J. stands for anymore."

She giggled again. A sound that filled his heart to bursting.

"You know you have to marry me, don't you?"

She jerked her head back, her eyes wide. "For real?"

He brushed her soaking hair out of her eyes. "Yeah. This is as real as it gets."

# EPILOGUE

"You take my breath away," Rafe whispered as he danced B.J. into a quiet corner of the Tompkinses' family room.

Soft, slow music played in the background, candlelight cast romantic shadows on the walls, and the look in his eyes as he held her touched places so deep inside her that B.J. couldn't form a response. She felt filled with the best that life had to offer.

Love was good.

Love was . . . life. Life as she'd never known it before. Just as she was seeing Rafe in a way she'd never seen him before.

"There is so much to celebrate," Ann had declared, and she and Robert had gone all-out with the postponed engagement party by making it a formal affair.

That meant the BOIs had to step it up a notch. Since these guys never did anything halfway, they'd all shown up dressed to the nines. In camo and face black they were imposing. In jeans and T-shirts they were hot. But in white tie and black tux, the lot of them were beyond description.

And the women . . . B.J. thought Stephanie looked gorgeous in a red silk floor-length gown. Jenna was stunning in emerald green and Crystal . . . B.J. had had a moment of serious envy when Crystal had appeared on Johnny's arm wearing a knockout mini cocktail dress in a deep saturated blue satin.

The showstopper for her, however, was Rafe. His dark skin and eyes against his starch-white dress shirt and black tux . . . well, let's just say there was at least one other person besides Rafe who was breathless.

"I can't wait to get you out of that dress," he whispered in her ear as he looped his arms low at her back and swayed against her.

"That works out just fine then, because when I bought it, it was with you undressing me in mind."

She'd ripped a page from Brittany's book and splurged on a clingy, black, strapless jersey crepe. Reed, the consummate flirt, had even approved with a long, low whistle.

"If you don't stop looking at me like I'm a piece of chocolate," Rafe murmured, bussing his nose against hers as she looped her arms around his neck, "we're going to have to leave the party early."

"Not a chance." She smiled up at him. "I haven't nearly had my fill of you dressed like this."

"Like a penguin?"

She grinned. "Like Bond. James Bond."

He laughed and spun them in a circle.

"Too bad Sam had to miss the party," B.J. said, snuggling against Rafe.

"Oh, I think he's happy as hell right where he is."

Sam had gotten the call from Abbie that morning. This was it. The baby was coming. The always cool and collected Sam Lang, rock solid and steady in a fight, had been so shaken up, he'd let Ann make his flight arrangements and allowed Robert to drive him to the airport to catch his flight to Vegas.

"Sam just called!" Robert announced suddenly, and the room grew quiet with expectation as Ann turned down the music and joined him, a huge smile on her face.

Tears of joy sparkled in her eyes when she addressed the expectant faces circled around her. "It's a little boy." She smiled up into Robert's eyes. "And his name is Bryan."


"Damn. She did it again," Doc grumbled around the unlit cigar he clamped between his teeth and mourned the loss of his money as Jenna scooped up a pile of poker chips that for the most part had once been his.

With the announcement of Bryan Samuel Lang's birth, the toasts had begun with enthusiasm and now, late in the evening, everyone was feeling pretty mellow. And with Doc present the inevitable poker game broke out.

Colter looked every bit the rakish high roller in his western-cut black tux even though he'd undone his tie and loosened his starched white collar.

"If you can't run with the big dogs," Jenna teased and, laughing, returned Crystal's high five, "maybe you'd better go home, puppy boy."

"Do not play poker with these women," Doc warned the room at large.

"D'you ever think you just might be a lousy poker player?" Savage—who looked pretty spiffy in his tux—suggested.

"D'you ever think about keeping your thoughts to yourself?" Doc shot back, and thumbed his black dress Stetson farther back on his head. "Ante up, ladies and gents."

The night had digressed into laughter, trash talk, and well wishes.

Brothers, B.J. thought, watching them interact. They truly were brothers, with Nate and Ann and Robert Tompkins assuming a parental role of sorts. Add Jenna, Crystal, and Abbie to the mix and they became a family. A family she was now fortunate enough to be a part of.

She still had to stop and take a deep breath every once in a while, give herself permission to enjoy the wealth of love that Rafe had brought into her life.

"Do you get the feeling that Steph and Joe made a connection while they were lying low and hiding out?" Rafe asked B.J. as they snuggled on the sofa, feeling happy and tired.

Yeah. She'd noticed the looks the two of them exchanged. "How do you feel about that?" she asked, and immediately wished she hadn't let the old, distrustful B.J. resurface. Rafe, however, just rolled with it.

"Happy as hell," he said easily, and kissed her. "There's a lot more to Joe than he lets anyone see. I'm glad Steph was able to recognize that."

"And I'm glad you didn't give up on me," she whispered.

"Give up on you? Let me tell you something, Beatrice Janine."

She clamped her hand over his mouth, hoping no one had overheard him. "Oh God. I knew I shouldn't have told you." But he'd been inside her at the time. She'd have told him anything, given him anything.

He laughed and pulled her hand away, kissed her palm. "Let me tell you something, *Beatrice*." He humored her by whispering so only she could hear. "Giving up was not an option. I was going to let you think about things for a while, but if you hadn't come to me, I promise you, I would have been back. And I would have worn you down."

"It wouldn't have taken much," she confessed. "The truth is, you had me at 'What part of you're tied up and we've got the guns don't you understand?'"

"Charmed you even when I was playing the bad guy, huh?"

"Yeah, well, don't let it go to your head."

"Not my head, no. My heart."

Enjoy the following excerpts from
the first three novels in
Cindy Gerard's Black Ops, Inc. series!

## SHOW NO MERCY
*Gabriel Jones's and Jenna McMillan's story*

*Buenos Aires*
*11:15 p.m.*

"Tonight? Are you crazy?" Jenna shook her head at Gabe. "I'm not flying anywhere. And I'm sure not going home."

Just as soon as she got hold of her laptop, which she'd left in her hotel room, she was going to fire off the bombing story to Hank.

He'd be over the moon, once he was convinced she was fine. Well, almost fine. Exhaustion and physical stress had done a number on her. Her adrenaline reserves had let down long ago. So had her deodorant.

She had no idea what was keeping Gabe on his feet.

In the past thirty-six hours they'd survived a bombing and made a round trip from Buenos Aires to Bahia Blanca with very little sleep. Her muscles had launched into full bitch mode.

Gabe looked like hell—in a raw, twelve-hour-stubble, determined-alpha-male-on-a-mission way.

*Damn him.*

Jaw set, eyes hooded, he stood beside her in the elevator heading up to her hotel room. The room she hadn't seen for almost two days. A hot bath and a change of clothes would go a long way toward making her feel human again. Then she'd get to work on that story.

If Jones had his way, though, they'd grab her stuff and head for the airport in the car waiting outside with Sam at the wheel and it would be *"Hasta la vista,* baby."

Well, she wasn't Linda Hamilton and he wasn't the "Governator."

Besides her story, she had unfinished business with Gabriel Jones. Something about possibly falling for an enigma. A mystery man whose life expectancy, because of his chosen profession, was most likely on par with that of a daylily.

God. Wouldn't he love being compared to a flower? A giddy laugh bubbled out. The glare he shot her said it all. Jones didn't do giddy. As a rule, neither did she.

She needed food. Fast. To help get her head back on straight if nothing else.

The elevator stopped on the seventh floor. The doors slid open with a rattle and a whoosh.

"Okay," she said, stepping out into the dimly lit hallway, "I know we've already had this conversation, but it was so much fun the first time, let's do it again."

"Let's not."

"No, really. I insist. You say, 'I'm putting you on a plane back to the States.' Then I say, 'Are you crazy?'"

"This is not a joke."

No. It wasn't. Just like seeing him this way wasn't funny. Knowing he gave a rat's rear leg about the prospect of her leaving him wasn't funny, either.

"Look," she said, trying another tack as she caught up with him, "thanks for walking me to my door. Sam's waiting for you in the car, and he's gotta be bushed, too, so you can both go on your merry way."

"For the last time, you need to back away from Maxim and get out of Argentina."

"Okay. Let's get something straight. In the first place, you don't tell me what to do. In the second place, I came here to do a job and I will do it. And in the third place, it's not like *I'm* being threatened here or anything. I mean, that bomb wasn't meant for me. You're not talking, but I think it's pretty safe to assume that Maxim was the target."

"Yeah, and you're just itching to get caught in the crossfire if someone goes after him again, aren't you? Damn it, Jenna. You're being stupid about this."

She stopped. Turned on him. "No, I'm being professional. I walked away from a story because of you the last time I was here. I'm not walking away from this one."

He reeled slightly. Fatigue could have been the

cause, but she knew the moment she saw his face that fatigue had nothing to do with his reaction.

In that same moment she knew something else. This battle-hardened warrior, this professional soldier wasn't as immune to death and destruction as he'd like everyone to think. He struggled with the same images she did. He saw the same charred bodies, the same bloodied corpses.

He felt the same kind of horror. The only difference was she could afford the luxury of regret. He couldn't, and there was nothing she could say to make him know she understood.

Key in hand, she eased around him toward the door to her room.

"Wait!" His voice was sharp as he grabbed her wrist and kept her from inserting the key in the lock. "Let me check it first."

"Oh, for God's sake. You know what?" She was tired. Of everything. Of him thinking he could tell her what to do, of him making it clear that he didn't want or need anyone—specifically her—in his life. "You've lived too long on the 'dark side,'" she said, putting a lot of theatrical woo-woo in the last two words. "I'm tired, I'm hungry, and all I want to do is eat, shower, write my story, and go to bed."

She jerked her hand away from his, shoved the key in the lock and pushed the door open—and came face-to-face with three gunmen.

Before she could react, Gabe hit her from the side, tackling her to the ground as the blast of a gun echoed into the hallway.

She waited for the pain, visualized her own blood, then realized that nothing hurt. Nothing but her hip where she'd landed on the floor with Gabe on top of her—again.

She struggled to get up.

"Stay down!" he ordered. "And roll! Get the hell away from the door!" he choked out through a hacking cough.

"Wha—" *Oh God.*

A horrible odor hit her olfactory senses then and she realized why he was choking. She gagged on a mouthful of air. Her eyes started burning. Her gut convulsed into dry heaves.

Gabe gagged, too, as he half-dragged, half-pushed her back toward the elevator, where the air was blessedly fresh.

Jenna lay facedown on the floor. She squinted toward the sound of Gabe's tortured breathing, barely able to make him out through the tears. He'd rolled to his side facing her door, using his body as a shield between her and whatever or whoever might still be in that room. He'd wedged the hilt of his Butterfly firmly between his teeth and he'd drawn a pistol she hadn't even been aware he'd been carrying. The barrel was trained on her open hotel room door.

"Cell phone," he gritted around the knife. "Pocket."

With her eyes pinched shut against the lingering burn and streaming tears, Jenna attacked his pants, searching pockets, and finally found the one with his cell phone.

Later, she'd think about the lean hips and flat gut

and all that male heat she'd encountered. Right now, she was shaking too badly to even be embarrassed that she might have grabbed something that definitely wasn't his phone.

"Punch one," he ordered.

She did.

"Lang." Sam answered on the first ring.

She could take it from here. "Men with guns. In my room."

A split second of silence. "Anyone hurt?"

"I . . . I don't know. I don't think so."

"On my way up." He disconnected.

She closed the phone, lowered her head to rest against Gabe's back, right between his shoulder blades. Right where he was solid and strong and his deep breaths were proof that he was alive and that he planned to keep them both that way.

Finally she drew a breath that didn't feel like it dragged over razor blades. She braved peeking over his shoulder. A buckshot pattern, roughly the size of a softball, had shattered the top of the door.

"Where are they? And not that I'm complaining, but why aren't they still shooting at us?"

"Because they're probably long gone. Are you hurt?" Gabe asked with enough urgency that she realized he must have felt her shiver in delayed reaction to the hole in the door.

"No. No, I'm okay. What about you? Are you hurt?"

"Only if you count the fact that you damn near ripped off my plumbing groping around for my phone."

She made a sound of exasperation. "Now? You pick *now* to become a comedian?"

"It's all about timing," he whispered back.

## TAKE NO PRISONERS
### *Sam Lang's and Abbie Hughes's story*

Abbie spotted the gay cop cowboy the minute she came back from break. It was hard not to. The guy was incredible looking. While she felt a little kernel of unease that he'd turned up again—at the casino where she worked this time—she wasn't going to let it throw her off her stride. The Vegas Strip wasn't all that big. Not really. There were only so many places for people to eat, sleep, and gamble.

When he drifted off twenty minutes or so later without so much as looking her way, she chalked it up to coincidence. Just as she found it coincidental that the tall, dark man who'd been playing the slot beside the golden boy ambled over to the blackjack tables.

Big guy. The western-cut white shirt and slim, crisp Wrangler jeans told her he was a real cowboy. The kind who made his living in the saddle, not the kind who just dressed the part. He was confident but quiet with it, she decided, as she dealt all around to her full table, then cut another glance the big guy's way.

He stood a few feet back from the tables, arms crossed over a broad chest, long legs planted about shoulder-width apart, eyes intent on the action on the blackjack table next to hers. On any given night there were a lot of spectators in a casino, so it wasn't unusual that he stood back from the crowd and just watched. What was unusual was that between deals, her gaze kept gravitating back to him.

What was even more curious was that when one of her players scooped up his chips and wandered off, leaving the third-base chair empty, Abbie found herself wishing the tall cowboy would take his place.

What was up with that? And what was up with the little stutter-step of her heart when he ambled over, nodded hello, and eased his lean hips onto the chair?

"Howdy," she said with what she told herself was a standard, welcoming smile.

He answered with a polite nod as he reached into his hip pocket and dug out his wallet. When she'd paid and collected bets all around, he tossed a hundred-dollar bill onto the table.

Abbie scooped it up, counted out one hundred in chips from the chip tray, then spread them on the green felt tabletop for him to see. After he'd gathered them in and stacked them in front of him, she tucked the hundred into the slot in front of her.

"Place your bets," she said to the table of seven, then dealt the first round faceup from the shoe. When all players had two cards faceup, she announced her own total. "Dealer has thirteen."

Her first-base player asked for a hit, which busted

him. When she got to the cute quiet cowboy, he waved his hand over his cards, standing pat with eighteen.

You could tell a lot about a person from their hands. Abbie saw a lot of hands—polished and manicured, dirty and rough, thin and arthritic. The cowboy's hands were big, like he was. His fingers were tan and long with blunt, clean nails—not buffed. Buffed, in her book, said pretentious. His were not. They were capable hands, a working man's hands, with the occasional scar to show he was more than a gentleman rancher. Plenty of calluses. He dug in.

She liked him for that. Was happy for him when she drew a king, which busted her. "Luck's running your way," she said with a smile as she paid him.

He looked up at her then and for the first time she was hit with the full force of his smile. Shy and sweet, yet she got the distinct impression there was something dark and dangerous about him.

Whoa. Where had that come from? And what the heck was going on with her?

Hundreds—hell, thousands—of players sat at her table in any given month. Some were serious, some were fun and funny, some sad. And yeah, some of them deserved a second look. But none of them flipped her switches or tripped her triggers like this man was flipping and tripping them right now. It was unsettling as all get-out.

"Place your bets," she announced again, then dealt around the table when all players had slid chips into their betting boxes.

Whereas the blond poster boy had been bad-boy

gorgeous, there wasn't one thing about this man that suggested a boy. Abbie pegged him for midthirties—maybe closer to forty, but it wasn't anything physical that gave her that impression. He was rock-solid and sort of rough-and-tumble looking. Dark brown hair, close cut, dark, *dark* brown eyes, all-seeing. Nice face. Hard face. All edgy angles and bold lines.

Maybe that was where the dangerous part came in. He had a look about him that was both disconcerting and compelling. A presence suggesting experience and intelligence and a core-solid confidence that needed no outward display or action to reinforce it.

Clint Eastwood without the swagger. Matthew Mc-Conaughey without the long hair and boyish charm—and *with* a shirt on, something McConaughey was generally filmed without. Although, the cowboy *did* have his own brand of charisma going on because sure as the world, he was throwing *her* for a loop.

"Cards?" she asked him now.

"Double down."

*Smart player,* she thought, and split his pair of eights. She grinned again when he eventually beat the table and her on both cards.

"I think maybe *you're* my luck." He tossed a token in the form of a red chip her way.

"Tip," she said loud enough for her pit boss to hear, showed him the five-dollar chip before she pocketed it. "Thanks," she said smiling at him.

"My pleasure."

He spoke so softly that the only reason she understood what he said was because she was looking right at him. The din of the casino drowned out his words to anyone else at the table as the rest of the players talked and joked or commiserated with each other.

The next words out of his mouth—"What time do you get off?"—stopped her cold.

She averted her gaze. "Place your bets," she told the table at large, thinking, *Hokay. Quiet doesn't necessarily mean shy.*

The man moved fast. Which both surprised and pleased her because it meant that all this "awareness," for lack of a better word, wasn't one-sided. It also made her a little nervous. Her first instinct was to give him her standard "Sorry. No fraternizing with the customers" speech.

But then she got an image of a devil sitting on her shoulder—a red-haired pixie devil with a remarkable resemblance to her friend Crystal. *"Don't you dare brush him off. Look at him. Look! At! Him!"*

She chanced meeting his eyes again—his expression was expectant but not pressuring—and found herself mouthing, "Midnight."

A hint of a smile tugged at one corner of his mouth. "Where?"

She didn't hesitate nearly long enough. "Here." *God, what am I doing?*

"Cards?" she asked the table.

He gave her the "hit me" signal when she came around to him.

He broke twenty-one, shrugged.

"Sorry," she said, liking the easy way he took the loss. "Better luck next time."

"Counting on it." He stood. "Later," he said for her ears only; then he strolled away from the table.

"Dealer pays sixteen," she said absently as she paid all winners and surreptitiously watched what was arguably one of the finest Wrangler butts she'd ever seen get lost in a sea of gamblers.

## WHISPER NO LIES
### Johnny Duane Reed's and Crystal Debrowski's story

It was business as usual tonight at Bali Hai Casino on the Vegas Strip, which meant that every nut job and wacko who could arrange bail was on the prowl. Crystal Debrowski figured that in her seven years working casino security, she'd pretty much heard every come-on line written in the casino crawlers and lounge lizards handbook.

Her latest admirer—a Mr. Yao Long, according to the business card sporting an embossed Komodo dragon emblem—had come a long way for a letdown.

She glanced from Mr. Yao to the man who appeared to be his bodyguard. "I don't believe I caught *your* name."

"Wong Li."

A Jackie Chan look-alike, Wong appeared to do all of his boss's talking for him. Talking that included pro-positioning Crystal at a one-hundred-dollar-minimum blackjack table where she was filling in for one of her dealers who'd gone on a quick break. Crystal was about ninety-nine percent certain that the gist of Yao's offer ran somewhere in the neighborhood of: Him, lord and master. Her, concubine and sex slave.

"Please tell Mr. Yao, thanks, but no thanks," she told Wong.

Because she perpetuated the sex kitten image—a girl had to have some fun, especially if that girl was thirty-one years old and lived in a world where few people took a petite woman seriously—Crystal cut Yao a little slack.

That didn't mean she was going for his insulting proposition. And it didn't mean she liked it. She'd pretty much had it with the opposite sex. Her newly adopted motto was: Men. Can't live with 'em, can't tie 'em to a train track and wait for Amtrak to do the deed. Chalk her disillusionment up to a string of bad relationships.

Johnny Duane Reed was a recent example. That cowboy had heartbreak written all over him and she'd be damned if she knew why every time he blew into town she ended up naked before he ended up gone. Reed always ended up gone.

The latest case in point, however, Mr. Yao Long, did not look happy right now. But then, it was hard to tell for certain. His expression hadn't altered since he'd appeared thirty minutes ago with his bodyguard.

"Did he understand that my answer is no?" Crystal's gaze darted from Wong to Yao as she turned the table back over to the dealer. "Because, I'm thinking that if he did, now would be a really good time for him to leave."

Mr. Yao, all five feet, four inches with salt-and-pepper hair, Armani suit, and Gucci loafers, continued to pierce her with eyes the color of onyx. His expression never wavered.

"Did *you* understand that my answer is no?" She averted her gaze from Mr. Personality to Wong.

"Mr. Yao understands your response but respectfully rejects your answer. Mr. Yao is quite taken with you. He expresses regret that you are reluctant to allow him the opportunity to get to know you better but must insist on your cooperation."

"Is he, like, texting you or something because I never saw his lips move." This was so ludicrous it was almost funny. The next words out of Wong's mouth, however, sobered her.

"Miss Debrowski, please understand it would not be wise—"

"Wait." She cut off Wong with a hand in the air as unease shifted to alarm. She didn't wear a name tag, yet this man knew who she was. "How do you know my name?"

"Mr. Yao makes it a point to know everything. He is a very important and powerful man in our country."

"Yeah, well, in my country it's neither polite nor acceptable for any man—important or otherwise—to impose his attention where it isn't wanted.

"Max," she said when the twenty-something security guard walked to her side. "Please escort these gentlemen out. Their business here is concluded."

"You will regret this," Wong said softly.

\* \* \*

Three weeks later, Crystal knew she was in deep trouble and she didn't have one single clue how it had come to this.

First the counterfeit chips had shown up on the floor, then one of her sections came up short for the evening shift's take. Tens of thousands of dollars short. Computer security codes were breached by hackers. Dozens of other little, yet vital security glitches—all on her watch—had her pulling her hair out.

So yeah, she became a subject of intense scrutiny. And no. She had no explanation, just a lot of sleepless nights trying to figure out how this was happening on her shift.

Then the unthinkable happened. Last night, twelve of the thirteen gaming tables under her direct supervision had been flooded with counterfeit twenty-dollar bills. Whoever distributed them had taken the casino for close to two hundred K.

Now here she was, standing in her boss's office. "You don't seriously believe I'm stealing from you?"

Gilbert sat behind his massive mahogany desk. "I don't want to, no. But given the circumstances, Miss Debrowski, we have no choice but to place you on leave without pay."

She swallowed back anger and frustration and tears. "I understand." Actually, she didn't, but given the fact that the only case she had to plead was ignorance, what else could she say?

Gilbert pressed the intercom button on his phone. "Send them in."

The door opened. Crystal looked over her shoulder to see two uniformed LVPD officers walk in.

She turned back to Gilbert, her heart pounding. "You're having me arrested?"

Her boss had the decency to look remorseful. "I'm sorry."

"And here I thought I was the only one who got to use handcuffs on you."

Crystal looked up from the corner of the jail cell four hours later to see Johnny Duane Reed grinning at her from the other side of the bars.

*Perfect.*

Grinning and gorgeous, Reed was the last person she wanted to see, specifically because until today he *had* been the only one who had ever gotten to use handcuffs on her.

A vivid memory of her naked and cuffed to her own bed while Reed had hovered over her was not the diversion she needed at this point in time.

She'd ask him what he was doing here but figured she already knew. "Abbie called you."

"I was visiting the ranch," Reed said. "I was there when you called her."

It figured that Reed would be back in Vegas and not bother to come and see her. Not that she wanted him to. Not that she cared.

"I need a lawyer, not a . . ." She paused, groping for the word that best described him.

"Lover?" he suggested with that cocky grin.

"Not the word I was searching for," she grumbled, but let it go at that.

"If you don't want him, sugar, I'll be happy to take him."

Her cell mate shot Reed her best come-hither hooker smile. Reed, of course, couldn't help himself. He winked at her.

Jesus, would you look at him. Hair too long and too blond. Eyes too sexy and too blue. Body too buff, ego too healthy. Standing there in his tight, faded jeans, painted-on T-shirt, and snakeskin boots, he looked like God's guilty gift—and he knew it.

So did Crystal. What she didn't know was why she was so glad to see a man who played at life, at love, and at caring about her. That was the sum total of Reed's commitment quotient. He played at everything.

"How you holding up, Tinkerbell?" he asked gently.

Oh God. He actually sounded like he cared.

"Careful, Reed. You might get me thinking you give a rip."

He had the gall to look wounded. "Now you've gone and hurt my feelings."

"Just get me out of here," she said, rising and meeting him at the heavy, barred door.

"Working on it," he said. "Abbie and Sam are right behind me. They'll arrange bail."

"Bail's already made."

Reed looked over his shoulder at the jailer, who sauntered slowly toward them with a set of keys.

Crystal backed away from the bars when the barrel-chested and balding deputy slipped the lock and slid open the door with a hollow, heavy clink. "Someone made my bail? Who?"

He shrugged. "You'll have to ask at processing. I just do what I'm told."

"I've always had this prison-chick fantasy," Reed said confidentially as Crystal slipped out of the cell. "You know—sex-starved, man-hungry."

"Stow it." Crystal marched past him, ignoring his warped sense of humor. She was tired and terrified and doing her damnedest not to let either show.

"Hey, hey," he said gently and caught her by the arm. "Looks like someone could use a hug."

Yeah. She could use a hug. She could use a hundred hugs but now was not the time, this was not the place, and Reed was not the man she wanted to show the slightest bit of weakness to. "What I need is fresh air."

"Sure. But first, do a guy a favor. Make my fantasy complete. Tell me that you and the sister there had a hair-pulling, nail-scratching catfight and I'll die a happy man."

"Screw you, Reed."

He dropped a hand on her shoulder. Squeezed. "Now you're talkin'."